NEFARIOUS

A PRIDE & PREJUDICE VARIATION

NICOLE CLARKSTON

Illustrated by JANET TAYLOR

Illustrated by RLSATHER SELFPUBBOOKCOVERS

Edited by J.W. GARRETT

WHITE SOUP PRESS

PROLOGUE

I pressed my fingers to my temples and sank lower in my chair as another moan sounded from behind the door. None of it had been my fault, but I bore the blame of it. Between the deepest groans, it was my name she cursed in her agony.

Footsteps raced from the basin to the bed, voices echoed low and strained, but the sounds of despair went on unabated… weaker now than when they first began all those hours ago.

I ought to have felt sorrow, guilt, fear… a father's desperation or a husband's anguish… but I was simply numb. Maids came and went—I could hear the door to the main hall opening and closing repeatedly, but I could only hold my vigil in the adjacent sitting room, a powerless wretch who knew not even his own mind.

The hands marched round the face of the clock, and the room grew quieter as they advanced. Then, what I had most dreaded and longed for came in a moment. The door creaked, and Mrs Reynolds stepped softly into the room behind me. I never turned to face her—there was no need.

"The babe?"

I heard her sigh. "No," she whispered.

"And Mrs Darcy?"

There was a long pause, then; "Mrs Darcy's suffering is over."

I blinked, staring at the wall, and swallowed. "Then we are both free."

CHAPTER 1

*S*ix months later

I STOOD before the steps of my family's crypt, frozen in place by emotions so strong I could barely draw breath. I studied the carved letters... and I could step no closer. Months of mourning had clarified my feelings, and now, I knew what I wished to say and think and do. What had I felt this year and a half since she had come into my life? It would be impossible to catalogue the tumultuous whirlwind that had been my sentiments. Each moment had been so changeable, and each day I had treaded upon glass, but no more. Now, I knew my own mind; I unclenched my teeth and the words that had simmered so long in my heart tumbled forth.

"They say it is wrong to speak ill of the dead. But I will speak—I will! I am finished with the pretty falsehoods of polite manners. All those things I longed to say to you in life, but never dared, for the sake of my precious dignity—would you have listened, my wife? But now, you shall hear, for the truth is... I hated you. Oh, how I hated you! Even in death, I hate you still. If not for the scandal, you would not grace the hallowed crypt of my ancestors, for you are unworthy to share an eternal resting place beside them."

The cold stone yielded no response.

"I was a good man once; honourable, the pride of my family, and no shadow ever besmirched my character. I shall never be so innocent again, and I lay the fault for that at your feet. I curse the day I ever laid eyes upon you! You, with your second-rate arts and allurements, your studied charm, and the way you teased—as if a bit of whimsy and flirtation were sufficient to secure me! Ah, but they were, were they not? You and your abominable family saw to that.

"Your family!" I felt like roaring, thundering against the dead and beating that stone slab with my fists… but instead, I lowered my tones to a contemptuous snarl. "Their behaviour, connections, interests… yes interests… all deplorable. And I, the scion of Pemberley, was forced to align—no, degrade myself—to you and to them through a marriage not of my making! Your mother's machinations were your undoing and I glory in the fact that you are now paying for your misdeeds. She should be proud that her matchmaking skills—nay, let us call them what they were—compromising tactics, were so successful. I feel no shame in saying that everything about you disgusted me. I despised your voice, the colour of your hair, that twisted smile and even your very name!

"Worse, I loathed the gossips hinting at a compromise and the rumours of an increasing bride that necessitated a hasty nuptial. As if you could have tempted me! Yet, half the matrons of the ton were counting on their fingers in anticipation of the blessed event. Who was the father, my unfaithful bride? Whoever he was, he was cleverer than I, to sully your bower and yet escape the noose. You were nothing to him but a light-skirt… an easy conquest. A whore, my wife. How dare you come to me unchaste!

"My one satisfaction is that the babe could never have been mine. My hands are clean, and your bastard will never bear my name. And I?" I brushed off my sleeve and turned away. "I am finally free, and I shall be happy without you, Elizabeth Darcy."

One Week Later

"Darcy! I had not looked for you for another month yet. What the devil brought you from Pemberley so early?"

Charles Bingley rose from his chair, hand outstretched to grasp mine. "Egad, but it is good to see you! How long are you in Town this time?"

I could not be easy until the footman had closed the door. Bingley's house was one of the few places where I might be free to speak without fear of some reprisal, but only when his sisters could not hear. After that reassuring click, my shoulders dropped, and I could finally fill my chest with air. "For good, Bingley. At least long enough to put these last months behind me. I've no plans to return north again for some time."

Bingley's ruddy brows rose, and he poured us each a drink from his decanter. "Yes, I should think. You have finished mourning, now, have you not? You will be seeking a new mistress for the house, I presume."

"For my house or for my bed, I care not which," I grumbled, and drained the brandy as if it had been water. It might as well have been.

Bingley's polite smile became something of a grimace. "I do not believe I have ever heard you speak so, Darcy."

"And so I never have, but you see before you a changed man. I shan't be pressed into marriage again at the whim of any other, and certainly not for the begetting of an heir. I've time enough for that. What I want is good company, a bit of feminine cheer, and to seek my own pleasure for once in my life. Be that with lady or madam, I shall do precisely as I wish, and devil take the hindmost."

A low whistle sounded upon Bingley's lips. "Well... I say... ahem, I had counted on your advice regarding the estate I am leasing. You did receive my letter, I presume? But I suppose with such a resolve, you would rather remain in London."

"I had your letter the day before I left. Hertfordshire, is it? You do rush into things in a dreadful, headlong manner, Bingley. Have you even viewed the property yet?"

"Yes, I spent a day looking about the area. A capital situation, Darcy! It is just what I want—a quiet neighbourhood, a house with some fashion about it, and the perfect setting for my plans."

I swirled the last drops round the bottom of my glass. Hardly any colour either. "You still hope to breed hunters?"

Bingley lifted his shoulders in a show of bashful self-deprecation. "I always have, you know. No money in it, I understand, but what care I for that? And a man cannot do without land, of course, so at last I shall have everything I need. You said I might buy a few of your mares. Also, I was very much counting on your advice, if you can spare it."

I grunted, somewhat obligingly. Bingley's humble request was as good as a challenge to my honour, whether he knew it or not. "When do you take up residence at this luxurious palace of yours?"

Bingley fairly beamed. "I leave in two days. I planned to ride ahead of the carriage. Oh, do come, Darcy. Why, the half-day's ride in fresh air alone will do wonders for you! You will come, will you not?"

"I may as well, but why so soon? How can it even be ready?"

"Oh, as to that, the house came with trained servants, and they are making the preparations as we speak. I wish to be settled before Michaelmas, while the weather is still fine. I understand the shooting is spectacular! I believe this will be the first season I have not come to Pemb—" Bingley broke off, clearing his throat, and quickly refilled both our glasses.

"The past is done," I insisted, perhaps a little too loudly, because Bingley flinched. I lowered my voice. "I intend to cleanse my life of the stench of that woman. It will be as if she never was!"

"Of course, Darcy, of course!" Bingley fingered his glass nervously. "Colchester is hosting a soiree tomorrow evening. All the finest debutantes, as well as some of our old mates. I told him I would attend... I am sure he would welcome you, if he knew you were in Town."

"I was invited."

"Brilliant! Then you will come? There are sure to be any number of ladies worthy of your attention. Perhaps…."

"I might begin my search for amusement on the more respectable side of town?"

"Well—" Bingley grinned sheepishly—"I thought perhaps you might want to start slowly, you know."

I narrowed my eyes. "Caution is warranted, naturally. As I recall too well."

I STOOD AGAINST THE WALL, trying to avoid the temptation to admire the draperies. Bingley had immediately offered his arm to one lady after another—most of whom looked beyond him towards myself, the highly eligible widower. Calculating, disingenuous, mercenary trollops….

I made a noise in my throat. I had been a fool to think I might find what I sought in the drawing rooms of London. Here, I was assured of nothing but the very thing I despised. Elizabeth had been my equal, had she not? And her family knew precisely what they were about, grooming her to be thrown directly into my path.

I gagged faintly as a lady passed by wearing a similar fragrance to *hers*. Why, even the mere thought of her name made my brow grow cold and my stomach turn. *No!* Every female with family and standing only desired one thing from me, and I would never fall prey to such again. What I wanted was a simple woman, one who understood that her place in my life was retained at *my* pleasure and would therefore take pains to secure it.

From behind the wall echoed the irregular clinking of billiard balls. As always, the gentlemen too intoxicated or too married to join the ladies on the dance floor had retreated to that masculine refuge. I glanced over my shoulder, considering. Bingley twirled by in the quadrille, clasping hands with a stunning, lively brunette. Both looked my way: Bingley with open delight, and the lady—a Miss Charlotte

Bevan, if I recalled correctly—with lowered lashes and a curve to her lips.

That cemented my decision, and I slipped from the room. *Women!* The whole blasted lot of them could wait one more day. A footman opened the door and a wave of cigar smoke and male laughter washed over me like the enveloping darkness of a sanctuary. I stiffened my spine and strode into the room as if I were the master of it. Indeed, I was in a way, for most of these men looked to me as their superior in status, or fencing, or wealth, or some other matter of consequence.

Colchester himself was leaning over the table with a smouldering Havana clenched between his teeth. Beside him stood Ramsey and Carlisle, both old school fellows I had not expected to encounter this evening. I frowned but said nothing. Carlisle nursed a drink, while Ramsey twirled a cue and held forth with idle gossip.

"... they say Winslow is strung. Can't stay away from the gaming hells, I hear. His estate is...." Ramsey fell silent then and nudged Carlisle with his elbow.

Colchester missed his shot and glanced up to learn why the temperature of the room had seemed to drop. The master of the house straightened then and pulled the cigar from his mouth. "Darcy! I had not expected you to really come. Welcome, old friend!"

"Thank you, Colchester." I nodded to the men I knew as my eyes scanned the room... and then stopped dead. "Benedict," I breathed, the hair standing on the back of my neck. "How dare you show your face here?"

The other scoffed. "I ought to ask the same of you, Darcy. It is I who bear the grievance, not yourself, but—" he sighed, smiled tightly, and offered a formal bow—"I would never embarrass my host in his own home."

"You speak of grievances?" I stalked towards him. "As if the contrivances leading to your family's ruin were not of your own making? As if there were any honour worth defending in that wretched string of syllables you call your family name?"

"Here, now!" Colchester interrupted. "Darcy, have a drink. Let us put this unpleasantness aside."

"Indeed, Darcy." Benedict shot his cuffs and squared his shoulders with a jerk. "Fancy that! A man walks into a friendly game and practically throws down a challenge, with no provocation whatsoever!" He gestured roundly to his fellows, drawing a few knowing smirks. "Ought you not to be still haunting your own bloody house, rather than casting your gloom all about London? If I did not know better, I would think you did not sincerely mourn your late wife. Damned indecent, man."

"Indecent?" I hissed. I ought to have turned away, preserved my dignity, but I had enough—nay, a good deal too much. "Mourn a whore and a parasite?"

Benedict's complexion drained to a pasty white. "That is my sister whose honour you defame, sir! Would you disgrace the dead so?"

"I speak only the truth. Her disgrace was her own." I shot a hard glance over Ramsey and Carlisle. "Honour? Such a virtue ought never be pronounced in the same breath as her name!"

"Darcy, Darcy…" A hand clapped on my shoulder.

"Keep out of this, Ramsey," I growled. "My business is not with you."

"Come on, old fellow, let bygones be bygones, shall we?" Ramsey urged.

"I wonder at you, Ramsey. And you, Colchester! Know you what deceitful filth you have invited into your home?"

"Come, Darcy, you speak as if he is a farmer or a tradesman!" Carlisle laughed.

My lip curled. "Farmers and tradesmen come by their earnings justly."

"Enough!" Benedict thundered. He rushed to stand before me, his frame quivering with rage. "I know too much about you!"

I could not restrain a snort. "He who digs in the dirt often finds himself covered with it."

"Blackguard! Tomorrow at dawn. Let us settle the matter!"

"Darcy!" Colchester protested, coming to stand between us. "Benedict, be reasonable, man!"

I paused—not in uncertainty but contempt. I stared back at Benedict before offering my reply and took perverse pleasure in the anxiety and confusion growing on his sallow face. Benedict was panting, his eyes dilated, and nostrils flared like some over-wrought ewe. Still, I kept silent. After a full minute, a few uncomfortable chuckles arose from the lookers-on.

"Do be serious, Benedict," I retorted at last, my voice dripping condescension. "We both know you cannot hit a stile at ten paces."

"I will have satisfaction, Darcy!"

"I will, as well. The satisfaction of witnessing your failure, and the satisfaction of a better life than I was sentenced to, shackled to Elizabeth Benedict."

A throat cleared, and I glanced over my shoulder. Bingley had just entered the room and looked as if he were trying to pretend he had not heard the slurry of insults. "Ah, Darcy, if you do not mind, I should like to make an early start for Hertfordshire tomorrow. Shall we?"

I smiled, an expression that caused even Colchester to stiffen in apprehension. "Indeed."

BINGLEY WAS RIGHT. The crisp air, the rolling scenery, and the thrill of swift horseflesh had been just what I needed. And the quiet. Bingley chattered more than most men, but he was virtually mute compared to his sisters, who trailed some distance behind us in the carriage. I hoped this Netherfield Park he had leased was very large, fitted with many a spacious room in which one might lose oneself.

"There it is!" he exclaimed, standing in his irons and pointing. I drew rein and squinted. Indeed, I could just make out an amber glint in the distance which must have been part of the roof. Over the next forty-five minutes, Bingley became a fount of information as each crested rise brought more and more of the house and property into view. At length, we stood in the drive as Bingley's new stable hands rushed to take our horses.

"Well, Darcy, what do you think?"

My initial impression wanted not a moment. The facade of the house was good, the columns well-formed, but some flaws leapt out to my attention. "I think," replied I, "that the western windows will require some repair. See the water stains? Was there any concession regarding that in your lease contract?"

His brow furrowed. "Why, no, I do not recall any mention of it."

"Then the responsibility will fall to you."

Some pleasure fled from Bingley's face. "I see. Well... I have it from the agent that the house has been vacant for over a year but has been well-maintained for all that. I certainly hope the fellow spoke the truth."

I pressed my lips together. "Let us hope."

Bingley nodded as he doffed his hat and looked up at the windows, looking crestfallen and nervous.

"It is a fine property," I offered by way of consolation. "The grounds are more than adequate, and the styling of the house appears to be everything it ought. Come, I should like a tour."

A flash of his habitual delight surfaced, and he gestured expansively. "Then let us see it!"

By the following afternoon, I had assured myself that my friend had not been entirely unfortunate—rash as had been his judgment in taking the place. Netherfield Park was almost grand in its proportions, and a more thorough inspection of the property yielded only a few issues of concern, most of which were trifling. It boasted comfortable drawing rooms, a dismal library, a respectable ballroom, and gardens after the more modern style rather than the glaringly formal arrangements still displayed at outdated estates. A cursory ride about its borders brought mercifully few complaints regarding the management of its croplands and tenant houses. Most importantly, it was surrounded by pristine fields and coveys perfectly suited for Bingley's wants—and my own if I am to confess it, for we were more often out of doors than in.

Avoiding Bingley's sisters had become something of an art I had perfected over the years. Mrs Hurst was a simple enough matter, but Miss Bingley was quite another. After much practice, I believe I had persuaded her that I was an obsessive ornithologist, a word I was obliged to define for her on more than one occasion. This brought the double blessing of Miss Bingley making a show of searching her brother's meagre library for reference material, while leaving me free to gaze out the window in peace. She was little more than an annoyance—certainly not the sort of woman clever enough or devious enough to cause me any true concern—but I remained cautious, nonetheless.

On the second day of our installation at Netherfield Park, a rather pompous, curious fellow named Sir William Lucas introduced himself, and graced us with an invitation to a public Assembly the following week. We could do nothing but accept, though I am sure Bingley did so with more enthusiasm than did I.

Sir William's arrival seemed an incendiary of some sort, for in his wake trailed an assortment of local gentlemen. No doubt they had all produced too many daughters and were eager to pass them off. It was my good fortune that I had purposed most of that day for letters to various stock breeders and to my own stables, on Bingley's behalf, so I met none of them.

By the sixth evening after our arrival, I had made efficient work of the immediate tasks at hand. Bingley would soon be the proud owner of a magnificent stallion and sixteen fine mares, eight of which were already in foal. I had also secured for him the services of a top stable manager and, as a gift, a smart-looking pair of pointers.

By morning we filled the kitchen with goose and pheasant, and by afternoon we admired the wheat, hay, and fleece produced by the estate. I wrote to Georgiana twice, and to Richard once. On the whole, we were an amicable party, taking our ease as we might. Mr Hurst ate and drank, the ladies talked unceasingly, and Bingley was as gratified and contented as I had ever seen a man.

I, on the other hand, was bored and irritable. My agitation over my apparently stagnant life was rotting away the final shreds of my good sense. For the first time in my memory, I did not dread the upcoming Assembly.

"Oh, Mr Darcy, how shall I endure the evening? I am quite certain that someone will tread upon my gown in an assembly such as this. The very idea! I simply do not know how I could have it mended, either, for I am sure there is no one here with adequate skill. I declare! Is that a cotton frock that girl is wearing?" Miss Bingley gave a throaty laugh. "How quaint. I believe I can guess your thoughts as well."

I reclaimed my arm from Bingley's sister on the pretence of offering her some refreshment as the first wave of waiters passed by. "I would imagine not."

She smiled and leaned close as she accepted the glass. "You are thinking how insupportable it would be to spend many an evening in such... tedious company." She blinked and sipped daintily.

"Indeed, the company is tedious," I agreed. "If you will excuse me, Miss Bingley."

I had the pleasure of seeing her start in surprise as I bowed my regrets. Naturally, I would be obliged to dance with her that evening, but I had no intention of making Caroline Bingley my first and only conquest. In a room full of modest, country gentry and tradespeople, it was not impossible that I might discover a fresh-faced, empty-headed, and preferably buxom beauty—sufficiently in awe of me to appreciate the compliment of my notice, yet possessing just enough grace and comportment that I need not be ashamed to be seen with her.

I'd no thought of marrying the wench. It was simply an Assembly —one night, after all! I had no expectations that any in this region could successfully contrive to ensnare my honour. I did not even know precisely what my own intentions were. I knew only that I was hungry—starved—and by heaven, there must be some pleasant women left in this world!

I was suffering from the deplorable affliction common to all healthy young males, and I am afraid my difficulties were compounded by a decade of gentlemanly conduct even a monk could not fault, followed by a year and a half of daily frustration such as would drive a saint to swear. Would I have been so eager to seek the comradeship of these simple country females, had I been in full possession of my good sense and faculties? Unlikely, but that realisation offered little help for me just then.

I would have had to be blind and deaf not to notice the stares and whispers I attracted. "Ten thousand a year" was the phrase hidden by each fluttering fan, and many a maid and matron cast their eyes up and down my person. Well and good, let them know who I was. These were not people of the *ton* who felt they might grasp at equality with me. They were no threat at all, and for once, I decided that I would employ the renown with which I was received to my own ends.

I sought and found Bingley amidst a cluster of local notables, all vying for an introduction at the courtesy of Sir William Lucas. I was, however, too late in making my way towards him, for he was leading a young lady away from her family to the set. His expression was alight with the usual merriment... and then my eyes rested upon his chosen partner. By all that is holy, she was the most dazzling creature I had ever beheld! I felt my strides falter as I ceased to walk with purpose and began to drift in whatever direction afforded me the best view of her.

To call her hair golden would have been an injustice. It was the colour of honey, with the sheen of true Oriental silk, and even from a distance I could see a mesmerising rainbow of variegated flaxen shades dancing in the light of the room's many candles. Her complexion was flawless ivory with flattering pink stains about her cheeks, and her eyes... angels above, her eyes.... I never knew a woman could have eyes the exact shade of a high mountain stream. They were almost turquoise around the edges, but set amid their depths, like a prince's diamond, was clear-cut crystal, lending them a perpetual air of glory. She moved with liquid grace, her every step and gesture informed by elegant manners and a most becoming sense of modesty, yet warmed and brought to mouth-watering life by full, nubile femininity such as few London beauties could ever aspire to.

I had to know her. I was staring, and I knew it, but what cared I for the opinions of gentlemen farmers when Venus herself was before me? I followed Bingley and my goddess up and down the line—casually, of course, making some pretence of acknowledging those who must move from my path. By the end of the set, my awe-struck wanderings had brought me into Sir William's circle, but I scarcely attended my surroundings until he pronounced my name… twice.

"Mr Darcy? Oh, Mr Darcy, I pray you are enjoying yourself. We are all easy here, quite happy neighbours as you see. I do hope you find our little gathering a pleasing one."

"Indeed," I obliged him, my eyes still on the ravishing one in Bingley's arms, "everything I see is… appealing."

They were walking towards me now, the fair vixen casting thick lashes low over her porcelain cheeks as Bingley led her with the apparent intention to introduce her to me. I vowed then to secure for my friend at least five more of my best blood stock in appreciation for his kindness.

"Darcy! May I present Miss Jane Bennet of Longbourn. Miss Bennet, my friend Fitzwilliam Darcy of Pemberley in Derbyshire."

I do not recall if I repeated her name, nor what cordialities I may have uttered. All I remember is that a moment later I was leading her to the set, her small perfect hand resting gently on my arm. This time, her radiant smile was mine alone, and she was sweet enough to offer it whenever we faced one another. I would swear on my father's grave that charming expression never left her countenance even when she turned away, so pleased was she to have gained my attention.

She spoke little, which suited me well enough. If a woman had nothing meaningful to say, she ought to keep quiet lest she become like Caroline Bingley… or the former Mrs Darcy, whose mouth had been ever brimming with vanity and idle caprice, and even outright vitriol. Far better a woman who could hold her peace when the situation called for it, rather than cultivating her escort's humiliation and disdain.

What my enchanting partner lacked in verbosity, she more than recovered in physical magnetism. Each time our hands passed one another, my nerves tingled with fire, and each time she stepped near, the soft fragrance of rose petals warmed my senses.

And her curves! Michelangelo himself never sculpted a more voluptuous figure. She was like a radiant golden pear—firm and yet velvety soft, the ripened fruit that begs to be plucked, then dribbles sweet juice down a boy's chin on one of those nostalgic afternoons of delicious liberty. Ah, yes, she recalled every youthful pleasure. By thunder, this might be just the sort of woman I sought, this backward country miss with no designs whatsoever, and every innocent seductive quality a man could dream of.

The set ended all too soon, and it was the first occasion in memory that I felt a twinge of regret as the final notes died away. I led her back to the side of the room, but not before securing a second set later in the evening. That it would engender talk troubled me not at all, for this was a woman worth knowing better. She thanked me very properly for the pleasure, and I stepped away as her next partner came forward. I am afraid I was gazing raptly after her, for Miss Bingley managed to startle me.

"I see you have found the company rather less tedious than you had feared, Mr Darcy. Tell me, did she entertain you with tales of cows and pigs?"

"I was well entertained," I answered evenly. There was no help for it, so I offered her my arm and faced my obligatory half hour of bitter banality, for it would be some while before I could partner with my enchantress again. Mrs Hurst soon put herself in my way, and so I danced a third with her, then retired to watch my angel as one usurper after another led her up and down the set. Polite creature that she was, her eyes never strayed from whichever gentleman she partnered, but I consoled myself that her smiles seemed less warm than they had been in my own company.

"Come, Darcy, I must have you dance again. I must!" Bingley appeared at my side, after escorting his most recent partner to her friends. She remained there, mercifully distracted by feminine chatter rather than impertinently seeking an introduction to myself, and I paid her no further notice.

"Upon my word, I have never seen so many pleasant girls in all my life… some of them uncommonly pretty!" Bingley enthused. "Come, I must have you dance. I cannot see you standing around in this stupid manner."

"I have already danced with each of your sisters, and with the only handsome girl in the room, as you well know. It would be a punishment for me to stand up with any other."

"Oh, Darcy, she is the most beautiful girl I ever beheld! I knew you would approve. I mean to dance with her again, but of course, I must wait my turn. But come, Darcy, there are many other attractive ladies. Her younger sister just there is also very pretty, and most agreeable."

"Which do you mean?" I asked, wondering if Venus could possess a twin.

"There," he pointed to the lady he had just led from the floor. She inclined her head towards her friends, but already I could see that the elder sister had claimed all the family beauty before any other daughters could be born. Her stature was moderate, her figure average if not slightly flawed, her unruly tresses a dull chocolate, and her complexion ruddy from the dance. She had hardly a good feature in her face, and more disturbingly, I overheard an arch lilt to her tones which implied a fancied wit. Another woman who thought herself clever! I shuddered.

"Perfectly tolerable, I suppose," I lied, "but not handsome enough to tempt me. What is her name?"

"Elizabeth Bennet."

"Great hounds of Hades! Could there be a more unfortunate name in all of Christendom? Little wonder she is slighted by other men. I would not dance with her if she were the last woman in the world!"

The joy drained from Bingley's face. "Oh, dear, forgive me. I had quite forgotten… well, or, Miss Charlotte Lucas is a very amiable girl."

"You are wasting your time with me, Bingley. Go back and enjoy the smiles of your partners. I intend to wait for Miss Jane Bennet to be at liberty again, and I shall not put myself in the way of any woman less appealing."

He shook his head as he walked away. "Very well, Darcy."

I resumed my pleasant observation of Miss Bennet, undisturbed for the moment, and reflected upon what vagaries of inheritance and parenting might have produced both an angel and an imp from the same family. One the tempting fruit, the other the very branch that is cut from the tree for a switch! Perhaps one was a foundling.

As I mused on this likely conclusion, the dark one happened to pass by me. She did not acknowledge my presence openly, but there was in her countenance a peculiar knowing expression, a stifled flare of amusement, and a quirk to her lips.

I straightened, making certain that by no posture or aspect of mine would she sense cordiality on my part. She, however, passed by in complete unconcern, which alarmed me even further. No woman ever made a pretence of ignoring me unless she thought to lead me on by playing the coquette.

There could be no doubts about it—Miss Elizabeth Bennet was living, breathing danger in feminine form. I would do well to avoid any room where she might be in company. My trouble would be in pursuing her sister at the same time.

CHAPTER 2

Darcy,

I must confess myself surprised to hear from you so soon. I thought you would have sworn off all society and closed the doors of Pemberley until Easter. I am glad you accepted Bingley's invitation. The fresh air and easy company will do you much good.

I have been nearly always with my regiment, so I cannot answer your questions pertaining to the family. There is talk that we may be sent to Spain, but I think there is nothing in it. Let us hope, eh?

I had a letter from Georgie the same day I received yours. Perhaps it is time to take her from school, Darcy. All her friends have gone, and she is too old for the schoolroom. She ought to go on tour, or at least have an establishment of her own. You needn't choose Bath, but Lyme or Ramsgate might do. I may ask Mother for some recommendations for a suitable companion if you like. I only suggest that if you do not undertake to find someone, Aunt Catherine will.

Darcy, I know it is callous to mention it, but I must. The last year has been hell, and you have been little like yourself. Heaven strike me for penning the words, but I am relieved on your behalf. I dearly hope that nothing remains of your former troubles, and you may lay it all to rest. Find some diversion to occupy your thoughts, for I know how fearsome a creature you can become when ennui strikes. Every man needs a purpose, they say, but absent that, a woman will do. If Hertfordshire is in short supply, my mother would be more than happy to lend her aid in securing the requisite cure. Or, if you do not like the sort of girls she would find, I might be of service in seeking some companionship for you.

I am afraid I must keep this brief, but I would rather write sooner than delay a week. Give Bingley my best, and do try to avoid his sister if you can.

Richard Fitzwilliam

I folded Richard's letter and tucked it away. Brief or no, it was cheering to have word from my cousin. There were few souls whose society—even from afar—held such comfort for me, and I would reserve the pleasure of reading his note again later.

I rose and wandered to the window, casting my eye over the gentle roll of the landscape all around Netherfield. Richard was correct, and I had left Georgiana at school far too long. She should have come away a year ago, but at the time, the reasons for keeping her there, and away from Pemberley, had outweighed any other considerations. I would have been glad of her company after... but I doubted she would have found mine agreeable.

Her letters had begun to sound despondent of late. It was not her way, and I had sensed some melancholy whenever she mentioned her friends leaving while she remained. Guilt nibbled at my conscience, but what the devil was I to do about it before? Now, however, was the time to right that wrong.

Perhaps what Georgiana needed was an extended holiday with family. Yes, that would be the very thing. I could ask Lady Matlock to... I frowned. No, I longed to see her myself, and I was certain she would share that sentiment. The girl I had last seen at Easter had grown tall and mature. Surely, she could hold her own in company by now.

I resolved to speak to Bingley about the arrangements later that afternoon, before we began our preparations to spend the evening at Lucas Lodge. That decision made, I purposefully turned my thoughts to Richard's other suggestion. A wise man, my cousin. A woman's companionship was precisely what I wanted, but not just any woman would do. These few days away from Pemberley and away from the temptations of London had cooled my blood, and I had recalled my senses somewhat.

I blessed Bingley for his timely invitation, for had he not drawn me off, I might already have acted rashly. I understood by now that what I wanted was not just a warm body, but a warm heart as well. I had enough of the devil, and it was time to fill my life with an angel… and I knew just where to find one.

"My dear Mr Darcy, we are so delighted to see you again. Why, I was just saying to Mr Bennet that we have never had such charming neighbours! I do hope you intend to stay some while in the area. I have made Mr Bennet promise to save you all the best coveys, so if you have shot all Mr Bingley's bids, pray, do not hesitate to come to Longbourn. My, what fine weather we have had! Do you not agree, Mr Darcy? My dear Jane, of course, is too much the lady to run about out of doors as some other girls do, but she does enjoy a good ride on occasion. If only she had someone to escort her! For you see, Mr Bennet rides but seldom, and my younger daughters not at all. I imagine you must ride a great deal, Mr Darcy?"

I managed not to curl my lip in public, but my inner being was recoiling. *This* was my angel's mother? Were all mothers equally vulgar and silly? The lady's husband—for I believed at first glance that Mr Bennet's only identity was as his wife's husband—stood not far away with a tea saucer in one hand and not a word of reproof on his idle lips. Surely, she was his *second* wife. There could be no other logical explanation.

She was still tilting her head and fairly quivering like a puppy who demands attention. "I do ride often, madam," I answered her. "May I ask if you have been introduced to Mr Bingley's sister, Mrs Hurst?"

"Oh! Does Mrs Hurst ride as well?"

I was sure Louisa Hurst would punish me somehow later, but my only thought then was escape. It was shorter work than it might have been to extricate myself from the matron's company, for her real object was as obvious as my own. Miss Bennet was on the far side of the room conversing with Bingley, and I paused to draw breath before I approached. She truly was as lovely as my first introduction had led me to believe. Many a woman can dazzle in the ballroom, but in less romantic lighting, without the pulse-lifting swirl of the music, and under the close scrutiny of an intimate gathering, her beauty rapidly diminishes. Not so with my fair Una, the pure maid of unmatched virtue.

My feet floated in her direction, my heart likely thundering loudly enough to drown out even Sir William's voice. I could already feel her silken hand, hear her sweet tones as she pronounced my name... but there was the dark one from the Assembly, the barely tolerable one passing before me.

No gentleman would permit a lady to step into his path at such a gathering without acknowledging her, and so I snapped her a perfunctory bow. "Miss Elizabeth, I believe?"

I mangled her name badly through gritted teeth and lazy elocution. Nonetheless, it was sufficient to check her. She seemed surprised by the address, as if her object had been, like mine, only to cross the room seeking another. She blinked, tilted her head, and performed a flippant curtsey. "Mr Darcy. How do you do?"

I was in no mind to stand in the middle of the room with *her*, so my reply, I am ashamed to confess, was rather short. "Charmed." I began to move away, but found, much to my chagrin, that the half-second delay had lodged me amidst a bevy of lace and frills. Had she *planned* to interrupt my course, she could not have timed our encounter more precisely! It was worse than St James' on a feast day, for I could turn nowhere but six or seven young ladies surrounded me.

I discovered the cause an instant later, for the rugs were being rolled away. Somewhere, a hand of only moderate talent struck up the harpsichord, and a line began to form. As to how I had missed the fact that an impromptu dance was being got up, I can only plead distraction. In any case, I was not entirely disappointed, for this, surely, was my chance to claim my lady's company.

That was when I saw her standing up with Bingley. For a moment, I wished that leg he had broken when we were youths had not set *quite* so well, and that he still suffered a limp.

I resigned myself to stand, as always, in the corner of the room. Corners, I had discovered, afforded me an advantageous position. I could be nearly invisible to others, but I could see almost everyone who might dare to approach, long before they were close. Such as Miss Elizabeth, who stood not fifteen feet from me, engaged in some lively conversation with Miss Lucas. I kept a wary eye on her with as much attention as I could spare from her sister's graceful form.

"What a charming amusement for young people this is, Mr Darcy! There is nothing like dancing, after all. I consider it as one of the first refinements of polished society."

Sir William had caught me entirely unawares—it seemed that despite my strategic posture, my facilities had been amply taxed by admiring the one woman and guarding against the other. I made some rather uncivil reply, and I am grateful that I cannot recall the particulars of what I might have said.

Sir William, however, was undeterred, and he pressed me for information regarding myself, my dancing habits, where I had my abode, and then, most mortifyingly, he called out to the dark faerie I had watched with such suspicion.

"My dear Miss Eliza, why are you not dancing? Mr Darcy, you must allow me to present this young lady to you as a very desirable partner. You cannot refuse to dance, I am sure, when so much beauty is before you."

He drew the young lady close, and out of gentlemanly fairness I conducted an earnest search for this beauty Sir William ascribed to her. I did catch a remarkable glint about her eye—a rather fetching one, if I had been disposed to admire women with mischievous proclivities. I was spared from further survey by the lady herself.

"I thank you, Sir William, but I am not inclined to dance. Please do not suppose that I moved this way in search of a partner."

"But you can see that Mr Darcy makes no objection," Sir William urged, despite the fact that my hands were still clasped behind my back.

She smiled, and then those dark eyes fastened upon mine. I could not quite repress a shiver. "Mr Darcy is all politeness."

"He is, he is! And why not, considering the inducement? You cannot refuse to oblige us for one half-hour."

"Indeed, sir, I have not the least intention of dancing. Miss Bingley, however, would make an exquisite partner, do you not agree, Sir William? I do not think it neighbourly to permit a newcomer to our midst to stand on the edge of the room, simply because our own young gentlemen are not acquainted with her."

I narrowed my eyes, but she appeared innocent to my displeasure. Her words had been uttered just loudly enough that Caroline Bingley had overheard her name and was now looking in our direction.

"Indeed, Mr Darcy!" Sir William agreed. "Pray, sir, do bestow upon us the honour of seeing you dance with the fair Miss Bingley. I would consider it a compliment to my house, one that by your own profession is so rare that even St James' cannot boast."

They had me neatly trapped. Miss Elizabeth turned quietly away as if she had not just waged and won a battle that would have made Napoleon proud of its elegance. As I moved to perform the duty they had appointed for me, I caught the faintest smile just before she began to speak with someone else. Whatever triumph she imagined herself to have achieved, whatever motives would have inspired her to match me with Miss Bingley, I could not guess.

I only knew that Miss Elizabeth Bennet terrified me as no woman ever had.

AMONG THE NEW introductions made at Lucas Lodge had been one Colonel Forster, whose regiment had been recently quartered in nearby Meryton. Little disposed as I had been to speak to any apart from Miss Jane Bennet, I had found his company rather less than disagreeable. Bingley, naturally, had been delighted in the acquaintance, and two days later we, along with Mr Hurst, were invited to dine with the colonel. This might have passed with little enough consequence, save for a most interesting debate between the ladies of Netherfield.

"My dear Louisa, we simply must have some amusement. Why, with the gentlemen all away, we shall have nothing whatever to do."

"Indeed, Caroline, for no good can come of two ladies left too long alone. We should not be friends by morning. Shall we not invite someone to dine with us?"

"Why, yes, dear, that would be the very thing! But whom shall we have? I declare, I have seen little beauty and no fashion at all in this abominable country. I can think of no one whose company would not be… eccentric."

Bingley had been poking the fire, and he looked up at that precise moment. "What of Miss Jane Bennet? She is a lovely girl with pleasant manners."

I raised my eyes from my book but made no other response. I am afraid, however, that Samuel Johnson no longer held my interest.

"Indeed, Caroline! Let us have Miss Bennet, for of the young ladies in the neighbourhood, her company would be the most credit to us."

"Oh! Not Miss Bennet," cried Caroline. "Why, I had heard her to be a reputed beauty, but I see nothing in it. And I am certain she cannot string six words together! Surely, another would be better company."

"Why ever so? Is she not the very picture of all that is gentle and ladylike?"

"But her connections! And that mother! I suppose you saw how they all conducted themselves. I think I could take a liking to Miss Elizabeth, for she seems a clever young lady, but the rest of them!"

Bingley continued to poke the fire, but I noticed that his motions were becoming agitated, and he prodded the embers with a vengeance seldom wrought upon hot coals. I expected that he, as I, would not have wished for his sisters to associate with such an artful, inelegant creature. A pity he lacked the courage to set his sister straight on the matter, but Mrs Hurst spared him the trouble.

"Nay, I shall defy you Caroline, and declare Miss Jane Bennet a dear, sweet girl, and I should not be afraid to know her better."

I hid a faint smile as I tried to resume reading. I would not see the lady, naturally, but just knowing that she would be in this room, admiring these walls and touching these furnishings, sent a puerile shiver through my being that I would have denied with my last breath. Perhaps later that night, after our return, I might sit again on this very sofa and catch that rose fragrance....

"Why, then let us compromise, Louisa. Would it not be more fitting to invite both ladies? A table of four is ever so much merrier than a table of three, is that not so?"

"If you insist, Caroline. Let the invitation be sent."

I sighed.

HOURS LATER, I handed my hat and cape to the footmen and looked curiously about. A good many candles still burned as if the occupants had only just quitted the main rooms. Had the Bennet ladies truly stayed so long at Netherfield? No doubt it would have been the designs of the insidious younger sister, intending to place herself in the way of two single men. The elder certainly would be innocent of such a scheme; moreover, she needed no such devices.

Miss Bingley greeted us on the stair, her thin lips tight with some annoyance. "Charles, thank goodness you are come home. Miss Bennet is ill, and we have put her up for the night. Louisa thinks we ought to send for the apothecary, but I think no such measures are necessary. Might you speak some sense to her?"

"Miss Bennet ill?" Bingley replied with some concern. "How did this come about?"

"Oh! That mother! She sent Miss Bennet alone on horseback in the rain, and the foolish girl caught a dreadful chill. I declare, her lips were blue when she arrived."

"She came alone?" I repeated.

Caroline shook her head in disgust. "Miss Elizabeth sent her regrets, as she claimed to be feeling poorly. I do hope they have not infected us as well with their illnesses. Charles, this is what comes of removing to the dirty, wet countryside."

"But what of Miss Bennet?" he asked.

"Oh! Louisa is with her. We have made her comfortable, I daresay, and sent word to Longbourn of her indisposition. I expect it is nothing more than a trifling cold, and it shall be cured utterly the moment she is assured of your safe return from Meryton," she pronounced with a decided sniff.

"I am certain Miss Bennet must have been earnestly afflicted, if it is as you say and she arrived wet and freezing," I chided her.

Her eyes widened. "Of course, you must be right, Mr Darcy. Let us hope that the morrow brings about an improvement."

I gazed up the stairs. "Indeed."

The next morning, however, brought no improvement. It needed all my self-control not to wait outside her door, as Bingley did. He was the master of the house, and of course must take an interest in the welfare of a guest. With breakfast came word that Miss Bennet desired to send a note to her family, and that the apothecary must be called. I am afraid that my book suffered a deal of neglect all that morning, for coupled with the knowledge that my fair one was ill and terribly uncomfortable was the realisation that she would be required to stay at Netherfield. Under the same roof as I.

The apothecary came and went, pronouncing Miss Bennet's ailment not dangerous, and my own elation knew no bounds. Could the angels have smiled upon me any more beneficently? She would soon be well, yet what host would hear of a lady travelling home in less than three days after such a fright? Surely, she would recover fully enough in that time to sit by evenings in the drawing room. Aye, her mother was as cagey and dogged in her methods as the most seasoned London matron, but what of that?

Had I not seen far worse? And I had no intentions of courting the mother.

Miss Bingley seemed to be the only person who was not gratified by Miss Bennet's presence in the house. She took to haunting the same rooms as I, gazing out the same windows and attempting to draw my notice by identifying—usually incorrectly—whatever birds she saw. By mid-day, I had seen enough swallows and skylarks and sparrows, by Miss Bingley's account, to fill a book, so I stepped out of doors. It was as well that I did, for I was then spared the mortification of any witnessing my reaction to what transpired next.

I stood on a small rise just outside the orchard, overlooking the fallow fields in the distance and breathing deeply, as I had not done all day. But... was that a figure walking over the fields? I squinted.

Indeed, it was. A woman's figure, possibly one of the tenants' wives. I watched longer, this singular personage who chose to wade through the ploughed and muddy furrows of earth rather than walking round by the road. Her attire was too fine for a farmer. What the devil?

She was looking down, carefully studying her way, and thus was almost upon me by the time I recognised her. Egad, it was the minx herself! I started back, thinking to return to the house, but it was too late. She stopped, not ten paces from me, her boots and petticoats sinking into the soft ground. "Mr Darcy!"

I tried to conceal the fact that I was gritting my teeth. "Miss Elizabeth."

She curtseyed, and I could not help but note how the dampness was seeping at least six inches up her skirts. "I am come to inquire after my sister. Is she still unwell?"

"She is."

She pursed her lips, and those interesting eyes made some sort of flicker that I could not understand. "Would it be too much to see her?"

"Not at all."

She was simply staring at me, and for a moment I had the impression that we were engaged in some battle of wills, the rules of which I had yet to learn. She crossed her arms and arched one brow. "Might I ask you to take me to her, sir?"

It was probably obvious by now that I was, in fact, clenching my jaw and trying not to roll my eyes. "Very well." I gestured, and she came the remaining distance out of the field with a graceless series of hops and leaps, landing at last beside me on the grass. She then proceeded to march briskly ahead of me to the house as a woman with an object often does.

I followed, sucking air through my teeth. A short visit, that was all; enough to assure the family that Miss Bennet was well and in the arms of friends. After that, she would be gone, and I could carry out my suit undisturbed.

"WHAT DO YOU MEAN, 'Miss Elizabeth intends to remain at Netherfield'?" I lowered my book, a rock forming in the pit of my stomach as the worst doom was pronounced over me.

I had taken myself out for a long ride with Bingley shortly after Miss Elizabeth's arrival. No sense in encountering her more frequently than necessary. That she remained all that while had been hardly a surprise, for I expected a meagrely dowered young lady in want of a husband to be holding court in the drawing room the moment we returned, bewailing her sister's condition and batting her eyelashes at us.

In this, I must confess that I was surprised. She never came below all afternoon, and it was now growing late. The carriage that had been intended to take her home set out instead to collect her belongings for an extended stay.

"Indeed, she is to remain," preened Miss Bingley. I thought she looked rather smug. "I have given her the room adjacent to Miss Bennet's. I daresay she was most relieved by my offer. Why, it is only the least that any good hostess must do, and Miss Eliza did so dote upon her sister. It would be an unkindness to send her away."

"What of the report of her own indisposition yesterday?"

"Oh! Some misunderstanding or other. I would warrant that her mother kept her home so she might have satisfactory reason to put Miss Bennet alone on horseback, and the fool girl was simple enough to comply."

My fingers gripped the edges of my book more tightly. "You would declare her at fault for the admirable trait of obedience to her parent? I do not censure her for riding on horseback. A lady ought to enjoy the out of doors, as it is good for her constitution. Miss Bennet could not have known it would rain before her arrival."

Miss Bingley's lashes fluttered, and she favoured me with a sweet smile. "Indeed, for over such a short distance, who could have known the weather would turn? But I do agree with you, for a young lady who could be taken ill by such a mild storm must have been in need of much exercise."

I fixed my eyes on the page before me, biting my lips together.

"But you know, Miss Eliza's cheeks were rosy and healthy this morning. I daresay she suffers no such malady as her sister. A girl of Miss Bennet's frail constitution must find it comforting to have so hale a one for her attendant. What do you think, Mr Darcy, were you not pleased to see Miss Elizabeth's arrival this morning?"

I felt a knot forming on my brow—the same one that often accompanied conversations in which I would rather not partake. "Her skirts were six inches deep in mud, and her hair blowsy and wild. Oh, her eyes were bright enough, and she seemed in no way to be troubled by her exertions, but on the whole, she presented a figure that could only be described as untamed and conceitedly independent. I would never permit *my* sister to make such a spectacle of herself."

Miss Bingley laughed. "I thought her quite a hoyden as well, but an entertaining one, to be sure. I believe I shall endeavour to offer her some assistance where I may—you know, a bit of fashion advice and such niceties. I always am in great demand for my opinions on matters of culture."

I frowned and nodded, then returned my attention to my book. It would have been supremely rude to feign my own illness and retire to my chambers, but I will not claim I was not tempted. The only excuse

I can offer for the fact that I remained where I was is my own vanity. I was not afraid of her... but my stomach was dashed unsettled, and I was continually obliged to wipe my palms.

The Stygian vixen came down for dinner, and Bingley, generous host that he was, lent her his arm to walk to the dining room. Mr and Mrs Hurst followed, then I brought up the rear of the procession with Miss Bingley. We were a small gathering, but still Miss Bingley insisted on using the formal dining room to impress her guest. As we stepped through the door, a wave of nausea crashed over me, and I could nearly have claimed illness in earnest.

Everything in my being rebelled, and I felt my inner parts churning as they had not done for some while. It was the strangest sensation that I had been there before—another country house party, another intimate set of friends, another massive table ostentatiously set... and another chocolate-haired Elizabeth with a head full of schemes I could only guess at.

"Mr Darcy?" Miss Bingley had stopped and was regarding me in some concern. "You look fearfully pale. I do hope Miss Bennet's illness has not caught you as well."

I forced myself to steady my breath. "I am quite well, Miss Bingley." I claimed my seat before all the blood rushed from my head, and the others filled their places. Caroline Bingley sat at my right and Mrs Hurst on my left. That placed *her* directly opposite me where I could not look up but that her face was the first I saw. She dipped her head in acknowledgment when our eyes met across the table, and I do not care to imagine what she might have read in my countenance. As I could hardly breathe properly, her opinions were the least of my concerns.

I lacked the courage to look at her again. How dare she smile and laugh as if hers were the lightest of hearts! Who was she to be so charming with everyone else, this earthy sprite who so cruelly recalled every wrong ever done me? How had I so sinned that the very spectre of the only woman I had ever despised would have settled in our midst and infiltrated my nearest—nay, my *only*—circle of friends?

As the first course was carried away, she chatted amiably with the family, and even provoked Hurst to some discourse on his favourite dish. The most astonishing moment of all was the startling realisation that Caroline Bingley seemed to be promoting Miss Elizabeth's rather dubious qualities and intentionally seeking her as a conversation partner. I would have expected my hostess to object to yet another young lady taking up residence in the house, and certainly to her presentation upon arrival, but Miss Bingley seemed to attribute some virtue to Miss Elizabeth that only she could see.

"Upon my word!" Miss Bingley trilled in response to something Miss Elizabeth had said. "I should not have thought it possible! Can you really have an aunt and uncle in trade? No, my dear, I shall not believe you. You are the very picture of everything cultured and refined."

"I?" chuckled the enchantress, with a nearly convincing degree of sincerity. "I am afraid my arrival this morning was anything but elegant."

"Such a charming trait, your self-effacement! But you must not belittle yourself, Miss Eliza. Why, you recall to mind one of my dearest friends from school, Miss Esmerelda Templeton. She always was the most fashionable lady you can imagine, and I recollect how she used to follow the hounds with her brother. Every week, she would come up with her face splattered with mud and—would you believe it—*dirt* under her fingernails! But she carried it off in such a way that we all thought the more of her for it. I daresay that is your gift as well. What do a bit of the outdoors on your clothing or less than fashionable relations signify?"

"I make no pretences to fashion, Miss Bingley. It is true, my uncle lives within sight of his warehouses in Cheapside, but I do not judge him for earning his living any more than I seek peculiar attention for my habits of walking out."

"Of course not! Naturally, your uncle must be the most generous and intelligent of men. And none could cast disingenuous behaviour at *your* feet! Your intentions I can guess well enough, for certainly you were moved by concern for your dearest sister. Any other consideration must be second."

"You are most kind, Miss Bingley. I have rarely been received so warmly into any house. It is a fine recommendation of your generosity and hospitality."

Miss Bingley seemed to grow an inch taller at the compliment, one which had seldom been extended to her with any sincerity, and fluttered her lashes in my direction. Fortunately for myself, I had just swallowed my sip of wine, otherwise I would have choked.

What game was this black elf about? For each time I dared look at her, I noticed something new. I understood well enough that twinkle in the eye, the slight but significant emphasis she placed on certain words. And there was that small dimple by the side of the mouth that denoted a woman who held some private amusement. I expected at any moment she would meet my eyes meaning to share a secret laugh at Miss Bingley's expense... but she never did. Whatever her other motives were, she seemed content to lavish goodwill upon one whom she could only perceive as competition.

Or perhaps... perhaps *I* was not her intended target, but Bingley. Of course! She must have already observed my interest in her sister. I had hardly been guarded in my admiration, for I cared little if anyone noticed. Yet, if any woman in this region might be inclined to devise some scheme to her own ends, it was the female ruffian opposite me.

So, she expected that one courtship would naturally lead to another, did she? I regarded her narrowly, and she happened to look up just then. An ebony brow quirked, and I thinned my lips in reply.

En garde, Mademoiselle.

CHAPTER 3

A gentleman understands well enough when he possesses an adversary. There is a certain tightness of being, a guarded-ness that sets his toes upon the edges of his boots whenever his rival is about. A wary look, an odd phrase, and the battle is carried forth, often beneath the unsuspecting noses of others present. A particular word may provoke a public fissure where the friends of one begin to denigrate the companions of the other, and a rash gesture might eventually lead to a feud spanning generations.

Ladies are even more dangerous.

The trouble with the female persuasion is that a man never quite knows where he stands with them. Did Elizabeth Bennet realise, as she so blithely chose a book from the side table, that the simple act had confirmed her villainy in my eyes? Naturally, she could not know that it was a particular favourite of mine that I had brought from London—a gift from my father upon attaining my majority. But devil take it, she ought to have seen the bookmark and understood that someone else was reading it. And when she twirled the blue satin ribbon from my Cambridge days round her fingers as she read, did she comprehend why my responses to everyone else's conversation suddenly became clipped and irascible?

She could not have chosen a more innocent-looking activity for herself, nor yet so effectively raised the challenge to my face. That she meant to encroach where she was not wanted was obvious. Where she presented a vulnerability for me to exploit was less so. I could not very well issue insults in a room of polite conversation, so I determined to say nothing at all. Let her feel my disdain for her strategy and struggle to uphold the appearance of rosy unconcern. *Engagement. May the match commence.*

It is difficult to maintain a contentious frame of mind when one's opponent refuses to approach the matter with any degree of gravity. Nonetheless, I prevailed, even as one of her slender fingers left off trailing the edge of the page to trace out a particular passage I had marked long ago—in the days when I had still been myself. A chill raced down the back of my neck as she blinked those strangely eloquent eyes, pursed her lips, then glanced curiously in my direction.

I knew the page and quote by heart, for Johnson's cynical observation had once been a source of much derisive amusement for me—

> "Men know that women are an overmatch for them, and
>   therefore they choose the weakest or the most
>   ignorant. If they did not think so, they never could be
>   afraid of women knowing as much as themselves."

Heat pricked my face. My reasons for noting the passage were much different in those days than they would have been now—*then*, I had been merely ignorant. Now, I hardly knew what I thought, and could hardly imagine what a sheltered young lady's perception might be.

I welded my lips and steeled my resolve. What mattered it what she thought? *Keep your sword up, man.* Her gaze had scarcely touched my own when she hastened to glance away, and I congratulated myself for having fixed on a facial expression that was at once inconspicuous to others and inhospitable to the enemy. A pink stain rose upon her cheek, and she refused to look in my direction again.

Contented, I shifted in my chair and turned my attention to the letter I wrote to Georgiana. *Point.*

All this while, Miss Bingley had flitted somewhere at the periphery of my consciousness. Restless and without any particular entertainment of her own, she sought to make me her amusement by coming to sit near me. She leaned upon the arm of her chair, cupped her chin on the back of her hand, and watched me for long minutes in silence. When I, in some annoyance, glanced up, she purred, "How fast you write, Mr Darcy."

"You are mistaken, I write rather slowly." It was true, and all the more so because I wrote with my off hand—a habit my first school master had assiduously tried to correct, until my father bade him to let me be. But still, it took great care to avoid smudging my carefully penned words.

Bingley laughed and made some cheerful jab about how I laboured over my words. Had he looked my way as he spoke, rather than at the cards in his hand, he would have known that I was not to be antagonised at that moment. The minx was listening, and I could tolerate no levity in her hearing. I bent my shoulders even more intently to my task.

"How many letters you must have occasion to write. Letters of business too, how odious!" Miss Bingley was lamenting.

I forget the precise exchange that followed, for my answers were purely reflexive. I only discovered a moment later, to my horror, that I had lowered my guard enough to confess that I wrote to a sister. Caroline Bingley's fond descriptions of Georgiana, and the absolute necessity of speaking warmly of my sister in the presence of others, punched a hole in my impenetrable armour. Heaven forfend I should display any tenderness in my bearing while my adversary looked on!

Miss Elizabeth's brow had lifted, a sure signal that she was listening to our conversation, but her eyes remained studiously fixed on my book. Odd, how their colour seemed to shift with her moods, the changeful jade. In the fields this morning, a decided greenish tint had brightened them. At the moment, they were nearly perfectly black as they roved Johnson's prose, but the pace at which they moved had slowed considerably. A slight pinch in the flesh round the eye... indeed, she was reconnoitring, and I was her unfortunate target. What intelligence she thought herself to be mistress of, I could not say, but like any wise combatant, I sought to misdirect her next assault.

Caroline Bingley was now pacing the room, her steps always in a horseshoe pattern around my chair. "I declare, Georgiana Darcy has not her equal for elegance and accomplishments. Miss Eliza, I am sure you could not help but think fondly of her, if you knew her."

The sinister eyes raised, and my persecutor feigned a benevolent smile. "Indeed, she must be a remarkable young lady to have drawn such praise. She is very young, I presume?"

"Not yet fifteen, is she, Mr Darcy?"

"She is just turned sixteen," I answered without looking up.

"How the years have flown! Is she much grown since I last saw her? Is she as tall as I am?"

"She is now about Miss Jane Bennet's height, or a little taller."

"Ah, you are so good, Mr Darcy, to recall our poor guest upstairs. How does she do this evening, Miss Eliza?"

Miss Elizabeth at last closed my copy of Samuel Johnson and set it aside to partake in the conversation. Perhaps she had sensed that more than one person in the room waited with deep interest upon her answer, for her hands came to rest in her lap, her expression sobered, and she blinked thoughtfully before replying. "I am afraid she is not at all well, Miss Bingley. She was very uncomfortable this evening."

"What is this?" Bingley cried from his card table. "Shall we send for Mr Jones again?"

"Oh, no, that will not be necessary. I believe she only wants rest."

Bingley, good fellow that he was, did not appear convinced. "You will inform us if her condition worsens, will you not? At the first sign of greater distress, we shall call for Jones—day or night!"

She bowed her head. "I thank you, sir. I expect she will rouse shortly, and I will be certain to report anything of concern."

"What a considerate sister you are, Miss Eliza," Miss Bingley crooned. "I always say that family are the greatest comfort anyone could have. Do you not agree, Mr Darcy?"

I froze, gripping the pen so tightly that the quill crimped between my fingers. I drew in two sharp breaths, staring at the wall until I could be steady. *Family a comfort?* More of a curse! A punishment inflicted upon any with few to call their own, for those with enough to spare always determined to impose themselves, claiming the rights of true relations and usurping whatever might have existed before.

Bah! I closed my eyes. By now, Miss Bingley's comment had lingered so long that she assumed I had not heard, which was just as well, for at least she left me in peace. I turned the bent pen over in my fingers and tossed it aside to search in the drawer for another. I expected Miss Bingley would see my searching and offer to mend the broken one for me, but she was now engaged in some jest with Miss Elizabeth. I had begun to breathe easily again until I heard my own name.

"Tease Mr Darcy! Why no, my dear, it is impossible. The very idea!"

"That is a pity," Miss Elizabeth objected, "for I dearly love to laugh."

I could not let such a remark pass. I turned in my chair and fixed her with a hard stare. "You think it proper to ridicule someone who has made it the study of his life to avoid the sort of weaknesses that would expose him? To make light of an honourable figure, purely for your own amusement?"

Curse those eyes, they changed colour again as the ghost of a smile teased her mouth. Gold was a fascinating shade when set in chocolate brown. "Not for my personal amusement, but the enjoyment of the whole room. I hope I never ridicule what is wise and good. Most of my associates take much delight in their own follies, for none regard themselves so seriously that they cannot admit to some fault. Have you no faults at all, sir?"

"Faults? Mr Darcy!" Miss Bingley protested. "He is a man perfectly without fault."

I ought to have confessed then and there, but I could not bear to open my flank to the attacking forces. I narrowed my eyes and remained silent. My strategic hesitation, however, proved my undoing.

That cunning smile widened. "Indeed, you are to be commended for living so long on this earth without cultivating a few aberrations. I now no longer wonder at your lack of good humour, sir, for if I were similarly cursed with perfection, I should think myself the dullest person in the world."

Miss Bingley's mouth dropped open, and she stood stock still, doing nothing more complicated than blinking while she tried to digest Miss Elizabeth's volley. For her part, my foe rose nimbly from the sofa and took up my book with a smile. She drew near with a word to Miss Bingley that she would retire to look in on her sister.

As for me, she softly placed the book at my elbow and leaned low, patting the cover. "You are not so very difficult to understand, Mr Darcy," she murmured *sotto voce*. Then she straightened, dipped her head to her hostess, and left the room.

I growled and tossed the second pen aside, for it was now mangled beyond repair. What does one do with an enemy who simply laughs at the sword tip? *Touché, Mademoiselle.*

～

7 October 1812

Day Two of Enemy Occupation

I am perpetually amazed at the complexities of familial dynamics. I have in my library at Pemberley a most interesting publication called 'Theoria generationis' by one Mr Wolf, in which the author postulates that the formless egg, the component supplied by the female of a species, when properly fed by the nutritive essence provided by the male, is the basis for birth and inheritance. This seminal nourishment, he claims, this gentle bathing in vital sustenance, is the conclusive event that germinates life from lifelessness.

I have lived in this world some while; decidedly long enough to know that when creatures have consumed the nutrients required to sustain their lives, the end result is anything but germinal. Perhaps in time, what is left behind by the sheep has nourished the grass blade that sprouts, but the grass was already there. It certainly does not become another sheep. I must conclude that there is some greater force at work, some element that yet defies human understanding.

For instance, how is it that I am dark-complected and of large stature, yet Georgiana is fair and trim? How is it that Richard is nearly a masculine version of my sister, but his older brother, Viscount Milton, is more similar in appearance to myself?

More importantly, how is it possible that the most angelic of beings, the most beautiful and guileless of all creatures, can find herself in possession of a family full of abject contradictions?

Mrs Bennet called this morning with the rest of her brood to enquire after the health of her 'dearest child.' By this, I presume that she is not, to my dismay, Mr Bennet's second wife, thus indicating that my flawless Miss Jane Bennet did, in fact, spring forth from that matron's ample loins. There, however, the surety of familial connection ended. I might have been mortified at the mother's conduct in sympathy for her other daughters, but they seemed determined to outdo their parent by uproarious displays of indecorum, each more boisterous than the last.

The worst of all was Miss Elizabeth. Good lord, how it pains me even to scribble that name again! There must be some arbiter in the heavens who assigns names based upon character qualities, slipping them into the blankets of new babes before the parents quite understand what has happened. This one ranks among the shrewdest of her breed.

Nay, she did not speak in voluble tones, nor did she importune her host with presumptuous demands for a ball, nor prattle on about the costliness of the furnishings or the size of the room. She left all those impudences to her nest mates. Rather, she sat poised and nearly silent, indulging her sisters with a patient smile now and again as if they were unruly pups instead of ungoverned young ladies. When she did deign to speak, it was to offer some subtle redirection, preying upon the weaker minds of the others and bending them to her will. I hardly think their suspicions were roused, so masterfully was it done.

I confess myself impressed, but even more so am I wary of the vipress's capabilities. In the moment, one might have observed her apparently modest behaviour and presumed that she was doing what she could to defray the awkwardness of the situation. A more seasoned beholder, however, learns to wonder what she is doing that is less obvious.

I wonder how it is that she, with a quirk of her brow, can silence the most ghastly cacophony it has ever been my misfortune to witness.

I wonder how she can lead the unleadable; how Mrs Bennet, with her wandering and illogical turn of mind, can be neatly manipulated into some semblance of rational discourse at a mere word from her daughter.

And I wonder how in blazes she has tricked Caroline Bingley into nearly civil behaviour whenever she is about. Surely, it was not merely that incident at Lucas Lodge when she presented Miss Bingley as an appealing dance partner. What black magic does she possess?

Whatever it is, it seems apparent that people fear her, and not least of all myself.

I am eager for Miss Bennet's recovery. It is reported that her fever is abating, and to that, I say God bless Mr Jones and whatever that maid's name is who attends my fair lady. I have not spoken with her since her arrival, and it is in a tortured sleep I pass my nights, for her room is only a few doors down from my own. Occasionally, I fancy that I can hear the sounds of her own restlessness, but of course, that must be a delusion. I scarce know my right hand from my left, I am in such a state.

I chide myself for my utter lack of wisdom in falling for a woman after exchanging no more than a few dozen words. And from such a family as hers! But my spirit cried out when I first beheld her beauty, and my heart suffers a pang whenever her angelic sweetness crosses my thoughts. How can there be a surer indication that at last, heaven has smiled upon me? I was brought up with good principles; with duty and logic and every rational consideration laid before me. And what has duty done for me? I know this for a certainty, that it is incapable of securing those softer sentiments I have so long been denied.

If I must assuage the shades of my father's advice to me and perform according to duty, perhaps I shall count it my duty to rescue my fair damsel from such a family as her own.

I CLOSED my journal and set it aside, then turned my attention to the tray of letters Bingley's butler had just delivered. Nothing new from Richard, which disappointed me, and it was too soon to hear again from Georgiana. She would be ecstatic when she received the letter I had written her the previous evening, the one detailing all the arrangements for her to come to Netherfield. She was to depart from her seminary in Bath on the tenth with the family of her friend Harriet Smythe, whose father had made a rather timely offer of escorting her when they travelled on to Cambridge. A maid was to come from my London house to see that everything would be in order, and Georgiana should arrive by the twelfth.

She would need a new wardrobe, that was sure. Every new month seemed to add to her height and figure. I shook my head and covered my eyes for a moment, pushing back the grief over all the time I had lost with her. I had scarcely known her at Easter! But it was not only her form that had changed—the inner girl had, as well. Soon she would be making calls with Lady Matlock, or taking meals with the family and selected guests, and she must have the appropriate attire.

Something soft would suit her. Creamy muslin, perhaps with a lavender ribbon like the one Miss Jane Bennet wore... no... no, it was the *other* sister who favoured that shade. How could I make such a mistake? Ah, well, no matter. I would gladly escort Georgiana to the modiste in a month or two when we returned to Town so she might dictate her own preferences.

That decision made, I proceeded to take each letter of business in its turn, never permitting myself to set one aside in preference to the one beneath it. This was a discipline my father had taught me, and one that I had recommended for Bingley time and again... to no avail, for his desk would be a hopeless case were it not for his housekeeper. I kept up a steady rhythm, all the sooner to be finished with the task.

A letter from my steward confirming that the horses for Bingley had set out ahead of schedule, as the weather proved cooperative. That was well, and I replied with my approval.

One was from Mrs Reynolds enquiring about the disposition of certain furnishings that I had ordered to be removed from the house. I told her to burn them, and was only sorry that I was not there to witness the conflagration.

Another was from the Earl of Matlock… this I examined for a moment before breaking the seal, as if I could detect, simply by the weight and cant of the pen used for the direction, what my uncle's mood had been when he wrote it. Our last encounter had not gone well.

He still blamed me, and he made no secret of it either in private or public. Though it chafed maddeningly, I had no choice but to tolerate his abuse. For abuse it was, even when applied by a well-meaning relative, to falsely accuse a man of one thing when his crime was something entirely different.

The contents of his letter were precisely as I expected. Once more, I had neglected my family duties on various fronts. Once more, Lady Catherine was seriously displeased and applying to the earl to rebuke me on her behalf. And, once more, he was entirely wrong about everything. I read his letter, back to front and front to back, just as thoroughly as ever I had been taught to do… but I did not answer it. Such a reply must wait until I was in full possession of my reason and my temper was under good regulation. I did manage to set it aside without crumpling it, and for that, I congratulated myself.

The next letter, and the last of the stack, proved to be no less distressing. It was from my solicitor in London, and he wrote regarding a certain lady's complaint over her small annuity. I snorted in disgust. Even had I been fond of my former mother-in-law, her portion would have been considered bounteous beyond any expectation. Yet, this woman knew my true sentiments towards her, and hers were no warmer for myself, and still it was not sufficient.

In truth, my support was only so generous so that she might keep quiet. I wished never to hear of her even breathing in the same county as myself, and a woman such as she would only check her tongue for as long as she was well-supplied with funds. What she was spending them on, I could not fathom, but more than likely there was a gentleman involved.

My reply to my solicitor was brusque; I would not forward another farthing until the next annuity was due to be paid. It was a risk, but this would not be the last I heard of her if she did intend to create trouble. It was only the opening round of shots fired.

AT LEAST THE dark one left my book alone this evening.

She sat instead on the sofa beside Miss Bingley, engaged in needle-work while the latter endeavoured to educate her about the English Swift's plumage and migratory habits. Though I did not give two straws over the matter, I rolled my eyes when my hostess expressed her admiration for a specimen she claimed to have seen perched on a branch earlier in the day. She had the species wrong—again—the swift had long gone south for the season. This time, however, I did not appear to be alone in noting her absurdity. Miss Elizabeth's mouth turned up on one side as she worked an elaborate knot, but otherwise she maintained her composure disturbingly well.

"I do wish I had seen it, for it sounds lovely," Miss Elizabeth murmured patiently. "Do you have any illustrations, perchance?"

"Naturally! Oh, Mr Darcy," Miss Bingley summoned me, "wher-ever has that book gone? I declare, the maid absolutely insists on putting it up each time I have it out."

I glanced up, raised an eyebrow with a frown, and returned to my own book.

Frustrated, she made a show of stretching and yawning. "Oh, I suppose it does not signify! I do so dote on reading, do you know, but truly, it is not the first of a lady's accomplishments."

"Is it not?" Miss Elizabeth asked with mock innocence. I could not help listening intently—the better to understand my adversary, natu-rally. The hair stood on my neck as I sensed what Miss Bingley was too dull to notice. Miss Elizabeth was like a cat with her prey, toying and permitting some sense of victory before closing in for the kill.

"Why no, to be sure!" Miss Bingley protested. "To be considered truly accomplished, a lady ought to be thoroughly educated in drawing, sewing, and the modern languages. She must set an exquisite table, be well-versed in all the conversational arts, and, of course, consort with only the finest of company."

"That would satisfy your notion of accomplishment?"

"Oh, not at all. She must also possess a certain something in her air, and her manner of walking. A truly accomplished lady is born with a natural talent for such poise, but even less gifted ladies may apply themselves to the instruction of the masters, and to diligent practice."

"Indeed? And where does one acquire such instruction? You must have attended a rather exclusive seminary, Miss Bingley."

"Well—" that lady touched her décolletage and bowed her head modestly to her inquisitor. "I do confess that my own education was rather dear, but you know, one cannot treat the education of a lady too seriously. My seminary is well-known for instilling the model of feminine elegance and sophistication. I have frequently been begged to offer my advice to other young ladies, and I am always happy to oblige. I presume you have often been to town for the benefit of the masters?"

"No, never."

Miss Bingley blinked. "Never! But surely, you had tutors. I suppose your younger sisters must still have a governess?" This last, Miss Bingley intoned with an amused glance in my direction.

"I am afraid not."

"What! Five daughters brought up at home, without a governess? I never heard of such a thing. I wonder that your mother found time to manage the household, for she must have been quite the slave to your education."

Miss Elizabeth emitted a light, airy chuckle that might have been pleasing from one less foxy. "Not at all, I assure you. Any in our house who desired an education might have it. My father thought less of fine manners than the improvement of our minds, and to that end, he encouraged extensive reading for any who would apply herself."

I looked up at this and narrowed my eyes. The room seemed to be commencing a slow, tilted spin, for my head felt strangely light and my sense of equilibrium was unsteady. Long ago, in another life, I had uttered a phrase very like that to Georgiana when she had asked me what I considered most important for her to learn. I never expected anything from this woman I could so heartily endorse, and to hear her nearly quoting myself... I needed fresh air, and badly.

Miss Bingley was nothing if not an astute observer, and she quickly noted my attention. "Why, then..." she fumbled, but only for a moment. "I suppose your father must know what he is about, my dear. A young lady ought to have a great many books as her constant companions. I do believe you would agree, would you not, Mr Darcy?"

I lowered my book. I was still nearly seeing double, but I dared not show any sign of weakness. "Indeed, I would, but a haphazard approach to them I cannot endorse."

"You have supervised the education of your own sister, I presume?" This was Miss Elizabeth, who set her needlework to rest in her lap for a moment as she regarded me with that same tilted head and appearance of innocence.

I shifted my gaze to the saucy tart and could hardly bear to hold it without flinching. There was some keen archness there—were I not so edgy in her presence, I would have been fascinated, but instead, I was alarmed. I composed myself and made as steady an answer as I might. "I have shared the guardianship of my sister these five years with a cousin on our mother's side. I have respected and valued his advice, but any final decisions regarding her upbringing have been mine to make."

She lifted her chin. "You take your duty very seriously."

"I do. I cannot comprehend the neglect of a young lady's education in times such as these."

"'Times such as these?'" she repeated. "By this, I must presume you have not subscribed to the time-honoured methods of training up a young lady for Miss Darcy's education?"

I closed my book. "I desired her to cultivate her thinking by studying the great classics, as I had done. Georgiana is also fond of music, so her school was chosen to afford her such opportunities as would please us both."

A curve appeared on her lips. "And as we know, learning that is not pleasurable to both master and pupil is unlikely to serve after the years in the schoolroom are over."

"I disagree. How should a lad ever learn his letters and figures, had he not a strict master to stand over him with the rod?"

"Perhaps I ought to clarify my meaning. Necessary skills are *not* always pleasurable, but they must be attained, nonetheless. I speak of education beyond those basics, where one may choose to indulge—or not to indulge—in studies which might nourish the mind and soul. The hand holding the pen may be compelled to form correct shapes, but the mind must choose to understand Herodotus or Mozart or Botticelli. It must, of its own initiative, decide whether to create or not, and whether to ponder the deep mysteries or to be content to dwell in the superficial."

"That is only partially true," I argued. "A good many of my own fellow students cared nothing for the higher forms until made to examine them by a diligent master who guided their studies."

Her brows arched. "And pray, did all take to these studies when exposed to them? Were they all teachable?"

"Not all," I admitted.

She offered a gentle dip of her head as if we had both somehow come to the same point from opposite ends. "We are each of us gifted differently, I expect. Some have both the means and the appetite for such an education while others do not. I find many have different aptitudes, which are just as valuable in their way as a mind that can form arguments in Latin or compose an aria in Italian. I should think that a person's level of accomplishment, as you say, has more to do with their willingness to learn and be taught than any innate giftedness."

"Well!" Miss Bingley interjected at last—I wondered why it had taken her so long to insert herself—"none can say that you did not study the art of debate, my dear Miss Eliza. Louisa, let us have some music!"

I allowed one last look to linger on my opponent—this one puzzled rather than piqued—then turned my attention back to my book. Or, rather, my eyes turned to Samuel Johnson. My thoughts went elsewhere.

Mrs Hurst played skilfully. She had chosen a lively piece that diverted the rest of the room, and soon Bingley rose to his feet. He looked about and discovered that Miss Elizabeth's toes were tapping the air, so he extended his hand to her.

"Miss Elizabeth, are you not struck with the urge to dance a reel?"

An immediate smile warmed her face, but before she accepted his hand, she made one fatal error, betraying her true thoughts. She glanced at me.

"I am indeed, Mr Bingley. But what is any dance if there is only one couple? Would it not be twice as amusing if we had companions?"

I refused to look up at her, and most pointedly ignored Caroline Bingley, whose gaze I could sense boring into my brow.

"Capital idea!" Bingley cried. "Come, Darcy, you must stand up with us."

"Perhaps he would prefer not," suggested his partner. "I imagine he might mock our taste in enjoying such an informal, *haphazard* dance."

"He may be sour all he likes the rest of the evening. I care little for his disdain, for you know, he applies it rather liberally, and I have never yet suffered a mortal wound. Caroline, you must join us as well. We could all do with a bit of liveliness."

I reluctantly cast my book aside and took my place opposite my partner. Caroline's hands were, as always, clammy and a bit too cloying, but it was nothing I had not braced myself for. The moment of my undoing was when Bingley, with his characteristic spontaneity, twirled Miss Elizabeth into my path for an impromptu change-up of partners.

If I could have tugged at my cravat, I would have. She met my eyes only once, but there was such a look of comprehension mixed with curiosity, of deadly challenge blended with sportiveness, that for a moment I forgot to breathe. We spun round once, as did Bingley and his sister, and when I turned back to her, she was looking to the side. Her hands were warm and soft, but she would not clasp my own. A mere touch, like the caress of two sabres before a duel, and a few seconds later she was back with Bingley.

I was shaking. Good Mrs Hurst's music helped conceal the greater part of my distress, but every organ in my body cried out for relief from the oppression she had somehow inflicted upon me. Running to my room would avail me nothing, for her presence was in the very air of the house, her enchantment spread like a magician's cloak over all my companions.

I *had* to get her away from Netherfield.

CHAPTER 4

I could ignore her.

I excelled at that, or at least the appearance of it. In my previous experience, when a person felt themselves the interloper, the unwelcome guest, they did the noble thing and quitted the room. However, she persisted in that divan by the window, devouring one of Bingley's books—by all appearances perfectly unconscious of my pointed chilliness, or even my very existence.

For a full half an hour she held me at bay, entirely at her mercy. I could not leave the room without acknowledging her, for I would have to pass by her chair. I could not initiate conversation, for that would be an admission that I noticed her presence. And I most assuredly could not ask for the book she held, when I discovered it was the very one I had sought, for that would be the ultimate concession of defeat.

And so, I bided my time, each book that came to my hand more exceedingly dull than the last. Great heavens, what made the woman think she was welcome in the library? Of all the places I could go to be alone, this was typically the surest, yet she had breached the sanctity of my habitual domain. I needed a new tactic.

Where the devil was Miss Bingley? She vanquished pretentious ladies for sport! I expected some instinct of hers would have long ago sounded the alarm and sent her scurrying to defend her turf, as she saw it. But no—I was left entirely, mercilessly vulnerable.

The minx intended to cede no ground, that much was obvious. And by the way she had smiled at Bingley and he at her last evening while they danced, I knew my time was short. Bad enough that *I* had once fallen prey to one of her ilk. I would not be a true friend if I allowed her to ensnare the most easy-spirited and ingenuous of men.

The epiphany struck me like a brick. Caroline Bingley! And for that matter, Louisa Hurst! They would no more wish their brother to take up with a presumptuous country temptress than I would. And if I set their minds to work on that task, that would be all the less mental capacity they could spare for my own affairs.

The diversion would be useful. Miss Bennet should be down this evening, for I had heard only a short while earlier that her fever had gone, and she was regaining her strength. I would sit by her at the fire and watch in triumph as Miss Elizabeth's schemes towards Bingley failed spectacularly.

∾

If Caroline Bingley had any notion of how effortlessly I was able to turn her considerable jealous energies to my own ends... I doubt she would have minded.

No, the sad truth was that if it brought my pleasure, she would have considered it barely short of a sacred commandment. I ought to have felt at least somewhat guilty in permitting her to carry on so, but I had tried to discourage her for years, with little effect. Shameless and desperate as I was becoming, I decided to make good use of her wiles, though Providence might punish me later.

Thus, it was with no surprise that I saw Miss Bingley hurry for her muff and cape when I announced my intention to take a walk out of doors. Mrs Hurst's company was secured for propriety, and we set out among the hedgerows. The day was fine, and I was often in the habit of walking in the afternoons, so there was no suspicion about it. I had only to wait, so wait I did until the ladies began inevitably to abuse Miss Elizabeth. I did wonder in passing if all gracious hostesses truly disdained their guests as much as Caroline Bingley apparently disliked her own, but it was a point of curiosity I must satisfy at a later date.

"I declare, Caroline, did you see how she came in from her walk this morning? Why, I know she was suitably attired when she went out, but how she got in such a state before she returned, I cannot help but wonder. I think the girl must spend her time running or climbing trees!"

"Louisa, I could hardly keep my countenance! Were it not so early in the morning, I would have been fearful that another neighbour might call and see her flitting about the woods or cavorting with the pigs. What does she think she is about, running about so wantonly out of doors before eight in the morning?"

"I thought you liked Miss Elizabeth," I wondered aloud.

"Like her? Well, of course I *like* her, in the very same way that a Whig likes a Tory, or the English like the French. They are a respectable adversary, a perfect contrast, and one in whose presence our own qualities are so markedly set off. What distinction should there be in ourselves, had we not such an opposite?"

Mrs Hurst applauded. "Well said, Caroline! But I do think it rather unfair that you should tease her so. After all, she is only a simple country girl. She cannot know with whom she has to deal."

"Oh, quite the contrary, I think she does. That is why I like her so well. She is clever, and if you ask me, she fancies herself my equal. I find engaging wits with her to be rather stimulating."

"What do you mean she is clever? Do you imply that she has some hidden agenda?" I asked, smiling inwardly. It really was *too* easy.

"Oh, my dear Mr Darcy, I am sure you could never dream of a young lady insinuating herself among a gentleman's friends simply to put herself in his way. It would never occur to you, so noble and upright as you are! But I am afraid it is true, and terribly common, do you see. Is that not right, Louisa?"

The other sister nodded vigorously.

"Do you think Miss Elizabeth has designs on myself?"

"Oh! No, I cannot think so. Why, she must see how heartily you dislike her, and no girl in the world is fool enough to throw herself after a hopeless cause. But my brother, now he is another problem altogether, do you not think?"

"Bingley has been known to lose his heart to ladies too easily," I confessed.

"Indeed!" agreed Miss Bingley. "And he has been ever so solicitous with Miss Elizabeth, I am dreadfully afraid he might attach himself to the silly creature."

"What would be the harm in it? Her father is a gentleman."

Miss Bingley tittered a patronising laugh, stepping neatly into my little snare. "A very *modest* gentleman, to be sure. But you heard her yourself, she has relations in Cheapside! Oh, no, no, no! It is quite out of the question. We cannot allow it, can we, Louisa?"

"Well, naturally," replied her sister, "but what do you propose to do, Caroline?"

I felt a surge of satisfaction. I need not lift a finger. Bingley's sisters were quite devious enough without any assistance from me.

"Simple enough—" Miss Bingley tossed her head—"we must see that she does not sit near him this evening. I was succeeding marvellously well last evening until Charles got up that silly dance. I suppose it was my fault for asking you to play, but it is a mercy you broke off a nail so you cannot play again tonight. I wish I could say we might drive her away, but with that odious Miss Bennet staying with us, and still rather ill, we would be considered the rudest family in the neighbourhood, and that I cannot have."

"Why, Caroline, what can you possibly have against Jane Bennet?" cried Mrs Hurst.

I regarded Miss Bingley narrowly. Was she truly so small-minded that she could throw stones at perfection? I might have been angered, were it not so pathetic.

"Oh! She is such a deceptive, manipulative creature! I have known ladies like her. The gentlemen fall smitten at her feet, vanquished by the hundreds, but it is all a sham. Mark my words, no lady can truly be so angelic as she appears. There is some fearful dross tainting the gold, of that you can be sure. She quite puts me on my guard, I can tell you. Better to have four or five Miss Elizabeths about causing trouble than a single one such as Miss Bennet! It is a mercy that as soon as she is recovered, they shall be off."

I shook my head but held my peace. Miss Bennet artful and deceptive! One might wonder upon what grounds Miss Bingley could base such an accusation, but it was plain enough. She was positively green with envy and had met her superior in a country girl from Hertfordshire. The humiliation must, indeed, have been bitter.

"I cannot quite agree with you about Miss Bennet," sniffed Mrs Hurst, "but I do not object to letting Miss Elizabeth know her place. I am afraid I shall leave it to you, for I do not think I am equal to it."

"Nothing to it! You saw how easy it was last evening to trick her into betraying her own ignorance on certain matters. Surely, this evening will be the same. The girl absolutely does not know when to keep her mouth closed! I may simply…"

A rustling in the thicket arrested Miss Bingley's speech, and we all halted our steps. A moment later, Miss Elizabeth herself emerged from the brush, looking perfectly nonchalant as she strolled. Her face was cast upward to the heavens, her strides lusty and springy, and a beatific smile warmed her features as if she had just listened to the song of the winter birds coming to rest in the bare branches.

I could not help myself… I took a second glance. And then a third, to verify what I saw. I think I had never known a woman who looked so perfectly at home wandering out of doors, without hanging upon some gentleman's arm. It was the same as with the library—she simply went where she wished, did as she wished, and seemed to care little for the devices and conventions of others. It *must* have been some ploy… but it did not look like one.

She looked hardly surprised to see us, and I doubt not that she had heard something of Miss Bingley's tones, if not her actual words. Whatever she had, or had not, overheard, she gave no indication that anything troubled her. She swept us a playful curtsey. "How do you all do this afternoon? I have been enjoying the gardens. I never knew

Netherfield could boast of such lovely grounds. Even at this time of the year, they are so delightfully arranged that I should not have thought anything wanting."

"Ah," Miss Bingley stammered. "Ahem, my dear Miss Eliza! If we had only known you intended to walk out, we would have waited for you."

"I thank you for your consideration, but I am quite used to walking alone. I find it peaceful, do not you?"

"It is the finest amusement, to be sure," Miss Bingley averred. "A lady ought to enjoy the out-of-doors, as often as she can. It is good for the constitution. Oh, my dear, speaking of that, how does Miss Bennet this afternoon?"

"She was much improved, and I believe she will come down to the drawing room this evening if she continues to feel stronger."

"That is welcome news," I answered. "Please give Miss Bennet our well wishes. We shall hope to see her later."

She stared into my eyes for an instant, some iron hardening her flinty gaze, then inclined her head. "You are most gracious, sir."

Miss Bingley could scarcely abide that I was speaking to another woman and inserted herself again. "Would you care to join us, Miss Eliza?"

"I thank you, but no. You all look so happily situated just as you are, and the woods do ring with such *merry* conversation when intimate friends are permitted to remain together, without an odd addition to the party. I shall look in on my sister and see you all at dinner."

With that, she flashed a bewitching smile and was off, no doubt running and playing with the dogs or some other such nonsense.

The remainder of our walk was silent. Caroline Bingley's cheeks had taken on a greenish hue, and I wondered if she would be ill, while Mrs Hurst looked quite red. We reached the end of the path, and I tipped my hat to the ladies, then took myself to the stables for a long, long ride.

I was almost too mortified to show my face that evening. Could the crafty one have set us down more elegantly in our shameful gossip and scheming? And such a countenance as she had possessed! If she had been angry, which I am certain she had every right to be, she was too self-composed to reveal it. Painful as it was to acknowledge, I was forced to bow to her as my superior in that instance.

How greatly my own shame had multiplied! If my father had only known how far I would sink from the honourable man he had trained up, he would have disowned me on his deathbed. Today's example of my own nefarious ways was only the crown jewel in the last year and a half of my life—a year and a half of wretched backsliding such as I had never believed myself capable of.

Was there any return for me? I had to hope there might be. Each time I thought of the serene, innocent Miss Bennet, my thoughts had begun to dwell less upon her extravagant beauty and more upon how desperately I craved just an ounce of her sweetness for myself. I could not have mistaken it—the tender, gentle way she had looked at me, the simple kindness in every word for every person—she truly was the picture of grace. In her pure, radiant presence, my darkness must flee, must it not? For if any woman could see whether I still possessed some goodness, it could only be she.

Yet what good could she attribute to a man who insulted her sister at every turn? If she were as faithful as I believed her to be, she could want nothing to do with me. Plainly, I must make some amends, and I could only begin by forfeiting the battle with the younger sister. *Elizabeth.*

Still, I could not even think that name without bile surging into my throat. My heart would race as if for combat, and blood would pump to my extremities... and sadly, away from my head, leading me on to all manner of infamous behaviour. It would be so for as long as she was called by the same unfortunate name as that *other* creature.

Perhaps I should think of her by a different appellation, one that would not raise my hackles each time she crossed my mind. She was a warrior... almost regal in her manifold victories over me, so little effort did she seem to exert. *Queen Bess.*

I ridiculed myself—admittedly, the first time I had done so in a very long while. Such a title for a country maid! But when I encountered her later, I repeated the name as a mantra in my head until I could almost believe it and look at her without flinching. And she, oddly, seemed to pay me little notice. I could not decide if that relieved or frustrated me.

After we had all retired to the drawing room for the evening, Miss Bennet came down on her sister's arm. I rose to greet her, as did everyone else save Hurst, who was already dozing on the sofa. I was necessarily the last to speak to her, and I spared a moment to appraise her once more. Her eyes glittered with the final vestiges of her fever, and her colour was high, but she appeared strong enough for now. I vowed to watch carefully for any signs of fatigue, for I could not bear to think of her overtaxing herself.

Bingley, attentive host that he was, had set chairs near the fire, and Miss Bingley took Miss Bennet by the arm. "Come, Miss Bennet, sit with me. I have so longed to see you up and well, and I simply must hear more of you. I believe you were telling me about that precious little embroidery knot that all the ladies were so fond of?"

"Oh, dear Caroline," Mrs Hurst said, "you ought not tire our guest with your questions." She emphasised this remark with a sideways glance at Queen Bess, who was assuming a seat on the sofa… beside Bingley.

"Quite so, Louisa!" Miss Bingley agreed at once. "My dear Miss Bennet, would you not prefer your sister's company? Surely, she will best know how to make you comfortable."

Jane Bennet sighed in obvious relief—I could hardly blame her—and replied, "Whatever you suggest, Miss Bingley."

"But of course! Come, Miss Eliza, I do apologise for imposing upon you, but I daresay your presence would be more familiar, as our dear Miss Bennet has not yet regained her strength."

To the victor, the spoils… the conquering queen smiled faintly as she stood and moved to sit beside her sister, and I began to feel some concern that Miss Bingley and Mrs Hurst were waging the wrong war. They seemed set upon their course, however, and chose the nearest chairs to the Bennet sisters, effectively blocking both Bingley and me from the conversation.

"My dear Miss Bennet," Miss Bingley spoke in a velvet tone, "you have missed so many enchanting conversations these last evenings. We were speaking often of sisters and education, and I fancy you would have had much to say on such topics."

I rolled my eyes. Bingley, I noticed, was leaning forward on his elbows to better hear Miss Bennet's reply.

"I have four sisters," Miss Bennet answered.

Caroline Bingley's smile looked pained. "Yes, dear, I have met them... all. As well as your mother! Now there is a lady who speaks her mind—did we not say that very thing, Louisa? Tell me, Miss Bennet, was your mother's father in the same trade as your uncle?"

Miss Bennet blinked, and her starry azure eyes shifted to her sister. At a subtle nod from the latter, she blurted, "He was a clerk."

"A... a clerk?" Miss Bingley fanned herself and exchanged bemused glances with Mrs Hurst. "Why, that is very... democratic."

The minx laughed. "Jane, you forget, Miss Bingley is not familiar with your sense of humour. You do enjoy provoking people so!"

Miss Bingley's nose wrinkled, and her fan waved more quickly. "I am afraid I do not have the pleasure of understanding you."

Miss Bennet once again glanced to her sister, then drew what appeared to be a steadying breath. "A clerk. That was what he always called himself."

"Even until his death, when he was consigning the solicitor's office to our uncle Philips and his warehouse to his own son. Grandfather Gardiner always was rather modest," chuckled Miss Elizabeth.

"He owned both a legal practice and a warehouse?" Miss Bingley was gaping at her own sister.

"He was very wealthy," insisted Miss Bennet, with the sort of patent innocence that a child might possess.

"As a successful solicitor sometimes is!" interrupted Miss Elizabeth. "But how he would frown to hear us speaking so, would he not, Jane?"

Miss Bennet wetted her lips, watching her sister intently, and nodded. "Of course, we should not speak only of ourselves. What was *your* father's profession, Miss Bingley?"

Miss Elizabeth happened to be sipping from her tea saucer just then, and she seemed to experience some difficulty in swallowing. Bingley smothered an enormous grin, but the ladies both suffered a near apoplexy. Miss Bingley sputtered, Mrs Hurst covered her mouth with her fingertips, and I… I could not help but laugh. Silently.

Innocent Miss Bennet simply gazed at them in patient attendance. What a marvel she was! In all my years amongst the elite of the *ton*, I had never witnessed such a masterful reversal of an otherwise impertinent conversation, save perhaps for her younger sister's efforts. Miss Elizabeth was adept at the appearance of innocence until the moment she thrust her sword, and then that twinkle in her dark eyes gave her away. Miss Bennet, however, stretched credulity with her sweetly candid and open manner.

It was Bingley who recovered his powers of speech first and modestly made explanation. "Our family owns three textile mills in the north, Miss Bennet. My father had a true head for the business, and now I am left simply to oversee it from afar. Occasionally, I do wish I had something more to do with it."

"And why do you say this, Mr Bingley?" This was the troublemaker again, fixing my friend in that magnetic gaze until I quite feared he might be drawn in. "Have you been displeased by the present management of the business?"

"Oh, nothing like that." Bingley shook his head. "It is only that I think perhaps I ought to play a larger part, you know, live up to my father and grandfather's legacy and take some satisfaction in my role."

I scoffed. "What satisfaction would you hope to gain by spending your life in a stuffy, dirty woollen mill? Bending over ledgers all day long, managing labour strikes and supply difficulties—your nature would never bear it."

"How so?" he asked.

"Why, the master of such an enterprise must be hard, must not break when he is tried by his workers. You would bend at the first ill wind."

"It seems to me," objected Miss Elizabeth, "that in declaring him unsuited to such a task, you have only shown off Mr Bingley's kindly nature."

"Kindly he is—kind enough to be ruined by any who would wish to take advantage of him. He would be swayed by any argument, be it legitimate or no. And how, Bingley, do you think you would sustain a month of tracking production numbers and writing a dozen business letters each day? Do you expect anyone would even be able to read what you wrote?"

"It is only because my ideas flow so quickly that I cannot put them all down properly," Bingley retorted with a genial chuckle.

"You are rather proud of this defect of yours, claiming it stems from an active mind, but if you were tested in business, you would discover that this quickness you so prize would be valued only by yourself. Others would think you an undisciplined fool, but all the while you would pride yourself on your clever foibles and easy temper."

"You are not wrong," Bingley confessed. "It is true, I should rather keep everyone at peace, and it troubles me greatly when I find myself at odds with others. I do not consider that a weakness, however, but a strength of a sort. Why, I have learned a fair bit about personalities and discovering what each person wants. You would be surprised, if you thought for a moment, what a useful skill that can be."

"Are you a student of character as well, Mr Bingley?" Miss Elizabeth asked.

"I suppose so, if that is what you would call it. Perhaps it is some instinct I inherited from my father, but I am afraid I do not ponder deeply, as I suspect you do, Miss Elizabeth. I am content to see a situation for what is needed, and then to think on other topics as they please me."

"And there you go, Charles, always speaking on such indelicate subjects," Caroline Bingley sighed. "Pray, do not prattle on so, for Miss Bennet and Miss Elizabeth can have no interest whatsoever in your strange little oddities. Shall not we speak of something more suitable? Miss Bennet, do you play the pianoforte?"

Miss Bennet had been listening to Bingley's speech with peculiar attention, and now she blinked at Miss Bingley as if forcibly awakened from a pleasant dream. "I am dreadful on the piano. I hope you do not require your guests to perform, Miss Bingley."

Miss Elizabeth patted her sister's hand with a tender laugh. "Not until you are feeling yourself again, of course. But my dear, I am afraid you have grown too warm. Would you like to move from the fire?"

I narrowed my eyes and frowned at Miss Elizabeth. What had got into the troublesome creature? She seemed determined to direct her sister's conversations, and I could only think it a disingenuous means of drawing the attention back to herself. I snorted silently. The artful vixen! She had succeeded in forcing Mrs Hurst to trade seats with Miss Bennet, but Miss Bingley remained resolutely fixed in her chair between myself and Miss Elizabeth.

I could not move from my own seat without causing an uncomfortable disturbance, but hang it all, it was *Bingley* who was now speaking in low tones to Miss Bennet! He was nearly touching her hand, so closely seated were they, and those easy smiles, those light, beautiful laughs, they were all for *him*. It was all well and proper to be an excellent host, particularly when one's guest had been ill, and Bingley was without his equal in that regard. Naturally, he could offer and ask certain things which were not in my power, and I was pleased beyond measure that Miss Bennet's comforts were so well looked after. But I had never in my life envied Bingley until that moment.

I scowled faintly and leaned against the back of the sofa, draping my arm over the edge and kneading my fingers. Miss Bingley shifted, and I noticed that she wore a rather impressive frown herself... and then I caught Miss Elizabeth's eye. Well did I know that spark of triumph, that satisfied hint of a smile. It was in that moment that I understood.

She was not putting herself in Bingley's way. She was working to remove all barriers between Bingley and my angel. And I was her primary obstacle.

CHAPTER 5

Darcy,

Tell me you did not challenge Benedict to a duel! I could not believe my ears the first day I had leave and went to my club. They could have told me Boney had surrendered to Nelson's ghost, and I would have believed it, but you, practically spoiling for a fight and provoked to duelling words? I would not have credited it, but it is on every wagging tongue, and the reports have you choosing pistols. (Bloody mistake, for you could best him in a moment with the sword, but with a pistol, occasionally even a blind man gets lucky.)

I can only presume that since you have not asked me to be your second, the challenge was never carried off? But to hear the talk, you all but stripped off your coat and went to fisticuffs right in Colchester's billiards room! Egad, I wish I had seen it, but it was still a damned foolish thing to do. You were in a fix enough, old chap. I suppose I needn't tell you that.

I am afraid my sources were not entirely certain what instigated that little scene of yours. Some say you went there in search of Benedict on purpose to challenge him. Others say Benedict accosted you by surprise. Now, I am a military man, and I have learned that the truth between two conflicting reports is often somewhere in the middle. I had my suspicions somewhat confirmed when I bumped into George Wickham yesterday and he claimed to have heard several first-hand accounts. I understand he sees Carlisle and

Ramsey on occasion, though why they still bother playing cards with the bankrupt cheat, I cannot comprehend.

You will never credit this, so I am eager to be the first to tell you. Wickham intends to join the militia! There, now after you have picked yourself off the floor and read that line thrice more, here is the real shock. He is friends with a Lieutenant Denny, who is posted in Meryton, and so he is bound there in a few days. Is that not just a few miles from Bingley's estate? Soon you shall have the pleasure of our old thorn in the side to keep you company there in Hertfordshire.

Do me a favour, Darcy, and try to refrain from any public words with the man. One rumoured duel is quite enough, although Wickham would never have the spine to stand up to you. I presume that affair over Kympton was all settled long ago, but as I recall, other unpleasantries arose to divert your attentions about the same time, and so I do not think I was privy to the outcome. At any rate, I am sure you will not be surprised to know that he is joining the militia because he has pockets to let again.

Well, enough of Wickham. I saw Mother last night, and she asked after Georgiana. She expects to see you both at Christmas, but Father overheard and had some colourful expressions of his own about the terms upon which you would be received at the house. Not Georgiana, mind, but you. I shall do what I can to smooth the waters, but he is under some woeful misapprehension from which, I am sorry to say, I hesitate to disabuse him.

By the by, give our dear girl a kiss from her cousin, will you? I am anxious to see her, and quite jealous that I will have to wait until you come away from Hertfordshire.

Regards,
Richard

I set Richard's latest letter aside with a frown. I ought to have known that rumours would have been flying since that evening at Colchester's. They would have done so if that scene had played out between any two other men, but myself? My reputation had always been that of the reserved, the patient, the cautious, and I had blasted it, along with my dignity, in one ill-judged encounter.

The animosity between Benedict and myself was no surprise to anyone, least of all those present in the room. Still, I ought to have turned round and left the moment I saw him, even if it branded me some sort of social coward. The offended, however, are not often wise, and I was monstrously offended. I still could not reconcile myself to taking what would have been the more prudent course. Well, it was done, and I doubted any real harm could come from it.

I did have to laugh when I read of Wickham's new venture. Was this not the man who used to hide behind me after taunting the stable hands until they were ready to bruise him? And he, with a pistol in his hand, responsible for securing peace and order! The militia would find themselves in possession of a sharp-looking, smooth-tongued booby who swindled all the officers at cards by day and bedded all the local shopkeeper's daughters by night. He would probably not be unique among the ranks.

I read the bottom of Richard's letter once more and decided to write to the countess. I had been disgracefully negligent in my correspondence with her, and mostly because I believed her opinions to be in line with her husband's. Perhaps I had been mistaken there. Regardless, Georgiana would have need of her aunt, and I could not allow my personal trials to hinder her chances.

WHEN I CAME DOWNSTAIRS, I was surprised to discover that Miss Jane Bennet and... whatever I ought to call her—Queen Bess made me chuckle, but was mightily cumbersome... at any rate, the Bennet sisters were already in the drawing room. Moreover, they were quite alone. I greeted them from the doorway, asked after Miss Bennet's health, then hesitated. With no others to act as a foil, would I be imperilled by the vexing one?

I decided to chance it. With Miss Bennet's rapid improvement came the understanding that she would soon return to Longbourn, the fortress of the enemy. If I meant to know more of her, I would vastly prefer to deal with only one of her siblings rather than the entire cohort.

A gallant inspiration struck me. "I beg your pardon, Miss Bennet and Miss Elizabeth, but shall I ring for tea?" Truthfully, my notion was less chivalrous than strategic, for refreshment gave one time to collect himself, instead of staring at a lady waiting for some conversational revelation to lead his thoughts.

Miss Bennet looked up from her needlework and then curiously to her sister. I was not certain, but I believed the only signal that passed between them was a blink by Miss Elizabeth, However, Miss Bennet shyly accepted my offer. I called for the tea, then chose a seat somewhat closer to Miss Bennet than the other.

"Are you not riding today, Mr Darcy?" asked Miss Elizabeth.

"I went out at dawn."

"Yes, I recall that. I always walk the gardens first thing in the morning, so I saw you coming in. But is it not your habit to ride again just after luncheon on the days when you do not go shooting with Mr Bingley?"

I crossed my boots and shifted in my chair. "You are quite familiar with my habits, Miss Elizabeth."

She smiled and studied the tip of her needle to be certain it was sharp. "You are a creature of habit, sir, so it does not take long to learn your ways. Mr Bingley, however, is less easy to predict."

I raised an eyebrow. "For instance?"

"For instance, just now he might be in his study or on his horse, out with his hounds or with his steward, or simply wandering about in search of something to do. Do you never do the same, sir?"

"Search for something to do? I hope not. I always have enough tasks at hand without looking for more. When I have my leisure, it is because I have earned it. Bingley, on the other hand, is likely to have forgotten something he truly meant to do, and is trying to discover what it is."

She smiled in pure amusement. *"Those who have least to do are generally the most busy people in the world."*

I tipped my chin lower and examined her expression. I ought to have known that a woman who enjoyed Johnson would also have read Richardson. "Bingley has many qualities, though orderliness is not one of them. *The wisest among us is a fool in some things."*

She laughed at my retaliatory quotation. "Indeed. Yet, you still have not answered my question."

"Why I am not riding this afternoon? I had an unusual amount of correspondence to answer today, some of which pertained to my sister's imminent arrival."

"Ah, the famous Miss Darcy! Pray, tell us more of her. We shall be delighted to know another young lady in the neighbourhood."

Hah! As if I would permit Georgiana to associate with a sly, indecorous —"What do you wish me to tell you?" I heard myself ask.

"Why, we already know her age and stature, so let us try for something more interesting. Is she adventurous or retiring? Does she prefer much company or little? You have told us she is fond of music, so what can you tell of her tastes and preferences?"

I stretched my arm over the side of the chair and thought for a moment. "She is both adventurous and retiring, as you put it. She is fond of riding and travelling, but when indoors, she often seeks quiet. She does not prefer large gatherings unless she is among persons well known to her, and though her company is often sought, she is hesitant to put herself forward. Her talent upon the pianoforte is exquisite, but she does not care to perform to strangers."

"An ideal young lady, then," Miss Elizabeth surmised.

"How so?"

"Is it not desirable that a young lady should be both dauntless and reticent? Comfortable and yet reserved in company? A talent without equal who bestows such a gift on only one or two intimate listeners? I understood such a fine balance of contradictions was the expected comportment in society."

I frowned and thought for a moment. The sardonic little wit, she had captured the *ton's* expectations more adroitly than anyone I had ever heard. Indeed, her conclusion was correct, and perhaps Georgiana was in no way to be faulted for meeting the standard, but my sister had always lacked something.

Certainly, she was charming when she wished, and full of interesting things to say, if one could follow the vagaries of thought which inspired them. She was highly intelligent, disciplined, and considerate, so the blame was not in her abilities, character, or disposition. I never could put my finger on it, save to say that Georgiana never knew quite what to do with herself in company. She relied on others for social cues, sometimes laughing inappropriately or sharing more personal information than was fitting. The poor girl would be easy prey for one such as Miss Bingley or... well, there was a reason I had kept her away from Pemberley for so long.

The regal minx was still waiting for my answer, one of those slim dark brows bent upward and a curious half-smile turning her lips. "She is everything a young lady ought to be," I concluded.

She acknowledged my response with a simple dip of her head and turned back to her needlework. I tapped my finger on the arm of the chair, seeking something I might say to Miss Bennet. At last, I thought I hit upon something.

"Miss Bennet, I had heard that you enjoy riding. Perhaps when you are recovered, we may plan an outing?"

Her sapphire eyes widened, and she blanched a moment. "I... do like horses. They are peaceful."

"Peaceful?" I asked. "How do you mean?"

Her lips pinched, and she glanced at her sister. "I always know what a horse is thinking," she supplied at last.

I smiled. "Indeed, they are far simpler creatures than we humans. I do enjoy them for that." She nodded and again bowed her head to her work.

The door opened, and a maid pushed a tea cart into the room. I nearly gasped in relief, for I had not yet thought of what to ask her next. The conversation had nowhere else to go, for the lady seemed to have nothing more to say on the subject. Once tea was served, the needlework would be put aside, and I could command a little more of her attention.

Miss Elizabeth rose to do the honours, serving her sister first. She came next to me, but before she poured my tea, she drew out a single sugar cube and broke it in half with the spoon. She then dropped it into the bottom of my empty cup and poured a second cup beside it for herself. My cup she filled last, so that I received the very darkest and richest nectar from the bottom of the pot. I gaped at her in astonishment.

"What is this, Miss Elizabeth?"

Her lips puckered in a silent chuckle. "As I said, sir, you are a creature of habit. You always take your tea like this."

I was some while in recovering myself. Ought I to be flattered, or nervous that she already knew my ways so well? For I had never vocalised my preferences, knowing that no one would quite understand them. I simply broke my own sugar lump and made a practice of waiting until everyone else had been served before I permitted my cup to be filled. No one, save my own maids, ever knew that it was out of personal inclination rather than happenstance.

A flood of heat spread over my face as I accepted the tea from her hand. "Thank you," I managed. Then, all I could do was to stare at my cup. A worthy adversary, this particular Elizabeth was. Not like that *other*, whose narrow mind was only capable of grasping the size of my coffers. And she still somehow committed matrimony upon me! *This* Elizabeth studied me, seemed to comprehend me, and was always a step or two ahead of me. My saucer trembled as my hands shook uncontrollably.

A wiser man would have left the country then and there. A fast coach to London, with an express sent to Georgiana that Hertfordshire was no longer in the plans. Bingley and his new estate be hanged, I would be a fool to stay in the area another day.

But a fool, apparently, I was. An arrogant one, and a reckless one, too, for just as I had so stupidly done with Benedict in Colchester's billiards room, so I was doing yet again without remorse, or even forethought. Too many times in recent memory had I been forced to stay my hand, to silence my vindications, but no longer. I could not bear to lose ground when I felt my purpose to be in the right.

With that object in mind, I waited for Miss Bennet to lower her cup and spoke, my voice only slightly hoarse. "I am afraid we are not amusing company for you at present. How do you prefer to pass the time, Miss Bennet? Do you like to read?"

She seemed surprised that I was speaking to her again, and her lashes fluttered while she collected her thoughts. "I like... I liked *The History of Charles Grandison.*"

"Ah, I see that Richardson must be a family favourite." I nodded, brushing my lips thoughtfully with my finger. "I found it a more wandering plot than *Clarissa*, but of solid merit, nonetheless. Pray, what thought you of Clementia's resolve first to compromise on her religion for the sake of love, and then her reversal to hold fast to the faith of her youth?"

Miss Bennet merely blinked. She opened her mouth as if to speak, her brows worked in some confused manner, and she fell to toying with her cup.

"Forgive me, Miss Bennet," I apologised. "I had not intended to make you uncomfortable. I suppose that is an impertinent question to ask a lady."

"There is no need to apologise, Mr Darcy," Miss Elizabeth admonished. "We are not such fine ladies as Miss Byron, who scarcely recovers from one fit before she is preparing to swoon again. Jane, were you not just telling me the other day that you felt a lady—such as Clementia della Porretta or Harriet Byron—ought to base her choice of a partner both on affection and respect?"

Miss Bennet nodded. "Yes, yes, that is what I said."

"And, of course, Mr Grandison's character was immoderately good, so that his morality was never in question, nor his generosity and benevolence. Therefore, it remains only to secure the affections of the lady, who must feel that she can entrust her hand to one who will not rob her of her true nature—to one, rather, who would value, instead of set himself at odds with those things which are a part of her. For if he truly disagreed and could not tolerate her convictions, yet claimed that he *could* simply to appease her, then he would be doing them both a disservice."

"That *is* like what I said." Miss Bennet hesitated, then offered me a smile that shone as brilliantly as the sun. "Yes, she ought to feel that the gentleman can respect her as well as she respects him."

"And," I asked, my curiosity piqued by this unusual response, "do you think Mr Grandison would have—how did you say—'set himself at odds' with Clementia's religion? He agreed to compromise just as she did. You believe he did not know his own mind?"

"I do not..." She wetted her lips and then drew a hasty sip of tea.

"Jane," sighed Miss Elizabeth as she held a line of stitches up to the light to examine them, "did you not find Mr Grandison a rather inflexible, unchanging sort of man?"

"What do you mean by that?" I asked, forgetting for the moment that she had not spoken to *me*. "Why ought he to change? Is he not already a paragon of all man's best qualities?"

"Is he?" Miss Elizabeth challenged. "Did he ever grow by his experiences? I found his excessive goodness rather dull, for no one can be so faultless. Truly interesting people possess an abundance of flaws. The lesser ones deny them, the better ones are quick to own them, and the perfect ones..."

"What?"

She smiled. "They do not exist," she whispered.

"Then what do you recommend?" I demanded. "Your standards are high, indeed, if such a character as Charles Grandison fails to meet your expectations. Shall such a figure be denied happiness, in your estimation, simply because he is not 'interesting'?"

"I never claimed such. I only stated that if he were truly good, he would have learned something of himself and we would have seen his already sterling qualities improved through the course of the story. As we did not, I can only conclude that his character was not genuine, and it was merely a figment of the author's imagination. The ladies, now their personalities I am able to understand, but Mr Richardson ought to have studied the members of his own sex a little more before endeavouring to create one."

I lapsed into a vexed sulk, drumming my fingers on the arm of the chair and snatching occasional glances out of the window. The audacity of the woman, to claim that no man could simply be good without the bother of constant amendments to his character!

Miss Bennet was biting her lip, her sweet nature troubled by my obvious annoyance. But Miss Elizabeth had resumed her stitches, just as if the conversation had never happened, and just as if I did not steal glimpses of her thoughtful countenance each time she tilted it to examine her work. The woman really ought to do something about those wisps of hair that continually tumbled over her eyes, for it was maddeningly distracting the way she would brush at them, only to have them fall once more.

"Ah! Here you all are!" Bingley strolled into the room, wearing a broad grin and mud-splattered breeches. The two great pointers I had gifted him trotted at his heels, cutting a rather impressive figure. "Darcy, I was just looking for you. I am surprised to find you here. Miss Bennet, how do you do this afternoon?"

Bingley pulled up the chair closest to mine, and I at last drew an easy breath. I had been wrong to stare down the lioness in her den without a second, and I never intended to make that mistake again. Bingley would smooth the discourse, as he always did. I never would know his trick, for he was not the cleverest of men, nor the most worldly, but there was something in his air that disarmed the prickliest of conversationalists.

Miss Bennet seemed to blossom at once in his company, for her countenance shone and she readily set aside her needlework. "I am well, sir. Mr Darcy was kind enough to call for some tea, but I am afraid it is all gone cold now. Shall I ring for some more for you?"

"No, no, that will be quite all right, Miss Bennet—" Bingley shook his head. "Ah, what a capital way to spend the afternoon! A fine brisk ride, excellent company, and a quiet evening in to look forward to. I do enjoy going out, Miss Bennet, but I declare, there is no pleasure at all like staying at home. Do you not agree?"

"Very much so, Mr Bingley," she answered with a radiant smile. She put out her hand, and Bingley's pointer—the female—came to sniff her fingers. The bitch seemed to approve of the lady, for she licked cautiously at her hand and slowly curled up at her feet. I looked on in perfect satisfaction. Dogs were excellent judges of character, were they not? What better commendation could a person ask for than a dog's affection? I nearly laughed aloud when I remembered how many times my own dogs had bitten the former Mrs Darcy. I always gave them a fine juicy steak afterward.

"Darcy," Bingley gestured with his index finger, "I just came in from the south field and there is some sign of flooding. I spoke with the steward, and he said there had been a trench dug some years ago, but it is broken down somehow. I am afraid it will have to be re-dug before that field is utterly ruined."

"I believe I can tell you something of that trench," put in Miss Elizabeth.

"Really?" Bingley asked in interest.

"Yes, you see, your closest neighbour to the south is Samuel Bowers, the present master of Purvis Lodge. When Netherfield lay vacant, I am afraid Mr Bowers permitted his cattle and horses to forage on your lands. In doing so, they trampled that trench until it no longer functioned. There was some trouble with flooding last year too, as I recall, but no one bothered to repair the damage. I believe if you speak with Mr Bowers, he would be reasonable and help to pay for the work to be done over again. Should you find him less amenable, you may always take it up with my father."

"Your father?"

"Indeed, for he is the nearest magistrate. Quite against his will, I might add, but there it is. I am sure he would stir himself to be of some use in this matter."

"I say!" Bingley cried. "You have saved me a deal of trouble, Miss Elizabeth! I had set my steward about the task of discovering what to do, and now he needn't bother. Thank you!"

"You are quite welcome, Mr Bingley."

"Well! With that aside, what of more pleasant topics? Miss Bennet, now that you are recovering your strength, I hope I have welcome news for you. I have agreed—that is, I have decided—to host a ball sometime next month. What do you think, will it be well-received?"

She blessed him with a gasp of surprise and a very prettily worded approval. I tapped my finger on the side of the chair again and permitted my fancy a bit of rein. She would come, attired in her very finest, her golden hair a confection of curls and tucks that I could gaze at all evening and still discover something new with each glance. Her starlight blue eyes would sparkle just for me, and she would breathlessly accept when I begged—

"May I have the first set, Miss Bennet?"

I blinked. Those words had *not* come from my mouth.

Bingley was leaning half out of his chair and reaching for the tips of her fingers. "I apologise for being so forward—after all, we have not even set the date for the ball! But you are presently my guest, and I suppose we might say that it is in honour of your recovery that we are now prepared to begin planning it, and so… do you mind very much, Miss Bennet?"

Her porcelain cheeks were rosy with pleasure as she murmured a soft "Yes."

I must have been exhibiting a rather astonishingly sour face, for I swear, I heard a muffled snort from Miss Elizabeth. When I shot her a disapproving glare, she seemed not to notice me at all. She merely continued to scratch the ears of Bingley's male pointer, who was draping his massive head over her knee, thumping his great tail, and groaning in ecstasy as if he had just found the patron saint of all dogs.

I sat back in my chair and proceeded to scowl at the window. For all my trouble, all I had to show for this interlude was the knowledge that Miss Bennet liked horses, and may or may not have actually read the book she professed to like.

And she would dance first with Bingley at the ball.

CHAPTER 6

I was not even sorry to learn that the Misses Bennet had applied to Bingley for the use of his carriage after church the next morning. Apparently, there must have been something wrong with Longbourn's carriage—a broken mother came to mind— but the ladies had determined that they wished to go, and so go they would. I believe Bingley was the only one who heard their resolve with any true regret, although Miss Bingley feigned it quite handsomely, and Bingley's dogs trailed after the ladies even when the carriage pulled out of the drive.

My own feelings, I could not attempt to describe. I had never been so frustrated in all my years, at least not in such a way. I had naturally known the destruction of all my hopes, but in that former instance, there had been no crystalline drops of relief ever present to afflict my Tantalus. Here, my object had been before me, within reach at any moment, and yet I was no nearer—nay, I daresay I was farther away— than I had been five days earlier.

The worst of it was not my failure to speak more than a few short sentences to Miss Bennet in all those days. No, the worst, the understanding that was costing me sleep and twisting my stomach into knots, was the recognition that I was not equal to the one I had set myself against. Who was this persecutor who so deftly slipped between myself and the woman I wished to win? Why was she so set against me that she scarcely permitted me a moment of liberty before her sabre cut me off? Bingley, she did not object to, yet was I not the better catch for her sister? Was my notice a thing to be despised?

I spent most of the afternoon out riding or walking, doing all within my power to avoid Mrs Hurst and Miss Bingley while I stewed in my torment. Theirs were opinions I most decidedly did not need, particularly after that humiliating scene in the drawing room the previous evening.

Miss Bingley had obliged Miss Bennet, and later Miss Elizabeth, to take a turn about the room with her in order to show off her own figure. She would have been greatly dismayed to hear my whole opinion on the matter, and in fact, I was still infuriated with myself for ever confessing the truth.

And the truth was that Miss Elizabeth walked very well.

Bloody hell, what the devil could I have been thinking? But on my father's grave, it was true. Her steps were elastic, her carriage poised and easy, her manner pleasing....

Good lord, it was happening again! One stray thought, one moment of unguarded vanity, and I would be forever trapped!

I am afraid that my bitterness may have ruined the remainder of that last evening for my companions. Miss Bingley, ever eager to appease me and to display her finer qualities, had applied herself to the instrument for an exhibition which might have proved sufficient to frighten away the dourest of moods, but through the whole performance, Bingley and Miss Bennet sat close together and smiled at each other. She never even looked my way.

Matters had only grown worse when Miss Bingley coerced Queen Bess to play. Devil take me, but I did not hate it. Not even when Miss Bingley interrupted the minx's playing to give her a more complicated piece, one beyond her modest abilities. I could only watch how the sliver of her tongue pressed against her upper lip, how the faintest crease would come and go on her brow as she worked her way through it. And then, I had to excuse myself.

Mercifully, they were gone now, but all that Sunday afternoon, I paced and fretted, galloped and wandered, working myself into a lather as I brooded and fumed over the failings of my own flesh. When I finally did permit myself the relief of going back indoors, I ordered a hot bath and stayed in it until long after the steam had gone, and my skin had wrinkled. I gazed up at the ceiling, breathing deeply, and tried for all my soul was worth to sort out the mess I found myself in.

When I finally roused myself to dress, my valet informed me that Georgiana's maid had arrived earlier in the afternoon and was asking my approval of the room and the items she had brought from London. I sighed and agreed to look over the chambers, though I could not think what might be wanting. When I entered the room, however, I learned what the maid must have meant.

Miss Bingley, in an effort to show herself the welcoming hostess, had decked the room in an assortment of hothouse flowers. Irises, lilies, orchids, massive sprays of jasmine and geraniums—it gave me a headache merely to walk in the door. It was just as the former Mrs Darcy used to do, for that harridan had known how heartily I disliked the heavy fragrances and the waste of so many flowers. I grimaced, pinching the bridge of my nose, and asked the maid to have them all taken away.

"But what shall I tell the housekeeper?" she protested. "She said Miss Bingley was ever so insistent, sir."

"Tell her whatever you like. Let the flowers be set out in the common rooms or given to the tenants for all I care. Or tell her that Miss Darcy is sensitive to the pollen."

She bobbed a curtsey. "Yes, Mr Darcy."

"No, wait. Stay a moment." I looked about the room, imagining how ponderous all Miss Bingley's décor would be without the softening effect of the flowers. "Perhaps we might leave some welcome for Miss Darcy." I thought for a moment, then my decision seemed to leap out at me from nowhere. "Ask the housekeeper if she can procure some dried lavender."

"Lavender, sir?"

I nodded, slowly. I did not know from where it had been coming, but I had been noticing that light, earthy fragrance more and more of late, and it was one that carried fond memories from my boyhood. "Yes," I affirmed in a soft voice. "For both her room and my own. Lavender would suit very well."

~

TWO DAYS LATER, the world was bright again. Georgiana's party were to stop at the coaching inn in Meryton, and as I was impatient to see her, I determined to take my carriage to escort her the rest of the way to Netherfield myself. Bingley rode beside the carriage on horseback, but I sat inside, for I wished for her company on the return drive.

Meryton was only slightly larger than Lambton. It boasted all the usual establishments, as well as the typical gatherings of young people admiring shop windows, the day's gossip, and members of the opposite sex. There must have been half a dozen red coats on every other corner, and at least that many pale bonnets on the adjacent corners.

I ordered the carriage to pull up at the coaching inn, and Bingley secured his horse. We could not know how long we would have to wait, but the roads were all reported to be sound, so Bingley and I sat down inside and made ourselves comfortable. I was truly impressed that the owner of the inn seemed to know my friend quite well—even knew what Bingley preferred to drink, though he could have only been in the establishment once or twice before.

About forty-five minutes after our arrival, I saw the Smythes' carriage through the window. I recognised Gerald Smythe at once, for he had long been an associate of my father's. His daughter was only a year younger than Georgiana, and they had taken several holidays together over the last two years. I was greatly in Smythe's debt for his family's friendship to my sister, whether he knew it or not.

"Darcy!" he greeted me as he stepped down. "Good to see you."

"And you, sir," I answered. "Was your journey a smooth one?"

"Yes, yes, quite. Here we are, my dears!" He reached into the carriage to hand down his wife, then the young ladies followed.

I stepped up to help Georgiana, and my heart nearly stopped. My dear little sister, the child I used to bounce on my knee and discipline when she misbehaved… she was gone. In her place was this elegant creature who looked astonishingly like a woman… like our mother, in fact. I swallowed audibly. "Georgiana?"

Her gloved hand stretched out of the carriage and she lifted the brim of her bonnet, revealing a face as clear and bright as one of Pemberley's golden apples. She smiled, displaying her perfect white teeth and the little dimple near her mouth she had inherited from our father. She was… breath-taking. Tears welled in my eyes and I blinked them rapidly away. *How had I missed this?*

She was laughing as I set her on the ground, and even there in the midst of town, she was not too modest to stand on her toes and kiss my cheek. "Oh, Fitzwilliam! How I have missed you!"

"I have missed you too. It has been far too long."

She gazed up at me; her smile almost too large for her face, and looked as if she had a thousand things to say all at once. She turned away, however, and extended her hand to my friend. "Mr Bingley! I did not know you would come to meet the carriage. I am so delighted to see your new home. Is it far?"

Bingley doffed his hat and kissed Georgiana's glove. "About four miles. All good road, and in Darcy's carriage you will hardly blink before you are there."

She giggled and returned to me, resting her hands on my arms as if she would embrace me right there in the middle of the street.

"Had you a smooth journey?" I asked.

"Oh! It was ever so dull. But I suppose the best journeys are dull, for we would not like to have something frightful occur. Harriet and I invented games to keep ourselves occupied, and I fear poor Mr Smythe shall be glad to be rid of me."

Smythe was still standing nearby, and he bowed with a chuckle. "Not at all, Miss Darcy. It is always a pleasure. Darcy—" he put out his hand once more—"I wish you a pleasant afternoon."

"The same to you, sir, and thank you."

"Shall we see you after Christmas for the return trip?"

I looked down at Georgiana, then back to Smythe. "No. She is coming home for good."

Georgiana could hardly contain a squeal, and Smythe laughed and bowed to her. "Then perhaps we will meet in Town soon."

"We shall look forward to it, sir, and I wish you a safe journey." I shook his hand and steered Georgiana across the street, where my own carriage awaited us.

"Darcy! Miss Darcy! Now, this is indeed a pleasure!"

I stopped in my tracks, my spine stiff and a frown already etched into my brow. Georgiana turned curiously, but her face brightened when she recognised the man calling to us.

"Mr Wickham! I did not know you were travelling with Fitzwilliam." She curtseyed to him, and he received her hand with a gallant flourish.

"I am afraid matters are not what they might appear," he answered with that suave old grin of his. "I merely had the good fortune of being in the same town at the same time. Good afternoon, Darcy," he acknowledged me, somewhat less warmly. "I wondered if I might bump into you someday. I saw Fitzwilliam last week, and—"

"So I understand," I interrupted. "Good day, Wickham." I moved towards Georgiana to lead her away, but she only stared at me in confusion.

Wickham wore something of a bemused expression. "Er... well, I say, it is good to see you, old chap, and Miss Darcy, may I offer my compliments. The years have been exceedingly kind."

She blushed prettily and smiled up at me, and I could not deny her such well-deserved praise. How could I, when she ought to have heard such words from me nearly every day?

Wickham inclined his head as Georgiana thanked him for the compliment, then turned back to me. "I was just making the acquaintance of some friends of yours, Darcy. It seems you have made quite an impression, as you always seem to do... ah, here they are, over by your carriage, and Miss Bennet is already speaking to Bingley. There's a good chap! Oh, Miss Elizabeth!"

I turned, my stomach dropping into my boots. This day had been so promising not five minutes before! Now, I must speak with both George Wickham *and* Elizabeth Bennet, and I must do so in such a way that Georgiana did not think me an ogre or touched in the head.

She—not Georgiana—was tipping her chin to the side, those piercing eyes sweeping over me as her brow wrinkled. Then her expression smoothed, and her lips curved—how had I never noticed how pert and delicately sculpted they were? I swallowed hard and made a half-bow, avoiding that eerie gaze for as many seconds as I could possibly delay.

"Good afternoon, Mr Darcy," she greeted me, in a tone that sounded crisp and forcibly civil.

"Good afternoon, Miss Elizabeth," I repeated, my voice just as clipped as hers. "May I present my sister? Miss Georgiana Darcy, Miss Elizabeth Bennet."

The vixen's face softened instantly for my sister. "Miss Darcy, it is a pleasure. I have heard much of you. I hope your journey was not too tiring."

"Not at all, thank you."

"And Georgiana," I hastened to add, "*this* is Miss Jane Bennet."

Bingley and Miss Bennet left off their discussion of the fine weather, and Miss Bennet, my fair and modest one, appeared startled at the honour of an introduction to my sister. She offered a polite dip of her head, a soft "Charmed, Miss Darcy," and then cast her eyes low, sidling ever so slightly closer to her own younger sister.

I had hoped for a somewhat more auspicious introduction than that. Georgiana frowned, unable to understand, and peered anxiously at the more troublesome of the Bennet sisters for some encouragement. At that moment, however, we all heard a masculine voice call out, "Oh, Cousin Elizabeth! Ah, there you are!"

From across the street we saw him—the foppiest, shoddiest, clumsiest excuse for a man I had ever encountered. On each arm he escorted yet another of the hedonistic younger Bennets, and upon his face was fixed an expression something akin to a cat who had gotten into the cream. Who in blazes he could have been was a mystery, save for the fact that he had addressed the nettlesome one as his cousin.

My fair Miss Bennet now wore a fearful grimace, and even Miss Elizabeth was rolling her eyes. "I am afraid we must be on our way. Good day, Miss Darcy. I hope we shall see you soon."

And before I could even speak any words of farewell, Miss Elizabeth had drawn her sister away, walking not towards her family but on ahead of them, so that none could pause and continue any conversation.

"Well! That was extraordinary," Bingley commented. "Ah, well, Darcy, I shall see you at the house. Miss Darcy—" he tipped his hat to Georgiana, then less gallantly to Wickham, and mounted his horse.

I opened the door of the carriage for Georgiana and beckoned for her to take my hand up. Wickham, however, seemed determined not to be forgotten quite so easily. He followed her, then bowed extravagantly when she turned.

"I wish you a pleasant day, Miss Darcy. And Darcy—" he straightened, addressing me, "I am sure I shall see you again soon."

I turned my back and helped Georgiana into the carriage, wondering precisely how much it would cost to bribe the entire regiment to uproot and take lodgings in a different county.

∽

OUR RETURN to Netherfield was heralded by no less than the entire upstairs staff, all forced to stand and greet us on the steps as though Georgiana were the future mistress of the house. Mrs Hurst simpered, her husband yawned and went back to his port, and Caroline Bingley fawned and cooed over my sister as if she were some sort of pet. All the while, Georgiana's smile looked more wooden by the moment.

Later, much later that evening, I came to visit her in the sitting room that had been appointed for her use. Rather than the blissfully contented young lady who had just left the schoolroom behind forever, I found a restless, uncertain maid who paced the room enough times to put a cramp in my neck.

"Georgie, do come sit," I demanded at last. "May I ask what troubles you?"

Georgiana dropped into a chair; her mouth puckered in a confusion of feeling. "It is nothing... only... do you think Miss Bingley likes me?"

"Likes you?" I laughed. "Is that what concerns you? How could you ask such a thing? But of course she does—quite well, in fact."

"Does she? I mean, does she really like me, or is she just that way because... well, I never quite know."

"What sort of question is this? You see how solicitous she always is, ordering your favourite meals and being certain you have the best seats and whatnot. You have seen her greetings in my own letters whenever she was present as I wrote, and I included less than a quarter of what she desired me to."

Georgiana nodded slowly but appeared unconvinced.

"Has she ever been unkind to you when I was elsewhere?"

"No... but I always thought that if I were not your sister, she would not be half so nice."

I was ready with a rebuttal, but then I paused. I had always thought generous hospitality a good indicator that one person liked another, but that little revelation the other day in the shrubbery recalled me. Of course, Georgiana was justified in her doubts—did Caroline Bingley give two straws for Colonel Fitzwilliam's sister? She was older than Georgiana, and not nearly so charming, but her brothers were not marketable marriage material, either. Well did I know Miss Bingley's wishes, but it was insupportable that Georgiana might sense herself no more than a pawn in the other's schemes.

I thought for a moment. "Have you any reason to suspect that she does not like you? Anything specific?"

"Well... no. I would like to think she does. I suppose I cannot tell you anything in particular, I just wish I understood her. You know, what she really thinks of me."

"But why?" I scoffed. "What does it matter what Miss Bingley thinks?"

"Oh! It is not only her. I wish I knew what people mean when they say certain things, and I am afraid it worries me more than it should."

I sighed. "People are not so very difficult to understand. They all want something, and the sooner you discover what it is, the more readily you will comprehend them."

Her head tilted and those blue eyes widened. "Do they, really? You are not being cynical with me, are you, Fitzwilliam? I am afraid that rather than reassuring me, you have given me even more cause for concern."

"And why would that be?"

"Well… what is it that you want?"

"What do I… good heavens! What a conversation for a girl just returned from school this very day."

"Oh." She lowered her eyes, blushing. "Did I say something wrong?"

"No! I…" I pressed my fingers to my brow and shook my head. "Of course, you have said nothing wrong. I had simply expected our first several conversations to be of a different nature. I have missed you, Georgie, and I wondered what you have been doing at school—things you did not put down in your letters."

Her teeth flashed in the briefest, most bashful of grins. "My piano master told me I was good enough to tour the Continent. That was very fine, was it not?"

"Why, Georgie! That is splendid praise! You should be very proud."

"But… I shall never do it, shall I?"

"Well, no. I have always envisioned quite a different future for you. But you ought to be pleased with all you have achieved, nevertheless."

"I suppose," she agreed. She was quiet for a moment, then asked "How long shall we remain at Netherfield?"

"Are you already anxious to escape?"

"Oh, no, it is lovely, but I do miss Pemberley. Please tell me we mustn't wait until spring before I shall see it again."

I frowned. "My plans are not fixed at present. I expect we will return to London for the winter, and I hope you may call frequently on the countess. Then, if circumstances are agreeable, perhaps I will resume my Easter visits to Rosings this year. I had not expected you to come with me, but perhaps we could discuss it?"

"But what of Pemberley? Do you not need to oversee the spring planting or the flocks and herds?"

"The steward has all that well in hand. There is no need for me to do more than write my instructions and respond to any questions he might have."

She sagged against the arm of her chair in disappointment. "So, it shall be summer before we return home?"

Summer. How long could I delay? I could think of nothing that would induce me to return to that hell, but for Georgie... No, even for her, I could not consider it!

Perhaps one day, if I were ever rewarded for my long suffering with the hand of love, I might find the courage to return. If I crossed the threshold once more with the sort of woman who was the antithesis of all I had formerly loathed—someone kinder than I deserved, gentler than my nameless fears, and wiser than any rational fellow would think prudent in a wife, then I would truly be a rich man. Such a woman would sweep all the past away and make everything new again. Then, and only then, could I once again call Pemberley my home.

Georgiana had grown quite still at my hesitation. She shifted in her seat, nibbling her lip as her eyes scanned the walls.

I sighed. "I had hoped that you would be pleased to spend some weeks with our friends here at Netherfield before we settle in London for the winter. Is the room to your liking?"

"Oh, yes," she nodded energetically. "It is very pleasant. I like the lavender particularly. Do you remember how mother used to keep it around?"

"Indeed, I do. That is why I requested it for you."

"Thank you," she smiled shyly. "Have you made many friends here, Fitzwilliam? It seems a very nice place."

"What friends do you expect me to make? I am already with my friends."

"Oh, now I know you must be teasing!" she laughed. "I meant among the neighbours. What of the Bennets you introduced me to?"

"Ah, those neighbours. We met them at a local assembly, then Mrs Hurst and Miss Bingley invited Miss Bennet to dine while we were out one evening. She fell ill while she was here and was required to stay a few days while she recovered."

"Oh, dear! But she appears quite well now."

"Yes, her illness was not serious, and she seems to have mended well."

"Oh, I am glad. I thought she was ever so kind. Do you like her, Fitzwilliam?"

My face flushed—right there, before a child of sixteen, I was blushing like a schoolboy! "Like her?" I sputtered, a little too defensively. "What manner of question is that?"

She lifted her shoulders, the picture of innocence. "I thought there was something… I could not decide how she was looking at you. That is the root of my worries, I fear. I simply do not know how to understand the things people mean to say, when they do not say them."

"Well, what do you think she would have said, if she had spoken all?"

Georgiana's brow pinched in thought. "That she was annoyed with you for some reason. But she was willing to be kind to me, even if you are not her favourite person."

"Good heavens! I hope you are quite wrong. Wherever did you get such a notion? No, Georgie, I am sure Miss Bennet could never think or act duplicitously. In fact, I doubt she has ever looked disapprovingly on anyone in the whole course of her life."

"Oh," she sighed dejectedly. "You see, there I go again! I thought I quite understood her. The other sister, now I would understand if you said she tended to be a little unfriendly, but I thought Miss Bennet seemed quite welcoming… to me, at least, if not to you."

"Of course, and I believe she would go out of her way to make herself welcoming, but I hope I have done nothing to give offence. As for the other sister, I would not call her 'unfriendly,' precisely. I am not certain what to call her, save that she seems to delight in vexing me."

"Vexing you! But, how could she? I never would have guessed… she spoke hardly a word, save to Mr Bingley."

"Hold a moment. Are we speaking of the same sister?"

"Well, I thought we were. Miss Bennet is the sister I met first, is that right? The one with the lovely brown eyes and the smile that looks as if she is about to laugh?"

"No! That was the younger sister I spoke of, Miss Elizabeth. Miss Jane Bennet is the elder. *She* is the kind and generous one, and I think you would like her very much."

"Oh." Her eyes fell to somewhere around my waistcoat. "Then I was wrong again."

"No, no, think nothing of it. How could you possibly form an accurate impression in only a moment? No one could expect you to read the thoughts of a stranger."

"I suppose. So, I shall try to learn more of Miss Bennet, if you think I would like her. Do you think it would be proper for me to call on them?"

"I think it would be more proper if they called on you first. You have been introduced now, so surely, they will come soon. Brace yourself, my dear, there are a good many Bennet sisters, and the younger girls all lack your breeding. But for all that, I would make no objections if you wished to associate with the eldest. In fact, our own Miss Bingley could benefit from her example of feminine accomplishment and deportment."

"No!" Georgiana giggled and covered her mouth. "Do you mean that Miss Bingley does not truly possess that 'certain something in her air and manner of walking' that she is so proud of? Perish the thought!"

"Let me only state that she ought to have stayed longer in school."

Georgiana collapsed in a fit of laughter, then snuggled into my chest when I offered my arm... just the way she used to do.

I kissed the top of her head, holding her tightly. I felt a great lurch in my chest, and the oddest notion occurred to me. Hope had not been fully extinguished from my terrestrial frame, though all the hubris and depravity of this earthen sphere had spared no pains in testing me.

The ever-present torrent in my veins finally slowed, and a once-dead part of my heart began to beat again that night.

CHAPTER 7

The brood of vixens wasted no time in descending upon Netherfield. I expected at least two days to pass before we heard more of them, but the ladies were announced the very next morning.

I thought Georgiana would float away in transports of delight, so wide was her smile at the news. And who could blame her for preferring Miss Bennet's company to Miss Bingley's? The poor child, she had almost nothing but the latter for nearly twenty-four hours, and already her eyelid was beginning to twitch.

Though my own preferences were for only one of the Bennets, I would willingly have borne the entire family just for the privilege of seeing Georgiana with her. Alas, the visiting party was made entirely of ladies, and we gentlemen were not welcome. I tried to appear nonchalant as I locked myself into the library.

I would like to claim I had some lofty purpose for my seclusion. Truly, I had only chosen that room because there was a hidden door along the back of it, through which one could occasionally catch voices from the drawing room. Not that I would lower myself to such a posture, naturally! But a man does not wish to feel himself alone all the time, does he? And who was I to blame if the books I preferred were located along the back wall of the library?

Ten minutes later, I still held two unopened tomes in my hands, and an impartial observer might have considered my foray into the library entirely unproductive. I had, however, learned to distinguish the tones of each inhabitant of the adjacent room. The loud, braying laughter, for instance, that was the youngest Bennet—the one who habitually neglected to wear her fichu and appeared astonishingly well-grown for her years.

The nervous giggle was her next older sister, who never went anywhere but that she clung to her younger sister's petticoats. The dead corner of the room must have belonged to the middle Bennet, who possessed a social ineptitude of truly magnificent proportions. I occasionally wondered if she and I might have managed to survive an entire evening together without the necessity of a single word exchanged.

By no means could I have mistaken the most voluble occupant of the room—the shrill, often distressed and never restrained tones of Mrs Bennet. Beside her, Caroline Bingley's false patronising and Mrs Hurst's long-suffering sighs sounded almost sophisticated. Then, there was Georgiana—I groaned when I picked her out again, laughing out of turn, then apologising for her *faux pas*. But then, my heart took wings when I heard Miss Bennet gently change the subject...

Wait... No, it was not Miss Bennet, but Miss Elizabeth's easy voice offering consolation and grace! And Georgiana responded in tones that echoed warmly through the wood against my ear. I could not understand all the words, but the feeling behind them I could comprehend well enough. *How very odd.* I kept listening.

Ah, there *she* was. Miss Jane Bennet had made hardly a sound in that din, but then she was asking Georgiana something—I specifically heard the word "Bath". There was Georgiana answering with energy, and Miss Bennet replying as the rest of the room fell quiet. I believe it was Miss Bennet who mentioned the ocean, and that topic occupied them for a half a moment. It was enough to make my throat swell with pride… and then that promising exchange came to an end when Mrs Bennet had to add her enthusiasm for the prospect of sea bathing. *Damnation!*

I leaned closer to the wood and even closed my eyes, straining to hear my favoured pair. What a kind and true friend for my sister Jane Bennet would be! Alas, the more dominant voices insisted upon drowning them out and crushing any budding felicity they might have shared. Miss Bingley and Mrs Bennet were bantering about something, then they brought Georgiana into the midst of it… and then, there it was again—that playful voice, *the wrong one*, sliced through the milieu with almost military precision to permit Georgiana an easier response. *What madness was this?*

"Darcy! Hah, I have found you out at last. What the devil are you doing in here?"

I dropped one of the books I held, so great was the shock Bingley's arrival had occasioned. As I recovered it, I glanced at the spine with a frown, as though it had given way and could account for my unwonted clumsiness.

"Bingley, what are you about, startling me so? I could have damaged this fine volume."

"Oh, now I know that for a falsehood, for you appraised this library yourself the first week we were here, and informed me it held not one book worth more than a six-pence."

"I was being facetious."

"And is that what you are doing now? Or are you trying to memorise…" he bent at the waist to examine the title in my hand… "*Common Varieties of European Wheat?*"

I shelved the book. "I presume you had some reason for searching me out just now?"

"Indeed, I did, and I suspect you have the same. What do you say we join the ladies? I know quite well what you can hear through that door, and I suppose if it were my young sister receiving some of her first callers, I would be anxious for her as well. Come, Darcy, they cannot object if we walk in together for the last few moments of their call. What do you say?"

"I think it ought to be counted impudent of us to presume so, but I doubt Mrs Bennet and her entourage would protest."

"Just as I had hoped." Bingley led the way, brave soul, and we both bowed to the ladies at the door. "Forgive us for the intrusion," he protested, "but we wished to offer our own greetings."

Mrs Bennet was quick with her welcome. "No intrusion, it is no intrusion at all, is that not right, Miss Bingley? Why, it is your own home, sir, and who would object to encountering the master when calling upon his family?"

"You are all graciousness, madam," Bingley bowed again.

To my dismay, I saw now that my sister's company had been claimed on both sides by Miss Bingley and the frightful one. Egad, small wonder that Miss Bennet and my sister had shared little conversation, with a social schemer to Georgiana's left and a virtual enchantress to her right! Wellington himself could hardly have extricated his person from such a precarious situation. What wiles had my poor sister been subjected to?

Georgiana was searching my expression, and I touched her gaze with a look of mild encouragement, but then my eyes were seeking out... oh, no, not *her*...

Ah, yes, the fair Miss Bennet sat on the opposite sofa beside Mrs Hurst. Mrs Bennet had claimed the far end of the furniture, but there was a space at Jane Bennet's elbow, just inviting enough that an enterprising gentleman could take up his stance next to her seat.

Bingley must have seen it as well, for our shoulders brushed as we both stepped in the same direction. This time, I was the more successful, perhaps because my strides were longer and more determined. Bingley glanced my way with a peculiar expression I could not read, then fell back to take a similar position between Miss Elizabeth's seat and Miss... good heavens, what was that silent sister's name?

Now. Now, man, this is your chance! I cleared my throat. "I am gratified to see you looking so well after your recent illness, Miss Bennet."

The lady scarcely turned her head, but I could see her eyes roll up in my direction to peek at me through the delicate golden spirals at her temples. "I am quite well, Mr Darcy."

"I am very glad to hear it."

There. I had expressed my gallant concern and demonstrated my allegiance by speaking only to her. My lady could now feel secure in my affections, for in such a gathering of females, even a lingering glance could incite rumours of an impending engagement.

"And you are not troubled by the cold at all?" Bingley asked.

Miss Bennet lifted her chin and smiled openly. "Not at all, sir. Have you not found the weather unaccountably warm this season?"

"Most pleasant," he agreed. "It puts me in mind of the last year my father was alive. He was fond of the outdoors as well, and he knew his time was short. What a blessing that mild autumn was! Why, I think we rode out nearly every day, and twice on some days. I thought he would be happy to simply perish out there in the fields, with the reins still in his hand!"

"Charles!" snapped Miss Bingley. "What can you mean, speaking so irreverently of the dead?"

I cast my eyes politely in another direction, but Miss Elizabeth's voice rose in Bingley's defence. "What can be irreverent in such a pleasant memory? It sounds as though that autumn was a gift to you both, Mr Bingley."

"Indeed, it was, or I shall ever think of it as such. I say, I have a splendid notion. What do you all say to a picnic while the weather remains fine? We could take the carriage out to Oakham Mount and set our baskets near that great old tree."

"Charles," chorused his sisters, "how could you even suggest it? A picnic in late October? Perfectly out of the question. We would all catch our deaths!"

"Oh!" Mrs Bennet interjected, "My girls are of sturdier constitutions than that. Never troubled by a bit of weather, are they? Young ladies raised in the country are always hardier, you know... most vigorous, of course," the lady finished with a knowing smirk and a wink towards her eldest daughter.

Poor Miss Jane Bennet tried to shrink in her seat, but it was Miss Elizabeth's flushed cheeks and sharp tongue that caught my notice... or perhaps, just perhaps, I might have already been watching her.

"Quite robust indeed," she quipped. "Why, we Hertfordshire lasses are veritable pioneers, always wandering hither and thither. Nothing short of a respectable rain shower or a bit of wind could bar us from ranging the countryside in search of adventure."

The youngest sister snorted. "What a good joke, Lizzy! Rain, indeed. Why, that never stopped you before!"

"Yet, it need not be a consideration now," Bingley put in with a laugh. "Why, I was consulting my almanack just this morning, and we are promised fine weather through the end of the month."

"Then," said I—to my own surprise, I must confess—"I propose an outing. Miss Bennet, I believe you have mentioned that you enjoy riding?"

Her shoulder arched away as she turned to look up at me. "I do," she confessed slowly.

"Capital!" Bingley exclaimed. "What of it, for those of us who are willing to venture out—perhaps Tuesday next? What do you say to a riding party, Miss Bennet?"

"Why, I... that would be delightful, Mr Bingley, but my father's horse is lame at present."

"Miss Bennet, I believe I have the perfect solution," I offered, with a nod to Bingley. "My friend has recently purchased a few of my best mares, and they arrived a few days ago. There are at least three among them that are proven ladies' mounts. You would be quite safe on any of them."

"Just so!" Bingley added. "What do you say, Miss Bennet? You are most welcome to your choice—the sorrel, I think, or perhaps the bay."

"Oh!" Georgiana cried, "is Bunny here?"

"Yes," I answered, "as well as Robin and Nightingale."

Miss Elizabeth emitted an amused chuckle. "Do you usually name your horses after other animals?"

"No, I choose a name that suits. Have you never noticed that names tend to define a character?"

"I think rather that the character defines the name," she answered pertly, with a lingering challenge to her look.

Hang it all, but it is possible that I could have smiled at her ready retort. I may have even chuckled.

"Oh, Lizzy," huffed Mrs Bennet, "enough of your tongue! Why must you interrupt everything? The gentlemen were speaking to Jane!"

"I believe Mr Bingley was speaking to the whole room, Mama," she replied smoothly, but there was a decided hue to her complexion that had not been there previously. For a moment—only a moment, of course—I pitied the lass. I knew something of unremitting humiliation at the hands of a relative, and hers were decidedly problematic.

Miss Bingley ceased glaring at Mrs Bennet to scold her brother. "Charles, you simply cannot go forward with this scheme. Why, Miss Bennet has only just recovered from her illness. Even should it not rain, and I cannot think that it would not, it is far too cold for a long outing. You must not think of it!"

A slight movement caught my... *no, that was not true...* I was already staring at the rogue Bennet sister, wondering what she would do next. It was like watching a master chess player at work, just before he decimates one's own chances, for the fascination of the thing so readily overcomes the disappointment of the loss. Miss Elizabeth's gaze rested easily on one of Miss Bingley's elaborate floral arrangements, but her lips were moving so subtly that almost no one could have noticed.

She was mouthing something to her sister. I glanced at Bingley and then every other face in the room, but all other eyes were on Miss Bennet.

Jane Bennet seemed to hold her breath, nodded very faintly to her sister, then spoke out bravely. "I am quite well, Miss Bingley, and I am not troubled by a little cold. If Mr Bingley is offering to escort me, and Mr Darcy will vouch for the horses, I would be most obliged to accept the invitation."

A glimmer of congratulations flickered in the minx's eyes as she smiled at her elder sister... and then she happened to glance up at me, and all pleasure fled from her expression. I looked quickly away, hoping my face did not look as warm as it felt.

"Alone!" Mrs Bennet was protesting. "Oh no, my dear, you cannot go riding with two gentlemen! You must take Lizzy with you, I absolutely insist."

Miss Elizabeth shook her head, her lips faintly pale. "I must beg off, Mama. I had promised to help Charlotte—"

"Nonsense!" the matron objected. "I cannot help it if Charlotte Lucas must put up her own candles and herbs. I'll have none of my girls doing such menial tasks. You cannot allow Jane to go alone!"

"Oh, they will not go alone," Georgiana chirped, quite surprising me. "May I come with you, Brother?"

I gravely nodded my permission, though my inner being was nearly dizzy with elation. An outing with Miss Bennet nearly to myself, and the easiest two chaperons in all of England? Nothing could be more auspicious! Better yet, Miss Bingley's pointed disapproval and the dark-haired siren's obvious reluctance would see them safely left behind for the day. I could not have arranged it prettier myself.

THE FOLLOWING Tuesday dawned clear and bright—nothing short of a miracle in late October. My spirits rose with the sun, and I felt sure that this, at last, was the heavenly sign that felicity might be within my grasp.

I dressed meticulously, my core humming with anticipation as I tried to imagine how gracefully my fair one would sit a side-saddle. Could there be a more elegant way to display a lady's poise and figure than the faint twist to her slim waist, the proud set of her shoulders, the curve of her delicate neck, and the light touch of her taper fingers upon the reins? How fortunate the gentleman who rode beside such an angel! Indeed, this would be an afternoon to remember.

Precisely at noon, Bingley's coachman met us at the door with five horses. I stopped and counted the mares, then looked at Georgiana in confusion. "I thought you requested Bunny to ride. Do you anticipate changing your mind? Why are there three horses with side-saddles?"

"Oh, did you not hear?" Bingley asked. "Mrs Bennet sent over a note that Miss Elizabeth's previous engagement no longer stands, and that she desired to join our company."

I closed my eyes, and only a monumental effort kept me from groaning aloud and muttering curses of frustration. Did she *always* insist on chaperoning her sister? How was I ever to be rid of the vexatious creature?

"Brother?" Georgiana stepped near to me. "Is something wrong?"

I sighed. "No, nothing at all. Shall I help you mount, Georgiana?"

Bingley and I each led one of the saddled horses, and we set out at a brisk trot for Longbourn. When we arrived, Mrs Bennet was naturally the first to greet us. She was wringing her hands in almost triumphant glee, and I felt a sickening lurch in my stomach. Perhaps I would do better to remember some pressing business and take my leave… but then *she* appeared.

Miss Bennet came just behind her mother, and she was, indeed, the image of perfection. She wore a dark green riding habit that fitted in all the right places and accentuated all her most remarkable features. Her black hat and veil barely concealed the coils of golden hair or the becoming blush as she greeted us, and anyone would agree that this was a lady who could dazzle both in the ballroom and in the countryside. She curtseyed very properly and then turned to make way for the one behind her—the only dark cloud I had seen all day.

Miss Elizabeth was not smiling, for once. Her considerable charm was drenched under a heavy cape, for that was what she appeared to be wearing. Clearly, her riding habit was the product of some hasty alterations and was still too loose about the shoulders. The pleats fell in the wrong places round her waist, and her manner this day seemed no less uncomfortable than her attire.

Her cheeks were pale and drawn, and she walked beside her father, who appeared to be watching her with some concern. She placed her hand on his forearm and nodded half-heartedly, then she raised her eyes. Though she greeted us, she was looking only at the horses with an expression no one could misread as anything but unadulterated terror.

"Elizabeth!" Georgiana called from the saddle. "Elizabeth, come ride this horse!"

I looked back at my sister in astonishment. When had they come to first-name terms? They had met only twice!

Miss Elizabeth hesitated, her eyes shifting until she accidentally encountered me, and then she turned rapidly away. I discovered then that I had somehow overlooked the remaining tide of Bennets flowing out from Longbourn's front door, as well as that rumpled popinjay I had seen in Meryton.

"Now, quite seriously, Cousin Elizabeth," he said, "I make no objections to a lady indulging in such an outing. Why, as my patroness herself has expressed on many an occasion, such exercise is fruitful for the body and soul. No, indeed, I am much in favour of ladies taking the air. Now, for myself, of course, the office of a parson rather demands that I preserve my dignity, and as such, it is far preferable that I should restrict myself to the carriage, or foot travel, for mine is not a physique well-suited to riding. However, I should not stand in the way of a lady's pleasure—"

"Mr Collins," she interrupted, "I thank you very kindly for your encouragement, but I fear I am keeping my party waiting."

He removed his hat and bowed deeply. "My humblest apologies, Cousin Elizabeth! And may I have the exquisite pleasure of an introduction?"

"Oh! Some other time, Mr Collins—" Mrs Bennet waved the man off. "Now, look sharp, girls, you must not keep Mr Darcy and Mr Bingley waiting!"

"Mr Darcy!" he cried, looking back and forth between Bingley and myself until he settled upon me with an appearance of surety. "The Mr Darcy of Pemberley in Derbyshire?"

I bowed faintly. "The same. And who might you be, sir?"

He stepped forward and removed his hat with a flourish to perform a deep, courtly bow. "I, sir, am William Collins, and it is my most unique honour to have been bestowed with the living at Hunsford in Kent by none other than your aunt, Lady Catherine de

Bourgh." He spoke the name with such reverence, I half expected him to fold his hands and lead the assembled party in a hymn.

I thinned my lips in some approximation of congratulations. The presumptive oaf was still beaming and apparently waiting to hear some praise for himself or his good fortune, but already his character was perfectly fixed in my mind. The simple knowledge that my aunt had chosen him told a great deal, and none of it flattering.

"It is, indeed, a happy coincidence, Mr Collins," Miss Elizabeth agreed, "but I am afraid we must be off if we are to make the most of this fine day."

"Oh, then far be it from me to restrain you, Cousin! No, Mr Darcy, I shall be content to wait for another time to speak to you, for I am quite certain that there is a great deal to be said about the graciousness of Lady Catherine de Bourgh and the wonders of Rosings Park, sir— yes, indeed, much more than we would have time for at this moment."

I glanced at Bingley, whose countenance bore a look of innocent astonishment at this pompous fellow. He blinked at me, then recalled himself to address the ladies. "Well, Miss Bennet and Miss Elizabeth, shall we be off? Which mount suits your pleasure?"

"Try this black mare, the one Fitzwilliam was leading," Georgiana called again to Miss Elizabeth, and the latter made her cautious way to the mare's side. "Her name is Nightingale. She might look large, but she is very gentle. She and Bunny have been friends since they were fillies, so you will be quite safe beside my horse."

I turned back to Miss Bennet and cursed myself for looking away for that one instant. What a distractible fool I was proving to be! Bingley was already helping the lady to mount the bay mare, so there was nothing for it but to see Miss Elizabeth into the saddle before Mr Collins opened his mouth again.

I bent to offer my hand for her boot. Miss Elizabeth clamped her teeth into her lip and seemed hesitant to touch me, as she must do. A pity I could not have simply led her horse to a mounting block! But even if it would have been gentlemanly, it was not possible, for the only block I saw was home to what appeared to be a newly potted plant. I rolled my eyes in disgust. Mrs Bennet knew her craft, that much was plain.

Miss Elizabeth had closed her eyes for a moment of composure, then she nodded briskly to me, indicating that she was ready. My heart seized, and only a valiant effort kept me from clutching at my chest. Which of us was the most mortified was a stiff contest—she blanched in dread of the horse, and I was nearly dead with terror of *her*. She stepped up nimbly enough, but the mare stomped one foot, and she clutched unsteadily at the saddle, half-dangling from the pommel and half-standing on my hand.

I cleared my throat, for that was all I was capable of doing... and that was when I smelled it. *Lavender.*

I almost reeled back in horror. *Impossible!* Yet, not only was that poignant aroma sweetly permeating her hair and clothing, but some earthier notes lent it warmth and fullness. Something pleasant, something that... that *matched*. Something that should have been there all along to complete the floral tones. It could only be Miss Elizabeth herself.

I fumbled, and though I am loath to confess it, I quite dropped the lady. It was fortunate that she still clung to the saddle straps, but she yelped in surprise, and even Georgiana cried out in alarm.

"Forgive me," Miss Elizabeth was muttering, her eyes shifting between myself and the horse. "I am afraid I am not practised at this. Perhaps it would be better if I stayed."

I tried to swallow, but it required at least three attempts before I could claim success, and my voice was raspy and unsteady when I did so. "The fault was mine, madam, but the choice is yours."

"Oh, Lizzy, what ails you?" called Mrs Bennet from the doorway. "Why, you are brave enough while climbing on rocks and trees, what difference if it is a horse? Perhaps Lydia should have come instead of you."

"Please come, Elizabeth!" Georgiana protested. "We will have such a merry time once you are mounted. You will see!"

I waited, praying for the first time in my life that my sister would be disappointed. Miss Elizabeth closed her eyes and appeared to be meditating on the merits of a quick death from a fall versus a more lingering one from the humiliation of her mother's scorn.

"Dear Cousin Elizabeth, shall I call for my boots?" offered Collins. "I would be most pleased to escort you on foot for your outing, and perhaps we might catch up with the party at their destination."

She gritted her teeth. "That will be quite all right, Mr Collins." After a few nervous pants, she nodded again to me, and I hoisted her up—almost too fast, for she was obliged to cling to the pommel to keep from being tossed over the other side. At last, we had her settled. Her knuckles were white on the reins and she was leaning unnaturally far forward, but she insisted that she was well.

I think I fell away from her rather than walking as a proper gentleman ought. Good Lord, I certainly hoped Bingley would be at hand when it came time to help her dismount! I drew out my hand-kerchief and dabbed my forehead before turning to offer my courtesies to the rest of the family as we departed.

The younger sisters had already wandered away in either boredom or jealousy. Collins was still talking, but no one was listening. Mrs Bennet stood in the doorway, waving a bit of lace as if her daughters were never to return, and Mr Bennet... he was looking straight at me, and he appeared to be laughing. I chose not to ask why.

The five of us fell into step along the drive, but it was an odd arrangement. Bingley and Miss Bennet had started out first, and took the natural lead, but there was no easy way for a third to ride beside them without appearing conspicuous. Georgiana held back beside her new friend, which left me alone in the centre of our little group. I could hear everything that the ladies behind me spoke of, but not a single word uttered by the pair in front of me. Bollocks, this would not do!

My mount wove a serpentine path down the drive as I craned my neck and strained politeness, trying to draw close enough to catch the conversation between Bingley and Miss Bennet. My urgency was only doubled by what I thought I heard behind me. Miss Elizabeth's typically saucy, playful voice carried a decided hitch, and her usual quick repartees sounded choked and forced.

Dash it all, the last thing I had looked for on this day was to learn to pity the Bennet minx! Yet, I did feel badly that a woman who was so plainly terrified of horses had been forced into it by her vulgar mother.

The best means I possessed of ensuring that the situation was never repeated was to distance myself as far as possible from the lady. Let my sister stay back and be her companion, for I had no intention of becoming a lackey to the one woman in all the world who set my hair on end and made my blood simmer with agitation.

Rude or not, I put heel to my mount and rode up on the left side of Miss Bennet's horse. She turned in some surprise, then smiled tightly. An uncomfortable glance over at Bingley, and then she fixed her eyes straight forward without a word.

That was when I prayed for a sudden cloudburst to put an end to this whole, awkward ordeal.

CHAPTER 8

*M*iss Bennet sat a horse with a graceful ease that rivalled Georgiana, whom I had instructed myself. Nay, she surpassed even my sister in one regard—Miss Bennet glowed with the full flower of feminine maturity. Though Georgiana was well grown, beside Miss Bennet she was still merely a child, flush with promise. Jane Bennet set the standard for womanly radiance, and I reflected pleasantly on what a sterling example Georgiana would have in her as a sister.

Unfortunately, the lady herself seemed unaware of my designs. She scarcely glanced my way and only spoke to me when I asked something directly of her. Her modesty was most becoming, for she could not have failed to note my interest. Surely, she meant only to excite me to a more positive declaration of my affections, and I admired the lady's reserve. However, I was shrewder than that.

What would it profit me to impress her with my attributes, my manners, and my most profound admiration, if her own heart were not similarly touched? No, no, it would not do. I must have her entirely devoted to me, and not merely for my personal consequence. If I were to put my neck in the noose once more, it should be to gain a wife of my own choosing who could fulfil my happiness by her sublime harmony with my own spirit. And what better choice than a woman who had already declared her desire to respect and love her future husband? Indeed, the lady had fairly told me what must be done to win her, and I would not stray from the steady course I had set.

And so, I rode at her left, while Bingley persisted at her right with the sort of tenacity I had only witnessed from him on the hunt field. She could not offer an observation on the path or the weather that he did not counter with some jest calculated to make her smile. Most frustratingly, he was maddeningly successful.

At last, I interjected with some question of consequence which was naturally designed to turn the conversation more to my own interests. "How do you like the mare, Miss Bennet?"

She was a moment in answering—in fact, it was Bingley who made some gesture to turn her attention my way as I repeated my question. She started and flicked her eyes shyly to me. "Very well, as I told Mr Bingley when we first set out. He seems quite proud of his new horse."

"As he should be. Her sire was a champion at Newmarket, and her dam was my father's favourite hunter."

"She is a fine creature." She smiled and looked straight ahead.

"Do you ever take fences?" I asked.

"Yes—low ones, such as the wall bordering our cow pasture. I would not have you think me a perfectly accomplished horsewoman, but I can manage the path well enough."

"Capital!" Bingley cried. "We can make a right jolly ride of it. What do you say, Miss Bennet? Darcy and I like to circle round the lowlands surrounding your southern field, then the rise to Oakham Mount. I thought we could return through the woods, by the river. Does that not sound a pleasant way? There ought to be no fences so large that you will find them troublesome."

"Yes, indeed, it sounds lovely, but... I am not certain that everyone in our party will be comfortable with the route."

"You are concerned for your sister? But what do you think, Darcy, are there not low places where one could go round the easier path rather than leaping a fence? I had not noticed."

"I daresay there are," I replied. "I have never known a fence in this country that is not down in some place or other. Surely, the needs of all can be accommodated."

"And how shall Miss Darcy fare?" he asked, with a pointed jerk of his head in my sister's direction.

"Georgiana is very accomplished. She will see to Miss Elizabeth's safety and enjoyment far better than any other could possibly do— save perhaps yourself, Bingley. I do believe Miss Elizabeth enjoys your company."

My friend narrowed his eyes faintly, and, for the first time in his life, he did not appear to be smiling. "Yet *you* are the better rider, and, as you have pointed out, you are also more familiar with her mount. I mean no disrespect to your sister's abilities, but in case our party should become separated, they ought to have a gentleman with them. Do you not think it wise to keep close by?"

I glanced to Miss Bennet, who was biting her lips together and peeking at me out of the corner of her eye. Her rosy cheeks were all the evidence I required that our present conversation was distressing her. *Very well, my lady.* If I could not please her by my company, I would prove the more gallant gentleman by looking after her wretched sister. I tipped my hat with a tight smile and drew rein, falling back in the group into the abyss of vexation.

As I did so, up ahead of me, Bingley and Miss Bennet flicked their riding crops and their horses picked up an easy canter. I scowled. *Perfect.*

"Oh, Fitzwilliam," Georgiana called from behind me, "I do so long for a good run! But let us not, just now, shall we?"

I turned in the saddle as they caught me up. "As you please."

Miss Elizabeth was sheer white, her expressive eyes a startling black in her ghostly complexion. I could not help but wonder how many minutes it had been since she had drawn a proper breath of air. The cords of her neck stood out intermittently as she ground her teeth, and her lips were some sickening shade of grey.

"If you would prefer to gallop, Miss Darcy," she offered in a raspy voice, "pray, do not be detained on my account. I know the country very well and can easily follow at my own pace. Do not be concerned for me, Mr Darcy. Please, go on as you would if I were not present. I do not mind."

"But your mount would," I informed her. "I suspect you have not seen a horse that has been left behind the rest, but they become a great deal more difficult to manage."

She drew a shaken breath, and her eyes became even larger, if that were possible. "Oh," she whispered.

"Oh, do not fear, Elizabeth, we shall stay with you," Georgiana soothed. "Fitzwilliam is a splendid teacher, and he will never ask you to do more than you are comfortable doing."

"Is that how you recall your lessons?" I asked her. "For I assure you, I did indeed ask you to do more than your comfort would have allowed. How do you think you learned to test the limits of your own abilities?"

"That is precisely as I would have expected, Mr Darcy," Miss Elizabeth rejoined. "Tell me, are you the sort of instructor who chides and belittles your pupil until they grudgingly perform as demanded?"

I twisted round to stare at her. "I certainly hope I never belittle anyone."

One coal-dark brow quirked. "Never, sir?"

"Absolutely not. I do not know what I could have said or done to give you such an impression, Miss Elizabeth."

"You are quite assured of your innocence?"

I squinted at her, the prickles forming along the back of my neck. That arch tone, I knew it all too well, but, in my folly, I waded directly into her trap. "I am."

Some life had returned to her features, and I caught that characteristic spark to her eyes. She pursed her lips. "Interesting," she mused.

"What can you mean, Elizabeth?" Georgiana asked. "If I did not know better, I would think my brother had insulted you. Fitzwilliam is chivalrous by nature, and, though he might hold high expectations, he is never unkind or unreasonable."

"Is he not? And does he never make presumptions about a person before coming to know them better?"

I fixed my eyes on the road and thought for a moment. "It could be said that my opinions, once formed, are quite inflexible."

"And do you take great care in forming these opinions? You would not, for instance, decry another person based on their status in society, or their appearance, or, perhaps, even their very name?"

I stared stupidly back at her. *Good lord, she had heard me.* Perhaps I had underestimated her as an adversary, but I had never expected her to nail my flesh to the wall quite so bluntly.

"Georgiana," I mumbled hoarsely, "can you still see Mr Bingley and Miss Bennet?"

She shaded her eyes. "They have slowed down, but they will be over that rise in a moment. Shall we catch them up?"

"A jog-trot should be sufficient to keep them in sight, I think," I answered, and I felt my cheek twitch as Miss Elizabeth ensnared me in her leaden gaze.

"But what about Elizabeth?" Georgiana protested.

"We will be just after you," I promised. "You need not go far, for Mr Bingley and Miss Bennet will wait for us when they discover that we have fallen behind."

Georgiana pouted but chirruped to her horse with an unhappy "Very well," to me and a sympathetic smile for Miss Elizabeth. As she jogged away, I tried not to look at the lady who remained, but I could feel her heated gaze boring into my temple.

"You have been biding your time for some while, waiting to confront me over my offence that night," I observed quietly.

"In fact, I have not."

I turned. "How is that? Clearly, you must have heard me."

"But it does not follow that I accepted the insult. You may have spoken it, but the choice of claiming it as a personal affront was my own to make. You are not worth troubling myself over."

Well, that stung. My brow clouded with hurt, and I could not decide why, but I lashed out in the only way I knew. "You claim you did not suffer over my words, yet you were quick to recall them at the earliest convenience and present them as proof of some perceived ill will of mine."

"Only because you have made it plain that you consider yourself above the mean arts. You declare yourself a man of virtue—very well, sir, I ask you to answer the accusation and defend your actions, if you can. I care nothing for my wounded pride, for I am quite prepared to continue regarding you as merely an object for my own amusement. But an affectionate brother, and…" she lifted her eyes meaningfully to the horizon… "one who would count himself a worthy suitor ought to be able to examine his behaviour towards the opposite sex with some degree of equanimity."

I drew up my horse and faced her squarely, and she halted her own mount to glare back at me. "As you have been so frank, so shall I be. I doubt we will ever be friends, Miss Elizabeth. Your dislike of me was fixed from the beginning, as was mine for you. My reasons are my own, and I daresay I have lived enough in the world to form my own opinions. Rarely am I wrong. But I will answer your accusations to clear my own character, for you are quite right that I care for my sister better than any other could, and that I consider myself a desirable match for any lady I should find worthy of my attentions."

Her expression flashed indignantly. "Pray, sir, speak on! I am most eager to learn what is so offensive about my person and name that you could think yourself justified in all your ways!"

"Your person, I do not object to. Another man might consider you quite handsome, in fact."

"Nay, that will not do!" she protested. "I recall your words exactly, if you care for a recitation."

"That will not be necessary. I had early noted the charms of your elder sister and found every other woman in the room paled in comparison. If your memory is so exact, you will also recall that the only other ladies I danced with all that evening were those of my own party. And so, I did not single you out for my particular disdain based upon your appearance or manners."

"No! it was far worse. My manners are my own to conduct, and I even have some hand in my appearance, for my toilette and my choice of gown make a deal of difference—"

Here, I almost interrupted her. Toilette and choice of gown? The finest maids and seamstresses in all London could not match their skills to the natural fire that kindled in her sharp eyes in this moment! How the swarthy queen did come alive when she was provoked! The very air all about her snapped, the magnetic essence of her being intensified, and even that lavender scent seemed to swell like a thundercloud. Egad, the woman could have worn sackcloth and ashes and she would still have transfixed the hapless observer! But she was not finished, and I was not quick enough to defend myself.

"—No! You chose to insult me based upon nothing more meaningful than the name I was given at birth! A grouping of phonemes and syllables that have nothing whatsoever to do with my character, my disposition, my prospects, or my aspirations. What can you have meant by it, sir? No gentleman could ever make such an outrageous statement and have any hope that others would not hold him in contempt! What can possibly be so offensive about my name that you would issue a verbal slap to my face in such a public way?"

"Such was not my intention. I never meant you to overhear my words. I spoke them out of my own preferences, and it is not incumbent upon me to explain myself."

She gaped incredulously. "So that is it? You simply brush off my complaints as if they are of no consequence? How, sir, do you expect to vindicate yourself in my eyes as an appropriate match for my sister if you care so little for the opinions of her family?"

"You go too far, Miss Elizabeth!" I snapped. "I have given Miss Bennet no cause to be uneasy in my company, nor have I openly declared any interest in her! I seek only to recommend myself to her good graces until such time as we know one another better."

"Your manners do little to recommend you, sir. Do you hope to win my sister's affections by bragging on your wealth or discrediting those around you until you are the only person in the room deserving of your own approval? If you expect to succeed, then I submit to you that *you* do not know my sister!"

She yanked the reins and made an inexpert lurch in the saddle as she furiously compelled the mare to move off. Her whip flipped ineffectually about the horse's flank, and her body bounced... rather interestingly… as the poor mare scurried forward. Then, almost as soon as she had dashed away, she pulled up.

"Oh, botheration!" she hissed.

"What is it now?" I demanded, but no explanations were necessary. I looked up in time to see Georgiana's hat cresting the top of the next rise before she disappeared. And just before us was a three-foot stone wall, bordering the extremity of Longbourn's field.

Miss Elizabeth tugged at the reins and had her horse pulled around to me before I realised what she was doing. Her left foot clapped the horse's side, and her face bore an expression of grim determination as she pushed past me.

"Where are you going, Miss Elizabeth?"

"Home!" she retorted. "I shall wait for the party to return. I am certain you will enjoy the ride better without me."

"That may be true, but what of you? I cannot allow a lady to ride off by herself. My personal feelings do not enter into it."

"And what of mine? I refuse to attempt that leap, and I am no more eager to have your company as I ride half a mile in the other direction to find the gate."

I blinked. "Half a mile?"

"Stupid, how stupid of me to forget!" she was muttering under her breath. "It is never any bother on foot!"

"Look, is there not some low part of the wall you can attempt?"

She whirled back. "Attempt! If you have not noticed, sir, I can barely stay aboard as it is! The only reason I agreed to this ridiculous misadventure was to look after Jane, and Mr Bingley is presently doing an admirable job of that."

I narrowed my eyes. "You meant to keep me apart from her."

She flung her hand in the air. "Ah, so the thickest man in the world discovers the truth at last!"

"But why? Have I nothing to offer her? Am I a scoundrel that you would not trust me in the company of a lady?"

"*You*, sir, are a brute and a swine, so set upon your own wishes that you would squash the interests of any that were not in accord with yours! Have you even noticed that Jane is uncomfortable in your presence? Do you think she could be content with a man who understands only his own appetites when he looks at her? If you do, you are indeed more of a fool than I thought."

My ire was hot, and I hustled my mount forward to cut her off. "So, this is your opinion of me! I thank you, madam, for explaining it so fully!"

"Oh, we would be here a month if I meant to tell you all my thoughts about you! I have no intention of remaining so long alone with you. Now, leave me be, or if you insist on following me, have the good grace to hold your tongue so I am spared the humiliation of losing my temper further!"

I let her go—seething, wounded, and mortified. My fists clenched and my lip curled, and I could have spat upon the ground like a labourer. How dare she speak so to me! I was *the* Darcy of Pemberley, heir to a family name and heritage that spanned more than thirty generations and connected by marriage or blood to better than half the lords and ladies in all England! And who was she? A country nobody, a meddlesome fay whose only recommendation was her rather remarkable wit! And those bewitching eyes... and... *oh, hang it all.*

She was walking her horse sedately, but I could tell by the stiffness of her spine that if she had felt comfortable at any speed, she would have given me a fearful chase. I backed my horse, meaning to turn about, leap the wall, and wash my hands of the irksome creature, but I was not wise enough to leave off without a malicious parting sally.

"Give my regards to that lout Collins! You will be miserable as a parson's wife, and I pity you if you think *him* a respectable sort of gentleman."

She shot a horrified look over her shoulder. "*What?* How could you presume—"

"How should I not? The man was leering at you like you were a choice mutton, yet *I* am the one you castigate as a brute! But do, go back to Longbourn, and tell them all what a cad I proved to be! And be sure to also tell them you are a coward, too petrified of a greying old mare to keep to your sworn task of guarding the sister you claim requires protection!"

She stopped, her shoulders heaving, and then spun back to face me. In that instant, I felt the dead pit that had been burrowed in my core swell and burst, overtaking my organs and drowning my being in a tide of blackness. I wanted to blame *her*, to denounce her for the heartless witch I had tried to make her out to be, to call her to task for provoking me since the day of our first introduction... but a horrid sickness dizzied my head and left me faint. It was not her... never had been.

I was the wretch.

And I had made her cry.

"You are the most hateful man! How on earth do Mr Bingley and your own sister tolerate you?"

I closed my eyes. "Forgive me, Miss Eliza—"

"Why should I?" she interrupted, as hot tears splashed down her fiery cheeks. "Why should I not do exactly as you suggest, and tell everyone in all Meryton that you are arrogant, conceited, and utterly careless of the feelings of others? Would it even trouble you for a moment, or do you truly lack any feeling whatsoever?"

"I..." I sighed, shook my head, and held out a hand in entreaty. "I hope you will not find that necessary. Please, I had no right to speak to anyone in such a way, and most particularly not a lady."

"*Lady!* Do you realise, Mr Darcy, that you mumble to yourself when you are deep in thought? I believe your favourite appellation for me is 'Minx.' You cannot even accord me the dignity of my own name!"

"*That* is because—" I had whipped out my finger as if to poke it in her face and explain to her all my sufferings, all the loathsome images her very name and presence invoked... but the trouble was, I could no longer remember them. I could only think of the finest, most unforgettable eyes I had ever seen, filled with tears of shame and fury, and all by my doing.

I dropped my hand. "I cannot explain... no, I have no right to explain. It is... it is not your fault."

She opened her mouth, blinked her damp lashes, and wetted her lips in hesitation. "Do you expect me to forgive you on so slight an inducement?"

"No," I sighed. "But I do beg to be understood, whether I deserve it or not. I am not the man you think… to be truthful, I am not certain if I know what sort of man I am… but my intentions towards your sister are sincere and honourable, and I take no pleasure in having you for an enemy."

Her brow furrowed. "That is the strangest—do you mean that for an apology, sir?"

I lifted my shoulders. "Short of divulging information that is rather too personal, it is the best I can do."

She rolled her eyes and lifted her hand to turn her mount.

"Wait! Miss Elizabeth, truly, do you think it best for you to turn back now? Would it not be…. well, somewhat uncomfortable?"

She paused. "If you are speaking of my cousin's platitudes or my mother's frustrations, I can bear up. It is better than the present company."

"Then if it is my presence that troubles you, permit me to find some way to relieve your distress. Would you prefer to rejoin the rest of our party?"

"I would, indeed, but it is impossible! I might as well return home, for by the time we walked all round to the gate, we would be hopelessly left behind."

"See here…" I turned and evaluated the wall, then looked back at her. "You said it was no trouble on foot. Can you climb it on your own?"

"Easily. There is a stile just by that oak there, do you see?" She pointed, and I glanced over my shoulder.

"Good. I shall take my horse over, then return for yours, and we can mount again on the opposite side."

She stifled a snort. "And how well do you sit a side-saddle, sir?"

"Not well at all, but it is not so impossible for me to sit astride behind the pommel for the half moment it would take."

She stared at me strangely for a moment. "You really are a curiosity, Mr Darcy."

"Be that as it may, it would answer for the present difficulty. We would both prefer to catch the others, would we not? Certainly, we would rather spare ourselves the embarrassment of another solution."

She bit her lower lip, and those dark eyes thoughtfully roved the horizon. "Very well, let us get on with it."

We walked together to the oak, and the steps built over the wall, and I dismounted. *This* was what I had dreaded, for to hand her down, I must hold her by the waist... and a rather firm waist it was. The flare of her hips was everything it should be... and then she was marching away from me, leaving only the intoxicating scent of lavender burning my fingertips. *Heaven and earth...* my heart gave a great, traitorous flip, and I could do no more than stare after her.

A few moments later, I had cleared the wall with both horses, and she approached with a guarded darkness shading her countenance. "I think I can use that stone there to step up," she offered uncomfortably.

"It will not do. For Georgiana, perhaps, but—" I stopped when those eyes flickered dangerously. "Forgive me, I do not mean to slight your abilities. Pray, allow me to see you safely mounted."

Her tense indignation seemed to drain from her, and her shoulders fell. "If it is any comfort, the ordeal will be as distasteful for me as it is for you."

Except it was not distasteful. Quite the opposite. Perhaps... perhaps she was far from unhandsome. Perhaps I could even confess her to be rather fetching... in a disinterested sort of way, of course.

Still, there was something tingling in my shoulder where she had touched me, and my wrist, where her skirts had brushed, seemed pleasantly warm. An anomaly, surely... yet I could not help gaping at her after I had mounted my own horse.

She glanced self-consciously at me and tucked a wayward curl behind her ear. "I suppose I must thank you for your help, sir."

I cleared my throat. "Not at all, Miss Elizabeth."

All was quiet between us for some moments as we plodded our steady way up the rise. I kept noticing the edge of her brown eyes flicking in my direction every few steps, as if she were trying to match my horse's pace and keep just ahead of me, so she needn't look at me fully. Her lips worked tightly, and she swallowed once or twice with an audible sigh.

"I am afraid we must have some conversation, sir," she huffed at last. "We cannot very well be suffering in stony silence when we regain our party, or we shall have to face questions that are more uncomfortable than speaking to each other could possibly be."

"I am happy to discuss whatever you like," I agreed. "Perhaps we could talk of books."

"Oh, no, that will not do. I can never think of pleasant things when I am in fear for my life."

"Then perhaps you can tell me why you are so afraid? Even a complete lack of experience cannot account for fear such as yours. Have you had some accident?"

She nodded. "When I was seven, a horse ran away with me. I fell off, and my foot caught in the stirrup. I was nearly dragged to death, but a quick-thinking groom was able to catch the horse in time."

"That is dreadful. Little wonder you were frightened, but it is an extremely rare occurrence. Do you not know the adage that you must get back on when you fall, or the fear will consume you?"

"Indeed, and so I did, or so my father compelled me to do. The very next time I mounted a horse—and it was reported to be an exceedingly gentle creature—it would not go forward for me. When I followed my father's direction and tapped it smartly with the crop, the beast put down his head and sent me over his ears. I refused to have anything to do with horses after that, and my father could not argue. When Jane took her riding instruction, he permitted me to enjoy his library."

"And thus, I now understand not only your intense fear of horses, but your very great love for reading."

She looked over her shoulder with a sly twinkle in her eye. "And what of you, sir? What were you escaping when you first discovered the magical realm of books?"

I turned to her gravely. "People."

Her lips parted questioningly, but she asked no more, for the remainder of our party had at last come into view. They were standing at the edge of the world, overlooking the golden fields beyond their little knoll, and I understood then why all the locals spoke of Oakham Mount with a mischievous giggle. There could be no more promising locale in all of Hertfordshire for a pair of lovers to pass the afternoon, or to meet for a clandestine assignation.

Bingley had dismounted and was standing near Miss Bennet's horse, and Georgiana was waving with enthusiasm as we approached. Miss Elizabeth looked seriously to me and said, "Mr Darcy, regardless of our personal feelings about each other, I am quite fond of your sister. If you prefer that I not call on her, I shall not. However, I would willingly endure your occasional presence to know her better."

"You can endure me! That is indeed high praise for my sister," I retorted. "But I have no qualms about a friendship between you, so long as you do not presume to teach her your own opinions of myself."

She snorted and shook her head, and I was quite certain I heard her mutter "*Swine,*" under her breath.

"Lizzy!" Miss Bennet was calling to her sister. "Are you well? Oh, dear, I am sorry for going off as we did!"

"Fear not, Jane," Miss Elizabeth answered in a clear, unaffected voice. "Mr Darcy saw to my comforts quite nobly."

Miss Bennet shifted her gaze doubtfully to me. "Mr Darcy! Oh! That is… that is well."

"Well, indeed," Bingley added. "But do forgive us, Miss Elizabeth. I did not know how very greatly we had distressed you."

"It is no matter," Miss Elizabeth replied airily. "I hope I did not hold you back too much. I should be sorry if you could not enjoy your ride the way you had anticipated."

Bingley mounted his horse and tipped his hat to the lady. "Not at all, Miss Elizabeth. Let us take the rest of the ride gently, shall we?"

We turned and ambled off together, allowing the ladies to set the pace. Bingley and I held our horses to the rear, but I think I was the only one who heard Miss Bennet turn to her sister and say, "Why,

Lizzy, you look ever so much more comfortable than before! You see, I knew you only wanted one or two good experiences to overcome your fear."

"I would not call it a good experience, but a distracting one," Miss Elizabeth replied.

"However so?"

"Perhaps I shall say that my mind was less agreeably engaged, leaving little energy or thought for fighting with my horse."

Miss Bennet glanced hesitantly again at her sister, then turned her attention back to the path ahead.

I, however, spent the rest of the ride staring at the frightful enigma that was Elizabeth Bennet.

CHAPTER 9

*I*t was nearly a fortnight before I was forced into her company again. Both the elder Bennets had called on Georgiana and Bingley's sisters, and the calls were regularly returned, but I always claimed something more pressing to do. I suspect Bingley found his way into the drawing room more often than not, but I dared not show my face. Not even in hopes of speaking to Jane Bennet, for I could not bear to see her sister.

How her words galled and stung! She was wrong! Wickedly, scornfully and cruelly so! Unfair, unfeeling, and woefully mistaken about all the particulars of my life, my intentions… but, perhaps, a trifle justified in one or two respects. I had, after all, spoken rather harshly to her. But she had no right to presume the worst about me! How was I to help it if she alone in all the world had the power to aggravate me to words I would later regret?

No, regret was not a strong enough word. I would have walked on glass or held my flesh to the flame if it could only recall the ludicrous and hurtful things I had said. I could do naught but obsess over each phrase, each point where I had wounded her. For days, I became little better than a reclusive ogre, lurking in the library or escaping alone out of doors. I retired early after dinner and saw even my own sister as seldom as I could. My self-imposed brooding ensured that I had nothing to ponder but her reproofs and the most excruciating recognition that... perhaps somewhat... at least in some small way... she may have been right. Or, at least, not entirely in the wrong.

I had nearly made up my mind to go—to quit Hertfordshire altogether and forswear any lingering hope that Miss Bennet might prove the source of happiness I had sought. Each time I took up my pen to tell my London housekeeper to expect our arrival, something would arrest me. Some odd shift in the air, some piercing flash of memory and premonition—conversations not yet completed, smiles yet to be cherished, and ideas still to be conceived. And, so, I stayed.

The worst hours were those I tried to pass in my bed. I came to think of that horizontal plank as a torture device, so much sweat and angst would pour from me therein. I could not rest but my conscience would provoke me to transports of remorse. I could not close my eyes but I would see all the better dark lashes and playfully curved lips—not, to my increasing torment, Miss Jane Bennet's lips. Even Caroline Bingley's visage would have troubled me less, for I could have simply brushed it off as a lingering impression of the day's events. I held no uncertainty about Caroline Bingley—she was easily categorised as another in a long line of pretenders to my affections.

Miss Elizabeth was something else entirely.

Surely, my doubts and anxiety were only the product of my own conscience. I had behaved abominably. Would I have tolerated another man to speak even half my offences to Georgiana? I would have run the man through and felt justified in doing it! Yet I, in my ignominy, had stood there in the middle of a rolling field on a day perfectly curated to bring pleasure, and I had given pain to one who had never harmed me.

I owed her the most profound of apologies, and not only that, I owed her my humblest gratitude. So far as I could tell, she had divulged my infamy to no other. She certainly had a right to! But no, I could not be mistaken—no one treated me according to my wrongs. No irate father called to challenge me for distressing his child, and no loyal neighbours refused to receive me. Even my own sister seemed to think I had behaved heroically that day. If she only knew that far from acting the gallant gentleman, I had proved the very offender of the lady, her pleasant image of me as a good brother would be forever shattered!

It was, therefore, with an almost dog-like submission that I agreed to attend a party at the residence of Mr and Mrs Philips in Meryton. Never would I have consented to Bingley's eccentric notion to grace the humble attorney's home with my presence, but for one simple fact: I knew that she would be there.

Moreover, I would never be left alone at her mercy in such a gathering. Sleep-deprived and tormented as I was, I clung to the hope that I might be able to offer a word or two of my contrition in such a way that only she could understand, and then my conscience would be absolved.

How wrong I was!

The first sign of trouble was when Caroline Bingley initially refused to join us—declaring her preference for Georgiana's company at home—then altered her intention almost too late to send the proper notice to our host. My task would have been much simpler without her hanging on my every word, shadowing each of my moves, and acting as the unwitting foil for Miss Elizabeth to throw back against my defences.

The second sign was when George Wickham strolled casually up to welcome me to the party. Apparently, he had become something of an intimate of the house, and not only the Philipses, but the Bennets' entire family. The devil! What fantasies had he woven to so deeply ingratiate himself? They must have been persuasive lies, for I recall precisely Miss Elizabeth's hooded look from over his shoulder when my eyes sought hers. I should have left, then and there.

I had never liked such parties. I was not skilled at speaking of inconsequentialities with people I hardly knew, and I cared nothing for most card games. Even dancing would have been a relief, for the dancers themselves always provided entertainment for others, but the Philips's modest home was not large enough.

And so, I was obliged to stand in a corner and pretend to enjoy

Mary Bennet's pedantic efforts at the pianoforte until I worked up the courage to talk to someone. The one benefit I found in such an arrangement was that Caroline Bingley did not linger long at my elbow. No rational person would.

"Mr Darcy! Ah, I had so hoped to speak with you again soon."

I died a little inside, but I turned and managed not to scowl at Mr Collins. He was already halfway through his drink and sweating more than any man of the cloth had a right to do. He half-bowed, displaying a greasy crown and sloshing the contents of his glass.

"It is my very great pleasure to encounter you here in Hertford-shire, Mr Darcy. Why, only four days ago, I received a letter from my most eminent patroness, Lady Catherine de Bourgh, and I am delighted to inform you that she was in excellent health when she wrote her letter."

I bowed my head gravely. "I am very glad to hear it, sir."

"And, of course, you must be eager to learn of the fair Miss Anne de Bourgh! It is within my power to assure you that she is in the finest of spirits, and also presently enjoys excellent health. I, of course, took the liberty of declaring my good fortune to the ladies in making your noble acquaintance, and, I flatter myself, none could be more honoured by your beneficent notice than my humble self. Ah, fairest Cousin Jane!"

What luck! Miss Bennet herself happened by, and for once, Bingley was not lapping at her heels like a forlorn pup. She paused, her eyes flitting uncomfortably between us, and apparently decided that I was the proper gentleman to curtsey to first.

"Mr Darcy," she offered softly. "I hope Miss Darcy is well this evening."

"She is. I believe she was sorry not to attend."

Miss Bennet smiled, then looked off to the side. Another uncom-fortable smile, then she dropped a parting curtsey and found some weak excuse to wander away.

Idiot. Why could I never think of anything to say to her? It was true; she offered little help, but why could I not return with a ready, engaging riposte the way I so easily did with… Damnation. I sighed when I glanced to my left and found Miss Elizabeth watching me, and she was not alone.

"Darcy!" Wickham called. "We've two empty chairs just here at our little table. Come, will you not have a drink with an old friend and a charming lady?"

I arched a brow. "I did not know you considered me a friend, Wickham."

"Well! What else should I call the son of the man who nearly raised me? We are all friends here, are we not, Miss Elizabeth?"

I shivered when her inscrutable gaze passed over me. At that faint softening about her eyes, I perceived a flicker of optimism for myself, but at that hardening of her lips, my inner being twisted in apprehension. "If Mr Darcy has not better amusement elsewhere, I hope he will not find our company disagreeable."

"It would be my pleasure," I lied, and I drew up the bloody chair.

Wickham summoned a maid to pour a glass for me and to refill theirs, and then he leaned back in his seat. "Can it really have been over three weeks I have been in Meryton, and have seen you but once, Darcy? A pity, for I had hoped to encounter you more often."

"I do not know why. I seldom pass through Meryton, and we would have little to say to one another in any case."

"You certainly do not hold with polite discourse, Mr Darcy!" interjected the lady. "I thought it was the established form to at least pretend pleasure in the resumption of an old acquaintance."

"Oh, Miss Elizabeth, do not trouble yourself about Darcy," laughed Wickham. "I believe he quite delights in making himself intractable. Adds to that air of mystery and aloofness he has worked so hard to cultivate, do you know."

"You are above your company, sir?" she asked.

"I said nothing of the kind."

"Yet, you have as much as announced that you have no use for the society of a man you have known since your youth!"

"There, there, Miss Elizabeth, pray, leave my old friend be," Wickham soothed. "We all perform according to our gifts. I may not have been blessed with wealth, but I have an abundance of goodwill.

Let us not create a scene in Mr and Mrs Philips's drawing room, shall we?"

She subsided, but there was a fire simmering in her eyes when she looked up. Somehow, I had crossed a line with her—no longer was I merely the pitiful victim of her beguilements but the focus of her enmity. She loathed me and had no qualms about telling me as much.

Well. That would make matters easier, I supposed. At least there would be no tears. I could withstand her hatred, but not that, not ever again! I could even be content now, secure in the knowledge that if my own behaviour had been inexcusable, so too was her foolish allegiance to a rascal.

So, why was it that the compassionate smile she bestowed on Wickham seemed to stab me through the viscera?

I refused to acknowledge his look of triumph as both waited for my response. I stared instead at my drink, casually swirling it about the glass. "You are mistaken, Miss Elizabeth, if you believe I have unjustly shunned a former companion. Mr Wickham has no doubt told you many of the particulars of our acquaintance, but I daresay there are certain matters he has neglected to share, out of good taste. Were they all known, perhaps you would not judge me harshly for not seeking Mr Wickham's company when I discovered him to be in town."

"Ah! The magnanimous lord of the manor. I told you, Miss Elizabeth, my friend always has good reasons, or at least reasons that sound good, for all his deeds. But really, Darcy, is it so very dreadful to share a few moments in pleasant company, reflecting on bygone days? I recall a time when it was not so distasteful to you to rub elbows with those of lesser status than yourself. Why, your long-standing friendship with Mr Bingley can attest to that."

"Mr Bingley is not only blessed with such happy manners as allow him to make friends easily, but also the personal integrity that makes him capable of keeping them."

"Ah! The first blood drawn." Wickham patted his chest in a display of gallows humour directed at Miss Elizabeth, but she was narrowing her flinty gaze at me.

"You speak as though neither of you can possibly possess both of Mr Bingley's virtues. I wonder, sir, which is your deficiency? Are you declaring your manners to be flawed, or is it the integrity that you lack?"

"You are an unusually perspicacious observer of human nature, Miss Elizabeth. I shall leave the final verdict to you."

"That will never do," protested Wickham. "I propose a little game —a test, if you will, and Miss Elizabeth shall be the arbiter. We shall take turns, Darcy and I, relating certain facts to either exonerate or convict ourselves."

"And what possible merit can there be in that?" I objected. "I never asked for your approval, and I have no interest in laying all my affairs before another so wholly unconnected with myself."

"There, do you see, Miss Elizabeth? My old friend speaks the truth, for he is indeed above our humble stations. We will only succeed in vexing a very great man."

"A great man?" she repeated with a questioning look.

"Oh, yes, indeed! But my friend here may have been too modest, Miss Elizabeth. Such is often his way! Perhaps you did not know of his estate or consequence, but I assure you, every unmarried lady in London certainly does. How tremendous was the rejoicing when he left off mourning the late Mrs Darcy and returned to Town!"

I shifted in my chair. "Your comments tend to the ungentlemanly, sir."

"Oh! Forgive me, Darcy, I did not mean to… why, Miss Elizabeth, I see that my words have been a revelation to you! Did you not know my friend was a widower?"

She was peering at me with a newfound depth of curiosity, and perhaps even… was that empathy? "I did not."

"Why! Most peculiar of you, Darcy. But I suppose I ought not to be surprised that the general knowledge of your past has been kept quiet."

Miss Elizabeth's eyes narrowed.

"If it has been kept quiet," I retorted testily, "it is only because those friends whose guest I am understand that it is not a subject I care to have discussed."

"Then I regret that we have caused you pain in your time of sorrow," Miss Elizabeth answered, cutting off some greased platitude from Wickham with an arch firmness he could not rebut. Sometimes, the woman could be an angel. She had bowed her head but then looked back up with a furrowed brow. "You must miss her deeply."

This was too much. "It is not as you presume," I replied quickly. "I have other reasons to desire some privacy on the matter."

"Indeed, Mrs Darcy was… a memorable woman," Wickham added with a grin. "I do not think you would have fancied her, Miss Elizabeth, but I assure you, her loss has created a deep void for many. Why, I spoke to just such a mourner less than a month back—how they do lament! Such a tragedy to lose both mother and child in that way… why, Darcy, I see that I am angering you! Forgive me, old chap. I thought you would be glad to have a bit of sympathy. I see I shall have to tread more carefully if I am to avoid offending you."

"I will thank you to keep out of my personal affairs!" I snapped.

"He meant no harm, Mr Darcy," Miss Elizabeth cried. "None could expect you to relish talk of losing someone you loved—"

I snorted and rolled my eyes, then quickly covered my mouth with my hand.

"… Do you mean you… did not love her?" she asked hesitantly.

"My dear Miss Elizabeth," Wickham gestured dismissively, "surely you know that to a man of Mr Darcy's station, marriage is a duty rather than a pleasure. How opposite we are, are we not! I a poor soldier with few prospects, he one of the greatest men in the kingdom, and still neither of us may marry where we please."

"You would not be so restricted, had others behaved according to honour," Miss Elizabeth declared, with a pronounced edge to her voice and a significant glance in my direction.

A bolt of fury lanced down my spine and I shot to my feet. "I can see that you are already prejudiced against me, Miss Elizabeth, and it will avail me nothing to introduce truth to this conversation. Very well, enjoy the company of this rogue! Let his lies tickle your ears and savour the honey of his words whilst you can, before they turn to gall!"

"Darcy!" Wickham protested as I turned to storm away, "you have it all wrong, old fellow! Do, sit down again. People are staring at you."

And then another voice brought the full nightmare into the light. "Mr Darcy?" Caroline Bingley said from behind me. "Oh, dear, Miss Eliza, what have you done to our poor Mr Darcy this time?" She slipped comfortably into the seat beside the one I had just occupied, and all three gazed expectantly up to me.

My fists flexed. I chewed my inner lip and cast my gaze round the room in search of someone—anyone—else to speak to. The only one who stood out was Mr Bennet, who was sipping from his saucer of tea and looking most impertinently back at me. I sighed and reclaimed the chair.

"Now, Darcy, as I was saying, I believe that was all a misunder-standing, am I not right, Miss Elizabeth? I had just this evening informed the lady that I was recently passed over for an opportunity to transfer to the Oxfordshire Regiment. I had hoped for better chances there, but, alas, another was in line before me."

Miss Elizabeth's brow quirked, but she did not deny his claim.

"Is that all!" ejaculated Miss Bingley, with a withering glance at Miss Elizabeth. "And here I feared you were being set upon, Mr Darcy."

"Oh, I am afraid we are still to blame for Mr Darcy's distress," Wickham apologised. "Though it was quite unintentionally done, I let slip some details about my old friend's recent loss that were news to our dear Miss Elizabeth. The fault is mine, not Miss Elizabeth's."

"Indeed!" She turned to look at me in interest. "Of course, Mr Darcy, you have our deepest sympathies. I had not wished to speak of it, but as it is now in the open... Why, I cannot think what it must be to lose your dear wife, and so soon! Pray, is there anything we can do to comfort you? Mr Wickham, sir, you sound as if you may have known the lady. Surely, she was a model of grace and sophistication. What a tragedy!"

"Alas, Miss Bingley," Wickham smiled, "I did not know her well, but I had a passing acquaintance with her—mostly through her family, you understand. She was truly nonpareil."

"Of course, she was! Just as she ought to have been," sighed Miss Bingley... and then the wench had the audacity to pat my sleeve!

I drew back and saw Miss Elizabeth's dark eyes following me. A faint line appeared between her brows, then she seemed to brush off whatever notion had troubled her. I thought I would be nauseous right then when she turned to smile again at Wickham.

"Sir, you have mentioned your wish to change regiments. May I ask what brought you to your current station?"

"Oh," Wickham stretched and smiled lazily, "that was nothing more than luck. You have met my friend Denny, and it was he who recommended it to me. Some gentleman's name had turned up by lot, and he wished to pay another to take his place. Terribly odd, I know, but—" he lifted his hands in a show of humility—"who am I to argue?"

With Wickham engaged in his preferred subject—himself—I grumbled some excuse and lurched to my feet. Though I had never stooped quite so low before, I found Bingley and informed him that I desired to leave the party early. His disappointment was keen, but he agreed. Within a quarter of an hour, we were mounting the carriage to return to Netherfield.

I never did manage to apologise to Miss Elizabeth.

~

14 November 1811

Darcy,

I was delighted to receive Georgiana's last letter. It sounds as if she has matured a year in just over a month. What are you feeding her there in Hertfordshire? You needn't answer, for I can guess it well enough. A hearty breakfast of your biting cynicism, a mid-day repast of Miss Bingley's excessive fawning, and an evening meal featuring Hurst's drunken snoring. Let me not forget afternoon tea with someone her own age, for my young cousin has confessed to making at least one friend. Little do I wonder which meal has brought the most pleasure.

If Georgiana has been writing to me more fluently and often, you have been doing so a great deal less. The last word I had from you, you were looking forward to a riding party or something of the kind. I say, did you fall and break your writing hand? Well, no matter, for I did not write to ask after your health.

Lady Catherine has come to London for the Season. Yes, yes, Anne came as well. That changed my father's attitude somewhat, for he is quite adamant that you and Georgiana shall spend Christmas with them. If you do not already have a letter from him to that effect, you may be expecting one soon. Fear not, I shall be there as often as I can, but I cannot guarantee that I will always be able to deflect our aunt's attentions. It would serve us both better if they all took it into their heads that I should wed Anne instead of you, but I do not hold great hopes. Perhaps I ought to work upon the lady herself, rather than our elders, eh?

I do have another rather serious reason for writing to you. I was at Tattersall's yesterday, and who should I bump shoulders with but the young Robert Benedict? He was with two or three other fellows, and I presume it was they who were bidding on the horses and not Benedict himself. Did you not once tell me that his father had left the estate entirely bankrupt? But you would not know it to see how the man carries on.

The moment he recognised me, he made as if to confront me. Thankfully, one of his friends restrained him, but not before he spat some rather distasteful slurs about you. I cannot say whether his accusations are generally believed, but I have not been the only one to hear them. I understand he spends a deal of time at the clubs and never has a kind word to say about you.

Your business is your own, of course, but you might consider returning to London. To anyone who cares to notice, your extended stay in Hertfordshire at this time of year may look as though you are hiding from rumours... or from facts. I know you consider yourself above the petty rivalries and scandals of the ton, but we still have Georgiana to think of. And, if I am not mistaken, you will eventually need another wife. It might be best if all of London did not begin to believe that you are the sort of man to plunder fortunes, mistreat women, or neglect your duties to a widow.

Well, do write back if you can bring yourself to it. I daresay you would far rather that I had information of you from your own hand than Georgiana's.

By the by, who is Elizabeth Bennet?

Richard Fitzwilliam

I FOLDED Richard's letter and set it on the escritoire, then made myself comfortable by the hearth in my room with a glass of brandy. Back to London, Richard said... for what? To bandy words with a puerile flibbertigibbet? To counter the prodigal dupe's accusations by broadcasting the truth of the whole bloody affair? Insupportable! I would only make myself the centre of the latest sensation, and the truth was far more damaging than the lies. My dignity was worth more than that.

Richard was correct about one point; I must eventually make peace with the Fitzwilliam family, and there was no better time to do it than Christmas. It would not be easy. The earl would press his demands, Lady Catherine would assert her wishes, and... and Anne would be there, waiting for me to offer my hand at last.

She could just keep waiting.

I drew a long sip of brandy, then twisted the glass about in the firelight. No, Anne would not do, could never be.... I blinked.

Could never be what?

Another burning taste of brandy as I thought a little longer. Anne was no Jane Bennet, that much was certain. She had not half Miss Bennet's physical appeal and even a smaller share of her sweetness. I squinted into the fire. Surely, there were more distinctions between the two...

I may have dozed off in that chair. I could not be certain, but awareness returned when I heard the echo of laughter from somewhere. A woman's laughter—warm and light, alluring and familiar. Perhaps it had been only my imagination, but it sounded for all the world like... like her.

Elizabeth Bennet.

Oh, good lord. It was not enough that the woman had invaded my dreams—or perhaps they were nightmares—for the last month or better, but now she was beginning to possess my waking hours. It was true, she was unlike any woman I had ever met, and even a stark opposite in many ways to the former Mrs Darcy, but why should that be counted a virtue? She was irreverent, she was unsophisticated, her wide-eyed beauty was unconventional, and that wit! Sharp-tongued, perceptive, amusing, discreet, graceful, faithful...

I pounded my forehead with my fist. Even when I meant to compile a list of her faults, she had corrupted my thinking so thoroughly that I only saw her many attributes! She was nothing but trouble. Exquisite, delicious, tempting trouble.

And she had taken George Wickham's part! That alone ought to be sufficient for me to wash my hands of her, save for the fact that an irrational sense of iniquity or—heaven help me—jealousy made my head pound every time I thought of it.

What had Georgiana told Richard about her? I could never ask. The very idea! I stroked my lip and stared at the fire until it scorched a blazing impression when I closed my eyes.

Then, I opened them with a sudden inspiration. That was what I must do! I had permitted myself to become distracted, but no more. I would fix my gaze on the right sort of woman, the one who did not terrify me—on Jane Bennet—until only her features remained in my mind when I turned away. It was not too late for me.

I returned to the escritoire for a fresh sheet of paper and wrote furiously. My tailor still had my measurements, and he would know precisely what I wished. I promised an extra crown if he could have everything done in time for the ball at Netherfield, for there could be no better night to win a lady's hand. I would then have the pleasure of returning to London an engaged man, and my relatives could go hang.

I set aside my pen and blotted the note with satisfaction. In less than a fortnight, all would be settled, and there would be no more of this Elizabeth Bennet nonsense.

CHAPTER 10

*W*inter finally arrived in Hertfordshire, and did so with a vengeance. The fields began to pile with snow drifts, and Bingley and I curtailed our morning rides to civilised circuits on the main roads. The ladies did not venture out at all except in carriages, and the last few days before the ball they stayed entirely indoors. Miss Bingley's great lament was that all her flowers must be chosen by proxy. Mine was that I could not so easily call on Miss Bennet.

I had determined upon a perfectly reasonable plan of action. Five times in the last twelve days, I had managed to see the lady. Twice she had called on Miss Bingley and Georgiana with her sister, twice our entire party had ventured to Longbourn, and once I had ridden alone —quite incidentally, of course. Mrs Bennet had made me most welcome, and Mr Bennet had even troubled himself to speak to me for a few minutes.

Miss Bennet had been, as always, uncomfortably reserved with me. Perhaps it was only because Mrs Bennet seemed to dote and hover over me, and Miss Bennet's sympathies were engaged on my behalf, but it was all dashedly awkward. It was more painful than usual, because her sister was not present to encourage her through her hesitancy or to deflect their mother's impropriety. I did not learn until I was prepared to leave that Miss Elizabeth had been out in the snowy garden with her youngest sister and George Wickham. Any pleasure I had hoped to gain by my visit evaporated instantly, replaced by insufferable brooding that carried well into the morning of the ball, three days later.

Georgiana would remain above stairs for the whole of the evening, which was only proper, and it gave me some relief. All the officers had been invited to the ball, including Wickham. Not that I could have supposed even *him* so audacious as to impress himself upon my own sister, but I would be occupied enough without the bother of protecting her. I stood in an upper window as the early guests began to arrive, adjusting my cufflinks and wondering if the cad would even have the courage to show his face.

He did.

Smiling and laughing with all his mates, George Wickham appeared to be the central figure in the troop of red-coated officers who filled the hall. He seemed to know everyone; calling local gentlemen and ladies by name whose acquaintance even I had yet to make. *The bounder.*

I did not have long to wait before the Bennet carriage arrived. The ladies stopped at the entry to greet their host, and almost at once, George Wickham was claiming Elizabeth Bennet's company. He swept her into the main hall, as Collins trailed hopefully behind with a barrage of his own absurdities and elucidations. Neither paid him any notice, preferring instead to gaze into each other's eyes as the rest of the room apparently vanished before them.

I needed a drink.

However, rather than to disappear into a dark corner with glass after glass of champagne for the whole night, I had other objectives. Jane Bennet was in the midst of accepting Bingley's arm into the crush of company, but I stopped before them and bowed.

"Miss Bennet, might I have the pleasure of escorting you into the room? No doubt Mr Bingley's duties as host will detain him some while longer at the door. Pray, allow me to seek some refreshment for you."

They both blinked—first at me, then at one another—and Bingley stepped back with a curious look at me. Miss Bennet watched him go, then smiled and curtseyed. "Thank you, Mr Darcy, that is very kind."

"Not at all," I insisted. We walked together into the fray, she adorning my arm like a silken ribbon on a stone statue. She felt delicate beside me—fragile, and perhaps a little timid. Her hand touched my sleeve no more than necessary, as if she were frightened, but then when others pressed all round, it was as if she wished to shrink away from them but dared not come nearer to me. Most paradoxical.

"Are you well, Miss Bennet?"

She flashed me a nervous glance. "Perfectly, sir."

"I am glad to hear it. I had hoped to beg the supper set of you this evening, if it is free."

I could see her swallowing. "I am afraid Mr Bingley has spoken for that dance, sir, as well as the first."

"Indeed?" A curious development! Bingley asking two of the most consequential dances of the evening of the same lady? This was more troubling than I had at first considered. "What of the second set, and the final? Might I have the pleasure of one or both of those, Miss Bennet?"

"I—I have promised the second set to my cousin, and the final to Mr Denny. I have only the first set after supper free."

"I see I should have spoken sooner. Very well, Miss Bennet, I shall patiently await the after-supper set."

She smiled tightly and said no more for a moment. I glanced around in satisfaction, comparing the lady on my arm to every other woman in the room. She shone far and above the r... except for *that* one, with the sparkling eyes and the laughter that sounded like music. But I must not look at *her*!

It was difficult not to, though. Her countenance was alight with merriment, and she was speaking animatedly to the admiring circle of officers surrounding her. Never had I seen her hair so richly dressed, her simple gown so painstakingly conformed to her curves. I could not help but remark how the dark sheen of her sumptuous tresses highlighted the life in her cheeks, the soft pink of her lips, and the snap and vigour of her eloquent eyes.

That was when George Wickham turned casually around and encountered my gaze from across the room. He smiled genially and made some salutary gesture, then fixed his attention on Miss Elizabeth once more. *The blackguard.*

Miss Bennet had at some point withdrawn her hand, and she stood beside me with her fingers laced, as if she were not certain what to do with them. She was leaning slightly, and I thought she looked as though she intended to move off, but surely, she was only resting her foot. Those dancing slippers must have pinched.

I gestured towards the orchestra, who were already assembled. "Have you any favourite dances, Miss Bennet?"

She started and looked at me as if I had just asked her to recite Plato. "I beg your pardon?"

"Your favourite dance. Do you prefer the Cotillion, by any chance?"

"I… my favourite dance…" She frowned, nibbled her lip, and said, "the Minuet?"

The Minuet! How dry and stilted! I could not decide if it were to my advantage or not that the Minuet was to be first, and that she would perform that dance with Bingley.

I concealed my disappointment and was about to make some clever reply when Miss Lucas approached and offered her hand to Miss Bennet. "Dear Jane, there you are! I was searching all over for you when Maria said you had arrived."

I shifted, stepping somewhat closer, and Miss Lucas looked up to me in surprise.

"Oh, Mr Darcy! Forgive me, sir, I did not see you at first. How do you do this evening?" She curtseyed very properly, then turned again to Miss Bennet.

"Mama was hoping to speak with you, if you do not mind, Jane. I hope I am not interrupting anything?" Miss Lucas glanced up at me again, and I could hardly deny her request. I stepped back and watched the ladies walk off together. There was something odd in Miss Lucas's manner. It was… *there*. A wink, barely discernible, shared with Miss Elizabeth across the room.

I stood alone and fuming for some minutes as Bingley found the ladies and joined them in some light frivolity. I had expected some displeasure on the minx's part when I made my preferences for her sister obvious for all to see, but I had not anticipated a network of Hertfordshire females, all allied against me. Perhaps I should have been thinking of her as a Queen Boudica.

I crossed my arms and eyed her warily through the crowd. How innocent and poised she appeared! She had joined company with some local girls and was listening to their prattling with a patient smile. That single brow arched in a way that told of her amusement, and one young lady—Miss King, if memory served—sought Miss Elizabeth's hand as she chattered nervously about some silliness or other. How tenderly she appeared to be advising her young friend…

"Have you ever meditated, Darcy, on the very great pleasure that a pair of fine eyes in the face of a pretty woman can bestow?"

I grimaced and flicked my gaze to the left. "I have not, Wickham."

"Really! My goodness, I could have sworn otherwise. Then perhaps it is the lady's figure, so light and pleasing, or her sprightly way of moving. I should think all that walking has made her quite hale and vigorous. What do you say, Darcy, shall I not have the most vivacious dance partner in the whole set?"

"That is not for me to determine," I answered evenly.

"Oh-ho, I see how it is! Come, Darcy, I know you too well to miss that unmistakable gleam in your eye whenever you look at Elizabeth Bennet. One might say that your taste has changed little, eh? Nearly the image of the first Mrs Darcy she—"

"Wickham!" I hissed, rounding on him. "Speak another word, and I will have you thrown out!"

One side of his mouth curved, and he squinted as he shook his head. "You are farther gone than I had thought, and still you refuse to confess it, even to yourself. But no matter, I shall distract the lady for you, if that is your wish. Nothing shall come between you and that bland goddess over there… except Bingley, of course."

I could not help the way my fists curled. Nor could I help an alarmed glance at her… at *Elizabeth*. The thought of her spending even one minute with Wickham inspired more resentment to burn in my breast than the knowledge of her sister's two planned dances with Bingley.

"She is a marvel, is she not?" Wickham goaded. "Clever, pretty, high-spirited… and sympathetic to the plight of the common man. I confess, I find that highly attractive in a woman."

I whirled back to him and snarled, low between gritted teeth, "Stay away from her, Wickham."

He made a face. "Whatever for? I assumed you would be glad to have the troublesome wench taken off your hands. I do not see you threatening Bingley, and I thought *that* was the lady you felt safe enough to set your sights upon!"

"Bingley has not a long list of bastards and abandoned women to his credit."

"Abandoned women! You ought to talk, old friend. Or, did you assume that the widowed Mrs Benedict would not speak of the great Fitzwilliam Darcy's wrongs against her? For shame, Darcy, robbing the woman of first her husband, then her daughter, and then leaving her destitute! You know, her son still refuses to speak to her because of you."

How I managed not to bloody the insolent bastard, I shall never know. I stalked a step closer, thrust my face into his, and growled, "I do not know where you are getting your misinformation, Wickham, but I will caution you only once. Stay out of my business, or I will buy up every last debt you have ever incurred, and have you thrown into the Marshalsea for the rest of your miserable life! And if you lay a finger on Elizabeth Bennet, I shall show you even less mercy. If you have the slightest notion of decency, *leave now*."

He stepped back, slightly paler than a moment before, and pretended to brush some dust off his uniform coat. "Well, then. I suppose I know where I stand. Ta, Darcy."

He sauntered away, the oily pestilence, just in time for the master of ceremonies to announce that the ball was about to begin.

IF I HAD FELT the uninvited twinges of pity for Elizabeth Bennet on that day she faced the mortal terror of horseflesh, this evening my stomach was crawling with sympathetic revulsion when Mr Collins claimed her for the Minuet.

Though it was far from my favourite, the Minuet was a graceful dance when performed well, and the lady did, indeed, perform it very well. So well, in fact, that I had nearly forgotten to notice the blonde beauty who stood in the set beside her. One sister was all grace and elegance, but the other… she was an enchantress, a siren, and I felt for a moment like Odysseus, lashed helplessly to the mast just so he could partake of her song. Every seductive step, every dip of her shoulders or sweeping arch of her neck was almost a sensual experience for the observer. I dashed a hand across my mouth, over my eyes, and discovered that I was sweating.

I would have found it necessary to leave the room, but the sinuous harmony of Elizabeth Bennet and the sweet violin was discordantly shattered by the bumbling oaf she met with each turn. At one point, he nearly trod on the hem of her gown, and at another, he actually collided with her and pushed her out of line. His clumsiness might have been excused as a simple lack of all grace, but I was watching the direction of his eyes whenever he stepped near to her, and it was making my ears hot. My teeth clenched, and I could feel my nostrils curling. The slithering eel! Who was he to think he belonged on the same floor with…?

I forced myself to close my eyes and turn away. I had no business becoming personally invested in Elizabeth Bennet or her dance partners! I had a clear object before me, and *she* was not it.

I swallowed another glass of champagne in a few reckless gulps, then composed myself enough to face the floor again. The torment was not even half over, but somehow, I endured it. At long last,

Collins was leading her from the floor, and I could see Wickham in their path, as he had just escorted the youngest Bennet sister to her friends. I looked quickly back to Miss Elizabeth, and that was when I saw something that truly made the blood fulminate in my veins.

Collins ought to have known better. The man was a parson, for heaven's sake! If I had not seen it with my own eyes, had not witnessed Miss Elizabeth's uncomfortable dodge, I would never have believed that a man of the cloth would brush his hand over a young lady's posterior in public. But so he did, and all good sense of my own was cast to the wind.

"Miss Elizabeth!"

She flinched and stumbled to a halt before me, which was understandable because I had appeared in her path of escape from the donkey. She curtseyed briskly. "Mr Darcy."

"Oh, Mr Darcy!" Collins flopped into an ungainly bow. "What a very great honour to bestow upon us, your magnanimous notice—"

"Collins, step away."

He blinked. "I... well, I beg your pardon, sir? If I have given offence—"

"You have offended the lady and disrespected your host. I shall not ask you again, sir. Step away from Miss Elizabeth."

"Well! I never... I say, Mr Darcy, I cannot know to what you refer."

"Would you like me to take the grievance up with your patroness?" I threatened. "I am certain she would find your behaviour just now *most* interesting."

His eyes widened. He drew a sharp breath, thinned his puffy lips, and bowed shortly to Miss Elizabeth before he lumbered away.

She was glaring at me now, those dark eyes almost black again. "Mr Darcy," she pronounced crisply, "in the future, if you decide to take upon yourself the mantle of the knight in armour, I will thank you not to create so *gauche* a scene as you have just done."

"Then you make a habit of permitting gentlemen improper liberties?" I snapped.

"I do not, but I could have taken the matter up with my father, without causing a public disturbance."

I snorted derisively. "Yes, and I am sure your father would have dealt with it handsomely, so long as it did not interrupt his reading."

She swept close, up under my chin, and so swiftly that I had not the time to shrink back. "*You*, sir, have no proper feeling! I am now more humiliated than I was before, because you approach everything with all the delicacy of a bull in a tearoom! Had you only been more discreet, you could have satisfied your misguided notions of chivalry *and* preserved my dignity!"

"How?" I scoffed. "Ought I have sidled meekly to you and begged the pleasure of the next set?"

"That would have served, yes! But everyone knows you have no preference for me, and I doubt you possess sufficient tact to ask in a convincing way."

"Have I not? Then try me. Or do you lack the courage, Miss Elizabeth?'

Her mouth puckered, her eyes glittered, and her jaw locked as she stared at me. "My courage rises with every attempt to intimidate me."

"Then I shall look forward to it, Miss Elizabeth!"

Her lips parted. "Have I just agreed to dance with you, sir?"

"If you wish to rescind your acceptance, then by all means, do so now."

She swallowed and nodded jerkily. "No, I accept. I have no intentions of sitting out the whole of the evening just for the pleasure of refusing you. I have the second set after supper."

I leaned down with a challenging grin, so close to her face I could feel her breath. "And here I had hoped for the supper dance. What do you think, Miss Elizabeth? Would we not have some fine debates over the white soup?"

She tilted her head with an arch smile. "I am afraid that honour will go to Mr Wickham, sir." She turned away, leaving me standing—swaying unsteadily—at the edge of the floor.

I glanced around, noted the curious looks from other guests, and excused myself for the next half hour.

~

It all rankled nauseatingly.

I knew I would not have endured the night if I had to stand by and watch Wickham dancing with Eli—that is, Bingley dancing the supper set with Miss Bennet, so I had offered up my soul on the sacrificial block. I danced with Caroline Bingley.

And ate with her.

And did my utmost to act interested yet aloof when she tried to drag me into some exasperated gossip over Mrs Bennet's outspoken vulgarities or the younger girls' blatant improprieties.

Nothing worked. For the whole of the meal, I only heard a single pair of voices—one tempting music, the other the very devil. Until that night, I had never known what it was to wish to claw out my own eyes and ears.

One moment of peace, could I not have so much? Just enough time to stop the madness spinning inside my head, to begin again on a clear path without the clinging vines of the forest trail pulling me back—back into the winding way, the mystical ramble, where every turn whispered sweet seduction, and one heart seemed tuned to my own...

Stop! I cried out in my head. It was lunacy to think of that darksome wit like some sort of confederate, slipping her hand into mine and embracing all the twists and mischances and splendour of this undertaking called life. Why, the woman despised me, and I thought little better of her! Did I?

I did know one thing for a blasted surety—I hated seeing her with Wickham. Hated how she smiled at him and credited his slimy words with good faith.

Hated the fact that she thought *him* the better man.

I had never in my life expected to be relieved when the master of ceremonies called everyone back to the dance after a ball supper, but this time, I was. Partly because Wickham was now showering his attentions on the very Miss King that Elizabeth Bennet had been encouraging earlier. Mostly, however, because I stood opposite Miss Jane Bennet for the first time all evening, and at last, my eyes had some proper place to land.

I had not meant for them to land on the one woman just to the left of her.

Bingley was partnering Miss Elizabeth for this, the Bonne Amité, and he, too, appeared to have some difficulty keeping his eyes on his own partner. Unlike myself, however, he could still laugh and talk, and he seemed to enjoy his partner's company. I made a valiant effort but was lamentably unsuccessful.

She tried to be friendly and personable. I am sure she did. I even attempted to encourage her, asking about the only thing I could think of—though why I asked her about her favourite flowers, I could not later recall. Roses. Why did every woman prefer roses?

I looked at her, standing opposite me in a line of others, and I could not help but think there ought to be some... some sparkle to the woman I had chosen. Should I not feel... *something*? Some pride, some instinctive draw? Had I not longed constantly all these weeks for her golden beauty, her heavenly gentleness? But now, in tasting this moment with her, this perfectly chaste sampling of connubial harmony, she was dull and flavourless. Like sweet apricot tarts without the salt; warm wine without the earthy spice. Oh, certainly she was the very image of all that was lovely, but... but....

Bingley and Miss Elizabeth crossed in the dance, and the minx was circling around me. I tried not to see her, but my very own body betrayed me. Just as a man can sense when he is watched, so my shoulders burned as she passed. My spine quivered and cringed, with prickles racing over my scalp, and finally... *damnation*, would this dance never end?

I was panting, and I could not see properly from the perspiration that beaded round my brows and stung my eyes. When she returned to her place, and it was my turn to cross paths with Miss Bennet and circle behind the raven-haired siren, something within me dashed against my ribcage and splintered. I... heaven help me, I never even saw Jane Bennet—I know I did not, for I nearly tripped over the poor girl. I saw only *her*—the one who had slowly robbed me of each defence, dismantling my pathetic armour bit by bit, until all my strength was as molten butter.

"Are you well, Mr Darcy?"

I blinked. Miss Bennet was rounding me now, lightly touching my fingertips and glancing up at me through shaded eyes—almost as if she wished she had not asked.

"What?"

I did not wait for her to ask again. I could not, for terror of where my heart seemed to be straying. At a moment when the dance called for only a light brush, I grasped her gloved hands with a jealous ferocity that made even Bingley turn his head in surprise. I cannot answer *why* I did it. In cases such as these, perhaps there is no just cause. I only knew that my grip on reason was slipping, and if I did not hold fast to *something*, there would be only one to catch me as I descended headlong into the lush hell of desire.

Miss Bennet's hands writhed out of my own, and she made an uncomfortable little gasp. She was looking away, her cheeks red and her lashes fluttering rapidly. I released her instantly, but not before I caught a hasty movement from my left.

Bingley. He had turned from Elizabeth Bennet, and both wore looks of shock, betrayal, and fury at my sudden audacity, but it was Bingley who was stepping out of line towards me.

"Darcy..." For the first time in our many years of friendship, I saw a dark line crossing his brow, and I discovered that he did, indeed, know how to clench a fist.

"To the left, Mr Bingley," whispered Elizabeth.

He recalled himself, but not without a last scathing glance at me.

When the dance was over, he stepped in front of me before I could offer to escort Jane Bennet from the floor. He whisked her away, and I never even gazed after her. I only saw one woman in the room—*Elizabeth*—and her eyes were an inferno of wrath and judgement.

In that moment, my doom was fixed.

~

THE ALLEMANDE. *Why did it have to be the Allemande?*

No doubt, it had been some wicked notion of Miss Bingley's,

possibly even a last-minute alteration. I could have survived a simple contredanse… perhaps… but to clasp hands with the most vexing female in all of Creation through nearly every step, to twirl her about in my arms and gaze into her bewitching eyes, would undoubtedly send me to an early grave.

For a moment, I believed the sultry one would refuse to stand up with me. Surely, we would have both counted it a relief. But her friends knew I had engaged her for this set, and other couples were forming around us. She declined to approach me, but neither did she leave the floor, so I was obliged to go to her and request her hand.

She cast a withering look at my outstretched fingers, then met my eyes with a cool expression. "Is it quite safe to give you my hand, sir? I should like to have it back later."

I swallowed. "I assure you, Miss Elizabeth, I meant no offence."

A chocolate brow twitched over stormy eyes. "Yet, you succeeded astonishingly well. Let us see what other talents you possess that you may not be aware of."

The dancers coalesced around us, but I fear I scarce saw them. I could not look away from her, for it would be a concession I could not afford to make. She stared back, unflinching and stony, as her body drew close to mine and she began to move. I held both her hands as we circled one another, and still I dared not blink.

"Tell me, Mr Darcy, do you always make it a habit to stare at a lady until she becomes uncomfortable?"

"Only if the lady is particularly bewildering," I snapped out reflexively, and instantly regretted it. I lifted my arm over her head—how fluidly she spun the pirouette under my hand!—and when she faced me again, I added, "I do apologise if I have made you uncomfortable, Miss Elizabeth."

She waited for me to complete my own turn, and retorted, "That will not do. I believe you were quite aware of the reactions your behaviour might provoke. Moreover, I think you are proud of your extraordinary capacity to perturb others."

We clasped each other's fingertips and twirled together, then fell into step *dos à dos*. Her shoulder was against mine, her hands warm in my own, and I had but to turn my head to nearly touch her face, just inches away. "Are you so determined to view each of my actions in the worst possible light? Do you so readily discount my position and understanding?"

She lifted her chin. "Your understanding is woeful, at best, and always has been regarding my sister. As for your position, it means less than nothing to me against the interests of one I love. Indeed, sir, your arrogance knows no bounds!"

"You mistake me yet again, Miss Elizabeth. I meant to say that I am no wet-behind-the-ears lad. I have moved among Society for many years, and never have I slipped so grievously as to offend a lady during a ball. My actions earlier were as startling to me as they were to Miss Bennet, and I deeply regret any discomfort I may have caused her."

"*May* have! Sir, the only reason I remained here on the floor with you rather than rushing to attend her is that I did not wish to deepen her humiliation any more. What cause could you have had for taking such a vulgar liberty and frightening her so?"

"I… I cannot tell."

"You do not even know!"

"I do. I simply cannot tell you."

"Then, sir, I am afraid we have nothing more to say to one another."

We separated for the moment to face another couple—she twirling nimbly in some strange man's embrace while I tried to force my eyes to remain on a blonde woman I had never met. A meaningless pirouette, a cold brush of unfamiliar hands, then we were back to our own places, and the one who commanded all my energies was staring at me across the set. Her blackened countenance left no ambiguity about her thoughts—if she had but held a sword, drawing my blood would have been a pleasure.

I regretted… oh, how I regretted… *what had I done?* I hardly knew myself anymore. I could not say where I had first erred, but I feared the litany of my wrongs was staggering. *I regret…*

Her eyes narrowed, and a fine line appeared between her brows. She mouthed *"What did you say?"*

I had no time to ponder her silent question, for it was again our turn to come together. Her hands slid against mine, and a new sensation washed through me. Warmth, but not merely the warmth of flesh. It was a sense of the familiar, the kindred… the homage of the sovereign and the possessed.

This was a fear I had not suffered before—the piercing moment of dread when clarity strikes at last, and a man discovers himself on the wrong side of all he had persuaded himself was right. The room spun with each turn, the laughter and noisome chatter of the other dancers receding into an almost drunken haze. It seemed the only part of the room that was not chaos, that I could understand, was the woman glaring back at me in icy silence.

"Miss Elizabeth," I rasped unsteadily, "I pray you, let us have some conversation."

"Do you seek to relieve your own feelings on the matter, or flatter mine?"

"I seek to make myself understood, and to mitigate our obvious discord. Or do you prefer that everyone believes us both to be unsociable and taciturn?"

"Surely you cannot claim such a criticism for yourself!" She twirled under my hand, her slim body flexile and musical as she swayed in the circle of my arms. "Or do you imply that we share such a fault, both of us unwilling to speak unless we can say something that will amaze the whole room?"

"Faith, I imagine we have more than certain faults in common, but for now I seek only to make what amends I may."

Her hands were warm in mine, her body pressed against my side again, and she tilted her face up. The fine muscles of her jaw stood out as she clipped back, "Then you are to be pitied, for you shall be disappointed on both counts. We, sir, are nothing alike, and it is too late for you to make your amends.

"A man such as you ought to have every advantage, every natural feeling of kindness for others. But from our first introduction, you have impressed me with your arrogance and conceit. I have told you this before, and you do not improve with correction. You hate everyone but those who you see as useful, for they are merely objects for your amusement! You take no pains to truly understand others— you simply expect them to conform to you. And you have the audacity to think yourself above reproach!"

"Are you so blameless?" I countered. "You wilfully misunderstand me, and then refuse to hear any sort of justification. Has it ever occurred to you, Miss Elizabeth, that no man lives or acts independently of his experiences? That simply…"

She looped herself in my arms again and shot a derisive taunt over her shoulder. "Simply *what*? What excuse have you to offer?"

I clenched my teeth. My hand flexed and burned where her fingers touched me, and the intoxicating tendrils of her scent scorched my senses.

"Simply…" I gasped, "… seeing you… being in the same room with you… I cannot bear it."

She whirled round to face me and violently whisked her hands away. "Then I shall not ask it of you any longer! Good evening, sir."

CHAPTER 11

*S*he... she left me!

My mind refused to comprehend. What woman would knowingly create a scene in the middle of a ball, then leave the floor—and eliminate her chances of dancing again the rest of the evening—just to escape my company? The remaining dancers paused—some hurrying out of her path, others simply filling the gap created by her sudden absence. I was in the way, but I could not think what to do. I stepped back from the crush, then looked about as I caught my breath.

Everyone was staring at me. Some whispered behind their fans. Miss Bingley and Mrs Hurst were turning to each other with an obscene blend of horror and glee—I could hear their squeals even over the music. Almost everyone was tittering something, but the loudest was Mrs Bennet, who was crying out her daughter's name in dismay. Her husband only surveyed me with pursed lips and one half-squinted eye.

I could not endure another moment. I wanted to escape upstairs, to strip off that outrageously expensive clothing and cast myself into the seclusion of my bed until morning, like Georgiana used to do when she was a girl. I could not go towards the stairs without marching through the thickest part of the crowd, so I retreated in the opposite direction—the only clear path in all the room.

The men's retiring room was down a hall and around a corner, guarded by a footman. I stepped inside, expecting the relief of solitude —or at worst, other men taking a few moments of ease after the flurry of skirts and perfume—and was met by none other than Bingley. He appeared to be in heated discussion with one of his neighbours, and both turned round when I entered. Bingley's face was red, and there was an uncomfortable silence when they saw me. I respectfully backed from the room.

All that remained was the balcony, in the opposite direction down the hall, and there I hastened myself. The November night was frosty, but the balcony was quiet, the very thing my tattered spirits craved just then. The moment I stepped outside, the cool air rushed about my face and brought a modicum of relief. To breathe for a moment, and to think, that was all I desired!

I leaned over a stone wall, my head hanging. A whisper stirred in the hedges, though the night was still. I closed my eyes, letting the calm of the outdoors soothe the unstable passions storming in my heart. Spasms of indignation and humiliation shook each misty puff of breath as I stared out over the frozen garden scape.

"Well, Darcy, trust you to make a fine tangle of things."

I glanced round, but there was really no need. "I have no business with you, Wickham."

"Pity, for I have business with you. I had hoped to catch you in a better humour, but your temper has only worsened all evening. I fear if I wait much longer, no man will be able to speak to you at all."

"Think you that I came out here because I desired to mingle? Whatever your cause, Wickham, you cannot prevail upon me to hear you favourably—and even less so just now!"

He tsked sadly. "Well, old fellow, perhaps you will be more amenable if I speak to your own interests. I hear that things went rather badly between you and Benedict when last you were in London."

"What business is that of yours?"

"Darcy!" he laughed, "it is in every way my business! For, you see, he thinks of me as a friend. I suppose word must get round about our lack of affection for one another, you know how it does. At any rate, he told me a number of things, in confidence of course. He was drunk, naturally, but some things he said would put you on your guard, if you knew of them."

I growled in exasperation. "And I suppose you are just the man to come warn me, for the right price."

"Well, be he quarrelsome or charming, every fellow must have something to live on, after all. Do you have any idea what pittance a militiaman is paid? I ask you!"

"No, I shall ask you. What happened to the three thousand pounds you received just over a year ago? How long did it take you to spend it all on loose women and betting tables?"

"It was nearly two years now, thank you very much, and I still say the living would have been worth half again what you offered."

"In point of fact, it is worth considerably less, but then, understanding the duties and sacrifices of a country parson was never one of your strengths."

"I was not born to it! Some men are, and then many others are formed for better things and denied them by nothing more than his father's name."

"Your father had a good name. It is a pity you chose not to follow in his ways. I tire of this conversation, Wickham. If you mean to irritate me until I submit and give you what you seek, I shall inform you that you lack the capacity to trouble me more than a fly."

"Ah," he grinned knowingly, "but I know one who does. Perhaps I might enlist *her* aid. After all, she thinks a deal better of me than she does of you, particularly after that rather memorable dance you just gave her."

I pressed my hands into the cold slab of stone that made up the wall and kept my peace, my chin tucked against the silk of my cravat.

Wickham watched me a moment, then appeared to gaze out over the gardens in commiseration. "You know, Darcy," he said at length, "I have always wondered about you. All that wealth—and you are not ill-favoured, either. Some women might even call you handsome. You could have snapped your fingers and summoned the best-dowered heiresses in all the kingdom to compete for your affections. A string of mistresses, too, for heaven knows you could afford a veritable harem. But think of the riches you could have claimed by marriage! A lord's daughter would not have been too high for you. You would not even have to charm the lady, for any woman would put up with a great deal to be mistress of Pemberley."

"Wickham," I sighed, "go trouble someone else, someone who does not become hostile at the sound of your breathing."

"And lord, there is that tongue! You really ought to mind it, Darcy, or it will cost you dearly one day."

"How so? You think I do not intend to discourage you? I would be best pleased if you left me."

He snorted. "You think you are my favourite person? That I sought you out to reminisce over old days? Egad, your conceit is breath-taking. It really is little wonder."

I raised an eyebrow, but refused to be drawn in.

"Aha, you will not ask! Very well, I shall tell you. I could not under-stand why, when the great and particular Fitzwilliam Darcy of Pemberley finally wed, he took to wife the single most disagreeable, pernicious, and vulgar woman in all England and the known world."

"Wickham—" I threatened.

"Certainly, the lady looked quite fetching at first. Lovely hair, a figure that any man would appreciate—if you do not mind me saying as much—but what a black-hearted witch!"

"Wickham!" I spun upon him, my fists clenched. "Leave!"

"Oh, come, Darcy, you cannot pretend you did not despise the cow. Everyone knew you did! I should think you would be glad of a friend who does not shrink from the truth and would condole with you. You were quite right to hide her away at Pemberley, for think of the disgrace she could have caused you in Town! But... well, it is a shame that she perished so suddenly. Some might even say—"

I cut off the last words he must have intended to utter, cuffing him in the shoulder and shoving him away from me. "Get out of my sight!" I bellowed.

He rubbed his shoulder—ever the consummate actor, for I had not pushed him hard enough to even wrinkle that sham of a uniform—but shook his head with his old oily charm. "I fear I have not quite done. You see, I do not believe half what I hear—although I do hear a good deal that makes me curious. By the by, how the devil did she ever ensnare you? You had thwarted far better women. Do you want to know what I think? No, how silly of me to ask. Now, before you sully that fine new waistcoat with my blood, just hear me for a moment."

"I am finished!" I declared, and threw off his staying hand as I pushed past him. "Sell your schemes and your lies elsewhere, Wickham."

He let me pass him, then reached out at the last second to spin me around. Wickham was only slightly smaller than I, and no doubt had been in more fights, so he could easily plant his feet and jerk me back.

"Leave off!" I cried, trying to yank away from his grasp.

"Not until you have heard me!"

He jerked again at my clothing, tearing at the ruffles of my cravat and refusing to release me. I gave him a bloody lip for a prize, and he finally turned me loose. However, now my knuckles were bleeding.

Wickham turned his head to spit, then felt his tooth. "Bastard," he muttered. "You think I do not see what you are doing?"

"And just *what* am I doing, Wickham?" I panted, shaking my hand.

He shoved his face up to mine. "Elizabeth Bennet," he hissed.

I turned back around. "That is the most preposterous thing I have ever heard."

"Is it, now?"

"You are mad!"

"Mad! Hah! Do you really think I do not know you after seven and twenty years? That I do not see how you are fairly slobbering every time you look at her? Fool yourself all you want, try to tempt yourself with that pale nymph of a sister, but you cannot deny that you have a suicidal fascination with a certain stamp of woman."

"Wickham," I snarled, my shoulders bunched as if I meant to swing at him again, "leave me be!"

"Hang on, Darcy, I was just warming to my subject! You see, you are a rather hot topic just now, and not only at the clubs. The ladies— by thunder! Do you know all the talk has you wedding the late Mrs Darcy only out of some dire need? Oh, you name it—Pemberley was bankrupt, or she slipped into your bed and... well, that rumour is not particularly inventive, but others are more dastardly. They say..." he crept close again as I bristled in heavy silence... "they say she had some dark power over you. Some destructive secret...."

I grabbed him by the lapels and spun him around to the door. "It is time for you to leave, Wickham!"

"Without even hearing me out? Because I see the truth! I can be a terribly useful help to y—" The rest of his protest was silenced as I shoved him inside the house and slammed the door.

My chest was heaving, but I strove to contain my wrath... to control... I clutched my head between cold, rigid fingers and grit my teeth against the howl of rage thundering in my breast. It was no use —a primal roar shook me, nearly doubling me forward, and then it rose away in the frozen night as a harmless puff of steam.

I straightened and closed my eyes, tried to reclaim some thread of dignity, but a sound caught my attention. Whispers, and the soft touch of leather slippers on stone... I whirled about, ready to cry, "Who goes there!" but I saw... and nearly retched.

Elizabeth and Jane Bennet.

The ravishing one tugged her elder sister close, tightening a wrap more snugly about the other while her own dangled loosely from her shoulders. Both ladies seemed to be just recovering from the shock of seeing me, but while Miss Bennet was hiding her face into her sister's neck, Miss Elizabeth was staring at me in open-mouthed mortification.

"Wh... what are you doing here?" I asked stupidly.

Miss Elizabeth straightened a little. "I came out to find my sister. We were just about to come back in when you arrived."

I blinked. "So... you were there..."

"For all of it." She swallowed visibly, then turned to her sister. "Come, Jane, you must go inside. You are far too chilled!" She refused to look my way again as she led her sister towards the door, but it opened before she could put her hand on the latch, and Bingley rushed out.

"Miss Bennet!" he cried in obvious relief. "Your friend Miss Lucas told me you had stepped out, and when I heard the door slam, I—" he paused and then surveyed our little assembly. "Darcy? What the devil is going on?"

"A simple coincidence, that is all, Mr Bingley," Miss Elizabeth explained. "It seems everyone was too warm in the ballroom. But we are quite cold now; I fear we walked too long. Sir, will you be so good as to see my sister inside?"

"Of course!" Bingley shot me a hard glance, but then his attentions were all for Miss Bennet. He helped Miss Elizabeth untangle their wraps, for it appeared that the latter had been sharing the warmth of her own outerwear, and then took the liberty of bracing an arm round Miss Bennet's shoulders as he escorted her in. Perhaps I should have felt jealous, but…

My minx, the troublesome siren, had remained. She crossed her arms, hugging her wrap about herself, and fixed her eyes on me with such a depth of understanding that I shivered.

"Do you mean to chastise me again, Miss Elizabeth?" I lashed out defensively. "Shall I ask why you considered it proper to eavesdrop on a conversation that was not meant for your ears?"

"I remained here, against my own inclinations and interests, so that I might apologise for doing precisely that!" she answered with heat. "As I told you, we were just rising from the bench to come into the house when you arrived. We did not wish to disturb you, so we waited half a moment, thinking perhaps you would go back in directly."

"And when I did not? Why would you not make your presence known?"

Her eyes glittered as she scoffed. "Sir, as cold as we were, the last thing either Jane or I desired was that anyone might suppose we had come out here for a liaison with you and Mr Wickham! We thought you went in with him when we heard the door slam, but then… well, sir, I only hope our mutual absence has not been noted."

My shoulders drooped, and I gestured to the door. "You should follow your sister, Miss Elizabeth. I will remain some minutes longer."

"A moment, sir, if you please? I should like to ask you something."

I hesitated, then relented. "You must have a number of questions."

"Yes, but…" she drew a shaken breath, and I could see the deep crimson rising in her cheeks through the light from the window.

"You are cold, Miss Elizabeth," I protested. "Perhaps some other time?"

"I doubt I shall have another opportunity to sketch your character. You puzzle me in the extreme, sir, but my question is not about you."

I gritted my teeth. "Wickham. You are still fascinated by the blackguard?"

"I never was 'fascinated'!" she retorted. "But you ought not to be surprised that I had judged him as the far more amiable of you. Is… is it as you say, that his character is corrupt?"

"Did you hear him deny it?"

She shook her head. "No."

"George Wickham only speaks the truth when it is part of a lie. He was given good principles as a youth, but chose not to follow them, nor even to give a pretence of it."

"Then I have been blinded, indeed!" she cried. "I thought him in earnest. What a fool I have been!"

I felt a stab through my core, and I stepped closer to her. "What has he told you? He did not impose himself upon you, did he? If he harmed you—"

"No, it was nothing like that. He presented a long summary of complaints about you, and I am ashamed to confess that he found a ready listener in me."

"Because he would slight me, you were so willing to believe him? I thought you far more intelligent than that!"

She looked down and pulled her wrap more tightly around her shoulders. "So did I, but had I any cause to disbelieve him? Have you ever shown yourself to be a gentleman for more than a moment?"

"I cannot claim to be proud of my conduct, Miss Elizabeth, but I have never sought to deceive you."

She studied me; those dark eyes black in the moonlight. "It is possible I permitted my own vanity to blind me, but... perhaps I was not the only one to misjudge a certain person based upon their impressions of another." That eyebrow twitched again, and she frowned. "Did you really hate your wife, sir? What woman would deserve such from her own husband?"

I sighed wearily and walked to the stone wall, hoping she would follow. "Hate is not a strong enough word. I have not sufficient breath to describe for you all the reasons, but I did try to treat her with the honour she deserved as my wife. She was... good lord, she was evil incarnate."

"And I remind you of her?"

I snorted, shaking my head. "No. At first you did, but no longer."

She stepped closer; her head tilted. "There is something I must know. The night we met, and you said those terrible things—"

"I was unfair," I answered quickly. "I cannot think why you would forgive me, but if you can, I would covet your absolution."

"It was my appearance that first put you off? I look like her?"

"A little," I confessed. "But there was more."

"My name? Why on earth would my name trouble you?"

I turned to face her and wetted my lips. "Her name was Elizabeth Benedict."

Her mouth opened to form a soft "Oh."

"Miss Elizabeth, if I may, I would ask your forgiveness for forming such an impression of you before ever giving you a chance to prove yourself quite different from what I expected."

She was blinking and her mouth worked in frustration. "But why would you do so? I cannot understand, sir. Even if there was some similarity, surely you are not such a fool as to think I was the same woman come back to torment you! You are heartless, and even stupid if you could—"

"Elizabeth!"

She stiffened in shock, and even I froze, astonished at my own error. I turned brusquely away. "Do you see? I can hardly command my own thoughts when you are near."

I heard a bitter gasp, and I glanced over my shoulder in time to see her dashing something from her eye. "Miss Elizabeth, I pray, forgive me."

"All this time? You were cruel and spiteful just to keep me at a distance because you saw only someone you hated when you looked at me? How could you? Am I so dreadful a person? Have I ever tried to put myself in your way?"

"No." I studied her, her soft features glowing in the moonlight, and confessed what I never would voice even in my own thoughts. "You terrified me."

Her brow clouded. "I! How could *I* be terrifying to a man such as *you?*"

"I… I do not easily forgive others their offences against myself. Though *you* have been blameless, my own character could be called resentful. Worse—I was so bitter that some part of me still wished to punish the one who had wounded me. Even though the resemblance was slight, and is even less so now, I saw something in you that I could not help but set myself against. Your cleverness, the way you so easily dismissed me. You are precisely…" I swallowed and closed my eyes.

"Precisely the sort of woman you have always disliked?" she finished for me.

I shook my head and could not meet her gaze. "Quite the opposite."

I dared to look at her, and she seemed to grow paler in the moonlight. "What Mr Wickham said, about you… ah… the way you saw me…"

"He knows me well, I am afraid. Far too well. You are precisely what I had first hoped *she* could have been, but just as each coin has two sides, so you are the light and she was the dark. And I, the ignorant wretch who swore he would never again touch the coin for fear of once being burned."

"So," she mused softly, but with a brittle edge to her voice, "Jane was no threat to you. You were so frustrated by the past that you sought to redeem yourself by intimidating and manipulating *her*?"

"Intimidate! I wished to…" I stopped. "By heaven, I do not know what I wished, but I never acted with malicious intent."

"But you did! You—you—"

"I gave you no end of difficulty," I finished for her. "I know it. You have done far better than I, for while I sought to dismantle all your tactics, you only desired to protect your sister. And how magnificently you did so! You ought to have lost your temper with me long before this."

She smirked and looked bashfully away. "Who says I did not?"

"Miss Elizabeth." I offered my hand, but she looked doubtfully at me instead of taking it. I held it there, extended despite her hesitation, and continued. "I imagine I will be returning to London soon, and you will be thoroughly rid of my presence. I wish you well, and I hope you will one day find it in your heart to forget all my impudence."

She blinked and drew a careful breath as her fingers cautiously touched mine, but instead of clasping my hand, she turned it over. "You are bleeding, sir."

A rolling, turbulent kind of fire lanced through my arm, across my shoulders, and, God help me, pierced my ignoble heart. I could only watch helplessly, breathlessly, as she drew out her own handkerchief to cover my bloody knuckles. Fingers, impossibly warm through her gloves, gently cradled my hand as she turned it over again and knotted the cloth in my palm. She then closed my hand and pressed it to my chest, then stepped back with an unsteady sigh.

I stared at my clenched fist, then looked back to her. "You have a surprising way of scolding a man who has knowingly offended you at every turn, Miss Elizabeth. Do I not richly deserve my injuries?"

She lifted her shoulders and wrapped her forearms tightly to her middle. "You are not without your faults, Mr Darcy, but Mr Wickham was wrong to affront you as he did."

I nodded. "Thank you, Miss Elizabeth." How I longed to say more!

What could I confess, if she would but hear me? Instead, I simply suggested, "You must be cold."

"Yes," she agreed. "I will leave you now."

As she turned away, I could not help but to stare longingly after her—rather like a pup I was, pathetically wishing she would glance back once more. She put her hand on the latch, and hope rose in my breast as she paused.

"Miss Elizabeth?"

She looked over her shoulder, her profile dark against the candlelit window.

"You... you will be on your guard against Mr Wickham, will you not? To protect your sisters?"

She bit her lip and nodded. "I will." Then, with quick decision, she pulled the door open and disappeared inside.

I saw her no more the rest of the night.

IF I SLEPT at all that night, it was a fitful, exhausting slumber. Her reproofs were more than I could bear. I had confessed to my wrongs, it was true, but I was not at all certain that I wished for her to believe my guilt.

That she, of all people, had been permitted a glimpse into my own vulnerability, my selfish failings, had the reverse effect that might have been supposed. Rather than gratitude for her apparent mercy, I felt only resentment for my own weakness—so much so, that I spent most of the night defending my actions to the most sympathetic and yet most demanding jury to be found: myself.

On the following morning, I came down to a quiet house. The family had retired in the wee hours and were likely still abed, but otherwise I would never have guessed the ball had even happened. The house had all been put to rights, and a modest breakfast awaited in the morning room.

I sorely needed the blackest of coffee, and for a mercy, a footman standing by offered to pour some for me. I observed him closely as he procured a cup and saucer. "You look more weary than I am, lad."

He looked all abashed at my notice. "Not at all, Mr Darcy. Forgive me for appearing out of sorts."

"Quite all right, who would not be? Have you had no rest?"

He gave me my cup and snapped back to attention. "Not until the family takes their morning meal, Mr Darcy."

"Indeed. Er, thank you, Mr…"

"Johnson, sir."

"Johnson. Thank you." I stroked my jaw thoughtfully and carried my coffee to a seat.

I had barely sat when Bingley appeared. He looked even more haggard than I—his hair only hastily combed, his cravat limp, and great dark circles under his eyes. He stopped in the entry, bracing both hands on the door frame.

I lifted my cup in greeting. "Good morning, Bingley. I am afraid I shall not be joining you for a ride today."

He was silent, but his eyes went to the footman, then back to me. "Darcy, I wonder if I might have a word with you."

I turned in my seat so that I could better face the open chair beside me. "Of course."

He shook his head. "In my study."

I frowned, but rose obligingly and followed him to the room, then waited for him to close the door. "What is this all about?" I asked.

He remained at the door, still turned away from me. "You bloody well know what it is about."

I nearly choked on my coffee. "What? Since when do you—"

"How dare you insult Miss Bennet?"

I sank into a chair. "It was not done intentionally, Bingley. I have already apologised to the lady and to her family, but if necessary, I—"

"How could you frighten her so! Did you even see her tears when she left the floor?"

I paused. "She was weeping? Whatever for?"

"Darcy! How could you claim ignorance? Are you so conceited that you cannot see how troubled she was the rest of the night?"

"I have admitted to my wrong, but was I not welcoming and chivalrous to her all the rest of the evening? It was a moment of madness, or weakness, call it what you will, but it is not as if I embraced the lady. Why would such a small matter provoke her to tears?"

"A small matter! Darcy, do you know what is being said of her?"

"No. How can anything be said of her?"

He stalked towards me. "Everyone is claiming that she intentionally set us against each other to incite one or the other of us to a display of jealousy!"

"Jealousy? That is preposterous. You and I would never—"

"Would we not?"

"Bingley?"

He strode to the window and raked his hands through his hair. "Darcy you are not the man you used to be."

"I know that well, but what has that to do with this present matter?"

"You are bitter. Surly. And practically ungoverned!"

"Ungoverned! Shall we talk of this new Master of the Estate attitude of yours? Who are you to take me to task as if I am a mere lad?"

"The master of this house!"

I fell silent for a moment. Bingley's face betrayed every symptom of discomfort—his pupils dilated, his complexion irregular, his eyes unable to meet mine—but his apparent rage had provoked him beyond his means to control. If I allowed him to calm himself, to speak his grievances and think clearly again, surely, he would be himself once more.

He continued staring at the floor by my feet another moment, then dropped his shoulders and paced back to the window. "Do you know, the Darcy I once knew would never have looked twice at Jane Bennet. For one thing, you never cared for her sort. I never once saw you admire a soft-spoken, gentle girl like her, and you never noticed the classic beauties. The witty ones, the unconventional ones, the 'accomplished' ones—bluestockings! Those were the ladies who always caught your eye."

"That is not true. I can count on one hand the women I consider accomplished and worthy of my notice. One of them is my sister, and another is the countess. Who are these others you claim for my particular attention?"

Bingley was pacing now and seemed as if he were so captured by his own thoughts that he had not heard my objection. "And another thing! You would have considered the Bennet family so far beneath you that any alliance would be 'reprehensible'. I am sure I have heard you say such a thing before. Therefore, a marriage would be out of the question, and the Darcy I once knew would never consider offering anything less noble."

"Nor did I now!"

He whirled. "That is not what you said in London!"

I subsided and fell to toying with my cup. "I know what I said, but you ought to know me better than that."

"Do I? Nothing you have done makes sense. You insist pursuing a woman who is terrified of you, and delight in offending her sister, who is a right honourable lady, and you do it all absolutely heedless of anyone else around you!"

My brow pinched. Had not Miss Elizabeth claimed the very thing last evening? But it did not make sense to me then, and even less so did it now, when I was already reeling and sleep-deprived. "Miss Bennet is terrified of me? I cannot understand this. When could I have frightened her?"

"Darcy! How can you be so blind? Do you not see?"

"See what?"

"You are everything that is intimidating and mortifying to her! You press her with questions she cannot answer, you make assumptions she could never satisfy—good lord, your entire manner is like a hurricane to a rose. She cannot understand how to respond!"

"Wait a minute, are you saying she is… simple? I do not believe that!"

"Simple! Not at all, but she is not like other women. She is so innocent, she believes—she truly believes—that all the world is as guileless and transparent as she. No, perhaps she is not a great intellect, but she is wiser than most. And she bears what you could never—" he growled and spun away, shaking his head as I sat in stupefied silence. "You simply will not see what there is unique and beautiful about her—rather, you insist on trying to make her match some standard you have that she could never meet. Egad, how can you not see this? Your own sister is very much like her, and still you do not understand!"

"How dare you compare the lady to Georgiana! Georgiana is a child, not yet even a woman, who must soon assume duties that frighten her."

"And Miss Bennet is a sheltered country maid, a mild, peaceful girl who suits my character perfectly, and who just happens to be the sweetest, kindest woman I have ever met. But in your world, she would be devoured. Life in your circle would destroy her—your personality would trample her, and everyone seems to know it but yourself. Have you not seen how she tried to discourage you?"

"Discourage me? She was the only one who did *not* do so. A woman who wishes to discourage a man should state her wishes clearly. I would have listened to a plain answer."

"She cannot, Darcy! Do you even understand the courage it took for her to return to the ball with me for the final set? A man who aspires to gain the notice and approval of a lady ought to trouble himself to learn her heart, but you will not! No one is worthy of altering your ways for, because you are always right."

"That is not true."

"Is it not? Shall I mention how grievously you have offended my neighbours? Is there a single one of them who can speak of you without recalling some insult you have done him?"

"I hardly know your neighbours!"

"And that, Darcy, is just the point. You have been here two months now and have met all the local principals more than once. Yet have you troubled yourself to know any of them? Do they not move in high enough circles for you?"

"I have come to know the Bennet family," I retorted. .

"Only because you lusted after Miss Bennet! Have you ever spoken to her father as an honourable man would?"

"I have had no cause to do so yet."

"Yet, you sought the company of his daughters, or at least one of them. What precisely did you intend? You claim you did not view her as a potential mistress, so what were your plans?"

"I meant to court the lady."

"That is not how a man courts a woman! That is not how a guest comports himself among his friend's neighbours! You have changed, Darcy."

"Have I? Or have I always been the elitist snob you seem to claim I am? Have I made a single complaint about Miss Bennet's family standing? If that troubled you before—and you never mentioned that it did—I should think you would be pleased by my recent enlightenment."

Bingley noted. "You are right, in former days you most decidedly would have thought the family beneath your notice. You would have warned me off Miss Bennet for myself, even, claiming her to be unworthy of me."

"And I still feel she would be. With a fortune like yours, you would be well able to marry up and improve your family standing."

"Yet you do not object to her for yourself!"

"I married connections once. That was more than enough for my appetites."

"Darcy you are both a more democratic man and a more selfish rascal. You now choose to offend indiscriminately." He turned away from me and crossed his arms, huffing in frustration.

I was silent a moment, then—"Have I offended you, Bingley?"

"Have you! When have you not offended me since your arrival in Hertfordshire? You belittle me before my neighbours, you insult ladies in my own drawing room, and you caused at least three scandals just last evening!"

"Three?"

"Are you aware," he snapped, "that Mr Wickham returned to the ballroom with a bleeding lip? He seemed to make light of it, but everyone knows where he got it."

I stiffened; my lip curled. "And you would defend Wickham to me? Even after knowing everything I have told you about him?"

"I defend no one, but I do task you with ungentlemanly conduct in my home."

I sighed. "Perhaps I owe you an apology."

"Perhaps!" Bingley paced the room again. "It is apparent to me that you are unhappy here in Hertfordshire, Darcy."

"What makes you say that?"

"I am not finished. I think… No, I am quite sure you would be more content in London."

I narrowed my eyes. "What was that… Are you asking me to leave?"

Bingley crossed his arms again, and his knuckles were white where they tucked into his jacket sleeves. His jaw muscles, too, quivered with uneasiness, but his voice was rock steady. "I am suggesting that Miss Darcy must long to see the rest of her family."

I stared blankly at the wall. "I cannot believe this! You are telling me I have overstayed my welcome? How often have you stayed at Pemberley for months at a time? And do you think everyone looked generously on your station or encouraged me to keep up our friendship?"

"Did I ever insult your friends and your neighbours? Did I ever intimidate or impose myself on a woman you fancied? I do not mind a bit of competition, if it be just, but I will not abide seeing you insult the woman I love."

"Love! You hardly know the woman! And you are so ready to cast off a friendship spanning over fifteen years?"

Bingley hung his head and uttered a broken sigh. "If the choice be between you and Miss Bennet…"

I nodded slowly. "Then I am properly chastened. I will send for my carriage, and Georgiana and I will depart by this very afternoon." I rose and began the slow, nightmarish march from the room, but Bingley's voice stopped me.

"Darcy?" Suddenly small and uncertain he sounded, and a note of grief trembled in his voice.

I paused and turned.

He seemed not to know what to say. His mouth opened, he blinked, and he closed it once more and tucked his fingers in his waistcoat. "Do write... when you can think of me kindly once more."

I thinned my lips. "I hope you shall do the same."

CHAPTER 12

*L*ondon
Two Weeks Later

"Darcy, is this where you have been hiding out? In the name of all that is decent, man, put on some candles."

I did not bother turning round when Richard invaded my library, but I did wonder precisely how he had bribed Hodges to let him in. Had I not told my butler I was not at home to anyone? I slowly sipped again from my brandy, ignoring my cousin's muttered oaths and imprecations when he stumbled over the pile of books I had been attempting to read.

"*Buggar*," Richard breathed when he reached my chair. "On second thought, forget the candles until you have seen your valet."

"Leave off, Richard."

"Perhaps an apothecary, too. What the devil are you doing here? And what is this… where are all the maids?"

"Leaving me be, which is precisely where I wish you were." I raised my snifter again, and Richard whisked it deftly from my fingers. "What is the meaning of this?" I snapped.

"Someone must do it, before you make a bigger ass of yourself," he reasoned, and finished the drink himself before I could reclaim it. "From what I hear, the only company you see all day is that stack of books and a bottle."

"A glass of brandy in the afternoon does not make a man a drunkard. I am not in my cups, and I have not been."

"Aye, if an afternoon glass is all you have consumed, but I challenge you to prove you were not intoxicated by some other means."

I snatched my glass away from him before he could accidentally swipe my head with it—the fool was gesticulating at me just as his father had always done to both of us whenever the impetuousness of youth brought down the earl's wrath—and banged it down on the side table. "Since when is a man to be condemned for improv—"

"Improving your mind through extensive reading? If a man's mind could be improved so much, you would have built a flying machine by now, or composed a volume of poetry, or perhaps even discovered a way to defeat Boney. You, sir, are a man with a demon, and I have come to cast it out."

I snorted. "If, by 'demon,' you mean a snarl of business frustrations and social obligations, I wish you would get on with it."

Richard took the snifter back and poured a measure of brandy for himself. "Business frustrations? How so?"

I sighed, and contemplated ejecting him from the house, but relented. "Last spring, I changed solicitors. I changed my bank, too, and also sold off certain shares to buy other investments."

Richard lowered himself to the chair opposite me. "I remember that. You were trying to make a clean break of things."

"Five days ago, I received a letter of resignation from Daniels, my present solicitor. The day after that, a letter came from the board at my bank, 'offering' me the opportunity to sell some of my holdings with them and pursue other investments."

"Indeed! Curious. Any notion of why?"

"A notion, of course, but nothing I can prove."

He leaned forward, resting his elbows on his knees. "You think Benedict's rumour campaign is truly influencing matters?"

I frowned and traced the glass of the brandy bottle with the edge of my index finger. "I think it must be more than rumours. How many personal scandals have been suffered without so much as a ripple in a man's financial interests?"

"You know how it is, though, Darcy. A fellow discovers that his friend is at odds with such and such other fellow, and they sever ties. It is likely for the best—you would not want some coterie loyal to a man who hates you to have their fingers in all your interests."

"So I have reasoned, but it is damned puzzling."

"I imagine it must be. Well, what have you done about it?"

"What could I do? I am withdrawing my assets from the bank and transferring my business, and I am seeking another solicitor. I wrote to Gerald Smythe—I suppose you remember him? He enquired after Georgiana and our winter plans, and when I replied, I asked if he could give a good character on his own man."

"A reasonable notion. What of Georgiana?"

"What do you mean?"

Richard gestured with the now-empty glass. "You bring her to London with nary a word of your expected arrival, then leave her with Mother and scarcely call to visit her."

"The countess asked her to stay! It only made sense, for your mother was the better one to supervise a new wardrobe and morning calls. You know how quickly Georgiana tires with too much coming and going, so we all deemed it wiser for her to stay in one place."

Richard scoffed. "And when was the last time you called?"

I sighed and rubbed the corner of my eye, which had begun to sting for some odd reason. "Three or four days ago. The earl and Lady Catherine did not welcome me when last I was there, and I chose not to trouble Geor—"

"Bollocks! You, Fitzwilliam Darcy, are in hiding. What the devil for? I have never in my life seen you back down from either my father or our aunt, and I cannot think why you would start now."

"Can you not? What good would I do Georgiana to bring constant strife to the house whenever I am in company there? Besides, as you have said yourself, perhaps it is best to let your father and Lady

166

Catherine believe that I intentionally crushed Anne's marital hopes, that I purposefully sought out and then executed the most insulting reversal of faith in our long family history. Let them believe I am a blackguard and a reprobate who dashed old alliances and family interest on a whim. No doubt the earl thinks me a libertine as well, such a slave to base desires that I sold off my good sense for a pittance. I would disabuse him of those misconceptions if I could, but we both know why I cannot."

"But that is in the past!" Richard objected. "Why, it is what… over a year and a half ago now!"

"And I am yet again a free man who has no intentions of satisfying their wishes. Once, I could have couched my refusal to marry Anne in a reasonable, respectful declaration of my preferences, without blasting my uncle's political ambitions. But not after all that has occurred, and the reprehensible manner of my 'betrayal,' as they consider it. Nothing short of a full capitulation will restore me to their good graces. As I have no intention of rendering it, I must remain at odds with them."

"To what end? You need a wife; Anne needs a husband. You are not holding out for some sentimental notion, are you? Pure folly, I say. No man remains infatuated with his wife after twenty years of marriage, so why limit your choices to start with? Besides, I cannot think of a woman in all creation who would think tenderly on you at this moment. Good heavens, Darcy, when was the last time you made yourself presentable?"

"Two weeks ago," I retorted, and reached to reclaim the brandy snifter. "Much good it did me," I muttered.

"What was that?"

I poured myself another finger full and reclined again in my chair. "Nothing. Pray, continue with your lecture."

"Well, as I was saying, at least with Anne, you know where her interests lie. And she is not an objectionable woman, after all—save for her teeth, I suppose."

"Not objectionable! What a sterling recommendation for a man to consider her as his wife! No, Richard, I married once where the bride was not of my choosing. I will not do it a second time. If that means Georgiana and her children will inherit Pemberley, so be it."

"Darcy! You would not leave that to her! Lose Pemberley to her husband's family? Be reasonable. No one said you must marry right away, or even that you must marry my father's choice, but there must be some decent way to go about it. Surely, you can find someone who will suit… if you trouble yourself to leave the house now and again."

I heaved myself from my chair and paced away. *Someone who would suit…* that was precisely the problem. Whom or what was this mythical creature to suit? Myself, or my expectations? And what a mockery if the last woman in the world was the very one who could satisfy both!

"What if you look beyond the *ton?*" Richard asked. "Some well-dowered tradesman's daughter, or perhaps even an American with a fortune of her own. Egad, how the cats at Almack's would put back their heads and howl!"

I cast an oblique glance over my shoulder. "I said I do not care for their opinions. I did not say that I meant to instigate a feud at St James's."

"Pity. That would have been worth seeing. But I say, you are so bloody choosy, you may as well broaden your search—particularly since, as you said, you married connections once. How many gentlemen take a pretty face rather than a long pedigree for their second bride? What of it? Did you meet no one promising during your whole two months in Hertfordshire?"

"No!" I clenched my fists, my shoulders tight as I squeezed my eyes, then released the breath I had caught. I shook my head. "Forgive me, but seeking a wife is the last of my present concerns."

Richard was whistling low when I turned round, his eyes wide and brow raised. "Well… I suppose it is no business of mine, after all. But Georgiana is, and the poor girl is nearly inconsolable whenever I see her."

"Inconsolable?" I crossed the room urgently. "What is this? Has she been unhappy? Why have I not been told?"

"Because no one else sees it. She hides it, just as well as someone else I know. But yes, since you ask, something is troubling her. Mother thinks it is only a product of encroaching maturity and credits her with a bit of seasonal melancholy, but I have read her letters for years. The girl I see in my mother's drawing room is diminished somehow. Low spirits, call it what you will, but something is wrong."

I frowned in thought. "You are saying she misses my company?"

"Perhaps." Richard sank down into his seat again and observed me carefully. "But when I asked her about Hertfordshire and the new friends she had made, it seemed only to make her the more despondent."

I looked away. "You have some opinion on the matter, naturally."

"Of course, I do, but with only patchy information, I shall not divulge what I have, with my humble abilities, pieced together. I do not care to be laughed at. No, I believe I shall pluck at a thread, and see what unravels."

I snorted. "Only one thread?"

He smiled. "It is rather a long one, and I expect the answer may require a couple more bottles of brandy. Have some Scotch sent up, too."

"Shall I also ring for dinner in here? You must think there is a great deal to tell."

"Oh—" he nodded—"I am sure of it. What happened in Hertfordshire?"

THE COUNTESS of Matlock was one of the few ladies of the *ton* who always managed to carry her way and yet remain respectable. She had married at the tender age of seventeen, after knowing the future earl less than a month. Within the year, she had given birth to my cousin the viscount, and her husband had inherited his father's title, placing her squarely at the centre of London society.

She never faltered. As far as I knew, Regina Fitzwilliam, Countess of Matlock was born with silver hair and the rod of authority in her hand. She was not excessively affectionate with her offspring, which was right and proper, but let one of them fall into any trial or run afoul of some persecutor, and the countess would vanquish her foes until they were all prostrate in her drawing room—and do it all over afternoon tea.

I had, therefore, believed Georgiana fortunate to count herself among those few Lady Matlock selected for her personal interest. No one, not even the vipers of Almack's—the arbiters of social capital themselves—would risk denying Georgiana her rightful place in society with Lady Matlock at her back. Despite whatever might be said or supposed of my judgment, my 'radically unpredictable political leanings,' or my 'questionable temper,' Georgiana was as secure as any future debutante could be.

It seemed, however, that Georgiana herself was becoming the problem.

Just after Richard's unwelcome call, which lasted a good two hours longer than decency would have allowed, I returned to Matlock House with him to see Georgiana for myself. I was prepared for Lady Catherine to greet me the moment of my arrival, but formidable as Lady Catherine was, she was never able to foil the countess, if the latter desired something. At present, it seemed she desired to speak to me.

"Alone," she clarified just as Richard fell into step beside me. He knew well enough to submit.

My aunt led the way to her morning room, and I dutifully sat where I was directed. "I apologise if I am calling too late. I hoped to see Georgiana. Is she keeping well?"

"Georgiana is precisely why I must have a word with you, Darcy." The countess sighed and levelled a heavy stare at me. "I am lost as to what to do with the child."

"Lost? Has she been downcast? Surely not! Are you certain her health does not trouble—"

"Her health is superb. Would that I knew half a dozen other girls with her constitution! It is her manners."

"Her manners? Forgive me, Aunt, I do not believe I understand. Surely, she has not behaved unbecomingly."

"If your mother were alive," she said gravely, "she would hide that girl away at Pemberley for another year. Perhaps two."

"Georgiana is full young," I confessed, "but she has always been a sweet girl. I cannot believe she has been contrary."

"I did not say that. She is willing enough—some would say *too* willing. She tries, I do believe she does, but in the effort, she distresses herself so greatly that her bearing becomes forced and... irregular."

"But this is not a character flaw," I reasoned. "Surely, she only wants a bit of practice."

The countess narrowed her eyes. "She is in constant need of direction, blurting out inappropriate thoughts whenever they cross her mind, then suffering in the most unattractive remorse later. Why, the girl nearly burst into tears when the Viscountess of Sudbury laughed at one of her absurdities. It simply will not do, Darcy. She makes people uncomfortable."

"With all due respect, Aunt, there are far worse things than a bit of social anxiety."

"Indeed! My guests could return to their homes and spread word that Miss Darcy is off in the head. They could whisper about Town that she is an untutored and unsophisticated girl who will forever be shunned. But that is not very likely."

"Of course not," I agreed, relaxing somewhat. "Not likely at all. No one would dare—"

My aunt stabbed the ground with her cane—an affectation she employed merely for the prestige she could command with it. "Not likely, because I will not permit it to happen! Fitzwilliam Darcy, the girl is not fit to be among her own age mates, let alone society. You simply must take her back to Pemberley."

"To Pemberley! What can be done there? Surely, taking her back to Pemberley will do nothing for her."

"Neither will leaving her here and permitting her to completely humiliate herself."

"But what of a companion for her, as we spoke about before? Such a woman would be a valuable asset to her. She would learn much, and take comfort in another's guidance."

"I agree…" Lady Matlock conceded, "if she were taken away from society for a time and allowed to mature."

"But why not here? Perhaps she need not receive morning callers with you for some while."

"That will not do, for everyone now knows her to be my guest. And, I might add, the presence of an heiress who expects to come out next season has drawn a number of fine ladies with sons to dispose of. If I suddenly begin hiding her away, rumours will begin."

"You need not hide her, but perhaps judiciously choose whom she sees. Are there not some among your acquaintances who would be easier company for her than others?"

"One or two, at best. Lady Appleby, perhaps, and Mrs Morgan. They, however, are not blessed with unwed sons."

"Yes, but they still have tongues, and can attest to seeing Georgiana. That would do something to allay your fears of rumours. What if you invited those ladies to tea more often and then let her remain in her room at other times? She could still stay here in London with you."

"If she is to remain in London, she should return to her own house for now. No one will be expecting her to receive morning callers at her age. But I agree that she should have a companion with her. Nay, I absolutely insist upon it! I sent over a list of names a few days ago."

"Yes, I received them. I thought I would interview the two you recommended the most highly. Mrs Annesley sounded promising, and she is not so much older than Georgiana that they could not become friendly."

"You would do better with Mrs Younge. She has shepherded more girls through this time of life than any other you will find."

"You have just told me that Georgiana is not comfortable with everyone. Should I not base the choice of her companion on that?"

My aunt thinned her lips. "Do as you wish, but you must do it soon."

"I shall arrange to interview the ladies and hire one of them so Georgiana may return to Darcy house at once. Will that suit?"

Lady Matlock sighed and flicked a dismissive hand. "See that you do it right away. Yesterday would not be too soon."

"Of course." I rose from my seat and dipped a short bow to the lady. "I hesitate to ask, Aunt, but I very much covet your influence for my sister. Shall you still be willing to—"

"Fear not, I shall not cut the girl, Darcy. But perhaps rather than having her here as my guest, I will take her out. I will still be seen with her, but if we pass anyone I know, it would be no more than a few moments' interaction. I can easily orchestrate some distraction to her benefit."

"That will do nicely," I agreed. "What of the booksellers? She very much enjoys Hatchard's."

The lady pursed her lips. "I had thought of the modiste, but there, I suppose her wardrobe is large enough. At least in a bookshop, long conversation will not be expected."

"Excellent! Then it is all settled. Thank you, Aunt."

She allowed a demure thinning of her lips, and a soft hum. Her eyes narrowed speculatively. "And what of yourself, Darcy?"

"I beg your pardon?"

"Psh, foolish boy. Do not think me put off that easily. I know what your uncle demanded when you were last here. Was he a terrible beast?"

"You know my uncle," I offered with a rueful smile.

"He is dreadfully set on having you for Anne. If I were you, my boy, I would not hear of it. You are getting no younger, you know."

I winced. "Thank you for the reminder, but I am not yet thirty."

"Your grandfather lost his virility at the tragic age of five and thirty! Oh, do not look so scandalised, it is no secret. Surely, such shall not be your fate, but you do not own the future, Darcy. A pity your young heir was lost at birth, but you must have another!"

I cleared my throat. "Of course, Aunt."

"Quite so." She commenced a slow, measured circle about the room, tapping the air with her finger as though she were a conductor.

"Anne's health takes a frightful turn every winter. Why, it is only an excess of draughts that has kept her on her feet this year. She would be an unwise risk, if you ask me."

"My refusal to marry Anne has less to do with her ability to produce an heir than you might assume."

"But it is sufficient. I think you could appease your uncle if you found an acceptable young lady among the daughters of his allies in the House."

I drew a long sigh and blinked. "I will try to remember that."

She nodded gravely. "I hope so. I will present a list of names for your consideration. I intend to host a dinner at Twelfth Night."

I coughed slightly. "That sounds more like a threat than an offer, Aunt."

One of her hazel eyes narrowed and her mouth turned up on that side. "You are wiser than you look, my boy."

"Darcy! You did not expect to leave without speaking to your uncle, did you?"

I halted in the doorway. "As a matter of fact, I was not leaving just yet. I was waiting on Georgiana."

"Hmm," he said, "you may as well sit down."

I hesitated but entered his study and found Richard sitting there with his father. He rose to pour me a glass of smuggled Scotch and passed it into my hand with a murmur of, "I expect you will need this before long."

I nodded my appreciation and took the chair beside his.

"Now then, Darcy," my uncle began, "has the countess told you all the particulars of her plans for Georgiana?"

I lowered my glass. "Plans? She only mentioned her concerns."

"One and the same. The girl is a Darcy, and certain things are expected of her."

I cleared my throat. "So I can see. If this is your sideways manner of asking after my own plans, I am afraid I cannot satisfy you."

The earl banged his fist on his desk. "Cannot satisfy me! Darcy, what has become of you? Never had I seen a lad with better patience, more intention! Where other youths ran off after whatever fancy entered their heads, you were steady and clever! You could have had a fine career before you, boy. Why, there was talk of a seat in the Commons for you when Sir Robert chose not to run again for Chesterfield. But then, you pissed it away on that Tory tramp from Cambridgeshire!"

"I should have thought you pleased, Uncle," I answered drily. "Did not some of my former relations' partners agree to do business with you at last?"

"But at what cost! I'll not debate this again, Darcy. I have seen you destroy enough ties. It is high time to start rebuilding some."

I caught my breath at this. All I could think of was Bingley—my oldest friend, and the only one I ever won on my own merits rather than my father's standing—lost to me, perhaps for years, if not forever.

Bingley, with his face red and his voice strained to the breaking point as he cast me out of his house.

Bingley, who could not meet my eyes when I stepped into my carriage.

And worse still, that modest estate we had passed just as we had commenced our shameful flight… and the lone figure out walking its fields. Shading her eyes, and then lifting a hand in farewell as our carriage had passed.

Severed ties, indeed.

"Do not be too hard on Darcy, Father," Richard rejoined. "I have it on good authority that we should be seeing him a great deal more often."

"Oh, shall we?" the earl growled testily. "What, have you broken off with all your other friends?"

"Father," Richard interrupted, "have you been pleased with the work of your solicitor?"

The earl grunted. "How should I not be? His father worked with my father, and so on to his great-grandfather. The quality of his work is irrelevant, but loyalty—now, that is invaluable." He squinted at me. "Why do you ask?"

"Oh, it is only that Darcy was considering a more competent man for his own affairs."

I shot Richard a dirty look, but my cousin was happily oblivious. The cad, what was he about?

"And Father, how are your interests in tobacco?"

"Tobacco? Hah. Are you interested in selling off some of your other fool ventures, Darcy? Never get anywhere with that steam engine you were so keen on. I blame these infernal friends of yours from trade for putting such damned schemes into your head."

"Only considering my options," I answered evenly.

"Well. I might consider speaking with you—if you show yourself to be a reasonable lad."

"I am no lad, and I am afraid I have not excelled at reason of late."

The earl harrumphed and drained his glass. Richard spared me an apologetic look, then offered his father more of the Scotch.

Our tête-à-tête mercifully ended when the countess herself entered the study and announced that my sister had come down. I bowed my respects to my uncle, and Richard left the room with me.

"What was that all about?" I hissed.

"Only trying to distract him, old boy. You were getting carved up like a Christmas ham."

"The next time you decide to use my personal information to distract your father—"

"Shall I bring up something juicier?"

I turned a sour eye upon my cousin. "You can be assured: I shall never burden you with my confidences again."

Richard grinned and lifted his shoulders. "Only trying to help. By the by, did you not say that the lady who caught your eye was a ravishing blonde with delicate spirits? I never! Not quite your type, now is she? I do not wonder that you left off."

I set my jaw and kept walking. "I am not pining over Miss Bennet, if that is your implication. In fact, I have scarce thought of her since I left Hertfordshire. My mind has been otherwise engaged."

"Good, good. I am glad you do not suffer a broken heart—Lord knows you could do without that sort of hardship. Do you think she will marry Bingley?"

"Richard..." I stopped and faced him full in the eye. I wanted to thunder at him for his impertinence, but there remained in my breast no spark of indignation with which to lash out. "Frankly, I do not care. Good evening."

I stood on the crown of the small hill overlooking Pemberley's orchards, the sun warm on my back and the air alive all around me. Long grass licked the calves of my boots, and the trees stirred over my head with the song of the robins. Could I have ordered such a day, I could have imagined nothing purer, closer to the paradise prescribed in Eden.

I looked down and wrapped my arm about the one I found at my side. Sparkling eyes laughed up into mine and her own arm tightened around my waist. She stood on her toes; her face angled up. Somehow, she never needed to speak to make me understand her. My heart heard it all in the silence, and my spirit answered in kind.

A moment—or perhaps it was an eternity later—I turned from the crackling fire in my library when a small hand traced over my shoulder. I pulled her down until our limbs entwined, sighing in purest contentment when she let a book fall open on my lap. I leaned my cheek on the crown of her head and listened to her musical voice as she read to me, my eyes folding into twilight.

Even in sleep, I could sense her heart pulsing in time with mine. Her body fit securely in the crook of my arm, her head and tousled hair cast over my chest in the sweet rapture of the gloaming—the radiant darkness that falls after the slow burn of the day, after the final, desperate sunburst of eventide. She stirred, hummed softly when I whispered her name, and tenderly stroked my cheek when my palm found the small, yet decidedly rounded swell of her stomach.

I SHOT UPRIGHT, my bedclothes clinging to my drenched torso and my chest heaving. I brushed the damp hair from my eyes, then as an afterthought, swiped at my forehead with the dry linen of my nightshirt.

Again.

Twenty-seven nights together, she had haunted me. Twenty-seven nights, the last fifteen of which had been more fervid, more sensual than all the rest. Each night since leaving Hertfordshire, I had wrenched myself from the most vivid of dreams—wrung-out, empty, and grieving what could never be my own. It had all been so... so *physical.* I could still feel the warmth of her touch, the texture of her hand, the firm smoothness of her....

Saints preserve me!

I panted and scraped my face with savage fingers. Her fragrance filled my nostrils, and the sound of her laughter echoed against the walls of my room. And when I opened my eyes, it was as if her face had been burned forever into my corneas by a thousand hours of gazing into her light.

I threw off the counterpane and staggered to the basin. My face I could rinse, my body I could revive, but the bewildering craving remained. I ached, as I had never done before, to clasp the vapours of my dream to my breast and caress not empty air, but slim shoulders, thick hair, and... *heaven and earth*, how was it possible that I could not summon her by the sheer force of my longing?

I pushed away from the stand and fumbled in the top drawer of my escritoire for the small contraband article I kept there. A slip of white linen, still crusted with blood in the centre. I lifted it and drank in the scent—faint, and growing fainter, even as the image of the woman herself only clouded my vision more each day.

I sank to the rug before my hearth, and stared into the coals in a blind daze, the handkerchief twined through my fingers like a talisman. Surely, it was only the madness of lust. A hunger, a physical need that her arms might satisfy. Naturally! She was... may the heavens strike me dead for denying it before, but she was, beyond any doubt, the handsomest woman I had ever known. Whether she improved upon acquaintance, had worked some enchantment upon me, or I truly had been that ignorant, I dared not speculate. I did know that I would live out the rest of my days comparing every woman's face, every woman's figure and voice and manner of walking to hers.

Yes, simple, base carnality must be the cause of my low spirits. Odd, however, that the feelings she invoked seemed more holy than that. I rested my head back against the divan, blinking at the ceiling. What would I have wished? How could it have been, had I stayed in Hertfordshire?

The answer came slowly, unravelling like an embroidered knot. I desired her good opinion, her faith. Perhaps that was all? I had offended her gravely, and learned only too late that I had cost myself the esteem of the one woman in the world who could have been persuaded to hear me with intelligence and understanding.

Friends I had not many, but were I not such a knave, I might have numbered her among them. She would have lent ear to my woes, given sweet counsel and unfaltering confidence. We two—my gentle friend and I—could have then been at peace. Her head would rest on my shoulder, her breath would tickle my throat with each heavenly laugh. She would twine her fingers through mine, and then she would cup my chin and whisper something fit only for the most intimate of attachments, and I would lean over her and….

Merde.

I would have been a dastard and a fraud to persuade myself that I felt only the desire of kinship for her. Fool I, but the mere thought of her ignited every nerve, every sinew in my body. I was no better than my dogs, who salivated at the prospect of a savoury feast! But there was more… damnably more.

The Greeks called it *póthos. Aphrodisia, eros.* The appetite for the sensual, the forbidden, the sacred fruit. That alone I could have battled. It was a thing common to man, after all, and nothing I had not known and contended with since I was a tender youth. There were means of either indulging or diverting such a longing—particularly in London, where they abounded on every corner.

But I was too far gone, and I knew it already. I wanted—good Lord, how I wanted!—only Elizabeth Bennet. Any salve I reached for would only burn more than the wound. Only she could quench the searing flames that threatened to consume me, for it was more than her touch, more than her surrender I yearned for. I ached for her respect, her esteem… her love.

I bent forward, cradling my head against my knees. My breath shuddered against my ribs, and a whisper cracked my swollen lips. "I… I love her."

I clenched my eyes, and spoke more loudly this time, chastising the hearth, the furniture, any object that could bear witness to my humiliation. "See the great fool, Fitzwilliam Darcy! He who loathes and loves opposites who appear in the same form! He, who knows not his own heart until it bursts within him to punish him for all his arrogance! Watch—look on and pity the derelict man, the one who deserves neither kindness nor mercy! For he laughed in the face of love, slapped away the hand of friendship until none remains to even pour water over his wretched head!"

I sagged, gasping and trembling with bridled sobs. Like a child, I clutched my face down again to my knees, and this time, great scalding tears burned my eyes. I had brought this hell upon myself, and I would rot forever in it.

CHAPTER 13

*W*ithin three more days, I had secured the services of another solicitor, completed the transfer of nearly all my investment interests, and met with four candidates for Georgiana's companion.

The most promising of the lot, Mrs Annesley, was everything I might have expected her to be. Proper and reserved, her manner seemed perfectly suited to a girl of Georgiana's quiet and fragile spirits. However, I did not choose her.

In an effort to palliate the breach between myself and my Fitzwilliam relations, I heeded my aunt's advice regarding Mrs Younge. She seemed a modest young woman whose life had been a sad tale of misfortunes. Perhaps I was as moved by pity as anything else, unconsciously reading my own history when she spoke candidly of hers. Or, more likely, perhaps I was merely seeing what I wished, and was determined upon my course. Whatever the case, I offered the young widow the position.

The lady very delicately informed me that her own sister was in some straits and asked for the privilege of deferring her date of hire until just after Christmas. I agreed, and sent word to Lady Matlock that I had found just the right woman to guide and protect my sister.

Georgiana herself was delighted with the news, and though her companion would be just over a fortnight in coming to us, we collectively decided that Georgiana would remove to Darcy house at once.

The nurse of a neighbouring family, herself a widowed gentlewoman, was without employment for some weeks while her young charges travelled to Bath. She agreed to sit in the mornings with Georgiana, and I believe their pleasure was mutual when Georgiana took it upon herself to tutor the older woman on the pianoforte. Lady Matlock came nearly every other day after luncheon, and often they would be out until very late in the afternoon. I felt myself quite contented with this arrangement, and hoped it was a signal of better things for Georgiana.

My own concerns, however, had grown only more troubling. Since coming away from Hertfordshire, I had written to Bingley twice. The first letter received no reply, and so a fortnight later I had attempted a second.

To this, the only answer was a prettily framed note from Miss Bingley to Georgiana, in which the former expressed all her regret at their parting, and her very great hope that they might see one another in Town again soon. What Georgiana's feelings were upon receiving this note, I could not quite be certain. My own, I knew far too well.

Since boyhood, I had ever been given to much reflection, perhaps even excessive brooding. My favourite means of commanding my thoughts had always been to secure quiet time out of doors or in my library. Now, however, the clamour of Town made any foray outside my own door a public event, and I could not set foot in my library without other memories tormenting me. I certainly attempted it often enough, but on the first such occasion, my eyes fell on my old copy of Samuel Johnson.

And then there it was... that insidious fragrance again, the heat rising in my face; the pleasure of watching her—the way her eyes would come to life and her slippered feet would twist together when she was amused. I stroked the old cover, just where her hands had caressed its worn edges. The pages fell open, and the blue satin ribbon slid under my fingertips. I closed my eyes, heaved a weary sigh, and returned the book to its place on the shelf.

It was no better the second time I came into my library. Nor the third. The fourth attempt resulted in a new resting place for Samuel Johnson, tucked sideways behind two books on ornithology. Miss Bingley would have been pleased.

Within a few days, however, the infernal book had not only wormed its way out of exile, but had found a place of honour on my study desk. For long hours, I would be writing letters of business or making plans for my steward, but each stroke of the pen was hard won. At every heartbeat, every word, my eyes would flick again to the book until at last I would surrender and indulge my distracted spirits in a line or two… or more.

What might have been unbearably poignant I found instead to be soothing. Her eyes had lingered fondly on these pages, her mind found nourishment and joy within its leather binding. And that meant that something, at least, of mine had the power to give her pleasure.

Then I would scoff at myself, recalling my senses. Every time, I would slam the book back down on my desk, declaring it all rot, and apply myself to my work… only to lose my thoughts mere moments later. Such was my daily struggle, and such it was again on this day, until my addled brain found something more distressing than my own frustrated hopes.

At the bottom of this day's correspondence was a letter addressed in a feminine hand. I knew before I broke the seal who the sender was, and my ire snapped to life. Why had she not gone through my new solicitor? I had forwarded her the necessary information; she had neither right nor cause to send to me directly. Yet, there it was—a demand for more money, a threat of undefined proportions, and the mother of the former Mrs Darcy had affixed her name to the bottom.

And what was this? A claim that I yet held something in trust that I had not released to her as promised? The nerve of the woman! She had even secured a second signature beside her own from a witness—from Mr Daniels, in fact—my old solicitor.

I cast the letter aside and paced to my window. What was the devil woman about? As if there remained anything she could have called her own! Her husband's effects, those that had not gone to his heir, were now the property of his various creditors. The estate his son had inherited was heavily leveraged, and presently leased out to some wealthy businessman from the north to cover expenses.

I had not kept so much as a hair comb belonging to the former Mrs Darcy—indeed, I would have burned down that entire wing of my own house, just to be rid of her scourge. As Mrs Reynolds, my steward, and even Mr Daniels himself could all attest, there were no hidden jewels from the lost Benedict fortune still littering my property.

I fell back upon my desk all in a furious rush, determined to pen such a scathing letter to Daniels that in the future he would rather drown himself in the filthy Thames than submit another such complaint to me. In this effort I was engaged when the countess herself threw open the door to my study without so much as a preamble.

"Darcy, how do you do today, my boy?"

I rose hastily. "Good afternoon, Aunt. I am afraid you have caught me in the midst of a rather provoking correspondence."

She waved a hand. "Then I shall not keep you. I came to inform you of a most delightful happenstance. I have just returned from Hatchard's with Georgiana, and I daresay, the girl has found a remarkably tasteful Christmas gift for you."

My brow pinched in bewilderment. "Then I shall look forward to learning what it is."

"Oh, fear not, I have no intention of spoiling the surprise. No, do you see, what I wished to tell you is that we happened upon a very knowledgeable young lady in the store—a lady, mind you, not a shop-keeper's girl or any such nonsense. Georgiana seemed familiar with her; I think from school. You know how flighty these girls can be—although, I must say, this one seemed rather steady."

"That is well. I had hoped Georgiana would encounter some friend or other in Town this winter," I answered distractedly.

"Indeed, indeed. I have sent inquiries after the young lady's family, naturally, but I gave Georgiana my blessing to invite the young lady to call."

"To call? Here?"

She blinked and shook her head slowly. "You would not have it the reverse until her companion can attend her, I presume."

"Of course," I nodded, glancing in annoyance once more at the letter on my desk.

She tapped her cane on the ground. "I can see that you are thinking of anything but the present just now, so I will be straightforward. Since Georgiana first came to London, I had not seen her so at ease with anyone as this girl. Why, she was nearly poised and serene! Provided I learn nothing shocking of the young lady, I think her influence might do our dear Georgiana much good. There, now, I have said my piece, and I shall leave you to that letter that must be of such import."

"Forgive me, Aunt," I sighed. "I thank you for taking an interest in Georgiana's affairs."

She arched a brow. "I shall send word of what I learn of her. Meanwhile, you may expect Georgiana to receive a caller soon."

I thanked my aunt again and saw her to the door, then returned with all haste to my letter. The words had been on the tip of my pen, the heat of my indignation still causing the ink to flow onto the page with just the proper amount of umbrage.

Only after I had sealed the letter and sent it off with a footman did I realise that I had not even the courtesy to ask the name of Georgiana's friend.

For days, Richard had been prevailing up on me to accompany him to the club. I think his excuse of desiring my company for the prestige it lent him was rather flimsy—he knew that it was one way to extract me from the house. Moreover, he found it convenient to have me nearby if he ever ran low at the card tables. And so, to Brooks' we repaired.

Richard's game was Hazard. He was uncannily lucky most of the time, but I think a good deal of that had to do with how he chose his tables. It was all too common to enter the club at ten of the morning to find a dozen fellows who had been at it all night. Such men were loose, both with their money and their sense. He was not long in seeking them. Richard gave a jerk of his head, and I groaned when I recognised the men he had chosen.

Ramsey and Carlisle, and just in the midst of them sat Benedict.

Richard glanced over in question. I only set my teeth—it was too late to withdraw now. Richard swaggered over to the table, nodding in that half-mocking, half-appreciative way he had when he studied his prospective opponents. "Just getting started, I see?"

Ramsey laughed. "Seven bloody hours ago. No! Going on thirteen now. How are you keeping, Fitzwilliam? And Darcy! We have not seen you in here for some months."

I kept my face carefully neutral as I greeted them. I even managed a tolerably civil acknowledgment of Benedict, but it cost me sorely in dignity.

"Yes, Darcy, why is that?" Benedict jeered. "Too good for us, are you?"

I clasped my hands behind my back and peered sideways at him. "I might ask what brings you here, as well. I thought White's was your club."

"Was my father's club!" he snapped. "The wrong lot, that. Not for me, old boy."

"That's right, Darcy," Carlisle grinned. "Why, you above all men know something of a fellow trying to make himself over. Our friend here is not responsible for his father's decisions; surely you can make allowances for him."

Ramsey had been busily surveying Richard, his bleary-eyed gaze resting speculatively on my cousin's pocket. "Care to join, Fitzwilliam? Always room for one more. And what of you, Darcy? I thought Whist was your game."

"When I play at all," I answered. "More of a thinking man's game."

"Ah, yes, there is the Darcy we know, always ready with a backwards insult for us plebeians. Come on old fellow, surely you are not too proud to sit down with your friends."

"Oh, but he is, indeed," Benedict snorted. "I am not afraid of you, Darcy. What of a rubber? I see an empty Whist table just there."

"It would be an unfair game," I answered.

"Oh, ho! Too good for me still, are you, Darcy? Would you refuse to play with your brother-in-law?"

"You have been up drinking all night," I replied.

"That would not matter," Carlisle laughed. "Darcy always wins at Whist. One wonders if he possesses some secret know-how. Or just devilishly good luck."

"Do you imply that he is a cheat?" Richard bristled.

"No, no, naturally! But he has a… a gift, shall I say. I am afraid he leaves us mere mortals in the dust. You are quite right Darcy—unfair, indeed. But what of you, Fitzwilliam? I know you are always good for a game of Hazard. Care to join us?"

"Much obliged," Richard replied. He drew up a chair and seated himself.

Would that I could have gone anywhere else. I silently cursed Richard and his persuasive arts, dragging me where I did not wish to go, amongst men I could certainly do without. But now, I was trapped, for had I walked away, I would have provided only more fuel for the gossips. A cursory glance about the room sufficed to inform me that our presence had been noted.

Like enough, that had been Richard's plan all along, forcing me to appear in public with one widely supposed to be my enemy, so that the potency of the rumours might evaporate. *The blackguard.* I scowled at him whenever he cared to notice me, and kept my eyes above the heads of the others when he did not.

The game progressed in a rational manner, if one can consider a game based entirely on chance "rational." Richard's genius was in persuading his companions to higher bets than they would normally have given, all while managing to keep his own losses low. Somehow, he possessed an uncanny knack for rolling threes and elevens when his comrades could only produce sixes and sevens. I crossed my hands behind my back and mused fretfully that a man who took the time to master a game of skill could be considered dishonest, but a man with unexplained good fortune—and a genial face—was only thought "lucky".

"Fitzwilliam," Benedict asked at length, "have you seen Colchester of late?"

Richard busied himself arranging his coins. "I heard he is back in Yorkshire for the winter."

"Pity!" lamented the other. "He had promised to—well, never mind. I suppose I may see him in a month or two."

Richard glanced up. "Something of importance?"

"Oh, no, only he had promised to do me a small favour, one gentleman to another, that sort of thing."

"Something we could help with instead?" asked Ramsey. "Come now man, are we not your friends? Darcy here is even your brother-in-law!"

I shifted, turning my shoulder ever so slightly away.

"Oh, well," Benedict demurred, "I am not quite so sure it merits—"

"Come now, Benedict," Carlisle urged, "we are all friends here."

"Well, since you insist, he had offered to introduce me to his sister. Fine girl, as I recall."

Ramsey whistled low. "I hear she has a dowry of eighteen thousand pounds. That is as handsome a recommendation as any I can think of!"

"Yes, yes, very attractive," agreed Carlisle. "But I wonder that you don't look round a bit, old boy. I do think you could do somewhat better. Why, I know many a girl with at least twenty thousand. Indeed, I think most of the young debutantes in the town have at least that much! Is that not so, Darcy?"

I glanced sideways. "I would not know. I have not been acquainted with any of them this year."

"Yes, but you must know how it is. Why, your own sister has—oh, forgive me, I did not mean to sound indelicate."

I rounded upon him, hissing between my teeth. "My sister is not yet out. Kindly leave her out of the conversation."

"Now, no one is proposing to Miss Darcy, but she is sixteen, is she not? I only felt there might be others like her—only daughters of good houses, I mean."

"Here, now," Richard interrupted by banging on the table, "let us put an end to this talk. Not only is it disrespectful to my ward, but you have more than implied that Miss Darcy might make a good match for the man who was brother to her sister-in-law! Damned indecent, man."

"Oh come, Fitzwilliam, there was nothing indecent in it. And besides, no one was serious," Ramsey protested. "We are only advising our friend here that he might look around a bit more. Egad, if we cannot speak of debutantes and dowries and that sort of thing here, where the devil can we do it?"

Richard growled darkly and took up the dice for a new toss. He rolled an eight, which happened to be the main, then threw up his hands. "Well, gentlemen, that is another for me. Do you know, I think I shall call it an end here."

"So soon?" Carlisle objected. "Why, have you no stomach for a good game?"

Richard rose to his feet. "Nothing of the kind. I just remembered that Darcy here wished to make time today for a little fencing. If I am not mistaken, I owe him a round or two, and so I think we must be off."

Ramsey and Carlisle both expressed their farewells. Benedict, however, remained staring at the table as we took our leave. I made no overtures of friendship as we left. In fact, I said not a single word to anyone until we reached my carriage and barked out an order to take us not to Angelo's fencing parlour, but back to my town house. Once we were safely underway, I exploded.

"What was that all about, Richard? Did you truly drag me there for the express purpose of creating an incident?"

"Creating an incident! I think I was trying to avoid one. Best thing that could have happened was for you and Benedict to meet in public and not come to bruises over the affair. I call today a smashing success."

"The next time you take it in your head to improve my image, kindly do it without me!" I snapped.

"It was not for you; it was for Georgiana."

"Oh, yes, my sister whose name has now been sullied at the club, while she is still a child barely out of the schoolroom!"

"Her name is mentioned often enough there without you to hear it. You may as well be at hand to defend her for once."

"And what have you done? Tell me, how many do you suppose have made wagers about my innocent young sister and her thirty thousand pounds?"

"That was ill-bred of them, I confess."

"Ill-bred! Why, before I know it, rumours will start up that Benedict feels I owe him my sister's hand in recompense for the dowry I plundered from his own family! You do know that is what he believes—that I took advantage of his sister and spent all her fortune. I ought to show him the settlement papers!"

"You do take things so seriously, Darcy. It was nothing like that. How many times have you been at the club when men discussed the assets of one prospective bride or another? It is serious business, and where better to talk of it?"

"Georgiana is not a piece of horseflesh up on the auction block!"

"No one ever said she was! But come, old boy, it is not too early to consider the matter. You and I both wish to see her matched well when the time comes, so let us begin to look after the eligible gentlemen."

"Let me assure you, Benedict is not a candidate, nor are Ramsey or Carlisle. She deserves someone with a bit of delicacy. Why, I would not even give her to you if you asked."

Richard crossed his arms. "That was a touch cruel."

I covered my eyes and sighed. "Forgive me. I know you would not…"

"I would never consider it, if it eases your conscience. But what about Bingley? Would you give her to him?"

"I had once considered the notion, yes—if she cared for him. Connections be hanged, he is as good a man as ever I knew. He would be just the right sort to—" I broke off with a sigh. "Well. I think Bingley's interests lie elsewhere. It does not matter; I am sure there will be another."

"Yes," he retorted drily, "it sounds as if there will be quite a long line of them. Let us hope she matures soon enough for her own good. By the by, Mother said Georgiana had met some friend or other while they were out the other day. Did you know this?"

"Yes, she mentioned it day before yesterday."

Richard looked away, gazing out the window of the carriage. "Do you know who it is?"

"No. I meant to ask Georgiana more of it, but she was at her instrument that evening, and I was with my new solicitor nearly all day yesterday. I sent a note around to the countess this morning, asking for more information. I expect she will present me with her full findings by evening."

Richard drew back the curtain and tilted his head. "I foresee you are to learn the lady's identity sooner than that." He nodded towards the window, and I discovered that we had already arrived at my house. "There is another carriage, and the footman is getting down and waiting for someone."

An indecent curiosity overcame me as I peered out at the carriage. It was not one belonging to anyone I knew. It bore no crest, and though both vehicle and horses looked well kept, they were not of the first quality. In fact, I might almost have suspected that the carriage could have belonged to a tradesman.

We passed briskly into the hall and arrived as Georgiana was leading her guests out of the drawing room. Just behind her trailed a slightly matronly woman, with a good face and a modest manner. The lady paused in apparent surprise at our arrival, then turned around behind her to...

The blood pounded in my ears, rushed into my face, and paralysed my tongue. It was *she*—the one who tormented me night and day, who had the power to command my thoughts and inspire every feeling ever known to man to well up simultaneously in my mortal frame. My Calypso, my sword-wielding queen, the only woman on earth who could both pardon and condemn me in the same breath—my own fine-eyed minx. *Elizabeth.*

"Oh! Mr Darcy!" She curtsied deeply, her cheeks red. "Forgive me, we did not know you would be at home."

"Miss... Miss Elizabeth." I cut a hasty bow, too eager to raise my eyes again to her to allow for more. "It is a pleasure."

She looked away and gestured uncomfortably to the older lady. "Mr Darcy, may I present my aunt, Mrs Gardiner."

"Mrs Gardiner," I bowed again. "This is my cousin, Colonel Fitzwilliam."

"Delighted, Mrs Gardiner." Richard stepped forward and greeted both ladies, then extended his hand to Elizabeth to bow over her fingers. "Charmed, Miss Bennet. My cousin has told me much of you."

Those dark eyes warmed slightly. "Miss Darcy is very kind."

"Hmm?" Richard queried. "Oh! yes, Miss Darcy. My cousin."

I could have strangled him where he stood. I was not so blinded by Elizabeth's presence that I did not see the mischievous quirk to his lip, or the confused frown of Mrs Gardiner. A line crossed Elizabeth's brow, and I shot Richard a dangerous look.

"Well," she smiled tightly, "I am afraid we must be going. I do not wish to keep you." She curtsied to my sister, and Georgiana expressed her pleasure in the warmest of means.

She was leaving! Something squeezed mercilessly against my lungs, and I choked on my next breath before I could summon the strength to speak. "Er... Miss Elizabeth! And Mrs Gardiner—may I see you to your carriage?"

They paused and glanced curiously at each other. Mrs Gardner graciously inclined her head and thanked me, but Elizabeth appeared more doubtful. She cautiously accepted my arm down the steps, and Richard, bothersome miscreant that he was, offered to escort Mrs Gardiner on ahead of us. The older lady descended the steps and mounted the box first, while I waited with Elizabeth. She was looking down, her countenance still rosy with discomfort, and I daresay my own looked no less uneasy.

"I—" I cleared my throat, "I had not expected to see you in Town, Miss Elizabeth."

A pained look crossed her features. "Nor had I expected to come at this time of year, but my mother thought it for the best."

"Your mother?"

"Indeed. She felt it would be an ideal time for me to visit my Aunt and Uncle Gardiner." She paused, then slowly raised her eyes to my own. Her lips parted and one eye flickered, as if she meant far more than her words could possibly convey.

"Oh…" I nodded as if I understood, and it is possible that my assumptions about Mrs Bennet and her machinations were not entirely wrong. "Yes, of course. And your family are in good health?"

"Yes, they are in excellent health."

"And your sisters? They are all well?"

The corner of her mouth turned up. "Quite well, sir."

"And… all the others are still at home?"

"Yes, all." She bit her lower lip and her brow creased, then added, "Perhaps you have not heard the news. There is to be a wedding soon."

"There is?" I drew a shaken breath. Somehow, I had expected that Bingley would have at least sent a letter. Was my transgression so great that even the effusive Bingley did not count me worthy of hearing of his joy?

"Yes," she continued. "My cousin Mr Collins and my friend Miss Lucas. It was a surprise for us all—more welcome to some than to others."

"Oh." I nodded. "Yes, of course. And how long have you been in Town?"

"Three weeks. I expect I am to return home after Twelfth Night—fear not, sir, I shall not make a habit of imposing on your hospitality."

"No!" I cried, then lowered my voice when I saw Richard jump. "No, I beg you, please feel at liberty to call as often as you wish. Georgiana very much values your friendship."

She gazed up at me, golden flecks dancing in her dark eyes. She nodded slowly and offered a thin smile. "I thank you, sir. Good day."

I let her clasp my hand as she stepped into the coach, then I turned to the house, my steps leaden and dream-like. When I reached the door, I could not help looking back at the coach as it pulled away.

"Well," Richard mused, "that does explain a few things."

"Put a cork in it, Richard."

"What?" He threw a hand in the air. "A bit touchy, aren't we?"

"You are trying to draw conclusions that will lead nowhere."

"I said nothing! You did all the concluding yourself—guilty conscience, Darcy?"

I turned away and marched into the house. "What could you possibly know of it?"

CHAPTER 14

It was no easy task convincing Richard that there was not some woebegone tale of lost romance to worm from my lips. I was only able to be rid of him after I reminded him of his prior admission that he was due to report to his regiment by evening. Even as he went, it was with the vow of discovering some imaginary secret of mine.

I longed to speak to Georgiana, to learn her feelings and to ask her how this re-acquaintance with Miss Elizabeth had come about, but she had retired above stairs to dress for dinner. Therefore, I sought intelligence from the most reliable source in the house—my house-keeper, Mrs Elliott.

"Oh, yes, Mr Darcy," she answered, "Miss Darcy received her guest warmly. Very warmly, indeed. She asked me to show the young lady and her aunt to the library to search for a particular book."

"Do you recall which?"

"Something to do with *Quixote*, I believe."

"Cervantes?"

"No…" Mrs Elliott frowned. "The author was a Charlotte some-thing or other."

"Ah. Charlotte Lennox. I might have guessed."

"Yes, she expressed great fondness for the title, said she had read it from the circulating library but could never get it again. I thought to help the young lady look for it, but she found it before I could. I hope you do not object, sir, but Miss Darcy permitted her guest the loan of the book."

"Object? No, no, not at all! She may keep it indefinitely if it pleases her. What else happened?"

"Well, as Miss Darcy and Miss Bennet looked a bit more about the library, I spoke some with Mrs Gardiner—that would be the young lady's aunt, sir."

"Yes, I met her. Was your impression of her favourable?"

Mrs Elliott brushed her apron importantly. Few were the house-keepers who could claim that their masters asked their opinions on the guests, but I had known Mrs Elliott since I was in leading strings. There was a very good reason why I trusted the woman with the keeping of a house in Town, and it had little to do with her ability to set a fine table.

"Mrs Gardiner is a good-tempered soul, sir—quite respectable, not acting above her station. And exceeding fond of her niece."

"And her niece? Did she appear to take pleasure in her visit?"

"Oh, I should say so. Quite merry she was, and perfectly unassuming. She was very kind to Miss Darcy. And I never did see a young lady so impressed by a library!"

I felt a warmth stealing over my heart. "She liked it, did she?"

"Quite so—oh, she did nothing unbecoming; that is not what I meant."

"Of course not. I am familiar with Miss Bennet's fondness for reading." An overwhelming desire took hold of me, one I had not prepared myself for. How I wished to give her that room—to be able to please her, to offer her my pride, my own delight, and the hope of sharing something with a soul that might be kindred to my own. The notion was like a seed, burrowed into my core and blooming in an instant... then withering just as quickly when I realised she would not have it—or me.

"After the library," Mrs Elliott continued, "Miss Darcy took her guests through the gallery. Mrs Gardiner admired the busts, but Miss Bennet seemed particularly taken with the portrait of Mr George Darcy and Lady Anne."

"The one with my mother's hand on my father's shoulder? She liked that portrait? I thought I was the only one to see its merits."

"She declared they looked like goodly people, the generous sort—her very words, sir. I agreed with her and said yes, indeed, they were, the very best of people—you know how we all loved Lady Anne, sir—and that they left two fine children after their own likeness."

My brow pinched. "I am sure that much was unnecessary, though I know it was kindly meant. Miss Bennet will think I had put you up to it."

"Not so, Mr Darcy," she answered, squaring her shoulders pertly. "It is never an obligation to speak well of this house, but an honour. I'll not have any guests thinking poorly of the master and my dear mistress."

I sighed, then smiled. "I thank you for looking to our guests so diligently. Please, if Miss Bennet or her aunt should ever call again, see that they are accorded every consideration."

She curtsied gravely. "That I will do, sir."

~

HOURS LATER, Georgiana and I retired for a quiet evening before the drawing room fire. She played some at her instrument, which I am sure she meant for my pleasure, but I confess, I was more preoccupied than usual. After half an hour, she came to sit beside me. I had taken up a book, and she had a bit of needlework, and we fell to our own occupations for some while.

At last, she dropped her work with an unhappy sigh. "Fitzwilliam, have I done wrong?"

I looked up. "Wrong? How could you think that?"

"Well, you did not seem pleased that I invited Miss Elizabeth here. I suppose I ought to have asked you first, but Lady Matlock encouraged me to do so. I knew that you were not friends—"

"No, Georgiana, it is quite all right. As a matter of fact, I am delighted that you have found your friend here. This is your home, and you may have what guests you wish. Do not think you have done wrong."

"Oh, I am glad! I was ever so happy she could come today."

I closed my book and set it aside to give my sister my full attention. "Where did you encounter her?"

"At Hatchard's. I was looking for... looking for something, and like magic, there she was to help me find it. Or at least, she knew just the right person to ask, and she knew what to look for."

I smiled. "A valuable friend. What of her aunt, Mrs Gardiner?"

"Oh, she is simply lovely! They were together at Hatchard's, but I do not think Mrs Gardiner knew as much about books, because she said very little there. It was when they called today that I found her to be so delightful. Is she not a kind lady?"

"How could I know? I was barely introduced to her. But if you feel she is kind, and even Lady Matlock approves, who am I to object?"

"I am not sure..." she hesitated.

"Did Lady Matlock not meet Mrs Gardiner?"

"Yes, but I think she supposed that Mrs Gardiner was Miss Elizabeth's companion rather than her aunt."

"Hmm," I mused. "Lady Matlock said she would make inquiries after the family of your friend—though they are quite unnecessary now that I know her to be Miss Elizabeth. However, I can only assume she would have learned by now who Mrs Gardiner is."

"Do you think she will be very put out when she discovers that Mrs Gardiner is from trade?"

I sighed, frowned, then placed a comforting hand on my sister's shoulder. "Perhaps she will be, but rest assured that I am not. For the few moments I did see her, I thought her appearance and manner most pleasing. If she has Miss Elizabeth's confidence, and if you take pleasure in her company, that is enough to satisfy me."

The doubt in her expression cleared. "Oh, thank you, Fitzwilliam! I was sure you would not approve, I was so worried about it, but I did not wish to be rude to Miss Elizabeth. I did so wish to keep up our friendship!"

"I hope you shall. How did you find her?"

"I beg your pardon?"

"Was she… is she well? Did she seem… angry about anything when you saw her today?"

"Angry, why would she be?"

"I…" I fingered the weathered edges of my book in thought. "I may have given her reasons to think ill of me."

"Why, no. She said very little of you."

I frowned, unable to decide how I felt about that.

"No, we spoke mostly of other things—sisters, Town, and some books. She only mentioned you once."

"Only once? What did she say?"

"Well, she seemed to think you might have a reason to be discontented about your time in Hertfordshire. She hoped you were in good spirits, that was all. I felt it was odd, but I told her I thought you had been well. Did I do right?"

"Of course, you did well."

"Then, may I ask her to call again?" She clasped her hands eagerly under her chin.

"Again? Why yes, I assumed you had already done so. Why would you not?"

"I wished to be sure that you approved. I worried you might think…"

"Never mind what I thought. She is your friend, and if you take pleasure in one another's company, then far be it from me to interfere."

"What if I returned her call? I mean, after Mrs Younge arrives? I know I cannot go before. Unless you escorted me—what do you think, Fitzwilliam?"

I narrowed my eyes. "I think it best if we wait for Mrs Younge. And perhaps it would be best—perhaps Miss Elizabeth would be most comfortable—if I am not present when she calls."

Her face fell. "If you think that best."

"I do."

～

I HAD every honest intention of being "not at home" when Elizabeth called on Georgiana again. However, "not at home" can mean a variety of things. My butler knew that I would receive no callers, but I was very much within my own house. I was, in fact, once again closeted in my study with a blue satin ribbon clenched in my hand and a particular handkerchief locked in the top of my desk drawer.

When Hodges informed me that Georgiana's caller had arrived, I merely nodded, replied "Very good," and continued to stare out the window. I was a useless creature, wholly unable to even lift a pen while my thoughts strayed.

How I yearned to listen at the door to hear what she had to say about me! Perhaps she had nothing at all to say, and the prospect mortified me more thoroughly than her anger could possibly have done. I would sooner know… but no, had I not agreed with my own heart that would be ill-judged to encounter her again? I would leave her in peace. I would!

And thus, I was rather surprised to find myself haunting the outer hall a quarter of an hour later. All the proper sounds of farewell echoed from the drawing room, and I raised my hopeful gaze to the door. It wavered, then a footman thrust it open, and there she was— smiling, her cheeks dusky with pleasure, and those eyes—those eyes that had afflicted me for better than two months, sparkling and alive and practically close enough for me to discern the amber glow from their depths.

I did not call attention to myself, standing at the end of the hall, nor did I attempt to conceal my presence. My hope was all I reached out with, a panting longing that she would sense how desperately I sought her notice. She took two steps, then stiffened, and turned.

"Mr Darcy. I did not know you were at home. How do you do this afternoon?"

I attempted a hesitant smile and came towards her. "Very well. And you, Miss Elizabeth?"

"Quite well, as you can see, sir."

I opened my mouth to express... something... but I could only stutter inarticulately—"Did Mrs Gardiner not accompany you today?"

"No, I came alone. My aunt said she wished to remain at home to finish her preparations for Christmastide. I think—" her lashes fluttered, and she laughed softly—"that she truly felt Miss Darcy and I would prefer to do without her."

"Pray, do not feel Mrs Gardiner could be unwelcomed here. I care nothing for her connections. She is your aunt, and your good opinion of her is character enough. She shall always be well-received in this house."

She looked up with a slightly bemused expression. "I thank you for that, Mr Darcy. However, that was not what I meant. I believe she felt that the frivolities of youth were better served without too many mature ears present."

I laughed, and though I only discovered it later, I think it was the first time I had ever been anything close to easy in her presence. "Your aunt sounds like a generous woman."

"Yes, very much so. She is too modest to tell you, but she comes from Lambton, in Derbyshire. I understand that is not far from Pemberley."

"Truly? She is correct, it is only five miles away."

She smiled and braced one hand on her opposite arm as if she wished to be open and friendly, but could not bring herself quite so far. "She had much to say of your family. She said your mother was well-thought-of, and your father, too, had a good reputation as a fair and noble man."

"Does this surprise you?"

Her smile widened into that infectious laugh I remembered so well. "It does. With two such apparently sterling models to guide you, I confess to wondering if you had somehow skipped your lessons in proper deportment."

I made a show of grasping my shoulder and wincing. "Touché. Perhaps I deserved that."

"I am only teasing you, sir."

"Are you? Did you not once call me a swine?"

"Oh," her brows raised innocently, "it was more than once."

This time I could not help bursting out into a hearty laugh. "Again, I richly deserved that. Miss Elizabeth—" I sobered immediately—"I have long wished to make amends with you. My behaviour has been unpardonable. Please—"

She held up her hand. "It is not necessary, sir."

"But it is. Do you think to stop me from expressing my regret, so you may take pleasure in considering me a brute, as you have always done?"

"No. I am willing to accept the explanation you gave me before, that life has made you a bitter soul, with your first inclination to strike and wound before permitting yourself to be the prey again. While I do not understand, I can accept."

"But I would have you understand," I pleaded.

She paused, a doubtful look in her eyes. "Why? How could anything but pain result from furthering our understanding of one another?"

"I—" I hesitated, trying to collect my thoughts. "Your good opinion is bestowed only on the deserving, and therefore well worth the earning. Even should I never attain it, I would not have you alive in the world and thinking ill of me, if I could help it. I know I do not deserve your forgiveness—"

"But that is precisely what makes it forgiveness," she interrupted.

"Perhaps you are right," I confessed. "Then yes, if I may be so bold, that is what I hope."

She inclined her head. "You may have it, sir."

I blinked. "So easily as that?"

"I did not say it was easy. It is for Miss Darcy's sake… and for your own. I do not believe your heart is wicked."

"Just the rest of me?"

"I believe you could do with some improvement." She laughed again—that sweet music! What must a man do to hear more of it?

"They say that people improve upon better acquaintance," I offered in challenge.

She pressed her lips and tilted her head speculatively. "Or sometimes their faults are only more intimately revealed."

I stepped closer. "I am willing to risk it, Miss Elizabeth."

She curtsied. "Then, I look forward to seeing you again. Good afternoon, Mr Darcy."

~

SHE HAD AGREED *to see me!*

I tried not to think more of it than I had a right to, but hang it all, it was the most promising notion to light my soul in two years or better. It was some while before I was steady enough to cease trembling.

Had he seen me, Fitzwilliam would have mocked me without mercy. A man of seven and twenty, shaking like a leaf over a country maid! Yet, so I was, and unrepentantly at that.

I do not know precisely what I hoped. I cannot say if my meditations formed any rational pattern, or any straight lines could be drawn from the scattered thoughts that filled my mind. I knew only one thing—that Elizabeth Bennet claimed not to hate me. Better still, had offered to forgive me! Perhaps the anguish that had robbed me of sleep all these weeks would finally begin to dim until I could again be at peace.

I set about my work that afternoon with a feverish intensity I had not brought to my desk in many months. For the first time in a great while, I took satisfaction in the duties that made my life what it was— the order, the planning, and the care I must devote to all about me. All these things required one sentiment that I had so long been without, but now I was nearly drunk on it. *Hope.*

And so it was that I truly smiled and warmly received Lady

Catherine when she was announced later that day. "Good afternoon, Aunt Catherine," I greeted her. "I hope you are well."

"I am not," she retorted sourly, breezing into my study with casual familiarity.

I helped her to a seat and asked with all the bountiful kindness that seemed to be overflowing in my being that day, "How can I help?"

"This steward of mine," she waved a paper unhappily in my direction, "has no notion whatsoever of how to manage the coffers. Why, only today I received word that there is an outstanding debt in the village of some hundred pounds! I ask you!"

"A hundred! To whom? How could it have gotten so large?"

"That is what I should like to know," she sniffed, fluttering her handkerchief. "Stonemasons, of all people."

"Had you hired anyone?"

"No more than is customary for the autumn. The steward was to attend to matters as he always does, and then I received word of this!"

"Was there damage to the structures? Perhaps there is some good reason that the repairs were more extensive than expected."

"Only Collins's wretched fireplace. The thing smokes hideously, but it is only Collins, after all. It shall do well enough for him, so I ordered only a patch to the chimney."

I looked over the letter, then asked, "What do you wish me to do about it?"

"Why, I thought it was obvious! If you would only marry Anne, this would be yours to bother with and I would not be troubled in my old age over such a trifling matter."

"A mysterious debt of over hundred pounds is far more than trifling. I am willing to assist in any way I can, but I have been quite plain on the matter. I do not intend to marry Anne."

"Stuff and nonsense, Darcy! I shall send the earl to speak with you again. The union has been planned since you were both in your cradles. You ruined all my hopes once, but you are George Darcy's son, and surely you would not do so again."

I shook my head. "Anne has a fine dowry. Surely, she can attract any number of gentlemen. What of Fitzwilliam?"

She lowered her handkerchief and regarded me with scandalised eyes. "I will not take a soldier for my daughter! Ruffians and cads to a man! You have not had a daughter, Darcy, so perhaps you cannot know what it is to have a girl's interests weighing heavy on your head, but I do. A lamentable lot, but I bear it for my poor child."

"I am responsible for Georgiana. I quite understand, and I would not wish either my sister or my cousin to be matched to a man with whom she could not be happy. And, I assure you, I would make Anne miserable."

"What, are you a scoundrel and I did not know it? Fitzwilliam Darcy, what is this foolishness? Surely, you cannot overlook your duty as a gentleman. Anne deserves to be married!"

"And so, she does. But she does not deserve me—or rather, she deserves better."

"You have left her to wait so long that now there is no one else!"

"I beg your pardon, Aunt, but I have never consciously given my cousin any expectations. It was not I who asked her to wait."

"But you have! It has been understood all these years; it is your family duty!"

"Aunt," I sighed, "we have canvassed this often enough. I am quite immovable on it. Shall we not lay the matter to rest and put away the discord within the family? I will help you in any capacity I may, save for that one."

"You will? Do you mean to resume your visits to Rosings in the spring?"

"If I am welcome to do so."

"At last, some sense from you! How can you ever be expected to understand Anne's estate and properly take the reins one day if you do not show some interest?"

I groaned inwardly and closed my eyes for the briefest of seconds. "My interest will not be as you wish it could, but I will come. I will even bring Georgiana, if she wishes it."

"Well! It is about time you let her family see her more. I do expect to interview her companion before you choose one."

"The matter is already decided, I am afraid. The lady is to come in less than a week."

She frowned disapprovingly. "Fitzwilliam Darcy, I am most seriously displeased. Georgiana is my own sister's child, and thus far you have not shown proper deference to her mother's family. We have our rights where her upbringing is concerned."

"Indeed, you do, which is why Richard has been apprised of everything. Now, had you other matters to discuss today?"

"It would seem," she sniffed and produced a note. "Lady Matlock entrusted this to my hand when she heard I was coming to call. Something to do with the holiday, I presume. I took care to remind her that I am not a common errand boy, and I trust you shall speak to the same."

I accepted the note. "I shall discourage her from sending any more missives in such a way."

"See that you do. And I expect to be received for dinner soon. You have been returned from Hertfordshire long enough; it is time you welcomed us properly."

"Of course, Lady Catherine. I shall see to it at my earliest opportunity."

She left shortly after that, and I saw her to her carriage. All the while, she was muttering imprecations about duty and the follies of young people. I think she fancied it was all under her breath, but I heard her quite clearly.

After she had gone, I returned to my study, my steps only slightly less buoyant than before. My heart was still lighter than it had any right to be, for I had kept on my desk my copy of Johnson with that now somewhat frayed blue ribbon. The countess's note was beside it, and there I turned my attention.

DARCY,

The earl and I desire for you to join us for dinner on the Twenty-Third. In attendance shall be Lord and Lady Beauchamp and their youngest daugh-

ter, Lady Penelope Seymour, as well as Viscount Dalrymple with his wife and their daughter Maria.

Lady Catherine and Anne have other plans and will not be joining us that evening.

See that you arrive early.

I DROPPED the note with a heavy heart. I could not possibly decline, but nothing within me wished to accept the truth—and the truth was that I was Fitzwilliam Darcy of Pemberley, and my choices were not always to be my own.

MISS ELIZABETH DID NOT CALL AGAIN on Georgiana for some days. I began to fear I had offended her, or perhaps driven her off. However, on the third day, Georgiana received a note from her. She explained that Mrs Gardiner had been ill, and that she had stayed at home to attend her young cousins.

"Oh, how terrible!" exclaimed Georgiana. "But is it not good of her? I am sure her aunt values her very much."

I took the note she offered and read it myself. "I am certain she does. Miss Elizabeth is a devoted attendant. However, I am sorry that it deprives you of your friend's companionship."

"But it does not, do you not see?" she protested. "Here is proof of her affection, and that she was thinking of me even when she could not come. And this makes me cherish her friendship all the more, because I know how well she esteems those who are close to her."

"Then," said I, "you truly are wiser than myself." She giggled—still very much the child in the woman's body—and flitted off to amuse herself at her instrument. Oddly, she left Miss Elizabeth's note in my hand.

I would be a liar if I did not confess to reading it over again... and again. How very fitting was her angular, yet flowing script. Somehow, it seemed to suit that sweet wit of hers, her irreverent sort of grace... great heavens, I was a hopeless wreck! However, there was none about to witness my maudlin reverie, nor to mock me when I held the paper close to detect her fragrance. I wandered back into my study, the note clutched securely in my pocket until I could settle at my desk and read it again.

Her expressions of regret seemed sincere, and no doubt they were, but I wondered if it was *only* Georgiana she had wished to see. Then, I snorted and derided myself for such languishing indulgences. *Of course,* it was only Georgiana she favoured because she would be a fool to permit herself any regard for me. Elizabeth Bennet was no fool—that title was reserved for myself.

The following evening, I presented myself at Matlock house in full dinner regalia. I was relieved that Richard's older brother, Viscount Milton was in attendance, but Richard was conspicuously absent. No doubt, the countess had ordered him to stay away so that the full scrutiny of the ladies and their families might fall upon myself. Pity he did not disobey his mother in this instance.

"Darcy—" Dalrymple bowed slightly when I approached. "It is a pleasure to see you. I think we have not met in at least six years."

"Sir," I acknowledged him, "the pleasure is mine."

"You remember Lady Dalrymple," he gestured. "And this, of course, is our Maria. She has only just had her coming out," he added with a peculiar weight to his tone. I understood it quite well—I was to be given first choice of the young lady, before other gentlemen took notice of her.

Perhaps it was my own sister's imminent coming out, or perhaps it was something else that caused a twinge in my inner being, but I wondered what the young lady herself thought of being presented in such a way. She was handsome enough to look at, and to be fair, prettier than most. Some might even say she was prettier than—I winced. Perhaps some could think that, but not I. Never I.

Even if her eyes held any shape, even if her voice carried any expression, she lacked the quickness, the arch cleverness I could never again do without. She made a passable curtesy, pronounced my name with a demure batting of her lashes, and then stood quietly by—waiting for her fate like a mouse in a trap.

"A pleasure," I murmured as I bowed in reply. She said nothing.

Lord Beauchamp had been speaking with Lord Matlock, and I waited on my uncle's pleasure for an introduction, because I had never met the man. When Matlock performed the honours, Beauchamp acknowledged me with a brusqueness I had not expected. "Darcy," he grunted, "I remember your father. Good friends we were at Cambridge."

"I am pleased to hear it, sir."

He nodded. "You have my condolences, though I know it has been five years already."

"I thank you, all the same."

He thinned his lips with a low "Mmm. May I present my daughter, Lady Penelope?"

I bowed to Lady Penelope, and instantly found her to be entirely the opposite of Miss Dalrymple. On the surface she possessed every air of elegance, but when she opened her mouth, there was a coarseness to her I could not quite abide. It was as if she had studied her manner, learned that I had shunned all the delicate lilies of the *ton*, and had settled upon an alternate deportment for herself.

"Mr Darcy," she pronounced my name distinctly, "how do you do?" I almost felt as if she would grasp my hand and give it a good shake, but mercifully she forbore. She then proceeded to elucidate for me the various acquaintances we had in common and spoke plainly about their recent doings, their relations, their houses, and even their latest fashionable apparel.

She could not have chosen a duller topic. I appreciated her clarity and lack of reticence. Her directness might have been refreshing, had her mind been better informed, and her look softened by any sympathy—any humour that betrayed some depth of feeling. *Good heavens, was I to compare every woman on earth to Elizabeth Bennet?*

It seemed that such was my fate, for as the ladies proceeded on their fathers' arms to the table, I found myself comparing their manner of walking, their tone of voice, every aspect of their being to the one woman they could never be. Lady Matlock had taken care to apprise me thoroughly on each young lady's prospects, and I am afraid that is what they were reduced to in my mind.

Lady Penelope possessed a dowry of twenty-five thousand pounds —rather impressive, when one considered that her two elder sisters had been similarly endowed upon their marriages. Not to be outshone, Miss Dalrymple boasted a dowry of twenty thousand and a small estate in Shropshire that yielded another thousand per annum. Either, as Lady Matlock candidly observed, would easily replace the loss of Georgiana's dowry when the time came. Most importantly, a marriage to either young lady purchased the permanent loyalty of her father for Lord Matlock.

"Choose either of them," Lady Matlock had suggested, "and your uncle will gladly forget this scheme of you marrying Anne."

I think I would rather have chosen Anne in that moment, for at least with her, I knew precisely which brand of domestic disharmony would be mine the rest of my days. One thing I did know—I would be damned if I chose any of the three.

My initial impression of Lady Penelope proved well-founded. Clearly, she was a young lady who was trying very hard to attract my notice. She reminded me of Miss Bingley, the way she laughed too loudly or spoke too warmly and praised whatever I approved of whenever she had the opportunity. I decided to ask my aunt later precisely how many seasons Lady Penelope had had so far and whether the lady's other prospects were particularly horrid. I could think of no other reason for her to find myself so fascinating.

Miss Dalrymple was even less appealing. I studied her some while, trying to determine if she were merely shy or if there might be something else at work. If I had to guess, I would have declared her entire manner to be one of oppressive boredom. Perhaps she even loved another or had heard unsavoury rumours of me. She would not have been the first woman to appear intimidated in my company, but she did not *refuse* to look at me, as had Jane Bennet. She simply never *looked* at me—never warmed to anything, in fact.

Only when her mother devised some means to force the young

lady to interact with me would she exert herself, and then no more than necessary. I knew I had been mistaken before about Jane Bennet's preferences, but I was no simpleton. I could learn from my errors, and they very clearly informed me in this case. The young woman wanted nothing to do with me, and the feeling was mutual.

The dinner concluded in the usual manner, with the gentlemen remaining behind to light cigars and converse round a bottle of port. My cousin the viscount had taken a chair close to mine, and we listened in quiet amity to our seniors as they postured and held forth their various political stances. Eventually, I sensed Milton's eyes upon me.

"Something on your mind, Randall?" I murmured under my breath, intentionally omitting his title.

His expression never changed, and he even held his cigar pensively to his lips as they scarcely moved. "Only wondering what is on yours, Darcy."

I frowned and let my eyebrows lift in a non-committal response.

Milton released a puff of smoke. "I thought as much. Well, take heart. There are many other young ladies in Town for the season. I shall ask my Priscilla to look round for you."

"Your interest in my affairs is touching."

"I confess, my interests are the same as my father's. His troubles will be mine to inherit, and a bit of prudence from you could do a deal to ease my way. Particularly after that debacle of your first marriage." He shook his head and drew a slow draught of his port.

"I hope you do not think as your father does, that my actions were by any means malicious."

"I was not certain what to think. Father thought you were directly challenging his position. Richard tells me otherwise. Rumour informs me you had no choice in the matter…"

I lifted my glass and said nothing.

"Well—" he leaned back in his chair—"Mother wanted to invite Lady Sarah—you recall, daughter of Lord Dewhurst—but she had another engagement. We are sure to see her at Twelfth Night, though. Perhaps you might find her more interesting."

"I doubt it."

"Why? Do you already have someone else in mind?"

I set my teeth and would not look at him.

"Why, you do! Well, now this is absolutely priceless. Someone father would disapprove of again? I am all astonishment, Darcy! Thought you had learned your lesson."

I turned to stare hard at him. "If I have learned anything, it is that the interests of others do not always align with my own."

"Bravo, old boy. Well said." He raised his glass and tipped his cigar at me. "But do not do anything rash, Darcy. Remember, my father and I serve the interests of the country, and you…" he shrugged, "well, I suppose you serve ours."

CHAPTER 15

The following day, the household bustled with the business of putting up decorations. Georgiana had always been fond of the Christmas Eve traditions—the foods, the festive spirit, and the chance to bring something of the outdoors in. She had an eye for arranging the greenery, just as our mother had. I amused myself most of the day by watching her fill the role of a mistress, directing Mrs Elliott about where to put this or that little bit of decoration.

"Shall I hang a kissing bough here, Fitzwilliam?" she asked, standing on her toes and reaching as high as she could above the drawing room door.

"Whatever for? Do you expect me to invite some young buck to the house to show you how it works?"

She flushed crimson, even to the tips of her ears. "No! I only thought, you know, because it is so pretty, and everyone puts one up, and surely we will have other company to admire it."

"But we are hosting no parties this season," I protested.

She let her arms fall from where she had been displaying the bough and looked at the floor. "Of course. You are right. How silly of me."

"It is not as if we have a dozen callers each morning, either. I presume you will have some when Mrs Younge comes…"

She sighed. "I suppose."

"Georgiana, what troubles you? Come, sit here by me," I invited.

She hesitated, then put aside her greenery to seat herself on the opposite end of the sofa. Her entire posture was suddenly withdrawn and apprehensive, and her complexion, still red.

"Georgiana? What is it?"

"Well, it is just…" she bit her lip, fumbled with her hands, and lifted her shoulders. Still looking down, she sighed again, then all her words bubbled out in a great rush. "Why do we no longer do anything?"

"'Do anything'? Do you mean host parties? I did not suppose you were quite prepared for such an undertaking. We are invited to Matlock house for the principle festivities. Is that not sufficient?"

"But we have not celebrated properly for two or three years! I thought this year, since we were together, that…" A trembling sigh shook her, and she hastily dashed away a tear.

I stared, temporarily at a loss. She had been so cheerful just a moment before! Was she truly so fragile that a slight discontentment could shatter her good spirits? "Georgiana, I do not understand. I thought you were happy to be here at our own house this year."

She sniffed, a long and disagreeable sound, and lifted her shoulders.

I tried to keep my countenance, but I am sure I failed. If Lady Matlock did not know how to manage Georgiana when she became sullen and heartless, how was I to succeed? "Do you wish we were at Pemberley?" I ventured.

Dewy eyes rose hopefully. "I miss home. Why have I not been allowed to go back, Fitzwilliam? It has been over two years since I saw it. I never even got to meet your wife. Should I not have known my own sister-in-law?"

How to explain? I blanched—opened my mouth to speak, then closed it and stared at the opposite wall.

"Forgive me," she mumbled, and started to rise to leave me.

"Stay," I pleaded in a husky voice.

She blinked and sat back down.

"It… it was wrong of me, to keep you away," I confessed. "I knew it, and you cannot know how it grieved me."

Her brow wrinkled. "Then, why did you?"

"If I told you, you would not think well of me."

She stiffened. "Of course, I would! But tell me, Fitzwilliam, what did I do that was so wrong?"

"Wrong! You?"

"I know it must have been me. Your wife, she would not have liked caring for me, I know that must have been it. I know I was rash and difficult to manage, and no lady wants a child who—"

"Georgiana, you must cease!" I grasped her shoulder and looked deeply down into her eyes. "All this time, you blamed yourself?"

She blinked; her lips parted. "Why… what else was there?"

"Oh, Georgie," I groaned. "You are right, I did keep you from her, but it was not because I did not wish for you to come. I certainly did not care whether she liked you or not. It was to protect you from her."

Her eyes rounded, and the blood drained from her face. "P-protect me?"

"I do not wish to detail it all for you. I would rather forget, to never think of that black period of my life again. It was hell for me and would have been worse for you. At least in school, you were free."

"I was alone!" she blurted, then immediately covered her mouth. "I am sorry," she whispered.

"Speak! If this is how it has been for you, then speak. I think you have much to accuse me of."

She chewed her lip. "Why could you not at least tell me? All this time, I thought you did not want me! I tried to be cheerful, to be *better* —you know, what you wanted me to be, but I did not know how!" Tears were multiplying now, and I took out my handkerchief to soothe them away.

"Georgiana, it was never your fault. I wanted you with me, more than anything! I suppose my reasons make no sense to you—they hardly sound rational to me, now. If I had told you how wretchedly miserable I was in my marriage, you would have been scarcely less so on my behalf. Either you would have mourned day and night, or you would have taken to denouncing the faithless shrew in the hearing of others. You would have ruined yourself and made my own circumstances even harder to bear. I hoped that if you were only disappointed in *me*, you could still find happiness elsewhere... well, I see that I was wrong."

"But why marry her? I thought you chose her, that you must have loved her!"

"Far from it. I would spare you the sordid tale, if I could, but you will hear more one day or another. I would prefer that you heard it from me."

She only stared; wide eyes still moist.

"It was not of my choosing. And before you think of some compromise to the lady's honour, I would assure you that I did nothing of the kind."

"But then, what could have compelled you? Were you trying to protect her from something? I could believe that."

My mouth worked. "Her... myself... and even you." I sighed unsteadily, my resolve to tell her all crumbling just as rapidly as I had formed it. "Forgive me, Georgiana, I cannot—"

She looked away, trying to conceal her disappointment. "Richard said... he said it was not your fault."

"What was not?"

She lifted a helpless hand and grimaced. "I could not be sure. He just said 'it'. Did she lie about you, try to trap you? I have heard that such intrigues sometimes—"

"Georgiana," I interrupted, "it no longer matters. What you must know is that I thought to do right, but I only found myself going more wrong with each passing day. Then one day, I awoke and did not know my way back."

My sister squinted and regarded me with abject confusion.

"What I mean," I fumbled, "is that I am heartily ashamed of what I have become. I have been selfish—was always selfish, I am afraid—but I have also been bitter and cruel. A swine, someone once called me, and though the truth of it convicted me almost immediately, it was some while before I could confess it."

"But you are not! You are everything kind and generous."

"No…" I breathed out slowly. "If you consider me, what I have become, as 'kind,' then I have done you yet another disservice. I am afraid you must look about you a little better to discover the meaning of the word. I know few to whom it could be applied."

"Miss Elizabeth?" she asked hesitantly.

I felt a weight shift from my brow. "Yes. Think on her example, not my own."

MRS YOUNGE CAME to us on Boxing Day, a fact that gave me immeasurable relief—particularly after the uncomfortable scene that had arisen the evening before. We had been invited to Matlock House for the Christmas festivities, and the viscountess, Lady Priscilla Milton, had taken it upon herself to befriend Georgiana. That development initially pleased me.

Unfortunately, the encounter devolved into an a miserable episode for all in which Lady Milton declared that her own abigail could have arranged Georgiana's hair in such a way as to "overcome somewhat of the childishness about her face," and even, "do something about the way her eyes start out at you like a waif." I spoke my own approval of my sister's looks that evening, but Lady Matlock kept frustratingly silent, as if she meant only to observe Georgiana's ability to defend herself.

The conversation only grew more tense afterward, with Lady Catherine's opinions blending with Lady Milton's to create a toxic cordial of thinly veiled invectives and slights, all directed at some aspect of Georgiana's appearance, manners, or sheltered upbringing. Lady Matlock did stir herself to add one or two comments designed to turn the exchange, but never did she utterly quench what Georgiana must have perceived as a slurry of insults.

There had been little I could do, for never were Lady Milton's words quite so scurrilous that I could take up the challenge. Subtle and almost Machiavellian she was, her speech laced with double entèndres that Georgiana and the rest of the room well understood, but that could be easily excused at any bold-faced objection such as I was capable of making. My poor sister!

I had determined to call for the carriage early, but by that time, matters had got so far that to withdraw Georgiana then, so gracelessly, would only humiliate her as the obvious loser of the skirmish. And so, I waited for my chance to pointedly declare myself fatigued, but Lady Milton had then begun to espouse the newest fashion in sleeves. "But they would not do for you, my dear Miss Darcy, for you are much too tall and broad of shoulder for them to look quite right."

Georgiana, already flushed and self-conscious over her height, at last abandoned her efforts at good manners. Tears brimmed up in her eyes, and if she had not swatted the viscountess' picking fingers away from her arm, I would have. It was her next outburst that sent us home early on Christmas night.

"But at least I am not grown fat, with a great wattle at my throat like some others!"

I could hardly blame her. How dare Lady Milton utter a single phrase in mixed company belittling a girl's appearance? Had she no decency, no memory of her own girlhood? She was cruel, heartless, and bitterly unrepentant of her behaviour, and when tasked with this accusation—by myself—she scoffed and declared that she "was only trying to help. The girl ought to be able to withstand a bit of well-meant criticism."

How I longed for the ability to issue a verbal set-down that would close her mouth for weeks whenever I entered her company! The entire business was her fault for needlessly provoking Georgiana. But it was Georgiana's childish eruption that caused my uncle to shake his head gravely, Lady Catherine to cry out in peals of horror, and Lady Matlock to level that granite stare at me as if to say, "I warned you."

Consequently, my sister and I endured a cold, silent carriage ride home on Christmas. What was I to say? She was already weeping and refused to look at me or hear my words of chastisement.

And so, when Mrs Younge arrived the next morning, I had a squadron of maids and footmen standing by to assist her in settling, so she could immediately set about her work of shaping my young sister into a creature I could take into company. When I led in Mrs Younge to introduce her, Georgiana had been writing a note, her eyes red and sniffling occasionally, and she hastily tucked her paper away. She bore the aspect of a martyr, staring down the long road of fate.

I thought surely that a woman of Mrs Younge's lively spirits would revive the poor girl and put her in such a mood that I might, sometime later, have some success in correcting her. Mrs Younge was a fount of wisdom and instruction, which she bestowed steadily upon her charge with apparent good humour. I thought Georgiana well-suited, and left them to themselves. Progress, however, was too slow for my taste.

ON THE TWENTY-EIGHTH, we determined on an outing to the frozen Serpentine in Hyde Park. Georgiana had fond memories of our father taking her ice skating, and I was inspired to find some comfortable way of helping her become used to her new companion. It was to be only Georgiana, Mrs Younge, and myself, but when Richard heard of it, he begged leave to join us.

The park was, as expected, teeming with winter revellers. Fine ladies and gentlemen, a few children, and even smartly dressed merchants and their families had ventured out on the ice. Mrs Younge proved quite capable on ice skates, so Richard and I merely trailed close behind and permitted the ladies to take their pleasure. Mrs Younge seemed to be the only one speaking, for Georgiana herself only set her teeth and continued to place one skate ahead of the other. After a while, even Mrs Younge appeared to give up.

Richard nudged me after some minutes more and shook his head. We slowed, dropping a little away, and he said, "She is not taking to it. Perhaps anoth—" He broke off suddenly and held up a warding hand. "Darcy, look sharp!"

His warning came too late. A youthful squeal startled me from my far side, and I staggered in an ungainly attempt to avoid the inevitable. Something slammed into my leg, then I saw only ice and sky before my head and shoulders crashed into the frozen lake.

Richard's face appeared above me, and beside him was another I had never seen before. A broad-shouldered man, slightly grey about the temples, with earnest-looking brown eyes which were now wide with anxiety. I groaned, reached to assess the damage to the back of my skull, but before I could rise, a third face appeared—a face I knew as well as my own.

"Mr Darcy! Are you well, sir?" Elizabeth Bennet was crouching at my side now, tilting her head this way and that in an apparent search for blood. Her cheeks were scarlet against a pale countenance, and she looked beseechingly to both Richard and the strange fellow at my shoulder. "Will someone not help him up?" she implored.

"Straight away, madam," Richard answered, "just as soon as he appears lucid. At the moment, he looks to be all a-dither."

The bounder, I could have struck him soundly, but that would mean looking away from *her*. I swallowed and sat up. "Miss Elizabeth!"

"Sir," the strange gentleman interjected, "allow me to beg your pardon for my daughter. It is her first time on ice skates. Do permit me to help you up, sir, and pray, let me make what amends I can."

"Your daughter?" I looked about, and at last saw the child whose wild careening had knocked me from my skates. She clung to her father's arm, shrinking in either fear or embarrassment, but appeared otherwise unharmed. I stared blankly at the man as I shifted my feet under myself and pushed to a standing posture. From somewhere behind me, Richard found my hat and placed it in my hands.

"If you will allow me," Elizabeth drew close to the stranger and looked up at me, brushing a curl back into her bonnet. "Uncle, this is Mr Darcy, and his cousin Colonel Fitzwilliam. Sirs, this is my uncle, Mr Edward Gardiner."

"Elizabeth!" My sister's cry echoed from several yards away, even as I was preparing to greet the man. I never knew Georgiana could skate quite so fast as she did then, with poor Mrs Younge huffing to catch her. What followed was a flurry of introductions, stilted bows and abbreviated curtsies—for no one else wished to fall on the ice. I learned that Elizabeth and her uncle had brought three young girls to enjoy the outdoors, while Mrs Gardiner remained at home.

"Mr Darcy," Mr Gardiner said, "please accept my humblest apologies. Are you certain you are well, sir?"

"No harm done," I assured him. "It is not the child's fault, for I was distracted myself."

He smiled in relief. "Thank you, sir. I beg your pardon for interrupting your outing today. We will take our leave."

"There is no cause for that," I answered quickly. "My sister takes great pleasure in Miss Elizabeth's company. Will you not join our party, Mr Gardiner?"

I felt *her* gaze on me—there was a warmth from the side nearest her I could not describe, tingling my cheek, my ear, and pulling at my mouth until I sensed that a rather open, unsophisticated smile had grown on my face. When Mr Gardiner looked to his niece for her answer, it was my permission to do the same… and I do believe she was smiling back at *me*.

Her gold-tinted eyes swept over me from head to toe, then she tilted her head and held my gaze for long seconds. "I am not certain you would find the company of three small girls to your liking, sir. We would not wish to interrupt your pleasure, even as you claim a desire to please others."

"On the contrary, Miss Elizabeth, I find children quite enjoyable. One always knows what a child is thinking."

Her lips drew together in a restrained chuckle, and she graced me with a small dip of her head before looking back to her uncle.

"We would be most obliged, Mr Darcy," was Gardiner's reply.

And that was how I found myself ice skating beside a tradesman I had just met, with his six-year-old daughter between us and requesting to hold my hand. Mr Gardiner had attempted to deflect the child at once, but I happened to look up and see Elizabeth regarding me in some wonder. I gladly accepted the little girl's hand.

Mr Gardiner and I fell to the rear of our party. Richard gallantly occupied Mrs Younge while Georgiana and Miss Elizabeth skated just after them, with the two eldest Gardiner children trailing close behind.

I ought to have expected that Elizabeth would resemble a dancer on the ice. Her poise and strength, and that sultry magnetism I had sensed when we danced the Allemande, were as powerfully in evidence under layers of wool and frosty air as they had been in muslin and candlelight. *Angels on earth!* If I did not look away, I would fall again... or begin to drool.

However, I could look nowhere else. Possessed of easy grace and her own inimitable sense of gaiety, she infected everyone, and most of all myself. Some melodious quality to her voice raised it sweetly above the noise, and, I confess, I attended to her figure and her words with greater reverence than I did my own activities. Only when my foot encountered a rough patch of ice and my skate faltered did I collect myself sufficiently to notice my own companion.

Mr Gardiner looked curiously at me, then straight forward again.

I cleared my throat. "I hope Mrs Gardiner is recovering well from her recent illness."

"I thank you, sir. She is faring well but did not relish the thought of a day out of doors so soon. Otherwise, she is quite herself again."

"I am very glad to hear it."

We continued in silence for a few moments, neither of us perhaps knowing enough of the other to happen upon an appropriate subject. At last, Gardiner said, "My niece is quite fond of Miss Darcy. She speaks highly of her."

"Does she?" I smiled down at the ice. "My sister was hoping to call on Miss Elizabeth when circumstances were more amenable."

"Do, sir, and welcome. Mrs Gardiner has spoken warmly of her pleasure in the acquaintance, and we would be honoured to receive you. Though, sir, we would not expect any particular notice."

"I assure you, Mr Gardiner, the honour would be entirely ours."

Mr Gardiner turned to face me; his brows arched so sharply that his hat slipped further down his forehead. "Well, then, we shall await your pleasure, Mr Darcy."

I gazed back at him for a moment and realised with a shiver that Gardiner seemed to expect *me* to call with Georgiana. *Impossible!* I looked quickly away, but my eyes snagged and caught on their natural resting place—on the woman who owned my frustrated dreams, my hopeless wishes, my passionate regrets.

She whirled about on her skates at that moment, laughing and teasing the children behind her with a snowball she had just scooped up from the edge of the ice. Her arms spread gracefully; her lithe body swayed like tender music with each movement. Still laughing, she happened to glance my way.

I saw the mischievous gleam in her eye, the playfully wicked quirk to her lips as she raised her missile and appeared to take aim. So convinced was I that she meant to knock my hat off that I was almost disappointed when she spun suddenly back, and the snowball landed harmlessly behind her young cousin.

"You missed, Lizzy!" the girl cried.

She caught up to Georgiana again and looked back over her shoulder. "Did I, Marie? Perhaps I meant only to surprise you rather than to strike." Once again, those bewitching eyes tangled with mine. And then, she smiled. There could be no doubts this time—she meant to smile at *me*.

"Mr Gardiner," I managed a moment later, "would tomorrow be convenient for us to call?"

THE NEXT MORNING found Georgiana and myself bundled in my carriage and bound for Cheapside. She seemed tense and nervous, giggling occasionally without cause, but mostly she just stared out the window with her lip clamped between her teeth.

I was no less uneasy, but I dared not reveal it. I had brought the paper to occupy myself for the half-hour drive, claiming that I had much to do later that day and it would be my only opportunity to look over the articles.

"Are you certain you have time today, Fitzwilliam?" she asked at length. "I could have come with Mrs Younge…"

"I thought you preferred that I attended you myself for this first call. Besides, I should like to know more of Mr Gardiner if you mean to call frequently."

"You do not think—"

"Think what?"

"Well," her hands traced helpless circles about her lap. "I mean, we will not make them uncomfortable, you do not think?"

I lowered the paper. "How so? Do you mean to be impertinent to your hostess?"

She flushed and looked out the window. "I hope not. I was only thinking that because they live… and we… they shall not be ashamed, or made to feel… do you know?"

"I am afraid I do not. You think they will be uncomfortable with the gulf between our station and theirs?"

She nodded quickly.

"My dear sister, no one could think you above your company. Myself, I dare not vouch for, but I am sure that Mr Gardiner and I will find the means to speak on equal terms."

Georgiana offered a tight smile and then stared down to her lap. She hardly looked at me again for the rest of the ride. Slowly, the recognition dawned that it was not her own bearing she feared might be off-putting to our hosts, but mine.

THE LADIES ADJOURNED to the sitting room immediately upon our arrival, and Mr Gardiner invited me to his study for a drink of something sterner than tea. By that time, I was sorely grateful for it, because my hard-won equanimity had vanished the moment Elizabeth greeted us.

She was attired in a gown I had never seen—soft green, with a dark ribbon round her slim waist and a new amber cross dangling just at the pearly juncture of her throat and breast. It had become a peculiar fascination of mine to determine what colour her eyes were each time we met, and this day, I caught a distinct emerald sparkle within their chocolate depths. Mr Gardiner was obliged to repeat his invitation to his study, and gratefully I followed.

The study was not large, but well-lit and pleasant. Mr Gardiner apparently possessed a penchant for reading, for the shelves were full. A casual glance at the assembled titles revealed books chosen less for their capacity to impress a visitor than their facility of giving pleasure or information to the reader.

"Mr Darcy," said he as he poured, "I hope you do not object, but I have been wishing to ask something of you."

I braced myself, expecting him to request the usual favours and condescensions. Everyone did. "Of course, sir."

He fingered his glass. "How well are you acquainted with the Mr Bingley of Netherfield Park?"

I hesitated. "We have been intimate friends since Eton. I knew his father, and I should say I know him better than I do any other, save perhaps Colonel Fitzwilliam."

Gardiner nodded. "That is well. And you know no harm of the man? He would not be found in deceit or shameful dealings?"

"Never."

"And he is a gentleman, sir? I mean, of course, he is respectful in the company of ladies?"

I stiffened. "None could be more so. I would consider him the very finest of men, and I would beg to learn who has been making accusations of him."

A sly smile appeared on the man's face. "No one, so far as I know. But your ready defence of him assures me that no one will. You are quite sure that there is no dishonour in him?"

"If there is, then nothing else I know may be depended upon. You may be confident, sir, for Bingley is as true a man as was ever born. May I ask to what these questions tend?"

Gardiner chuckled and offered me a seat. He sighed, then shook his head. "I am sure you must have been acquainted with my brother Bennet during your stay in Hertfordshire."

"Naturally."

"Then you must also be familiar with his *laissez-faire* manner, particularly regarding his daughters."

I lifted a brow but made no reply. Gardiner only grunted and continued. "Bennet is sharp, none can deny it, but whether he can be troubled to act is another question."

I sipped my drink pensively. "You believe he would fail to protect his own daughters? I cannot think of a more reprehensible practice than the neglect of one's family."

"Oh, do not underestimate the man. He is exceedingly fond of his girls—well, the eldest girls, at least, and has a passing tolerance for the younger three. Moreover, he has means and arts you cannot imagine unless you know him better. However, I fear that his external manner is not sufficiently off-putting to someone who might wish to take advantage of an innocent girl like our Jane."

"You need have no fear on that head. Miss Bennet is, from all that I can see, most ably defended by her sisters, her neighbours, and by Bingley himself." I frowned and cast my eyes to my glass.

"I am very glad to hear it, Mr Darcy. Elizabeth had already given her assurances, but I do appreciate your candour. It is more relief than you can know."

"Then I am happy to oblige." And I was—truly. It was some measure of justification, to speak praise of my estranged friend in the hearing of another. I could have said more, much more, but not without plundering that well of vulnerability I had so diligently kept buried. I stirred faintly in my seat, then hazarded a different subject. "May I ask, sir, what is your business?"

He smiled broadly, the open, genial smile of one who could take pride in his life's work. "Oh, textiles mostly. I dabble in rice and spices and some other commodities—tobacco not infrequently, and books whenever I can get them—but that is the extent of it."

"No tea?"

"Well," he laughed, "that particular sword cuts both ways. My father contracted for the East India Company when he started the business. Our ships have carried their share of tea, but I expanded other trade streams and gave up the contract a few years ago. No more tea for us, as the Company does not look well on competition."

"I expect not."

Gardiner nodded and drew a sip from his glass. "Have you an interest in trade, sir?"

"A man would be a fool not to. My family also had a stake in the Company, but I sold out over a year ago."

"May I ask why? From a purely business standpoint, of course, sir. You are the first I have heard in a long while who wished to dissolve relations. Do you expect some great loss in the market?"

"My reasons were more personal. I lost my taste for it, you could say. At present, I am most heavily invested in industry—some of it to do with textiles, in fact."

"Indeed! How so?" Gardiner leaned forward, and I could see that I had stumbled upon his pet topic.

"Perhaps it is not specific to your textiles, but rather the larger infrastructure. Iron, coal, and last year I became interested in steam engines."

"Fascinating, is it not? And a sure success, if a man can weather a bit of difficulty from time to time. So I have advised others, but too often they have no patience, running out to seek something with a more ready return."

"Nevertheless, I believe the futures are optimistic."

Gardiner lifted his glass and I touched it to my own. "I could not agree more."

We remained in the study some while longer, and I became quite easy with this respectable, well-informed tradesman. In fact, he impressed me greatly with his acumen as we discussed matters of politics and the economy in a way I had not done in years. His experience and character were rare, for seldom did a man possess both knowledge and honour in his position. I was almost sorry when the quarter hour came to a close and he suggested that we seek out the ladies. Nevertheless, my body trembled in eagerness to return to *her* company, even if it should only be for a moment.

We found them in the sunlit parlour, all leaning over a little table, and quite oblivious of our presence. Mrs Gardiner was displaying some needlework recently done by her middle child, the one named Marie. Georgiana paid all the proper compliments, sighing over how prettily stitched a particular little flower was, but Mrs Gardiner was quick to deflect the praise. "It was not I who taught her, it was Lizzy."

Elizabeth looked on her protégé's accomplishments with a glowing, maternal sort of pride. "Oh, do not think I deserve the credit. She is a ready pupil."

Mrs Gardiner raised a sceptical smile to Georgiana. "Do not listen to a thing she says, Miss Darcy. I have tried to teach Marie this same stitch for two years, with little success. It was because she is so fond of Lizzy that she was willing to sit and listen."

Elizabeth laughed, and I felt a euphoric warmth steal through my core. I could listen to that melody every day and still crave more of it. The way her profile bent to the soft glow of the fabric, the shafts of light dancing in her hair and silhouetting her figure... I do not know if I sighed audibly, but I felt it in my soul. She was tipping her head affectionately towards Georgiana, her fingers tracing out a bit of the work that she especially admired, then her eyes flipped to us, standing at the door. At her obvious recognition, all three ladies straightened.

Georgiana nearly danced to me, beaming with sheer contentment. "Have you finished your visit, Brother?"

"I think we could have spoken much longer, but I fear overstaying my welcome."

"Impossible, Mr Darcy," Gardiner rejoined. "The pleasure was entirely mine, I assure you. We shall always be delighted to receive your company."

I thanked him, then turned to Georgiana with a reluctant air of finality. I dared not look at Elizabeth, for I felt certain I would falter, say something to humiliate myself, or even give the perceptive one a window into my feelings that I could not afford for her to see.

My sister looked to her hostess. "I suppose we must go. Thank you for everything, Mrs Gardiner."

"Did you wish to take the sketch with you today?" the lady offered kindly.

At a gasp from Georgiana, Mrs Gardiner explained. "I beg your pardon, Mr Darcy, but would you mind very much waiting a moment before you go?"

I made an agreeable answer and chanced a glimpse at Elizabeth. She was just shifting her gaze from me, as if afraid to meet my eyes, but her expression told plainly of her approval.

"Oh!" Georgiana pressed Mrs Gardiner's hand. "I would be ever so grateful, Mrs Gardiner."

"Then you may come with me, and perhaps you will help me find it sooner. Oh, forgive me, Mr Darcy, we have not told you the great mystery!"

Georgiana turned to me, a sheen making her eyes glimmer. "Mrs Gardiner knew our mother."

I regarded the lady in surprise. "Indeed!"

"Oh, not well, sir. My mother was an accomplished seamstress, and occasionally Mrs Darcy would bring her work—you know, when she could not go to Town. Mrs Darcy was always kind to our family, usually bringing some little treat for us when we were children."

Before I could express my pleasure in such warm praise for my mother, Georgiana was speaking again, nearly breathless, so quickly did the words tumble from her. "When Mrs Gardiner was a girl, she was practicing her drawing, and she thought to draw the prettiest lady she knew. And who do you think it was? She drew Mother, and she still has a little sketch she offered to give me."

"Mrs Gardiner," I replied, my voice strangely husky, "that is very kind."

"Oh!" Mrs Gardiner laughed, "You will not think so when you see the portrait, but it is yours all the same. I warrant it does not do credit to the subject. But come, Miss Darcy, let us not keep your brother waiting."

"By all means, take what time you wish," I offered. "We are quite at our leisure, and very much obliged by your thoughtfulness, Mrs Gardiner."

They went off together, but Elizabeth lingered hesitantly. She looked as if she would follow her aunt, but then she caught my eye, and apparently decided to remain. Mr Gardiner cast a peculiar glance our way, then cleared his throat and sought out a seat for himself on the opposite side of the room from where we stood. Elizabeth smiled nervously and gestured to a pair of chairs near the window. I was all too ready to assist her and then take a seat for myself.

She folded her hands in her lap and was looking steadily down at them for a moment. I cast about, searching for something I might say to raise her interest. "Miss Elizabeth, I—"

"Mr Darcy—" She caught her breath as our words seemed to collide in mid-air.

I tensed, but then she pursed her lips and an amused chuckle bubbled forth. "My apologies, sir."

"Not at all, Miss Elizabeth. Pray, speak what you wished."

"I only meant to... to thank you, I suppose, for your kindness to my aunt and uncle."

"Thank me! It is I who am in their debt—and yours. I cannot begin to express my gratitude for what you have done for my sister."

"What I have done? I have done nothing but form a friendship which gives me as much pleasure as it can possibly give her. She is a charming young lady."

I shook my head wryly. "Our family does not always agree with you."

"How so? If you do not mind, sir."

My brow pinched as I tried to form the words. "I think, perhaps, I shall defer to your expertise in describing her. You seem to understand her better than I do, so perhaps you can imagine how she conducts herself among those who offer criticism, both kindly meant and otherwise."

She blinked and sighed in understanding. "Oh. I wish there were something I could do to help."

"Perhaps there is. She has already improved greatly due to your influence. She needs guidance, some model of comportment, and I... well, perhaps I am the last person to whom she ought to turn for such advice."

She seemed to choke and covered her mouth as a snort of laughter echoed from behind her hand.

"Yes, yes, mock me if you will! I deserve no less," I retorted, but I could not feel affronted. Rather, I believe I was grinning like a simpleton, eager to laugh at my own faults if only she would treat me generously.

"I was not mocking you, sir. I find your self-deprecation amusing, that is all. Please, go on."

"I beg your pardon?" I was lost already, drowning in a sea of sparkling amber. How did she wield such power over my thoughts? If only she would keep looking at me that way...

She lifted her brows. "Georgiana?"

"Ah." I straightened self-consciously. "Yes, Georgiana. You have met Mrs Younge. I believe her to be well-qualified and agreeable, but she and Georgiana have been slow to form any sort of rapport. However, I have noticed that after your calls, or even after receiving a note from you, Georgiana's spirits are better, and she is more cheerful in Mrs Younge's company."

"You are asking me to call more frequently?"

I shifted. "I will take care to remain discreet, if my presence troubles you. But yes, if you can spare the time, I would beg your interest."

"My interest she has already, but am I quite fashionable enough society for Miss Georgiana Darcy? I doubt she would profit by it."

I held her gaze, and the right side of my mouth turned up. "I think anyone who would dare to slight your company a fool of the first order. As for Georgiana, there is none whose friendship I value more for her."

Her lips parted as she stared back at me. "Then... I would be honoured to spend as much time with her as I am able."

"My gratitude is more profound than you can know." I glanced at Mr Gardiner, happily engaged with a book at the other end of the room, and lowered my voice. "Miss Elizabeth, there is one more thing, if I may."

She tipped her head towards mine, and a bit of impishness tugged at her mouth. "A secret, Mr Darcy? I am all amazement."

"You know, perhaps better than almost anyone, the manner of my departure from Hertfordshire."

She blinked and nodded subtly.

"I—" another glance at Mr Gardiner—"I wish there were some way to make amends. With Bingley, with your family, with everyone. The thing is beyond me, and deservedly so, but there is one thing I would ask."

Her brows peaked, but she said nothing. I drew a shaken sigh and continued.

"I would know—I hope, at least—that Miss Bennet did not suffer any sort of... discomfort... due to my actions on the evening of the ball."

"I..." she released a soft breath, her eyes straying to her uncle for a scant instant before they returned. "I believe not. Her friendship with Miss Bingley has become strained, though it never was promising, and our mother was... somewhat put out, but it is nothing of consequence."

"Your mother was put out with Miss Bennet, or with me?"

"Neither." A wince crossed her lovely brow. "With me, if you would know. I am far too impertinent, as you are already aware."

I straightened and regarded her narrowly. "She believes you were the reason I left Hertfordshire? She blames *you* for—good lord. Miss Elizabeth, if you do not grow tired of my apologies, then I must offer one more."

She lifted her shoulders and shook her head, smiling dismissively. "It is for the best. Jane is strong enough now, and Mr Bingley is so kind to her. She no longer needs me."

"Why would she have needed you before? And please, before you answer, know that I have relinquished any interest I supposed myself to have felt for her. You were entirely right—my motives were selfish and driven by my own petty cares, the demons I thought to flee. I would have done her evil, and I am grateful that matters have come about as they have. But I never could understand. Why does everyone seem to feel she needs special protection?"

Her eyes widened. "You did not know?"

"No," I shook my head. "Should I have?"

She leaned closer. "Jane is deaf in her left ear."

Deaf! I blinked a moment, recalling every incident when she appeared to be ignoring me, when she stumbled at my long and pompous questions. How Bingley always sat or walked at her right when my own instincts were the opposite; the hesitant replies, the uncomfortable detachment.... "I have wronged her, indeed!" I breathed. "How did it come about?"

"She had a terrible fever when she was a babe, just before I was born. I suspect she does not hear well out of her right ear, either, but she does not know. She does not recall what it is to hear clearly. Consequently, she is terribly shy in company. It makes her very nervous when she does not know what is said, so much so that she stumbles and cannot make sense of the conversation. It overwhelms her, causes her to speak strangely at times, even to offend people. Some even swear she is touched in the head. You must think her dull or slow, but she is not! In fact, if you knew her—"

"You need not explain. I can well imagine."

She seemed to settle. "Thank you for understanding."

"Again, you offer thanks I do not deserve! Who should understand but I, who have been so unfeeling that I gave offence at nearly every turn? At least Miss Bennet never did it wilfully."

She tilted her head. "And you did?"

"With astonishing regularity, I am afraid."

A brilliant smile flashed. "But as we have established before, Mr Darcy, you were the unhappy victim of circumstances."

"And I, a grown man who has lived and moved in the world, was incapable of governing myself? No, it does not suffice. I knew what I was about and obstinately persisted in my arrogant delusions."

She arched a brow and pursed those velvet lips, as if she were a governess expressing pleasure at her pupil's discovery. "But as you have said, no man acts independently of his circumstances."

It was a test; one I would cut off my own arm to pass. I studied her pert look for a moment, the smile she attempted to smother, and then, cautiously, smiled back at her. "Do not try to acquit me, Miss Elizabeth. It is a fruitless endeavour."

"In fact, I have judged and found you guilty—if, indeed, the same man sits before me as I have known previously. On that point, I am yet uncertain. The man I knew in Hertfordshire was surly—contemptible, even—almost as if he *wished* to make everyone dislike him. He appeared to expect at any moment to be grievously wronged by some enemy… but I no longer see that man."

"That 'enemy' of which you speak is nothing more pernicious than an unfortunate past, and frightful memories which I ought to have laid to rest long ago. I am still far from successful in that regard."

"Such memories can be insidious, sir, and from what I know of the matter, the blame was not your own." She pouted faintly, and a fine line appeared between her brows as her eyes wandered over my face. "I pray you find peace. You must learn something of my philosophy; to think on the past only as it gives you pleasure."

I laughed quietly. "Then I shall have precious little to look back on."

A noise from the outer hall called our attention, and soon we could hear Georgiana and Mrs Gardiner returning. Elizabeth glanced in that direction, then smiled back at me before she rose. "Perhaps you must begin to make some new memories, Mr Darcy."

I followed her to the door, my heart thrumming at a breakneck pace. Was it possible that Elizabeth Bennet and I had just shared a few moments of conversation without once provoking each other to anger? And not just idle talk had we exchanged—no, it was soul-nourishing manna, the sort of intimate accord that I had shared with only a handful of persons in my lifetime.

Georgiana and the Gardiners were bidding their farewells at the door, and I turned round to find Elizabeth still close at my side. She looked up to me, then her eyes shifted, and a startled expression overcame her features. She began to step away, but too late.

"Elizabeth, you and Fitzwilliam are under the kissing bough!" Georgiana cried in delight.

"Oh, no," Elizabeth protested, "I am not, I—"

"It is bad luck to refuse, Lizzy," Mrs Gardiner added with a teasing laugh of her own.

She had gone quite pale, even to the lips, and she was staring at me now.

"I would never impose," I offered, beginning to step away.

"Fitzwilliam!" objected Georgiana. "You will ruin all the fun of it!"

Elizabeth drew a bracing breath, closed her eyes and nodded, as if she were waiting for me to cut off all her hair or pierce her with a surgeon's lance. "Bad luck is bad luck, Mr Darcy," she muttered between clenched teeth. "I would not wish such a thing."

"Nor I." I stepped close, but not close enough to touch her, and brushed a quick, imprecise caress to her cheek before jerking away again.

"There, Lizzy, that was not so bad," soothed Mrs Gardiner.

Mr Gardiner was shaking his head and chuckling. "Do forgive us, Mr Darcy. The ladies will have their sport during the festive season."

I spared him some vague assurance that I found the entire scene amusing, all in good fun, or something of the sort, but I could only stare at *her*. And my lips could still taste her sweetness.

She began to lift her hand to her cheek but pulled it down at once. Her complexion was flaming, her eyes great and dark with embarrassment, but her feelings… her feelings, I could not read. She stole one last shy glance at me before I left the house, and I think, but I was not certain… I think she may have been smiling.

CHAPTER 16

*E*lizabeth called on Georgiana the very next day, but I was out when she came. Just as I was out on the second day, and again on the third when I knew she would return. I had business, a great deal of business, and I also owed it to this public image Richard insisted that I must cultivate to make an occasional appearance at my club. Moreover, I had yet to find just the right gift for Georgiana for Epiphany, and...

I was avoiding her. I knew it, and damned myself for it, and for what she must think of me. A coward, likely, or worse; a rogue who would engage her in intimate conversation, displaying a familiarity readily apparent to her family—for our words had been low, our heads tipped close almost as lovers exchanging clandestine endearments. A disloyal rascal who would claim the privilege of kissing her cheek, only to disappear from her society. Ah, yes, a harmless flirtation, the kissing bough was claimed to be—nothing improper in it, to be sure, but had Elizabeth been any other woman, she would have expected me to call on her afterward.

What *did* she expect of me? This question left me wrung with sweat and twisted in my sheets, night after night. Occasionally, a ravishing sort of delirium would persuade me that if I should dress myself that very moment and make my appearance at her door, she would welcome me, absolve me of all my wrongs, and even permit me another kiss, and another... But how could she forgive an unworthy knave, generous as she was? And how could I ask it of her?

And so, I kept away, but each day when I returned to the house, it was as if my senses were trained like a bloodhound to detect the shadows of her presence. It was not merely that hint of lavender when I would sit in the chair she had earlier occupied, but something richer, lighter—a joy hovering in the air of my home. Her touch could be felt by more than myself, for even the maids who had brought her tea seemed—to me, at least—to be on the verge of laughter. That is, until they would see me and instantly sober.

The most tangible evidence that my enchantress had wrought her magic was in Georgiana herself. After only a few days, she was somehow steadier. Some silken threads now seemed woven between her and Mrs Younge, a kinship beginning to flourish where formerly a brick wall had dwelt. And I, for good or ill, persuaded myself that had I been present, this feminine camaraderie would never have been possible. Georgiana would have been more anxious to please, if she knew herself to be under my watchful eye, and Elizabeth would have... *would have what?*

I felt as if I understood her now even less than I had before. No rational being could swing from vile loathing and disgust to benevolent accord without somehow wiping out the memory of past wrongs. "Think on the past only as it gives you pleasure," she had said... was it possible that she truly was capable of it? It was a question I could not answer and did not dare ask.

"Well, Darcy, what do you think of all this?"

I roused myself from the letter I was writing as Richard escorted himself into my study—unannounced, as he usually did.

"What do I think of what?" I asked

"Have you not heard? Oh, I suppose not, if you did not go out this morning and have not yet read your paper. Why, the bonds bill, of course! Father is red as a cabbage over the affair."

"I am afraid you must be more specific. Which bonds bill?"

"Why, the East India bonds bill. Have you really heard nothing of it?"

"Very little. I thought that was rejected five years ago."

"No, indeed, it is to be read a second time. Wallingford put it forward this time, and he has a fair bit of support. Father is hot, I can tell you. A 'bloody waste' he calls it, 'throwing good money after bad'. Their monopoly cannot last much longer, with all the merchants crying for their share of trade, and what will Parliament have purchased us? A great anchor, that is what."

I tilted back in my chair and fingered the quill thoughtfully. "Quite a coincidence, this, because I just had a rather fascinating conversation a few days ago with Mr Gardiner on this very subject."

"Mr Gardiner..." Richard made a show of forgetfulness. "Oh, yes, I recall. The uncle of your fair damsel, is he not?"

I scowled and rose from my desk. "She is not *my* fair damsel."

"Whatever she is, she has your attention."

I wandered to the window, putting my back to him. "She is Georgiana's friend, and a lady worthy of respect."

Richard was silent for an uncomfortably long while, and at last I turned round to see what he was musing on. He touched a finger to his lips. "You know I would never torment you needlessly, but are you certain your judgment regarding her is clear? You are not trying to redeem something better left to rot, are you?"

"You think her name and appearance influenced my opinion of her? They certainly did, but not for the good. Rather, I thought her the very devil when we first met. I avoided her like a disease, as if she were the incarnation of... well, I was proved wrong, time and again. I shudder to recall my treatment of her, but she bested me even so, and in such a manner! I have come to believe meeting her was something of a gift, rather than a torment."

"A gift! How so?"

"If you possessed a blackened stain upon your past, you would do all within your power to curse it into nothingness, would you not?"

"No, for I am not the sort to brood and stew over his troubles. I prefer a bottle or a woman. But, go on."

"It does not serve, either your method or my own."

Richard fell into a chair, kicked his boots out and regarded me with a lazy grin. "So, what does work? Speak, oh, great sage, for I would lap at the fount of your wisdom."

I lowered myself to the seat opposite and propped my elbow on the side as I thought. "I believe," I answered slowly, "that poison requires an antidote, rather than more poison. Enmity and loathing can never be neutralised by hatred and vitriol, but by..." I furrowed my brow and searched for the proper word.

"An angel?" Richard supplied.

An angel... I allowed a slow smile. *Just so.*

"Well," Richard grunted, "Mother will be quite disappointed that all her matchmaking is bound to come to nothing. And Father! I think I will request a transfer to Spain before you tell him."

"I do not have an understanding with Miss Bennet, nor am I likely to. She is Georgiana's friend; a friend I heartily approve of."

He snorted. "Do not attempt that with me, Darcy! I have never seen you fall all over yourself as you do whenever she is about. You say the resemblance to the past no longer troubles you, so what holds you back? Connections, for I imagine she has none? Money? I warrant she is poor as a church mouse. Or is it something deeper? She has got to you, seen through something, has she not? Are you afraid of her?"

"What man in his senses is not afraid of a perceptive woman?"

"Hah! There it is. You and Father will have something in common after all—both wed to terrifying creatures."

I shook my head and pushed out of my seat. "Terrifying? Perhaps, but she is thrilling, rather than horrible. In fact, it has been some while now that I have considered her the most magnificent woman of my acquaintance. But Miss Elizabeth would never have me."

"What?" he followed me as I paced to the window. "Not have Fitzwilliam Darcy and all of Pemberley?"

I sighed and crossed my arms. "If she were the sort of woman to accept only my name and station, I would not have *her*. But Elizabeth... she is not such a woman. She has seen me for the wretched being I am, and I would not wish that on any woman—least of all her."

Richard whistled low and turned away. "Well, Darcy, you do have a dilemma. Best of luck with it, and all that. Meanwhile, are my dear cousins in want of a first-footer at midnight to wish you all luck for the new year? I should be happy to oblige, and even wear the proper boots, though I am not quite tall or dark enough to suit."

I permitted an amused smile and shake of my head. "We would count your appearance a blessing on the house."

"Then I must hie me home to make ready. Oh! I nearly forgot." He fumbled in the pocket of his coat and withdrew a folded note. "Mother has sent over her instructions for you regarding Twelfth Night. I trust you will make a smashing Julius Caesar."

I closed my eyes and tried not to groan. "I presume there is also a Cleopatra."

"Naturally. Lady Sarah, daughter of Lord Dewhurst."

EIGHTEEN HUNDRED AND Twelve dawned with a grey sky and a steady downpour. It was a day exactly suited for a warm fire and a brandy; a perfectly comfortable sort of day for a reclusive soul to retire into the deepest chair in the library with a familiar book to while away the hours.

Samuel Johnson was my companion, that silken bookmark now tired and ragged. I daydreamed quite as much as I read, my mind wandering from Hertfordshire to Pemberley and yet, not settling on either but spiralling upward; from there into my own sort of heaven. Somewhere far away from the toils and demands of London, somewhere I could turn to my bed at the end of each day tired rather than weary—satisfied in doing some good in the world, and... God help me, every image, every hope, involved *her* at my side. My fine-eyed minx, the sovereign possessor of my heart and the one to whom I would gladly ascribe any virtue to be found in me.

Sentimental fool that I was, I had taken to carrying her handkerchief in my pocket where I could stroke it now and again with no one the wiser. I drew it out now, tracing the simple, elegant lines of her initials. Lifting it to my lips, inhaling the last traces of her scent, I blinked away a sort of burning sensation from my eyes as that familiar hollow ache started to choke me again.

I knew the truth—had known it all along, though my obstinate mind had railed against it at every turn. I would never be content, never know fulfilment in life and deed, unless I confessed to myself what I wanted above all else. My goddess, my queen, my siren; the only one who could chastise me and make me love her all the more, whose gentle levity could inspire deep, restorative contemplation and whose gravity could illuminate my darkest cares.

Perhaps I had been wrong to avoid her. How many times had I erred in judging her? And yet, I persisted in assuming her thoughts would be like my own. What had I to lose in asking…?

My thumb had wandered from her initials and found a peculiar knot in the corner of the cloth that I had somehow missed before. I held it closer to my candle to inspect it. A memory knot, some thought she must have wished to preserve, worked in white thread. Why it made me ponder so, I could not say, but it held me transfixed. What would be so elusive to her sharp mind that she must provide herself some memento, to keep from forgetting?

I turned the cloth over several times, examining it from both sides and speculating the most preposterous notions. Then, I startled back when the flame from my candle leapt high, coming near my fingers and threatening to consume my precious keepsake.

Damnation!

I blew and tamped, then looked on in horror at the opposite corner of the cloth. Scorched and ruined, the edging lace was withered and blackened by the flame. I could not explain why, but my eyes stung—I wept over it. I, a grown man who could order a hundred more at a moment's notice, bowed my head and sobbed over a strip of white linen. Over my own foolishness. It seemed the closer I held something, the greater its peril. And I wondered, for I could not help but do so, what sort of omen this was for the year to come.

WE CALLED at the house on Gracechurch Street on the third, thinking perhaps the family would prefer a day of rest after the New Year's festivities. I went with the handkerchief in my pocket, hopeful that I might find an opportunity to return it to its proper owner and then speak something of my wish for... for more.

Mr Gardiner had gone to his warehouse that day. Though his presence would have called me away from the ladies, I was surprised at my own disappointment—most particularly when I found Elizabeth in a more sombre mood than I had ever seen. The spark seemed drained from her smile, her repartees sluggish, and her voice unnaturally subdued this day. She greeted me upon my arrival, but then seemed never to look my direction.

It was Mrs Gardiner and Mrs Younge who furnished most of the conversation, and though I was disappointed, I was pleased with the performance of my sister's companion. It was all Elizabeth, all her goodness and cheer that had made this possible. At each smile or carefully moderated response Mrs Younge managed to provoke from Georgiana, I would try to catch Elizabeth's eye to inform her of my gratitude. She never seemed to notice.

Perhaps she had the headache, though I had never seen her indisposed before. However, with the winter so grey and cold, and her aunt's recent ailment, it was possible that even my vibrant lady might suffer the maladies of the season. And so, I asked her as we made ready to take our leave.

"Miss Elizabeth, I hope you are not unwell."

She looked as if she had been trying to avoid meeting my eye and I had called her out. "Unwell?"

"Yes, you did not seem quite yourself today. I hope there is nothing the matter."

She shook her head and her eyes dropped. "No, it is nothing of importance. I thank you for calling today."

"You are certain?"

"Nothing is wrong," she repeated firmly.

Chastised, I took a step back and withdrew the hand which had been hovering near my pocket. This was not the day. "I hope you are not distressed over returning to Hertfordshire soon. I believe you said you would be going back just after Twelfth Night?"

She blinked and hesitated a moment. "I may stay on another few weeks. Perhaps longer… I very much enjoy the company of my young cousins, and my aunt has been gracious enough to ask…" She stopped and a soft breath escaped her as she raised her eyes to me at last.

At that look, I knew the truth. Bingley had not yet offered for Miss Bennet, though I could not think why, and her mother was growing anxious. Having Elizabeth back at Longbourn before all was settled was a complication Mrs Bennet would not tolerate. After her most beautiful daughter, as she loudly declared her eldest, had already lost one eligible suitor in myself, the lady did not mean to lose another.

"I understand," I answered. "Indeed, I am grateful to hear it, Miss Elizabeth."

Her eyebrows raised slightly.

I offered an encouraging smile. "Georgiana and I would be sorry to see you leave London."

She blinked, her lips parting softly. "Thank you for that, Mr Darcy."

I nodded. "Good day, Miss Elizabeth."

~

I DID NOT SEE her again for some days, though I know she called on Georgiana at least once while I was out with Richard. I stopped one day to ask after Mr Gardiner, but we learned that all the family were out. This time, it almost felt as if it were she avoiding my company rather than the reverse. I puzzled over this, but short of sending the woman a highly improper note or waiting at her door to declare myself, there was little I could do but to remain patient.

On the morning of Epiphany, I awoke and breathed deeply in relief. She would not be leaving London this day, and I still had time. Half an hour later, I was in the breakfast room, meticulously stirring my tea and turning over certain phrases under my breath.

"*You must allow me to tell you…*" No, too cold, too formal, and a trifle too insistent.

"*How ardently…*" Yes, that was much better. But, steady, not too fast.

"*Though the relative positions of our families…*" Surely, she would appreciate the honour I paid her. Only she could have brought me to such humility! But how to say it?

"*I beg you to relieve my suffering…*" Yes, she of great sympathy—such a plea might stir her heart.

I rehearsed it all again, muttering the words and shaking my head. *Dash it all!* I sighed and discarded the whole bombastic speech.

For the first time in far too long, I knew with absolute clarity how I felt, but the practice of putting it into words—gentle words to incline her ear rather than put her off—still eluded me. How was it a man confessed his feelings for such a woman, declared his intentions discreetly so that she might understand in a room of others, and bless his wish to speak more plainly?

"Good morning, Brother," Georgiana sang out, prancing up behind me and putting her hands on my shoulders to kiss my cheek. She had not done that since she was a girl.

I started, lowering my cup and rising to my feet to greet her. "Good morning, Georgiana. I say, what is that in your hand?"

"This, dear Brother, is your surprise. Oh, I cannot wait until you see it! I looked, and I looked, and I could not find anything you did not already own, or that would not be silly or dull." She dropped into the chair beside mine, nearly bouncing with excitement.

"I thought you were going to get me a silver chain for my pocket watch."

"You have a dozen already, and anyway, when I did go into the jeweller's with Lady Matlock, there was this terribly foolish fellow there dawdling about, trying to decide which pair of gold cuff-links to get. He was taking so dreadfully long that we gave up."

"So, what is this you have in your hand?"

"Oh, this?" She patted it with an impish smile. "You will just have to wait and see."

"In that case, I feel as if my gift to you shall be rapidly overshadowed. I propose that you open your gift first. Close your eyes."

"Whatever for?"

"It was a gift I could not wrap, so there must still be some degree of surprise."

She sighed, giggled, and clasped her hands in her lap with her closed eyes turned up like a painted cherub. I drew out the pencil sketch from my pocket, then tucked it into her hands.

She opened her eyes. "I do not understand. It looks like a chaise. Did you draw it?"

I scoffed. "How polite you are! No, this was drawn to order, by the man who is presently building it."

She studied it another moment, then her eyes widened. "Oh! Fitzwilliam! You are giving me my own chaise?"

"In a manner of speaking. I thought you would enjoy it in the parks this summer."

Her expression of pleasure faded slightly. "In London."

"Naturally, for it would not be suitable for long travel. It should be finished by early spring, but I thought you would like to choose the paint colour. Perhaps we could look in next week?"

Her lips tightened into a renewal of her smile. "Of course. Well, now I am disappointed, for this is ever so much grander than what I got you."

"A chaise might be large, but I have faith that whatever you have was chosen with greater care. May I see it?"

She held her breath and put the box in my lap. A book, judging by its weight and shape. My sister knew me well.

"I looked, and I even wrote to Mrs Reynolds at Pemberley to be sure," she explained, nervously wringing her hands. "You do not have one like it, and I am assured that there was not another to be had anywhere in London."

"Now you have me truly intrigued." I untied the ribbon and raised the box lid. It appeared at first a rather commonplace book of poetry. Leather bound, plain lettering on the cover. Thomas Campbell... I lifted it to examine the spine.

"*The Pleasures of Hope*? Do you know, I have never read it. I recall that Father had a few lines from this written down, but I believe that the copy must have been lent him."

She stood and leaned over me to turn the pages. "It is illustrated, see—a first edition, and this one must have been a gift, do you see? There is an inscription."

I turned to the title page, and, indeed, there was a note from the author himself to some unnamed person. "However did you come by this? There were only a few with such illustrations printed, and I have never seen one for sale."

She drew back, her countenance smug. "It was not for sale."

"Not for sale? But I thought you purchased it from Hatchard's."

"No... I encountered Elizabeth at Hatchard's and told her my trouble. She knew just the right thing, and where to procure it."

I leaned back. "Well?"

"It was her own."

"What—do you mean that you took a book from your friend, one of her personal possessions for my gift?"

"Oh, no," she protested, "it was not precisely hers. She said it belonged to her father, and he likes the newer edition better. He never read it and was quite happy to part with it."

"For a price, I hope. This is all very irregular. You would not take a man's private property?"

"Of course not. I traded, or rather Miss Elizabeth brokered the trade. Her father had been coveting a copy of Byron, and I had that dreadful *English Bards* that Richard gave me. Miss Elizabeth assures me he is perfectly delighted with it, and if his letters to her are to be believed, he reads it constantly. There, do you think it was fair? There is nothing inappropriate in it, I hope?"

"No, I am simply astonished at all your manoeuvring—did Lady Matlock know of this? How did you get it here?"

"Not... all of it." She bit her lip and offered a guilty smile. "Not the bit about where the book came from. Elizabeth had to write to her father to see if it was agreeable with him. That was why she came the first day she called here, to tell me that it was. I do not think she would have come otherwise, though I did say she was welcome, and Lady Matlock approved. I thought it so strange. Why should she not have felt welcome?"

I brushed my hand over the soft glow of the leather binding. "She ought always to feel welcome here. If she does not, the fault is not hers."

She looked quizzically at me, but immediately turned her attention to the book again. "Oh, Fitzwilliam, do you like it?"

"Like it... It is the sort of thing I never knew I wanted until I saw it, and then longed for it more than anything else you could have given me. Thank you, Georgiana." It was not merely the book of poetry, though I was pleased in the gift and delighted with how thoughtfully chosen it had been. The recognition that this gift had brought Elizabeth back into my life, into my home, made it my most cherished possession. *Pleasures of hope...*

Some while later, I had retired to my chair in the library and was conducting a leisurely amble through the pages before settling down to read it through. The opening lines I knew well, for they had been scribbled in my father's hand, and the paper kept in his desk when he gave me the key to it. My eyes touched fondly over them and then dived for more.

But what was this? The pages seemed to split in one place, and when I allowed them to fall open, I found a small marker. A slim, short bit of lavender ribbon.

That could not have belonged to Mr Bennet! *She* must have left it, loved the place where it was, perhaps even... could it have been her own message to me? Vanity, surely not. But I hungrily sought the page, nevertheless, and nearly sobbed aloud when I understood.

Where is the troubled heart, consign'd to share
  Tumultuous toils, or solitary care,
  Unblest by visionary thoughts that stray
  To count the joys of Fortune's better day?
  Lo, nature, life, and liberty relume
  The dim-ey'd tenant of the dungeon gloom,
  A long-lost friend, or hapless child restor'd,
  Smiles at his blazing hearth and social board;
  Warm from his heart the tears of rapture flow,
  And virtue triumphs o'er remember'd woe.

I LINGERED over that stanza for an hour or better, particularly the last lines. The final words echoed like a drumbeat in my ears, and for the first time in… perhaps it was years—I felt the warmth of fresh vigour flowing through my veins. Life, and purpose, and direction, these were *her* gifts to me, whether she had meant to bestow them or not.

All these, and yet more, something more priceless than diamonds. *Hope.*

TWELFTH NIGHT WAS a horror I could have easily done without.

Lady Matlock was celebrated for her fêtes, the tales of which revelries endured far longer than the headaches they created. The halls reverberated with merriment, festooned with every sort of greenery and colourful ribbon. The attendees themselves were fitted to the occasion, with not a few of Lady Matlock's characters sparing no expense to look—and act—the part.

My own costume was as minimal as I could make it and still please my hostess. I wore my typical breeches and waistcoat, but in place of my dinner jacket was a great draped sash of white fabric. I also conceded to wear a laurel on my head, but more I would not do. Lady Sarah had, according to the style of the evening, fairly clung to my toga throughout the whole of the affair. Her costume must have required far more effort than my own, and I wondered what her father had been thinking to permit such a sheer gown.

Viscount Milton had done the lady no injustice when he declared her fetching. I am sure I would have thought her pleasant to look upon, but her very presence simply irritated me. I tired of her coquetry within the first half-hour. By the time another hour had passed, I had settled it with myself that no more grating voice existed in all Christendom than that of 'Cleopatra'. By the end of the evening, I was perfectly persuaded that Lady Matlock meant to drive me to Bedlam.

It was, therefore, with a pounding head and infinite relief that I was at last able to summon my coach and return to my own home. However, when I entered my door, my feelings altered from relief to dejection when I observed the bareness of the walls. The servants had taken down all the greenery in accordance with proper tradition, and I stood below the empty arch where Georgiana had hung the kissing bough. Perhaps it was only fatigue, and the frustration of an entire evening spent where I did not wish to be, but once more the weight of all the world bore down on me as I stared up at the wall... Empty, just as the rest of my house was.

I dreamt about Elizabeth that night. I had dreamt of her so many times, but this was different from all the rest. Most often when she appeared in my dreams, it was as a bitter spirit, arms crossed in scornful rejection and holding me to account for all my offenses. Never could I earn her approval, and so often on such nights, I would lurch to a panting, weeping arousal, only to find an empty bedroom.

Occasionally, some sweet vagary of Morpheus would visit me in the enchanting form of communion. I could almost feel her, smell her, and cradle her warmth to my chest. On such nights, I slept better than any others, and would awake in the morning refreshed, if not restored. But this night, it was something entirely different.

I distinctly recall rain; the sense of being cold, and wet, and desperately out of place. And there was Elizabeth, not far away, but just beyond my reach—arms extended, imploring, begging something of me, but I could not understand what it was. Her beautiful face was drenched with tears—tears that shattered the final vestiges of my dignity and snapped something deep within. I cried out, either to go to her or try to bring her where I was, but when at last I reached her, she faded as my fingers passed through her image.

I was sobbing when I awoke, pleading for her not to leave. Unable to bear another such nightmare, I stoked the fire in my room myself, draped my shoulders in a blanket, and settled in for the rest of the night with Campbell's poetry. Tomorrow, I would go to her.

CHAPTER 17

J was beginning to wonder if the heavens possessed a wicked sense of humour, or if I had so thoroughly cursed myself in the past that no good plan of my own could ever come to fruition. I was bound for Gracechurch Street the morning after Epiphany, but the moment my carriage was brought to the door, a messenger met it with a note.

I brushed him off, not wishing for anything to delay my errand, but the young fellow stepped forward with an impertinence I found most peculiar. "The lady insisted I give this to you, sir, and I am not to return until I have done so."

"Very well," I relented, and took the note as I sat down inside. The direction, "Darcy" simply printed in block letters, gave me no clues regarding the sender. That bit of ambiguity may have been intentional, but wholly unnecessary, for only one lady would presume so. Still, I might have merely tossed it away, accounted it as nothing more than a nuisance, but for the words penned inside.

Darcy,

As you have declined to answer any of my previous entreaties, I now must take greater measures. Meet me at my apartment at half past. Bring a footman, if you wish, though you need have no fear that a woman of my age could form any designs upon you.

In case you should protest the hour or the inconvenience, perhaps I shall remind you that none of your doings of late have been secret. A pity you appear to have broken off with even that tradesman you once spoke so fondly of, but I understand there may be some new connection of interest. I wonder how well your treatment of a widow will sound to her ears?

THE NOTE WAS UNSIGNED, but Lady Benedict's hand was one that brought a fresh resurgence of all my bile and resentment. Devil take the woman; did she truly mean to threaten me? And was this... Elizabeth she referred to? *My* Elizabeth? My hand trembled faintly as I read that line over again.

So, I had been watched. Or informed upon, which seemed more likely, for to anyone merely observing the movement of carriages back and forth between Darcy House and Gracechurch Street, the connection was simply an attachment between young ladies. Someone must have... I narrowed my eyes, and my nostrils curled. *Wickham.*

I knocked on the roof of the carriage and gave my driver the new direction, then with my right hand, I angrily crumpled Mrs Benedict's summons while the left smoothed over my waistcoat pocket with regret. *One more day,* I promised myself, and I would ask to exchange her handkerchief for her heart.

LADY BENEDICT MUST HAVE BEEN a handsome woman in her youth. Even now, at the age of eight and forty, she remained striking. As it was with Lady Matlock, though a man would not necessarily declare her a fine, lovely creature, neither would he dare to call her anything less than remarkable. However, where Lady Matlock was a figure of authority and wisdom, Lady Benedict was a maleficent, a Jezebel.

When I considered the adage that daughters frequently resembled their mothers later in life, I never failed to burst into a cold sweat at the lifelong curse I was almost dealt.

I found her looking rather pale and unusually languid this day. The cause was readily apparent in a snuff box beside her, the lid of which still stood open. "Darcy," she greeted me with outstretched hand, gesturing to a chair. She did not rise from her seat, but continued to recline, regarding me under lowered lids as I approached. "How good of you to finally come."

"Lady Benedict. Forgive me for asking, but you look unwell today."

"Unwell?" She laughed—a lazy, abominable sound. "If I am, so must be every fashionable lady. Oh, what troubles you, son-in-law? Come, kiss your mother-in-law."

I clasped my hands behind my back and fixed my eyes on the opposite wall. "You wished to see me. May I ask why?"

She rose at last, pacing the room in a manner she must have presumed to be graceful, but it only looked lethargic. "Oh, Darcy, why must you be so dull? You know very well why I sent for you. What do you take me for?"

I refused to answer, and she turned back to me with a frown.

"Very well, then, if you are so determined to feign ignorance. You have those shares. You took them, I know it positively. They are not rightfully yours, and I would have them back."

Only my eyes moved, and I pointedly furrowed a brow. "Which shares do you mean?"

"Why, the East India Company stock! Sir Edmund purchased half a dozen in the last two years alone, to say nothing for the many he had before, besides the handful he inherited from his father."

"I have no knowledge of these, madam. I suggest you speak with your son."

The drugged haze she had exhibited upon my entry vanished at a finger-snap, and the woman's ire raged forth. "Robert will not speak with me because he assumes I have taken them! They were to be his, and I would give them to him. It was you! Are you so callous that you would steal from and then lie to a widow or a dead man's heir?"

"Lie?" I bristled, and my hands fell from behind my back. "That is a heinous accusation, madam. I trust you would not dare—"

"Unless I had evidence?" she interrupted. "I certainly have." She turned back to the table and took up a paper from beside her snuff box to present it to me. I scanned the signature at the bottom before reading the rest and nearly crumpled the paper in disgust.

Instead, I held it up, pointing an accusing finger at the name. "Daniels? You would take the word of a former solicitor who forfeited his duties?"

She lifted her long, elegant shoulders and tossed her head. "From what I understand, he had ample reason to wish no longer to be in your employ. Valid or not, can you tell me he does not speak the truth?"

I read the statement over, seeking the individual details. "He does. I sold fifteen shares over a year ago, and he even conducted the business for me. See here, sold for one hundred eighty pounds per share, with eleven shillings and nine pence paid to the Company by the buyer in consideration for the transfer."

"There, you have it in your own words!"

"But you know only half the truth. Daniels knows what I had, but not the source. The shares I sold were purchased by my great grandfather in seventeen fifty-six. He got the interest for a pittance, even sat on the Court of Directors for some time. Like many other families, we watched our fortunes grow—until I learned the infamy of the Company's means. This, thanks to your own son, whose letters I discovered among the business effects I was required to sort after Sir Edmund's death. These letters revealed far more than I would ever have wished to know."

She shook her head and lifted a dismissive hand. "Darcy, I should have thought you a wiser man than to believe the puerile ramblings of a boy away from England for his first time."

"A stay of five years in the Orient is hardly a boy's tour. He began his appointment as a factor for the company in aught-five, and his mentions of fortunes made in opium—" here, I slanted my eyes toward her own private vice at the table—"gave me great cause to wonder how the Benedict coffers could possibly be in such straits as I found them to be."

Uneven red patches rose in her cheeks. "How impertinent you are! You assume that just because you were permitted irregular freedoms in your wife's household, that you might have the pleasure of sitting in judgment over it?"

"I did not ask for the duty, madam." I returned my eyes to the wall, far above her head, and assumed an air of nonchalance.

"Oh, yes, the noble son-in-law!" she sneered, and began to slowly circle round me. "Because my own son, the proper heir, was out of the country and my husband lay dead, you assumed the role of the faithful counsellor, the scrupulous protector, valiantly performing as he must. I ought to have set the hue and cry that very night, instead of keeping silent and trusting our fortunes to you!"

"I wished you would have. That fate would have been less odious than my months of marriage to your daughter."

Without warning, she rushed to me, and slapped me across the cheekbone. I refused to wince, but she seemed to care little as she railed at me. "You are not so invincible as you think! I have other complaints. Where were you, oh great and honourable Darcy, when my daughter cried out for her mother in her agony? Where were you when she died trying to bring your own heir?"

One of my eyes narrowed. "I do not mock your grief, madam, but you do a wilful violence to the facts if you persist in that fabrication. Recall, that even she herself confessed the love of some other—or others, for I never learned the full truth."

Until that moment, I had never noticed that a woman's eyes could contract or reflect a flat glare like those of a cat. Her complexion changed hues, and she contorted her mouth as if she would spit on me. "You dare malign my own child! My only daughter, the girl after my own heart!"

"She certainly was," I shot back. "Tell me, Lady Benedict, did you even wait until Sir Edmund had grown cold before you found his replacement? Unless I am incorrect, your chosen amusement will turn on you the moment he discovers there is not another dime to be gotten from me."

She raised her hand and delivered another resounding crack to my cheek, but again, I refused to flinch. "Beast!" she hissed.

"If I am, you have made me so. I did not choose to align myself with you and intend to wash my hands of your society. Good day, Lady Benedict."

"You forget, Darcy!" she cried as I turned my back. "I know one thing more."

I stopped and could feel her drawing close by the prickling of my neck.

"What is this," she dropped her voice to a sultry croon that made my flesh crawl, "about another young lady? The very image of my own child, I understand."

"My affairs are none of your concern," I answered coldly. "And even if they were, I would answer you that anyone resembling your daughter would send me in search of a priest and a silver dagger." I was already walking out, but I heard every word of her retort before the door slammed behind me.

"You lie! You have seduced this other, won her favour and spun a web of deceit. Does she think you innocent, Darcy? I am not without my means, and I will have what is mine! I would count it as sweet gratification if it also cost you what is yours!"

I WAS A SHAKEN, seething, outraged wretch when I mounted my own carriage again. I ought to have gone home, settled my nerves, and waited for a better day, but Lady Benedict's threat echoed in my ears until they throbbed, and my stomach turned. "Gracechurch Street," I ordered my driver, then I proceeded to brood and storm about the whole confrontation.

That devious, loathsome she-serpent! If it were true, if she did possess the means to bend my Elizabeth's ear and whisper her perfidy, would Elizabeth believe her? Would she have any reason not to?

And so, like a boorish fool, I fairly raced up the steps to the Gardiners' house and insisted on seeing her. Alone, if she would.

I was shown to the drawing room and told to wait a moment; Miss Elizabeth was upstairs. I paced by the window, then felt it would be bad form to be prowling about the glass like some caged creature when she arrived. I tried sitting, but that posture only recalled a regent waiting upon a subject, and if anything, this situation was the reverse of that. At last, I settled on standing near a table, not far from the door, and staring at it as if I could will it to open.

She came, and she came alone. That is, she brought a maid who stood beyond the door, but remained out of earshot. She hurried to me and stopped just short of clasping my hand in entreaty. "Mr Darcy? Is something the matter with Georgiana?"

"With Georgi—er, no, Miss Elizabeth."

She sighed in obvious relief. "There is not bad news of some kind?"

"No, you may be easy on that score. It is another matter I wished to talk of." I attempted to gather my thoughts, but they still raged about like wild things, refusing to be tamed. Rather than speak, I am afraid I only stared.

She was regarding me strangely, but she gestured to the sofa at the far end of the room. "Will you be seated, Mr Darcy? Shall I have some tea brought?"

"Yes, thank you, and no, no tea, please."

We settled on opposite ends of the sofa; she smoothing her skirts and looking down, and I gesticulating with my hands as if they could form my words. "You recall," I began abruptly, "the evening of the ball at Netherfield."

Her lips twitched. "Vividly."

"You overheard certain things, things about…" I faltered and closed my eyes.

"Mr Wickham, sir?"

"Wickham." His name was almost a growl, and I felt my lips curl. "No—yes, rather, but it is not precisely he of whom I speak."

Her countenance seemed to darken—in embarrassment or anger, I could not say. "Your… ah, your former wife, sir?"

"Pray, do not accord her so much dignity. There is a matter I wished to set straight, and after that, I would ask—"

She held up a hand. "Before you say more, Mr Darcy, recall that I scarcely know you."

"Scarcely?" I repeated in mild consternation. "In fact, Miss Elizabeth, I believe you know me better even than I do, and you discovered my faults at first glance."

"But that is all. I am not well acquainted with your virtues, I know nothing of your family or life, and I do not move in your circles."

"That is not entirely true, for you are a gentleman's daughter, and I have told you more of my life—at least of my recent years—than even my own sister. If that is your objection, I beg you to hear me now."

She looked as if she would protest, but then nodded uncertainly as her hands pressed tightly into her lap.

I was nearly steady, my breath drawing now in deep trembles rather than uneven gasps. "Perhaps I shall begin by asking whether you credited my words to you that night as the truth."

She did not respond at once, and I looked urgently into her face, hoping to read her feelings. She was still hesitating... *why* would she hesitate?

"I cannot think," she answered cautiously, "why you would have attempted to deceive me. You could have gained nothing by it. Moreover, what I heard from Mr Wickham himself convinced me that *he* was not a man to be trusted."

"You only believed me because you could not believe him?"

"No," she arched her shoulders and squarely met my eye. "I had been trying to sort out the puzzle of your deplorable behaviour, coupled with the friendship of Mr Bingley, who is, as near as I can tell, a perpetually amiable kind of man. Miss Darcy and Colonel Fitzwilliam also display a fondness for you I could not understand, unless my first previous impressions of you were an incomplete picture. When I came to London and met your housekeeper, her appraisal of your character so nearly matched your own explanation that I could do little but concede."

I stared for a moment. "That is the measure of it? You only think me honourable because—"

"I did not say I found you honourable. That much, I have yet to determine."

I swallowed and looked down. "I see."

"Mr Darcy," she stirred, and then rose from the sofa, placing several feet between us. She would only look at her hands. "Clearly, you are distressed today, and I am sorry for it. But I must remind you that it is not seemly for me to meet with you alone. Shall I ask my aunt…?"

"Please, Miss Elizabeth, one moment more? There is another question I must ask you."

Her mouth pressed tightly, and she sighed. "If it is truly so important."

Important, she said. Could there be anything more vital? "Indeed," I answered hoarsely. "Quite so." I shifted, hoping by my posture to invite her to sit beside me once more. Those dark eyes fixed on me, never blinking, as she glided near and carefully lowered herself.

"Thank you, Miss Elizabeth." I bit down on my lip, then plunged ahead. "Have you had any contact with George Wickham since I left Hertfordshire?"

Her breathing stilled. "He—he did call at Longbourn just after the ball. I had not yet found an opportunity to speak with my father, and Mr Wickham stayed above half an hour."

"And did you speak with your father later?"

"Well…" her fingers toyed together in her lap, and her lashes fluttered. "My father found it terribly amusing—a fine tale, he branded it. Gossip, he thinks, for I did not feel secure in divulging the source of my information—nor, I think, would it have helped my cause. Particularly after the events of that evening, the sympathies of nearly everyone, and most especially my mother, were engaged for Mr Wickham."

I snorted. "I expect he employed that bruised lip to great effect."

"In-indeed, sir." Her eyes dropped again.

"But your sisters, you cautioned them, did you not?"

A crimson flush stained her cheeks. "You are already acquainted with my younger sisters' careless disregard for decorum. I am afraid that only Jane and Mary will be safe from Mr Wickham's flattery. My father thought the matter of small concern, for, as he says, my sisters do not have sufficient dowry to attract him."

"George Wickham cares little for a girl's dowry, but if she possesses other attributes without the mischief of good sense to trouble him—"

She gulped. "I understand. Is this why you called today, sir? Have you some particular reason to believe my sisters are in danger of being deceived?"

"It is not unlikely, but I was more concerned about *you*." I stared at her, watched those expressive eyes darken again, and my attention fell to her moistened lips. "Have you... have you betrayed any of your knowledge to Wickham himself?"

She shook her head. "I saw him only in the company of my sisters, and the following morning I left for London. But, how should I? To do so would be to confess that I was privy to your conversation, a thing I am not inclined to do."

"I suppose that is the best that can be hoped. I have reason to think he might seek your society again. He, or an associate."

"How? He is stationed in Meryton."

"As to that, even militiamen are occasionally granted leave. I would not put it beyond him to absent his duties entirely, if the inducement were strong enough. If he believed he stood to gain by 'incidentally' resuming your acquaintance and sowing his half-truths and falsehoods—"

"But why?" She shook her head. "It makes no sense. What would he wish to tell me?"

My throat tightened. "Anything that might damage me in your eyes."

Her face dropped into that old playful impassivity; one eyebrow curved faintly, and her lips drew together. "I doubt any lies can be more damaging than the truth, can they? Come, Mr Darcy, I have hardly been treated only to your more sterling qualities."

I could not help a half-smile. "You might be surprised. It is not merely he, Miss Elizabeth. My… my former mother-in-law… I shall hereafter refer to her as 'Lady B,' has been pressing for her own ends. She seems to believe that I stole her late husband's property—which I did not—and is willing to exact whatever unpleasantness or artifices necessary to obtain what she wants. I have reason to think she has been communicating with Mr Wickham, and you were the subject of their exchange."

Her brow contracted, her eyes narrowed, and she lifted her hands. "Mr Darcy, I can see that you truly are disturbed over the matter, but I do not understand. What possible motive could Mr Wickham—whom I have no expectation of ever seeing again—and a woman utterly unknown to me have in potentially harming my opinions of you?"

"Because…" I closed my eyes again, a chill of foreboding lancing through my breastbone and squeezing my heart. "They wish to cause me pain, and they could find no surer way to do it. Because what George Wickham said the night of the ball was true. Because blind and ignorant as I was, determined as I was to flee you utterly, I found I could not. You have bewitched me body and soul. I beg of you—"

She rose hastily, stumbling away. "Oh, no, no, no, Mr Darcy," she stuttered. Her hands were shaking visibly, her cheeks bloodless. "Pray, do not go on!"

I stood, followed after her, but stopped when she drew back again. "But I must! Please, Miss Elizabeth, I do not press you for an immediate answer. I understand my behaviour to you was abominable in the past, but I hope one day to earn your regard. I beseech you—"

"You have my regard, sir!" She was still backing away, her hands clasped behind her skirts and her face averted, as if she could not look me in the eye. "As my friend's brother—as my own friend!—and as a man who has suffered more than his share. I do appreciate the honour of your proposal, but it is absolutely impossible for me to accept. My feelings in every respect forbid it!"

"What can I do? I would lay every possession I have at your feet, swear my heart and my last breath to you! I care nothing for fortune or position, for family duty or even pride!"

Her chin lifted; black eyes glittered. "And this, sir, is but one of the reasons I can never accept you. Even now, these things are in your mind. How much more after a year, when you tire of yet another wife? How greatly will you revile me or my family when you see how your own dignity has suffered by the connection?"

"Tire of you? I love you! I told you," I cried in exasperation, "I despised her before I was forced to marry her! Can you not sympathise with that? Do you not see how an attachment borne for the sake of duty or pity would soon become toxic and intolerable?"

She was panting, slim shoulders heaving as she nodded. "Indeed, I do. I am sorry, Mr Darcy." She spun then and fled the room.

CHAPTER 18

 *wo weeks later*

"FITZWILLIAM DARCY, I am ashamed of you!"

I lifted my groggy head from the arm of my chair. Blinking, I rubbed my eyes as a shape materialised from the grey of the bookshelves in my shrouded library. The figure was speaking—lecturing, really—and I squinted again. "Lady Matlock?" I slurred.

"At last, you rouse yourself! I have been here above five minutes, staring at what I took to be your corpse. Georgiana, dear," she commanded over her shoulder, "you may leave the smelling salts. Run along, girl; it is not fitting for you to look upon a drunkard."

I staggered upright, tugging my coat to make a more respectable presentation. "I am no such thing."

"Are you not! It is more than a fortnight now since anyone has seen you. Lord Dewhurst expected you to call no later than last week, and Lord Matlock and Lady Catherine have each sent notes requesting your presence. Richard attempted to call thrice, at my behest, but even he came away disappointed."

"I have been occupied with other matters," I retorted as I attempted to straighten my cravat.

"Yes." She cast a dismal eye over my chair and the blanket that some footman must have thrown over me when he awoke to light the fires. "Dreadfully occupied, it would seem."

A maid brushed soundlessly past Lady Matlock just then with a cart, heavily laden with fresh tea, black coffee, and an assortment of cold meats. She bobbed a short curtsey, then poured both hot beverages. Looking down, she asked if anything else was wanted, then scurried from the room.

"There, do you see?" Lady Matlock sniffed.

"See what?"

"Your own people dare not trouble you. Georgiana tells me you have become little better than a troglodyte, seeing no one and taking no pleasure in anything. You will hardly even speak to her!"

"I took my evening meal with her just last night. How can she claim I do not see her?"

"You stared at your plate, eating and saying nothing until the poor girl left the room in tears."

"I was not in the mood for conversation," I pardoned myself, and swallowed nearly all the little cup of coffee. I stared unhappily at the remnants, then took up the tea. Too sweet by half, and not at all dark enough. I switched back to the coffee.

"Fitzwilliam Darcy," she shook her walking stick at me, "what has become of you? Are you going out to the gaming hells at night?"

"Aunt!" I protested.

She made a noise in her throat and shook her head with a heavy disapproval. "I am no mere girl, Darcy. Think you I do not know what amusements young men find for themselves? The bottle, the hells, or a woman, it must be one of these."

I looked away, unable to meet her gaze.

"Then you have a mistress. I ought to have thought as much. Come, now, you must not allow the woman to make such demands of you, and spare some of your energies for the waking hours."

"Lady Matlock," I sighed, trying to keep my voice as reasonable and respectful as I could. "I have no mistress. I have not been drinking heavily, and I have no stomach for the gaming tables."

"Then what is it, Darcy? You have poor Georgiana thinking that you are dying of consumption and Richard believing you have gone mad."

"Richard is nearer to the truth."

"And what is that?" she demanded.

"The truth… I have been up reading."

"Reading." Her lips puckered, and she scrutinised me through lowered lids. "For a fortnight together? I am no fool, Darcy."

"If I am not reading, I am often writing. There—" I indicated a writing desk—"you see my labours of last night."

She turned faintly, then looked back at me all askance. "Indeed, I am inclined to agree with my son. You are mad, Darcy. Pray tell me it is a passing sort of madness, for Lady Dewhurst and Lady Sarah were in my drawing room only this morning, and their impatience could hardly be concealed."

"I do not intend to arouse any expectations in Lady Sarah. I can scarce abide the woman."

"Very well, then. Miss Dalrymple or Lady Penelope—"

"I shall not be offering for either of them."

She hissed an exasperated sigh. "You may be assured, Darcy, I have thoroughly examined the credentials of each of the eligible ladies of acceptable position. If you are so determined to be particular, you will soon find yourself with only Anne as a suitable alternative."

"Then I shall not marry. I did so once, and it brought only disaster."

She rolled her eyes. "Petulant boy! George Darcy's son knew his duty. This… this changeful stripling I see before me is no Darcy! He is a phantom, a churlish waif of a creature who cannot exert himself to even choose his morning beverage, to say nothing for a wife! What, do you think you must form some special attachment to the wench? Choose one and let it be done!"

"Aunt," I sighed, "much of what you say is true. I have become a wasted prodigal, offending right and left and incapable of settling on any one object. If you must know, I did choose a woman I fancied—a woman not of the *ton*, but one whose society would be no discredit even to Lord Matlock."

"Indeed? Most peculiar. A woman not of the *ton*, Darcy? Whatever could you be thinking? What is she, some shopkeeper's girl? Do tell me your honour is not already committed."

The great ache that had been tormenting my stomach for weeks shifted somewhat higher, squeezing my heart as I confessed, "No."

"Then let it remain that way. Now, Darcy, I am not entirely without sympathy. I had a tremendous fondness for your mother, and I take most particular interest in her children. Heaven knows, my own brood are dull enough! At least you and Georgiana present me some intrigue, and a woman of my age must have her share of frustrations, else she becomes a tiresome old crone. I shall suspend any further talk of marriage for a few weeks until you have set your head straight again. Meanwhile, I expect you will be at home to Richard when he calls."

She left shortly after that, and I stood alone in the darkened library. *I ought to go up and dress*, I thought. *Ought to take Georgiana to the wainwright's to look at her chaise. Ought to do some blasted thing.*

I wandered numbly to my writing desk and surveyed the inane ramblings of the previous night. Good lord, even I could make no sense of them. They were absurd, scattered, maudlin—grotesque, even. The bitter effusions of a contemptible soul, too dense to understand that he had not even lost love—no, he had never had it to begin with.

My hand strayed over the disordered pages, touching each one as if trying to bid adieu but never letting go. With each page, my eye fell on her name, the name that had first been anathema and then sweet nectar to my lips. What a fool I was!

In a rush of self-loathing, I swept up the papers into my arms, crumpling them at random, and thrust them into the fire grate. The resulting blaze nearly scorched my hair, and I stood back, squinting into the flames. If only it were so easy to uproot the tendrils of her memory from my soul.

~

One week later

"FITZWILLIAM!"

Georgiana's cry of pleasure arrested me as I passed by the drawing room one day, and I turned back. "Good morning, Georgiana. You look as if you are going out."

"Yes, Mrs Younge and I are waiting on Lady Matlock. I wished to be fitted for a new bonnet, and our aunt desired to attend us."

"Very good. When is she to arrive? It is already quarter of, and it is not like our aunt to delay an outing."

"Well," she tugged on the fingertips of one glove, "I asked her to come a little later. I..." her eyes slid to Mrs Younge, waiting demurely on the sofa, and she lowered her voice. "I understand you had a restful night and were up early today, so I did not know if perhaps you had been told of our plans and intended to come with us. I heard you were dressing to go out, but Hodges did not seem to know where."

I drew near and took her hand. "My kind sister. Most thoughtful of you, my dear, but no. I have been too long without some proper exercise, so I am bound for the fencing salon."

"Oh!" she brightened. "When you see Richard, ask him if he will come. It has been ages since we have had him to dinner."

I nodded hesitantly. "Of course, if I should see him. Give Lady Matlock my regards, for I know she means to ask after me."

Georgiana giggled. "I believe she expected to see you before she goes, but of course, not if you are going out. How long shall you be? Oh! I know just the thing. I sent a note yesterday asking if Lady Matlock and I might call on Elizabeth and Mrs Gardiner this afternoon. Perhaps you could join us for that?"

"No!" I bit out, with far too much vehemence.

Georgiana jumped; her eyes wide. "I—I'm sorry, Fitzwilliam," she stammered.

I shook my head, holding up a hand of apology. "Forgive me,

Georgiana, I... forgive me." I turned like a coward and left the room, cursing myself for a bastard when I heard my young sister's bereaved gasp.

~

I HAD NOT BEEN to Angelo's in at least two years, but shortly after I entered the salon, the master himself, Henry Angelo, greeted me. "Mr Darcy," he bowed. "We are pleased to see you again."

I shook his hand. "The pleasure is mine, sir."

"Did you wish for a match? Young Henry is just returned from the continent and would be honoured to stand up with you."

"I thank you, Mr Angelo. I would count it a privilege."

He bowed again, gracious as always, and answered, "I will have him called. And now, I must beg your pardon, Mr Darcy, for I see that Mr Hastings and Sir Anthony are now prepared for their lesson."

I stood back with the other observers, and complete silence fell over the salon. The only sounds for the next several minutes were the light touches of feet, the metallic grazing of foils, and the strained efforts of the combatants. I was utterly engaged, admiring the skill of the fencers, when someone brushed intentionally against my elbow. Expecting the younger Angelo, I instead discovered Ramsey by my side.

We nodded to each other, and I turned my attention back to the match, but Ramsey leaned close and whispered, tight-lipped, near my ear. "I heard you had left London, Darcy."

I furrowed my brow and shook my head slightly in answer, never taking my eyes off the fencers. *A parry, a step back.*

"Word has it," he murmured softly again, "that you jilted Lord Dewhurst's daughter. No one has seen you since Twelfth Night, so we all thought you had left for Derbyshire."

I cocked an annoyed glance at him but refused to respond. Hastings was advancing on Sir Anthony. *Thrust—and a block.*

Ramsey fell quiet for a moment, seeming to watch as intently as anyone else, but then he tipped close to me again. "I say, Darcy, when did you last see Benedict?"

My upper lip twitched, but I held my tongue. *Feint. Touch, and a circle.*

"He was hoping to speak with you—says Lady Benedict had some rather distasteful things to report of you. Egad, Darcy, if they are true—"

I glared at him. "*If* they are true! What has that rodent to say that he cannot declare to my face?" *Riposte—and a dropped foil.*

Angelo rose from his instructor's chair at my outburst and was frowning in our direction. He gave a signal, and a lad came by with a penalty tray. I scowled at Ramsey as I drew the penny from my pocket, but he was smiling in cheerful resignation as he did the same.

Hastings bent to retrieve Sir Anthony's foil, and the match resumed. Ramsey fell mercifully quiet at last, but when Hastings finally bested his opponent and the whole salon rose up in complimentary applause, Ramsey turned to me.

"What do you say, Darcy, shall we have a round? Or did you intend to wait for Young Angelo?" His request seemed innocent enough, but there was in his eyes a certain brittleness, almost a feral hunger. To refuse him would be a concession of weakness, and I was in no humour to withdraw. I accepted.

Fifteen minutes later, we were both attired in the proper vestments and facing each other in the midst of the salon. Ramsey lifted the tip of his foil to salute me, and I answered in kind. He shifted his feet to adjust for my fighting stance and gave a nod.

"*En garde*," Angelo commanded, and I balanced on the balls of my feet. "*Prêtes? Allez!*"

Ramsey's first charge was fierce, a lunge from several paces back rather than the more purposeful steps I had intended. He made the point just before I slashed his foil away, then I snapped back to guard position. We both stepped forward, our foils poised for attack.

This time, I darted into his range and tapped his chest. He struck me back, and for some while we exchanged equal touches, advancing and retreating in synchrony, neither ever gaining more than one point on the other. Ramsey, being a smaller man, was decidedly lighter on his feet, but I was by no means defenceless. I knew my own strengths, as well as my vulnerabilities—my height was less of a disadvantage to me than it might have been, had I not studied twice as hard as others on my footwork.

Ramsey feinted forward and leapt back, intending to unbalance me, but I was watching his feet, and I was ready with a lunge. I gained the point, but he struck out to avenge himself and the ball tip of his blade drove into my upper arm. Ordinarily, this would have provoked an immediate order to halt and a penalty of a six-pence, but I had scarcely flinched, and we were moving too fast, turned slightly the wrong direction. Angelo, in the periphery of my vision, rose from his chair, but sat again without issuing the penalty.

I was beginning to breathe more heavily, the rapid cadence telling on me more than it ought. I had been too idle of late, and I began to labour. Even so, it was exhilarating at last to move, to fight, to engage my unslaked energies and raging sense of loss and failure for some physical battle. Ramsey's movements were tight, graceful, and perfectly balanced, but I was with him at each step. And I was angry.

Sweat dripped into my eyes as our silver foils clashed and slid together. Even my open hand felt damp and my shirt clung to my chest. Ramsey drew back, his tip high, and I prepared to meet his lunge. His knee began to drop, but before he thrust, he recovered and rushed into my range, swiping viciously with his blade.

I was able to parry, but only just. All my suppressed vexation simmered forth, and I lunged back in answer. Ramsey did not fall away but met me with an attempted riposte. I tipped my foil to the remise and cut through his defences, a move that provoked the heat of outrage to flare in his eyes. What followed, I can scarce recall, but I do remember my own passion. The friendly match was now become combat in earnest, and I was determined to win *something*, for a bloody change.

Ramsey seemed in no mind to be the loser, however, and our successive parries flew fast and brutal. He closed, ready to put my foil in a bind, but Angelo rose to his feet. "Halt!" he cried.

We both stood panting, in some wonder that our time was up. Or had Angelo stopped us? Ramsey was all politeness again as we saluted first each other, then Angelo, and surrendered our blades.

Most of the spectators were applauding our performance, and I raised a hand in breathless acknowledgment as we left the floor. Standing at the edge of the gathering, clapping slowly, we found Carlisle. "Smashing show," he greeted us. "Absolutely smashing. Darcy, old fellow, you have still got it."

Ramsey grinned and extended his hand to me. "I cannot recall the last time I enjoyed a match more. You really ought to come more often, Darcy. Excuse me, won't you?" He turned to a footman who was ready with a cloth and a drink for each of us, then a moment later he had gone to the retiring room.

"Are you finished too, Darcy?" Carlisle asked. "There is a Whist table, if you should be so inclined."

I waved him off. "No, I only came for a bit of exercise."

"Ah, suit yourself. Just as well, for perhaps I shall stop by the club instead and see if Benedict is about. You are quite certain you do not wish to join me?"

I shot him a derisive glance. "Did you expect me to?"

"No!" he laughed. "Not really. Oh, come, Darcy, Benedict is a good enough chap. You cannot persist in this vendetta forever."

"Vendetta?" I at last took the cloth from the footman and dabbed my brow. "It is not I who have instigated a campaign to blacken his name. I would be perfectly content to forget I ever knew him, but circumstances have made that impossible. I do not take lightly the volley of accusations from both son and mother."

Carlisle leaned close and dropped his voice. "Do you mean about the shares?"

I yanked the cloth away and narrowed my eyes. "What do you know of this?"

He shrugged, then with a jerk of his head, indicated for me to follow him away from the crush, out into the quiet hall. "Benedict is not a fellow to hold his tongue. He says his mother gave the vouchers for the interest into your care while he was out of the country, so you might be a voice among the General Court and thus ensure that a portion of the Company's lucre continued to flow into the family's coffers. Sadly, once Mrs Darcy died, your interests were no longer engaged for the Benedict family—his story, old boy, not mine."

I shook out the cloth I still held, regarding him—the conversation, really—in abject disgust. "That is a blatant falsehood. Only an imbecile would believe it."

"Well," he laughed, "Benedict is, at times, an imbecile. But you know, he was not there when it all happened. All he knows is that his father left him a letter in his will referring to them. No one seems to know what came of them, and there is no record of their transfer. Ramsey and I, do you know, we tried to counsel the poor fool, but he persists in his delusions. I tell you what, Darcy, I will see what I might do. Father is on the Court of Directors, so perhaps I might hear something to be of some help."

"If it is as you say, and there is no evidence of transfer, then what troubles him? As far as the Company is concerned, Sir Edmund's son and heir is still a beneficiary of the profits."

"Ah, but can he prove it? You see, there is no history of the transfer because there is no record that he owned the shares in the first place. That is where it is all murky, Darcy. Where have they gone? Sir Edmund's man of business gave a sworn statement that Sir Edmund had purchased a sizable interest from Archibald Doyle, some years back, but the poor fellow has been in his grave these two years past with no heir to verify the claim. No one seems to know anything but that."

"And that Robert, who ought to have made a fortune or two in his own right while in India, came back to London empty-handed," I grunted.

Carlisle grinned. "Just so."

"Sir?" A passing footman bowed and offered to take the cloth from my hand. I gave it to him with a gratuity, and he left us.

"Well, Darcy," Carlisle inclined his head as the footman walked away, "a pleasure, as always. Shall we be seeing you at the club again soon? Or did you mean to return to Hertfordshire?"

"Hertfordshire?" I had begun to walk off but lurched to a halt. "Why would you assume that?"

He shrugged again. "Idle curiosity, that is all. Afternoon, Darcy."

∼

"OH, BROTHER," Georgiana gushed at dinner that evening, "we had the most wonderful outing!"

I teased the ragout on my plate with my fork, but I had only managed a few bites. "Did you, now?"

"I found just the right bonnet for Easter. Oh, I know it is weeks away yet, but I fancied the style. It is the newest fashion, flared in the back a little, and it shall be trimmed with green and lavender ribbon."

I lifted my eyes, but they stung, so I looked down again. It was a moment before the ache left my throat sufficiently to speak. "That will look charming on you, Georgiana."

"And Mrs Younge found one for herself with a dark blue ribbon, and it does looks so flattering on her."

I glanced to the lady, who was smiling in pleasure back at my sister. That was one situation that appeared to be going well. "I am glad of it."

"After that, Lady Matlock took us to a tea shop, for we were all quite done in for a rest, but it was still not too late when we finished, so we called at Gracechurch Street."

I stared at my plate. This morning's announcement, that they had asked to call in the afternoon, had sounded to me no more than her girlish assumptions. That prospect had been dreadful enough, but to discover that her plan had been carried off—that Lady Matlock herself had graced the Gardiners' home and met with my own Queen Bess, sent a dead chill down my spine.

"Fitzwilliam, do you not like the beef?" Georgiana frowned, tasted a bit more of her own, and suggested, "perhaps if you sent for a bit of salt?"

"Thank you, but no. It is seasoned perfectly. How did Lady Matlock find your friend?"

"Oh, well, you remember, they had met before, so our aunt was pleased to see Elizabeth again. She had ever so many questions, though—about Hertfordshire, for she said a friend of hers had gone there recently and she had never stayed there herself, so she wished to know more of the shire and the neighbourhood round Meryton. And she asked a good deal about Mrs Gardiner, for I had told our aunt that she was from Lambton. They talked a long while about that."

"They appeared to get on?"

"Who could not get on with Mrs Gardiner?" Even Mrs Younge smiled at this, and I could do no less.

"After that," Georgiana continued, "Lady Matlock asked after Elizabeth's family a great deal. 'Five sisters,' she kept saying, as if she had not heard properly."

"She heard. Our aunt never drops a syllable without purpose. I expect she meant to mortify Miss Elizabeth."

"Oh, I do not think so, for they both seemed amused. Miss Elizabeth even laughed a little about what it was like to have so many sisters. That is, until she mentioned there was no brother, and the heir to Longbourn was Mr Collins, who is Lady Catherine's rector. Well, Lady Matlock frowned quite a lot about this. Do you know, I am not sure that my aunts are fond of one another. I always assumed they must be, but now I am not so certain."

I set aside my fork. "I have found the wisest course is to keep out of it yourself. Cunning as serpents, innocent as doves, as the saying goes."

Her expression pinched as she thought for a moment. "I never quite understood what that means. I suppose I shall have to learn."

I glanced at a footman and signalled for him to carry away my plate, only half-eaten. "I am still learning it, as well. It sounds as if you had an agreeable afternoon, on the whole," I said. Then, with what I imagined to be great slyness, I asked, "Miss Elizabeth was well today?"

Georgiana bit her lip pensively. "I thought she was, until just near the end of our call. Then, she looked suddenly as if she would be ill, and she kept rising to pour more tea, though no one wanted any. Do you recall that, Mrs Younge?"

The elder lady concurred with a nod of her head, but she remained quiet, as she usually did at table when I was present.

"I thought that was right. It was when Lady Matlock started talking more about Lady Catherine, and... Fitzwilliam, are you intending to marry Anne?"

I choked. I was neither eating nor drinking, but suddenly plain, dry air seemed too much for me. I turned my head to cough, cleared my throat and answered, in a cracked voice, "I am not. What would make you ask that?"

"Oh," she sighed, "I did not think you were, but Lady Matlock acted as if she were imparting some great secret to us, and she made it sound as if you planned to make an offer any day now to a certain young lady, and how she was quite certain that Lady Catherine would be terribly pleased for the good fortune of one so closely connected to her."

I felt the blood from my extremities pooling somewhere around my stomach, and I was glad now that I had hardly eaten, for I surely would have cast up my accounts. I lurched to my feet. "She said what? She had no right to speak in such a manner!"

Georgiana blinked as if she were frightened, and then something remarkable happened. She drew a steadying breath, looked me in the eye with a lifted chin, and pronounced, "That is what she said. If you do not like it, Fitzwilliam, perhaps you should ask Lady Matlock." She stood, dropped her napkin into the chair, and then she smiled sweetly at me as she left the dining room.

I swayed—grasped the back of my chair for support as the room lost focus around me and began to spin. *Good heavens, I had done it.* Somehow, through the most unlikely of means, I had succeeded in bringing Elizabeth into my home, but it was not her body. It was only her spirit, the seed of which had sprung up in the fertile ground of my sister's hungry, neglected soul and slowly, secretly, begun to flourish.

CHAPTER 19

I slept not at all that night.

I had hoped fervently that my exercises at the fencing salon would exhaust my body enough that I might fall, sated and fatigued, into my bed. Instead, my limbs tingled, my heart pounded, and I could only cease pacing to drop, for a moment or two at a time, into my desk and scribble mad words on yet another page.

Hour after hour I passed in this way, heaving and retching forth all my regrets, my anguish, and the great, yawning sense of emptiness that seemed to loom over all else. Then, when those sentiments were spent and my eyes grew heavy, the frenetic pace of my gait slowed, I sank down with my head in my hands. More words, more broken pens, but these were for her ears, not my own. And I wept over them far more than any others I had written.

You were right to refuse me.

OH, what that sentence alone cost me! I believe I dwelt upon it for half an hour, lightly tracing the pen-strokes over and over until I could no longer read it through my tears.

I have never given you cause to put your trust in me, and still I asked for that very honour. You have been wiser, more steadfast and truer than I. I justly deserved your censure, and your reproofs have inspired in me at least the dream of becoming a better man.

Yet, it was more than your faithful correction, more than your simple candour. I first loved your mind, for I could not best it. I love your beauty, for it is purely your own and of the sort that can never tarnish. I love your gentleness, the way you touch every creature around you, even those who are the most undeserving. I love your easy spirits and your enchanting humour, and how you alone possess the means to make me laugh at my own folly.

All these made me yours long before I was willing to confess how thoroughly I was lost, but one thing more secured my devotion. You forgave me. When I was unforgivable, you listened, though I am certain you did not wish to. You did not treat me according to my wrongs, did not banish me forever. You saw me wounded, and you had compassion.

Forgive me once again, my queen. You offered friendship I did not deserve, but I only craved more. I have grieved you, asked for more than is just, and no doubt injured you. Can you ever think on me with other than repugnance? Or shall you be better pleased to forget me entirely? I know that I shall never forget you, no matter how I might one day wish to.

I pray that if you remember one thing, it is this; that I shall always bless heaven for the pleasure of having known you. You have redeemed what was lost and made it beautiful in my eyes, a thing I would have counted impossible. You have restored my sister to me and cleansed me of so much of my bitterness, and I can never fully express to you my gratitude.

For too long I have kept what was yours, but now I return it, for I have no right to hold it. It grieves me to confess that even this simple article did not survive my affections unscathed, and you will find the corner charred. Better the handkerchief than you, my Elizabeth, and so please take it from me, and may it be in safer keeping.

To these confessions I will only add, God bless you, and please accept my sincerest wishes for your health and happiness.

Fitzwilliam Darcy

It was dawn by the time I signed my farewell, and read it over through dry, bloodshot eyes. It was not poetry. There was no meter or rhyme, no elegant phrasing; only the truth. She deserved that much, at least. I sealed it and laid it beside the folded handkerchief, then prepared to go out.

When the hour struck ten, I was standing on the steps of the house on Gracechurch Street. I smoothed my pocket, checked for the particular weight and softness that ought to be there, and then spoke to the butler.

"Miss Elizabeth is unavailable," he answered, "but Mrs Gardiner will see you."

I looked helplessly over his shoulder into the hall, but there was no other to declare it a misunderstanding. My spirits leaden, I accepted his offer to call on Mrs Gardiner. He showed me to that same fateful drawing room, the place where all my hopes had died, and I stood forlornly in the centre. I drew out the note and handkerchief and prayed that I could count on Mrs Gardiner's discretion and good character.

I was waiting nearly half an hour. During that time, I wandered aimlessly about the room, each lonely footfall sounding the death knell of every pure and perfect aspiration. After this day, I would see her no more, and she would likely sever ties even with Georgiana. But I must do it—I owed her this, and I could not shrink.

At length, I heard the door creak and turned around to face it. It was not Mrs Gardiner, but Elizabeth herself slowly opening the door. She came inside and closed it, then waited, the soft amber of her eyes fixed low as a rosy shame warmed her satin cheeks. She clasped her fingertips in graceful repose over her skirts, and murmured, "Mr Darcy."

I stepped eagerly forward. "Miss Elizabeth. Thank you for seeing me—I did not expect so much."

She raised her chin, and a tendril of her chocolate ringlets slipped from behind her ear. She studied me, taking in my state—for though my valet had done his best, I could not conceal my obvious fatigue from her. There was the slightest softening round her eyes, as she used to do when she would note something that inspired her sympathy; a movement of her lips that might have suggested pity, then she looked down again. "My aunt is waiting just outside."

"I understand." I turned the letter in my hand to present it to her. "Will you do me the honour of reading this? And this…" I placed the handkerchief on top, letting my hand rest on it for another pulse-beat and wishing I were not wearing gloves, so that I could touch it just once more. "This is yours."

She bit her upper lip, and I saw her lashes flutter before she looked up again. Her eyes, those precious gems, had filled with tears. "Thank you," she whispered.

"Elizabeth—" I swallowed, lifted my hand, and then hesitated before letting it fall again. "I did not mean to cause you sorrow."

She sniffed lightly and blinked, forcing a smile. "It is not that, sir. I do not expect I shall be seeing you again. I leave for Hertfordshire day after tomorrow to help my sister prepare for her wedding."

"To Bingley?" I asked hopefully.

She gave up blinking and dashed a tear from her own cheek. "Yes. She is very happy, and I am longing to see her."

I nodded and offered a sincere smile, looking intently down into her face. "If it is not too much, I hope you shall convey to her, and to Mr Bingley, my heartfelt congratulations. I never knew a couple more deserving of their happiness."

"Sir, have you thought of writing Mr Bingley yourself?"

I shook my head. "I have written. I regret to say that my offences have been too great, and he quite justly ignored my letters."

She looked down to the sealed note in her hand. "Perhaps you might try again, Mr Darcy. I believe your friend would be sorry not to have you by his side at his wedding."

"Miss Elizabeth, I shall always heed your advice. I will write my congratulations this very afternoon. If I am fortunate, perhaps he will even read them."

She wetted her lips in acknowledgment, clumped lashes blinking her approval, then shifted her feet as if she meant to excuse herself.

"One more thing," I begged, and was gratified at the way she stepped forward again. "If you are leaving London, and it is not too much, will you call on Georgiana one last time? She will... she will miss you."

"I..." Her eyes slid to the left, and she faltered.

"I will keep out of the way, or leave the house entirely," I offered. "Please come. I would not have my sister suffer for my offences."

She thinned her lips and inclined her head. "Tomorrow morning, sir," she agreed. "Good day, Mr Darcy, and... and God bless you."

"Mr Darcy?" Mrs Elliott entered my study and waited for my notice.

I set aside the business letter I was writing. "Yes, Mrs Elliott?"

"Sir, Miss Darcy has callers."

So, she had come. Even after my letter, she had come. I breathed a silent prayer of thanks. *Would that I could go to her.* Struggling for composure, I balled my fists under my desk and nodded to my housekeeper.

"Very good. Thank you, Mrs Elliott. Please inform me when her callers depart."

"Sir, they are not the party you said to expect. Her present callers are Lady Matlock, Lady Catherine, Lady Milton, and Miss de Bourgh. They are asking if you are at liberty to see them."

My stomach turned to rock. Of all the days for them to call! I was a moment in responding, staring at my desk, but I shook myself to make answer. "I will come."

Lady Matlock had assumed for herself the chair nearest the fire, a feat which apparently still rankled with Lady Catherine, who was occasionally sending sideways glances in that direction. She and Anne had therefore taken the nearby divan together. Lady Milton had claimed the sofa, with Mrs Younge on the opposite end and Georgiana pressed into the middle. The very air of the room seemed heavy when I entered, and my arrival did nothing to relieve that sensation.

"Ah, Darcy, there you are," Lady Matlock greeted me. "We were just speaking of Georgiana's presentation next year."

My sister's plaintive expression was impossible to ignore, but I only gave her the most cursory of glances before taking up my stance beside the fireplace. "Does that not seem premature?"

"Not at all," Lady Matlock declared, "but it was only an incidental conversation."

"What we came to speak of," Lady Catherine interjected, "was my imminent departure for Kent. The weather has warmed somewhat, and Anne and I wish to return to Rosings."

I nodded mildly. "When do you mean to depart?"

Lady Catherine drew herself straighter and levelled her chin at me. "Tuesday next. I believe that should be ample time for you, Darcy."

Anne, who seldom spoke and certainly never interrupted her mother, now joined Lady Catherine in staring expectantly at me.

"I am afraid," I answered slowly, "that may not suffice to host you for a dinner before you go."

Lady Matlock's mouth tightened, but she said nothing. It was Lady Catherine who issued an aggrieved sigh. "Darcy, you know very well that we have other expectations of you before we begin our travels."

"Indeed. As you are aware, I have been in contact with your steward regarding the stonemason's bill. I received his latest reply only yesterday, detailing each of the expenses. It seems the repairs were far more extensive than you had thought. I may present it to you at your convenience."

"The stonemason! Darcy, you know perfectly well what I speak of. You are no simpleton."

"Nor am I inclined to discuss this subject before an audience. You will find me rather inflexible on that point."

"Audience!" Lady Catherine scoffed. "Who are we but the parties most concerned with the match?"

"I had been accustomed to think of marriage as being an arrangement between two persons, no more."

"Then you are a greater fool than I had thought. The couple, and their resulting issue, are only a forfeiture; a pledge by their families, until such time as they become the elders who must form alliances for their own children. That is the natural way of things, Darcy."

"With all due respect, Lady Catherine, it is not my way. I intend no slight against my cousin, but I require much more consideration."

"What is there to consider?" she cried. "This is hardly the subject of a moment!"

"I mean it in the sense of value, in exchange for such a promise. You insist on viewing it as a transaction, and so I shall as well—you offer a dowry and an estate, should I choose Anne, but I am afraid that fails to meet my requirements."

"Darcy!" Lady Catherine rose, trembling, and lifted a hand in censure. "How dare you speak so of my daughter, in the hearing of others! Do you mean to wound her?"

"I attempted to demur so I could avoid doing just that, but you would not have it. Anne," I addressed her directly, "do you find me amiable?"

Her sallow brow wrinkled. "What does it matter if I do?"

"What a ridiculous question!" Lady Catherine protested. "You are her betrothed. It is her duty to find you amiable!"

"I am not her betrothed; I have made no such offer, and it gives me no pleasure to humiliate my cousin."

"Darcy is correct," Lady Matlock decided at last. All eyes turned to her as she arched her shoulders and leaned slightly forward. "No young lady wishes to be spoken of as an object in the hearing of others. Anne, my dear, we shall discuss this in private. Darcy, let us also speak of..." she broke off at a knock on the drawing room door. "Darcy, are you expecting other callers?"

I glanced round and called for the maid who had beckoned at the door. She entered hesitantly. "Sir, Mrs Gardiner and Miss Bennet are here to see Miss Darcy. I would have asked them to come at another time, sir, but you said before—"

"Mrs Gardiner and Miss Bennet? Let them be shown in!" announced Lady Matlock. "At last, we shall have some agreeable conversation." This remark was directed with scathing accuracy at Lady Catherine, who bristled visibly but held her peace.

I had promised to be away when she came. Even so, mine was the first face she sought as she entered, and the look that crossed her features was some combination of shock and... was that relief? Pleasure? I gazed back, hoping she could feel my regret, my apology, and not least my joy in seeing her once more.

Lady Matlock performed the honours, introducing Elizabeth as "Georgiana's dear friend." "But," she continued, "you must already know of Miss Bennet's family, Lady Catherine, for are they not kin of your new rector?"

I was ashamed to own that my aunt's reception was even more frosty for that bit of intelligence. Elizabeth could do no good that Lady Catherine would confess. She saw it at once—I recognised that bit of laughter in her eyes, the refusal to be intimidated, and my heart nearly burst in pride. Others might cower in fear or lap at Lady Catherine's hand like a dog, but not my minx.

Mrs Younge made a place for Elizabeth at Georgiana's side, and I had another chair brought for Mrs Gardiner. Then, the room fell utterly silent. Lady Milton picked at her gloves, Georgiana sat wide-eyed and tense, and Elizabeth did her best to take no notice of me. Her effort was a dismal failure, but I suspect my own was little better.

Lady Matlock seemed the only one not suffering the same discomfiture as all the rest of us. "Mrs Gardiner," she began cheerfully, "I recall that you hailed originally from Derbyshire. The Matlock seat is there, as you know, and I wonder if you agree with me that there is no more breath-taking country to be seen than the Peaks."

"I must concur," Mrs Gardiner answered. "I have been longing to tour it again, and Mr Gardiner has already begun to plan such a journey for this summer."

"Ah," Lady Matlock nodded her approval. "And shall Miss Bennet accompany you?"

"I am afraid not, your ladyship," Elizabeth answered for herself. "I am bound tomorrow morning for Hertfordshire, as my elder sister is to be married at the end of the month."

"Indeed! She is to be congratulated. But surely, your mother can do without you for a month or two this summer. I insist that if you should come to Derbyshire, you and your aunt must call on me at Matlock."

"I thank your ladyship most kindly for the invitation, but it is not presently in my power to accept."

"Then I shall write to your mother myself, if I must. We are always eager for good company during the summer months, is that not true, my dear Priscilla?"

Lady Milton's brow narrowed so sharply that I could have sworn her rather substantial nose had suddenly grown longer. "Naturally, if the company is, indeed, 'good.' I often find there is little of such to be had in the country. Rather confined and unvarying, is it not?"

"Not if one takes the trouble to observe those qualities that make each person unique," Elizabeth offered. "Each has their own desires, their own experiences and expectations. I find the unlocking of such human mysteries fascinating."

"How very singular," Lady Milton intoned flatly, as she toyed with a bit of lace from her gown. "I find that most are not worth the trouble."

"Then we must define 'good company,'" Elizabeth declared. "What do you think, Lady Milton?"

"Why, good breeding, to be sure," the lady pronounced with a decided sniff. "And suitable manners—that, I cannot do without. I abhor the backward ways of the local rustics."

"I must have my share in this as well," concurred Lady Catherine. "Let us not forget a proper education. Insupportable how so many youths these days are suffered to carry on, uncouth and with no thought for duty and family dignity." She flicked a contemptuous glance my way, then—"All that is nothing to the deplorable practice of neglecting the upbringing of young ladies. Who shall be the keepers of decency if even mothers cannot be troubled to restrain their daughters and commend to them all that is proper? I abhor such ignorance, and that is why I always exhort Anne to constant study of the disciplines she was taught."

"All these virtues must make for agreeable company, indeed," Elizabeth surmised.

"But not 'good' company?" Lady Matlock asked. "You are very sly in your omission, Miss Bennet, but you must have some additional qualities to define the term."

"I have, indeed. I am a great lover of much conversation, and I find it most pleasant when my companions are clever, well-informed people of an agreeable nature." She smiled faintly as she finished, and between measured blinks, her eyes found me.

A warmth stirred in my breast, a breath of something sweet and enticing that I could not resist. "And to all this," I suggested, "one must add something more substantial. A just and upright character, in whose confidence and benevolence one may never be in doubt." I watched—could not help it—and was gratified by the pleasure glowing in her cheeks.

"You are quite wrong," Lady Matlock decided. "I am afraid what you describe is not 'good' company at all—it is the *best*."

"All this talk of company," complained Lady Catherine, "but no one holds any standard. I should rather keep to my own counsel and not be bothered with indiscriminate guests turning up. I choose my companions with more care."

Elizabeth appeared to smother her amusement, her gaze flitting to Mrs Gardiner as the older lady twitched a brow in warning.

"What can you mean, Lady Catherine?" Georgiana asked—the first time she had joined the general conversation since I had entered the room.

Lady Catherine glared in astonishment at this show of boldness, but Georgiana simply gazed back, the picture of innocence.

"I mean this very thing," Lady Catherine snorted. "How shall I take pleasure in the attendance of guests when at every moment I am to expect some manner of affront? Young ladies suffered to carry on their impertinence in the company of their betters, no proper guidance. I blame these modern, romantic notions. Think of it! I heard of a family—" here, she dropped her chin and narrowed her eyes at Elizabeth—"that had *five* daughters. No sons at all—apparently the mother had not the decency to provide an heir—and the daughters were permitted to gad about without escort or thought for propriety. And no governess! All five out at once, and impressing their wanton ways on the entire neighbourhood. How shall any respectable ladies not be corrupted by such weak-minded company?"

Elizabeth was, by now, valiantly struggling to contain a peal of laughter. Perhaps others would not have known, could not have seen her mirth, but to one who had studied her ways, it was as clear as Lady Catherine's disdain. She caught my eye, and my own gaze dwelt a long while on that faint crease just beside her mouth. "With all due respect, Lady Catherine," she reasoned, "if such ladies are so irresolute that one feeble companion can sway them, one wonders whether their respectability truly was so faultless as you claim."

"You are very free with your opinions, Miss Bennet," Lady Catherine accused.

"I only speak as I find, your ladyship."

"And what is your feeling on an impressionable young lady who might be led astray by unscrupulous or vulgar friends?" Lady Milton asked, with a decided sneer in her voice.

Elizabeth shifted her eyes to Lady Milton, but in so doing, her gaze swept over me. Was it my imagination, or did she slow for that fraction of a second?

"Perhaps it would be better if I knew to what sort of young lady you referred. Has she already a good character? Has she any able protectors? Let us know all the particulars, so I might answer you as accurately as I may."

Lady Milton's cheek twitched slightly, and her tone was brittle when she answered. "A young lady of good family and moderate looks, possessing a substantial dowry and no experience of the world. What protection she does have is, at best, uneducated in the ways of feminine arts, and at worst, wilfully ignorant of the young lady's shortcomings."

"You submit a troubling prospect, Lady Milton," Elizabeth answered after a moment. "But you have not described for me the young lady's character, so I must make my own assumptions. I shall then believe that she is a gentle girl, quite modest and innocent with an engaging aspect and an honest heart. Such a young lady presents both a vulnerability and a strength."

"A strength?" Lady Matlock interjected with an amused tilt of her head. "This intrigues me very much. Do go on, Miss Bennet."

"Why, her manner renders her at once more vulnerable to those who would seek to manipulate her and more enchanting to those who would befriend her. It is likely that she has attracted both sorts in equal measure, and therefore, as many as would do her harm, she has just the same number who would defend her. As to her guardian, though you claim this person is untutored, his blindness to the girl's shortcomings is, in fact, the highest compliment he can pay her, for it is an assurance of his devotion to his charge. I am certain such a person must hold the young lady's best interests dear to his heart and would not suffer any real harm to come to her."

Lady Matlock was chuckling low in her throat, but her lips remained pursed, her eyes speculatively narrowed. "An intriguing argument you make, Miss Bennet."

"Indeed," sighed Lady Milton indifferently. She had resumed the examination of her glove tips and appeared to have done with challenging Elizabeth's wit. Even Lady Catherine and Anne were frowning and mute, staring across the room at no object in particular.

Georgiana, however, had silently clasped Elizabeth's hand, and her lashes were dewy as their fingers squeezed each other. Elizabeth lifted her eyes to me, and I met them with a congratulatory wink. To my queen, the victory.

"Elizabeth," Mrs Gardiner suggested in a low voice, "perhaps it is time we bade Miss Darcy our adieux."

"You are not leaving so soon?" Lady Matlock protested.

"I am afraid we must, your ladyship." Elizabeth and her aunt rose, and the rest of the room did likewise.

A panic surged in my breast; one I had not anticipated. I had made my farewells, kissed her fair image a hundred times in my heart, but this unexpected gift, this last moment of her gracing my home, had undone all my carefully wrought defences. I waited by, watching as everyone else took their leave of my ravishing one, and struggled like a child against unwonted sobs. I followed as Georgiana walked with her guests into the outer hall, hoping for just one more word, away from my aunts and cousins and their imperious ways.

Mrs Gardiner curtsied to me, and as she raised up again, there was a firmness in her look—caution, admonition, concern—but it was not without a degree of kindness that made me wish I might have merited her esteem. As she turned away, Elizabeth came to me at last.

She looked as if she would speak, but only drew a trembling breath and dipped her head.

I extended my hand. "Miss Elizabeth. We were honoured by your call," I murmured in a low voice.

She hesitated, then her gloved fingertips slid over mine as she curtsied. "Thank you, Mr Darcy."

I released her hand and stepped back, but she seemed to collect herself and leaned forward for some desperate confession. "I wished to tell you that I did receive another caller yesterday afternoon. A Lady Benedict."

My heart froze in my chest, and my next words sounded stretched and unnatural. "What came of it?"

"Nothing. She tried to introduce herself as a concerned stranger who had heard my name brought up and sought to give me warning. I... I am afraid I may have lost my temper."

I glanced to Mrs Gardiner, who was bowing her head and touching the backs of her fingers to her mouth. Her eyes were crinkled with laughter, but she composed herself quickly.

Elizabeth was still searching my face, and I longed to know precisely how she had blasted Lady Benedict. My Elizabeth must have been a fearsome thing to behold! It was an image that must remain purely in my imagination, but oh, what I would have given to know it all! Instead, I only nodded. "I am grateful to hear you were not taken in."

Her brow dimpled. "No. But my faith in another has been strengthened." She drew a shaken breath and curtseyed. "I must go now."

"Wait!" I almost cried out as she turned away, but my voice was husky and raw. She hesitated, and I stumbled about for some words to make her linger... only one moment would suffice. Anything so I might look on her for just a little longer! "I—I wish it were in my power to attend the wedding. Do convey my well wishes to the bride and groom?"

She glanced down and her smooth cheek dimpled in a smile. "You will be missed, sir. Perhaps your plans may change, and you will be able to offer your congratulations in person."

"I am not without hope, Miss Elizabeth."

She looked up one last time. Amber and emerald danced in her eyes, dark velvet lashes fell just once—an acknowledgment and a promise. "Goodbye, Mr Darcy."

I returned to the drawing room with Georgiana by my side. The room, and the voices therein, merely echoed in my ears as we resumed our places and tried, with sympathetic glances at one another, to rejoin the conversation.

"Well, I cannot abide such conceit," Lady Milton was declaring with a wave of her lace. "The idea that such a girl could sit in that very sofa, speak with such cheek and still remain ignorant of what we were truly talking of!"

I narrowed my eyes and my fists clenched behind my back.

"Obstinate, headstrong girl," grumbled Lady Catherine. "She knew very well that you were denouncing her. She simply did not heed, and is incapable of being corrected. I do not wonder now that Collins did not choose her. Georgiana, I absolutely insist that you cease any further contact with that hedonistic minx."

My sister gasped, but rather than desperately seeking my support, she took a moment to gather her thoughts. Her brow knotted, and she wetted her lips before making a careful reply. "Miss Elizabeth has been my friend—a better and truer friend than I have found elsewhere." She blinked slowly and did not fail to gaze significantly back at our aunt with her response.

Lady Catherine huffed in dismay. "You see, Darcy, what poor company has done already! Why, the girl is becoming as impertinent as that Bennet hoyden!"

"I do see, and there is nothing in Georgiana's conduct to chastise," I declared. "Moreover, Elizabeth Bennet is no hoyden. She was a guest in my home, as you are now. In my mind, that makes her your equal. As such, I will hear no insult to her."

Lady Matlock had remained silent, but that silver head of hers was inclined in some deep thought, her lips drawn and her finger tapping the side of her chair. "Indeed. I find Miss Elizabeth's society would be no discredit. No discredit at all."

CHAPTER 20

That February began as cheerless and grey as most months by that name, but for me, it seemed a time of rest before a new beginning. Perhaps it was simply my many years at Pemberley—watching the slow greening of tender grass after the winter, the tiny spikes of daffodils boldly peeking through the remnants of snow—but as I looked out of my window into the sodden and dismal world, I was not without some spark of newness stirring in my breast.

I spent more time in that first week enjoying my sister's company than I had ever done. I could not describe why it seemed natural for us to seek each other whenever we had our leisure, but for a change, I saw her far more than did Mrs Younge. It was not that we engaged in deep conversation or did anything of import. I believe we merely found comfort in being in the same room. Often, we simply sat at opposite ends of the sofa and read, trading volumes of poetry. Occasionally, Georgiana would turn to her paints, while I resumed an old hobby, long ago abandoned, of tying fishing lures. The material point was that we were easy with one another, and I believed—it was no vanity on my part to observe—that my sister grew bolder with each passing day.

Great was her elation the morning we received word that her

chaise was complete, and ready to be delivered. My coachman inspected it in every detail and pronounced it fit, so I ordered the horses and we prepared to go out for a first drive. Georgiana had asked for it to be painted white—a more appropriate colour than the black I usually requested, for it was of lighter build than many of its type. I had purposed it for her own use about Town, but I did not desire for it to be serviceable only for one task, such a pleasure phaeton only good for sunny drives to the park. It was, therefore, also suitable for short journeys and inclement weather.

"Is it really to be my own, Fitzwilliam?" she gushed as she admired the supple red leather, the brilliant brass, and the polished sheen of the paint.

"It is. You ought to have the liberty of your own vehicle, particularly as you are now going out more."

"But there are three other carriages to choose from. It was not necessary, Fitzwilliam. You do spoil me so!"

"Not so much as you deserve. I am doing what I can to make amends for this past year, Georgiana. You ought to have been taken from school sooner, perhaps even given your own establishment in Bath or Ramsgate or Lyme. Father always intended something of that kind for you, and it had been my original desire to carry out his wishes."

"Truly? I should have thought he would have wanted me to remain with family—perhaps one of my aunts for a year or so."

I chuckled quietly. "He knew them well, and he knew you. I fancy he meant for you to experience a bit of liberty from the family's expectations before you were thrust into the midst of them."

She giggled and spontaneously clasped my hand. "I was terrified of Aunt Matlock, but she is not half so dreadful as I once thought. I am still quite frightened of our uncle, though. And I do not think I could survive a week if I had to stay in the same house as Lady Milton." She shuddered, and I could not help but to offer a sympathetic laugh.

When we returned to the house, Georgiana immediately sought out Mrs Younge, and, with my blessing, took her companion out for a drive. I retired to my study and asked for the day's correspondence while I took my tea. They came together—the tea hot and black as tar, with just a hint of sweetness.

I savoured the dark elixir, gazing down into its shadowy depths. Intrigue, there was; richness, fullness, but something was missing. Perhaps I had lost my taste for the bitter. I dropped another full lump of sugar into the cup, then tested it, and found it precisely to my liking. Earthy and flavourful, yet uninhibited by any trace of the acrid bite to which I had become accustomed. *Complex and sweet...* I sighed and leaned back in my chair a moment as I finished my cup and dreamed of what might have been.

When I at last set my empty cup aside, I began to sort the day's letters. The earl had sent over a note, asking to speak with me at my earliest convenience. Like as not, he required another lord's support in some political matter and wished me to call on the miscreant's homely daughter. I frowned but schooled my hand and managed to send a reply that was civil and accommodating. I would go, I would attend my family duty, but I would not be made to answer for each of his ambitions. My respect only went so far.

A letter from Benedict followed. I nearly crumpled it before opening it, but I forced myself to do the noble thing and read the blasted paper.

Darcy,

I should like a chance to settle certain matters. Let us raise the white flag, shall we?

Do not fear that I have developed any liking for you, or that I might expect to call you a friend. As Wickham says, you are equally capable of giving offence or pleasing as you choose, though I imagine the effort of the latter is not palatable to you. You may be easy, for I shall not require any displays of friendliness.

Surely, you can sympathise with the distress of being alienated from what family you have remaining to you. I believe you alone hold the power to clear up this mystery with my father's assets so I may again be at peace with my mother. Carlisle has been counselling me, as I am sure you must have guessed, and his belief is that you are as ignorant of the affair as I am. However, you were there. I am left simply to hope that you might be a man of honour and will truthfully divulge what you know.

I shall await your reply, and I pray you do not find me as hostile as you found my mother.

~R.B

.

I ROSE from my desk to wander to the window. Could the vermin be in earnest? Was it possible he asked in good faith? It would be a first.

Such a humble note left me no alternative, lest I prove myself to be an ogre and a tyrant. I was no such thing; what was more, I was eager to lay the past to rest. If by a simple relation of the facts I could abolish the ever-growing rancour between us, I would do it, and gladly.

I was not without my reservations—after all, it was not as though there were anything new that I could tell which he could not have heard a dozen times already. But, perhaps a display of goodwill might suffice to end our feud and put the past behind me once and for all. I gazed some minutes more out the window; then, my resolve fixed, I sat down to pen an appropriate reply.

Only after all this did I permit myself to look at the last letter in the stack. My eye had caught the script when the letters had first arrived, and by no means could I fail to recognise Bingley's blotched and hurried penmanship. Only a monumental feat of self-will had compelled me to leave that letter on the bottom, but I was glad of it now. If I was to be so brutally chastised again by a man who seldom corrected even his dogs, I would clear my head of other cares first, so I might meditate on his just reproofs with all due solemnity.

Darcy,

I cannot tell you how delighted I was to receive your latest letter. I wished to write and give you the news myself, but I was uncertain how it would be received. God bless Miss Elizabeth for relating it all to you, and for confirming that you truly were as pleased as your letter reports.

I am the happiest man alive, of that I am certain. My dear Jane has made me the most blessed of men, and we look forward to perfect joy in our marriage. No one else knows, so I will tell you now; I spoke with Mr Bennet the very morning after you left Hertfordshire, but he requested that I wait to make a public declaration until a month or two had passed, and the events of the ball had been somewhat forgotten. I see the wisdom in it now, though you may imagine I fretted a great deal. My dear Jane is patient, and none could speak ill of her, but I imagine it was not her reputation or her feelings that concerned her father. I think, rather, he wished to be certain that I was as earnest and steadfast in my suit as I represented myself to be, and at length, I was able to persuade him.

Darcy, I have missed you sorely. Not a day has passed when I did not wish for the company of my friend or grieve the manner in which we parted. I was angry; I do not recall when I have ever been more so. But I also pitied you, for after you had gone, I thought of nothing else but the deplorable events of the last year or better. I am not sorry for speaking in defence of my dearest Jane, but I regret losing my patience with you, my friend. That your behaviour was so much the reverse of your accustomed character ought to have served to make me understand what you must have been suffering.

If you can speak to me again with equanimity, I would ask a very great favour of you. Will you stand up at my wedding? I have spoken with Jane on the matter, and, I suspect, her sister has added her own insights. You may be assured that she shares my hope for reconciliation and adds her own wishes that you might consider it an earnest and heartfelt request.

The ceremony is set for the twenty-fifth, and if you are able to come a week or even two before that date, I shall be eager to see you. I remain your friend,

Charles Bingley

I READ the letter thrice more, in such a rapture of jubilation that I nearly leapt from my chair and cried out in grateful triumph. Rather than startle all the maids, however, I set hurriedly about penning a reply. I accepted, and answered with the most profuse confession of my own sins to ever reach masculine ears.

I paused for only a moment, and that was to consult my calendar. If I saw both Benedict and the earl the next day, and settled certain other matters on the day following, I could easily arrive in Hertfordshire two weeks before the wedding.

I called for a footman to take all three responses at once, and paid an extra shilling for the express rider to Hertfordshire. Then I asked for another cup of tea and relished the darksome nectar by the fire with my new book of poetry until Georgiana returned.

"AH, DARCY," the earl grunted amiably as I entered his study the next morning. "Very good of you to come. Sit down... sherry?" He gestured to the decanter at the sideboard, but I shook my head.

"No, thank you, sir. You wished to speak with me?"

"Indeed." He drew out an elaborate cigar tin from his drawer and tapped out one of the brown lengths for himself, then offered one to me.

I waved this off as well, but the hairs raised on the back of my neck. There could be only one reason for him to seem so hospitable. He wanted something.

"Now, Darcy," he puffed, "what do you know about Hayworth?"

"Very little. I have never met him."

"A shame. What have you heard of him?"

I regarded my uncle carefully. "Whig. Wrote a labour bill that passed last session. Drives a fine curricle. Frequents Ascot in the summer, during which time his wife is rumoured to entertain her own... guests."

My uncle began to chuckle, the cigar clenched between his teeth. "I thought you knew very little."

"I do not know your interest in him, nor why you ask me. I presume you are hoping to gain his support, and that he has a daughter."

"Darcy," he scoffed and released a grey cloud of smoke. "If I wished to unite with every powerful family in the House, I would need far more nephews. No, no, the reason I ask is because he had a most intriguing tale. He is on the board of a certain bank, and he made some remark in passing about a particular gentleman—also on the board—whose doings seemed a bit suspect."

I shifted back in my chair; my face impassive. "What does this have to do with me?"

"Patience—I have not done. Now, Hayworth has been sniffing it out, for he would like nothing better than to bring this other gentleman up on charges but has had no luck. No one has been able to prove that this fellow might have dealt dishonestly, but there was a peculiar incident two months ago, where one of the bank's favoured clients suddenly pulled out his investments, with no explanation. Hayworth found a rather cantankerous letter of withdrawal written by the gentleman himself—not his solicitor, mind you—that made it sound as if the bank itself had caused some offence… need I name the author of said letter?"

I raised a brow. "You believe I can give evidence against someone on the board of the bank?"

"I was greatly hoping you could. The man in question, if you must know, is a thorn in my side already. A Whig, to be sure, but in name only. Never on the right side of the fence on any matter. I can respect a man with convictions who will put up a decent argument, but this fellow's only conviction is that his pockets ought to be as well-lined as possible."

"I thought that was the case more often than not," I retorted.

My uncle shook the ash from his cigar and pointed it at me. "You will not find a clean pair of hands in the entire House, but while some are merely covered in grime, others are dripping with blood."

I shook my head. "There is a vast difference between unscrupulous accounting and murder."

"Why do you think most murders are committed?" The earl examined his cigar in the light, then stubbed it out and leaned forward on his desk. "Hayworth wants to know why you withdrew from the bank so suddenly. What information did you have? You must have known something."

"Truthfully? Nothing at all. I received a signed letterhead insisting that I remove my accounts. This occurred during the same week that my solicitor left my employ."

The earl narrowed his eyes. "Do you still have the letter?"

"Naturally."

"And what of this solicitor? Did he have connections at your bank?"

"Daniels. No, in fact he was quite young, but I had a good recommendation of him, and at the time, was too impatient to look further. I settled on him and am sorry now that I did, because he proved untrustworthy. He broke confidence and has given evidence against me which was imagined to be harmful. You may be assured that I have taken actions to have his license revoked."

"Mmm. There is nothing else?"

"No... although I did question the calculation of a certain percentage last fall. I nearly forgot about it, for it was only a minor error, or so I thought."

"And when was this?"

I squinted at the far wall in thought. "Just after I came to London from Derbyshire. The day before the party at Colchester's. I left for Hertfordshire the next morning and thought no more of it. I never did receive any answer to my inquiry."

My uncle drew a long breath, his eyes no more than thin black lines and his hand covering his mouth. "Most curious, indeed."

"I presume that mine were the only accounts withdrawn."

"Perhaps you were the only one to notice something amiss. In any case, I would like to have that letter, and anything else you can think of."

"Certainly, but may I ask the name of this gentleman you mean to ruin?"

The earl frowned. "The present Viscount Wallingford, Percival Ramsey. I believe you are friends with his eldest son."

~

WHEN I RETURNED HOME, Georgiana was out—nothing at all surprising, given her new freedom. I was glad of it, for she would have seen my vexation and made herself unhappy over it all afternoon.

I had no affection for Wallingford, and would be pleased to see one more dishonest man brought low. Still, I had not settled it with myself that my own uncle was being perfectly truthful with me. I found the letter from the bank and had it carried to Matlock House, then proceeded to brood over the whole affair for the next hour.

Precisely at one o'clock, as my note had specified, Benedict arrived. He appeared slightly out of breath, as if he had walked all the way, but I did confirm later that he had arrived in his carriage. I seated myself behind my desk and offered him the chair before it, then steepled my fingers and waited.

"About time we sat down to talk things over," he began. "I have not been able to say a thing but that it gets misrepresented."

I lifted a brow. "That must be distressing."

"Indeed, it is. You cannot know what it is, to constantly hear the most abject falsehoods about oneself and know that no man of sense would give ear to the truth."

It needed all my patience not to laugh outright at his ignorance. "What did you come to say, Benedict?"

"You despise me. I know it, and to be truthful, I am not fond of you. However, I expect you may have had a poor impression of me when we finally met—you know, grieving as I was—and perhaps I did nothing to improve it when we would see each other in town. I found all my solace in the bottle, and I confess that I gave a fearful accounting of myself."

"You did."

"But you did little better," he cried, "and you were stone sober. I have never met a more hostile fellow!"

"Did you have a point to make," I asked testily, "or did you merely come here to rattle on your trivial laments?"

"Ah," he raised a finger, "I did. My mother, do you see. She believes there was something belonging to my father that had gone missing, and blames you for it."

"And do you?"

He shrugged. "Naturally, what else is there to think? But I have no proof, nor am I likely to get it."

"Because there is none. And, as the burden rests with you," I rose from my chair, "I am afraid we have nothing more to discuss."

"One more thing, Darcy, and this I must know."

There was such an urgency in his voice, an unaccustomed vulnerability about his face, that I slowly resumed my seat. "What is it?"

He leaned forward. "My sister, Elizabeth. What truly happened?"

I fell silent, my eyes resting on the polished surface of my desk as the clock ticked away. I felt my own pulse quicken; my nostrils flared, and even my palms began to sweat. "The babe came too early. The midwife did all within her power, but there was a... a rupture of some sort. Nothing could have saved her."

His face was ashen, but he thinned his lips. "That is not what I asked. What made you marry her in the first place?"

This, I could not answer so easily. I stared at him as that old nausea roiled within—all my helpless wrath, my visceral repugnance. And yet, like a silent friend slipping her hand into mine, some peace came to soothe me, even as I suffered the demon who battered my very ribs from inside. The vile one, the one who had so thoroughly blackened my life still disgusted me, and always would, but her grip of terror upon me had begun to slip. The hands of the clock marched on, and I began to breathe just a little easier.

He edged further up in his seat and placed his hands on my desk, his voice low and shaken. "You loathed her—everyone knew it. Good lord, I could scarcely abide her myself! My mother petted her, shielded her from everything, but you have no need to tell me what she was. It was true, what they said about her—about the babe being some other man's by-blow? Everyone says it. What the devil made you take her?"

"As you say…" I rasped, "the very devil himself. Fear…" I swallowed and steadied myself. "Look here, Benedict, I have already told you everything that is in my power to tell. What more would you have of me?"

"The truth! All of it! Am I not entitled?" He was out of the chair now, leaning forward on my desk. All his beseeching and pitiful agitation had now vanished. In its place was a bitter scowl, a sneer of contempt and challenge.

I rose to meet him, glaring back from my full height and with all the haughtiness of the Darcy heritage. "I am afraid you will find as many different versions of the truth as there are people to tell it."

"Darcy," he shook his head, his teeth beginning to glimmer, "I do not think you understand. I spoke with my mother two days ago. She received me at last, and she has an exhaustive list of complaints about you. The missing shares are only the beginning, for some of what she had to say…" he curled his lips back and inched closer to me, "is perfectly damning."

"Then let her accuse me to my face and be done with it. She has been demanding more money for months, and thinks with her idle threats that I will at last give in. Did she tell you that? Did she tell you what she is already receiving, and the debts that I cleared on her behalf? Or what about her consort? They are a well-suited pair, if I am not mistaken."

"You dare accuse my mother of taking a lover!"

"Her habits were no secret before your father's death. How should they be any shock to you now? But did you know it was your old friend Wickham who has been seducing her with his lies?"

He paled. "I will cut out your tongue for that, Darcy."

"Ask him yourself. You have known Wickham almost as long as I, and if you do not come to the same conclusion, you are a fool. So long as he thinks there is a fortune to be had from a woman, he will continue to bend her ear. But I have done enough, and will do no more. I have no qualms with showing you what I settled upon her—what *I* did for her! Not her ignoble husband, who ought to have made some provision, and not her son, who seems to have misplaced his own wealth." I straightened; my fists balled at my side. "I do not believe we can have more to say to one another."

He pushed back from my desk. "I only asked for the truth, Darcy."

"That is not what you asked. You wished for me to confess to some wrong, to give you some bit of information with which to ruin me. Very well, I shall give it, but you shall be disappointed, for the only wrong I ever did was to set eyes on your home estate in the first place. I believe you know your way out."

CHAPTER 21

I stared across the table at my sister, my breakfast forgotten before me. "What do you mean, you do not wish to attend the wedding? I thought you would be eager to see your friend again."

"So I am, but we will stay at Netherfield, will we not?" She looked studiously down, spreading a bit of jam on her scone.

"Of course."

"And you will not stay after the wedding. That would not be seemly, would it?"

"No," I confessed. "It will be a short stay, only two weeks, but why would you not wish to come? You have always been fond of Bingley, and I thought you were friendly with Jane Bennet."

"But I am not friendly with Miss Bingley," she offered in a low voice. She raised her eyes hesitantly, her teeth bared in a cringe.

"Be that as it may, she is tolerable. You have always borne up before."

She nibbled thoughtfully on her scone. "But if I am there, she becomes *in*tolerable. You know she does—always following me and telling me how wonderful I am at everything. I cannot bear it, Fitzwilliam! I cannot leave my room without her looking for me and trying to flatter me somehow. I try to play the piano and study some of my hard pieces—you know how I sometimes work through the difficult bits. I cannot even touch it but she and Mrs Hurst come to applaud my playing."

"Georgiana," I pinched the bridge of my nose, "all this may be true, but it never stopped you before. What is the real reason?"

She pursed her lips and traced circles on her plate with her fork, refusing to look at me.

"Georgiana?" I asked in a more demanding tone.

"Well, it is only that I am not even out, so I cannot attend some of the dinners and parties they will have, and you know, Mrs Younge is not likely to be comfortable among people with whom she is not acquainted."

"I disagree, for that exact scenario is precisely why I hired her."

My sister dropped her fork and proceeded to fidget with her napkin. "And Lady Matlock said I should start being fitted for a summer wardrobe—walking dresses, morning gowns, and I shall surely need a new riding habit. Did you notice that I am a full half inch taller than I was in November?"

"Georgiana." I crossed my arms and levelled a hard look at her.

"Oh, very well," she sighed. "I do not wish to go because I will be in the way between you and Elizabeth."

"In the…" I stammered, my eyes narrowed as if I did not understand—as if the very mention of my love's delicious name had not sent my heart plunging into my stomach.

Georgiana's mouth curved. "You heard me, Fitzwilliam, and do not pretend you did not! You have been silly as a goose around her ever since Netherfield. At first, I thought you hated her, but when I saw you watching her that day we went ice skating, I put it together. And then, there is that little bit of ribbon you carry in your pocket."

"Ribbon! In my pocket?"

She pointed, her clever smile widening to a wicked grin. "The left one. You toy with it whenever you are reading, and even sometimes when I play for you. Confess it, Fitzwilliam!"

"I do not deny that I think highly of her."

"Think *constantly* of her, that is more like it," she giggled, with all the precocious charm of fifteen.

"She is an enchanting woman," I offered defensively. "Clever and well-informed, able to converse about more than fashions and the weather. Anyone would value her company."

"Yes," she nodded, "or, at least, *you* certainly do."

"You do, as well. Come now, you have said yourself what a gracious friend she has been, and has she not inspired you to better confidence? She possesses a remarkable air about her. I believe there are few upon whom she would not make an impression."

Georgiana covered her mouth and a dreadfully unladylike snort issued from behind her fingers. "I doubt Lady Milton and Lady Catherine will soon forget meeting her."

I could not help laughing myself. It was true, was it not? All of it—I had been smitten from the moment she first walked by me in the Assembly, fine eyes sparkling in amusement at my foolishness when she ought to have been offended. The terror that had struck my heart in that moment, and the bitter enmity that followed were nothing more than my own vanity and loathsome stubbornness, and my unwillingness to confess what my soul had known at first glance.

"Will you make her an offer, Fitzwilliam?"

I drew a long breath and regarded my impertinent sister for a moment. "If I were ever welcomed to do so; yes."

"Why would she not welcome you? Did you not know that she loves you?"

A rush of blood pounded in my ears, burning the back of my neck. I felt hot and clammy all at once, unable to swallow or to speak. Gradually, and after much struggle, I forced my breathing to steady and my fists to unlock. Unreasoning buffoon that I was! "I am afraid you must be mistaken," I replied unsteadily. "Miss Elizabeth cannot love me—it is impossible."

She sighed impatiently. "You really are a goose, Fitzwilliam! Have you not seen how she smiles differently at you than she does at everyone else?"

"Indeed, I have, and you are quite wrong. She does so not because of any affection for me, but because she must force herself to civility in my presence. You were not privy to all our conversations, but allow me to assure you that she does *not* cherish some secret *amour* for me."

"Well, what about all the effort she put into helping me find your Christmas gift?"

"That was done as a favour to you, not to me."

Georgiana shook her head. "You did not see her enthusiasm, the way her eyes lit up, and she began to scheme about that book. She thought you would like it, decided it must be yours, and I think she would have walked all the way to Longbourn if she had needed to, just to bring it here."

"What you interpret as devotion is merely her natural generosity. At best, she views me as a project—an exercise in patience, if you will, and I maintain that her interest truly lies in you, not me."

Georgiana pinched her lips, a sliver of annoyance beginning to show. "How silly and blind can you be, Fitzwilliam? She is different when you are around. Oh, I do not know how to say it. She teases more, she is quicker and funnier, and she touches her hair all the time. And she watches you. Not constantly, not like Miss Bingley, but I always have the impression that even when she is facing away from you, she is perfectly aware of everything you are doing. It is something in her eyes—like she is looking back rather than ahead. That is the only way I know to describe it."

"Georgiana—" I dug my fingers into my own eyes for a moment, hoping the abuse might clear the rosy vapours from before them so I could see clearly. "You are a most affectionate sister, and as such, you think and feel what you believe everyone else must. Let me assure you, if I went to Miss Elizabeth at this very moment and fell to my knee, she would run from the room. I know this; it is a fact. I know also that it is all my own doing, and perhaps, given time, I might find a way to overcome her profound dislike of me. Perhaps we might even become friends, but—"

"But if I went to Hertfordshire with you now, you would see her less," Georgiana interrupted.

"How so? I would hardly see her at all, if it were not for you."

"That is here in London," she reasoned. "There, you will have Mr Bingley and Miss Bennet with you, and they will still require occasional chaperons, will they not?"

"You forget, we will also have Miss Bingley, Mr and Mrs Hurst, and any number of Bennet sisters. It seems to me that if you are so determined to secure for me time with Miss Elizabeth, you would do better to come, and perhaps your devious mind can contrive something to your liking."

"Nothing easier, Fitzwilliam. Miss Bingley and the Hursts do not care for the out of doors at this time of year. Miss Elizabeth is too kind to exclude *me*, but if she wishes to see you, Fitzwilliam—and I believe she does—I trust she is quite clever enough to find a way to evade *them*."

I closed my mouth and regarded her for a moment. "You have thought a long while about this."

"I am quite determined, Fitzwilliam. If the choice be either a short stay in Hertfordshire, seeing my friend only occasionally, or an entire summer at Pemberley with her as a sister, I know which I should choose."

"You are so certain! I am afraid you are bound for disappointment. Even if Miss Elizabeth does nurture some… fascination for me… and I think it unlikely…" I caught my breath and looked away, unable to confess while meeting her gaze. "She does not trust me."

I heard her rise, caught the shadow of her movement as she came around the table to embrace me from behind, as she had done in her days of girlhood. "I was right about you loving her, was I not?" she whispered in my ear. "You cannot even deny it."

I emitted a short, wry laugh. "I cannot."

"Then, perhaps I am right about her, too. Just go, Fitzwilliam. And be sure to write to me, just as soon as she accepts you."

MY TREPIDATION upon approaching Netherfield was overcome only by the hopes my sister's naive suppositions had given rise to. A burning sensation simmered in my throat as my carriage rolled into Meryton, and then my vision blurred when we passed the turn that would have taken us to Longbourn.

I leaned close to the window, my breath fogging the glass until I impatiently wiped the mist away. Perhaps some romantic fancy had persuaded me that I would pass her out walking, and she would wave at my carriage, and I would stop and go to her, and in a few moments, we could settle all our differences, and…

But the carriage rolled on, its progress unimpeded by my boots as I pressed them against the floor, like a child dragging its feet. When I arrived at Netherfield, it was with a tumult of emotion storming my breast. Bingley was standing on the steps, but until the door opened and I ducked my head out, I could only see the lower half of his body through the window.

"Darcy!" He rushed down, and almost before I had even touched the gravel, he had clasped both my forearms. "Punctual as always! I cannot tell you how pleased I am to see you!"

He released me, and I clapped his shoulder, my expression as sincere as I could make it. "Bingley, I am honoured. Truly."

The flesh about his eyes tightened and his effusive smile sobered to something more earnest. "Let us go in and have a drink, shall we?"

Bingley directed a footman to take my hat and greatcoat, and I followed him to the billiards room, of all places. "Caroline was dressing to come down and greet you," he explained. "I think she believes that you are typically half an hour late, like everyone else, so she is not ready yet. She will be down directly, but she will not come after us in here."

"You have become crafty since I have been away," I observed.

"I have had to. Caroline was not best pleased by my attentions to Jane, and neither was Louisa. Just getting out the door without them to call on her at Longbourn has required daily undertakings so onerous, I liken it to Nelson's siege of Malta."

I laughed heartily and sipped the brandy—a fine vintage, one he usually reserved only for his favourite guests. "Bingley, regarding Miss Bennet," I began.

"No, stop there, Darcy. I believe I have the whole of it from Miss Elizabeth, and I would rather not taint your arrival with woeful arguments or regrets. You are here, and it is all settled."

"I am afraid that is not sufficient for me. I shall never be easy until something is done to lift this cursed cloud from over my head. I was an ass—you were perfectly in the right in every respect."

He swallowed his drink slowly, pensively, and lowered his glass. "But I regret speaking as I did to you. Good heavens, you are my oldest friend, it is not as if I wished to lose that again."

"Again?"

"Yes, well…" he looked down. "I thought I should never see you again after you married before. I thought no one would ever see you again."

"Hmm. Nor did I."

"And, so," he reasoned, shrugging, "I knew you were a bit agitated. You have never been changeable before, but it was as if you carried a great thorn under your shirt that would press and provoke you at the oddest times. I thought a bit of gaiety, a little of our old sociability, might be the best thing a man could do for you."

"No. The best thing you could do for me was precisely what you did—to chastise me and make me see what a nefarious bastard I had been. I did not thank you for it then, but I do now."

"Well, then." He raised his glass. "To all-night balls and painful mornings-after. May we weather this storm as handily as we have others."

I returned the salute, and we drank together, falling into companionable quiet for some minutes.

"Bingley," I asked at length, "what of Miss Bennet? Shall she be troubled to see me? I would not distress the lady just before your wedding."

"She is well. Darcy, I cannot tell you what a jewel she is! Only yesterday when I took my leave, she pressed me to be certain you were properly welcomed. I had explained a bit to her—not much, not more than I could be sure of, but I did tell her that your marriage had left you quite unlike yourself. Gracious woman that she is, she expressed her hope that you would find happiness in a lady who could match you, and make you forget all the wretchedness of the past."

"That would be my wish, as well. You are marrying a kind and noble woman, Bingley. Would that all were so deserving of your good fortune."

"Do not give up hope, Darcy. What you must seek is a lady who is not afraid of confronting you, and who can go toe to toe with you when you err. Where you shall find her, I know not... or, perhaps..." He touched a finger to his chin, his brow furrowed. "No, impossible."

"If you thought to suggest your sister, I must protest," I grunted, then finished my brandy.

"In a manner of speaking, perhaps. Are you certain, Darcy? I should like to have you for a brother someday." This, he asked with a peculiar twinkle in his eye, a sly grin that was quite too devious for his typically open ways.

"Unless you were to suddenly change your loyalties to Georgiana rather than Miss Bennet, I do not see how it is possible for us to call one another brothers."

"Ah, well," he sighed. "Stranger things have happened."

"Oh, Mr Darcy, we are so delighted you could come back to us. Why, I was quite distressed that you went away before, without ever coming to one of my dinners. But Mr Bingley I am sure, can tell you that we are all quite agreeable here, and we do wish you would join us one evening."

Mrs Bennet clasped her hands like a girl as she preened before me. Bingley and I had called at Longbourn on this, the morning after my arrival, to pay my courtesies to the family. We had an entire circuit to perform, and I thought wryly that if every time a man went away, he must spend a week renewing old acquaintances, it was enough to make him never leave.

"You are very kind to offer, Mrs Bennet," I answered my hostess, but at every moment I was trying to peer over her head and beyond her. Each time my eyes would drift from her, she seemed so eager to discern the direction of my notice that she consistently got in the way. I gave up and looked squarely at her.

"But we were so sorry you went away before," the lady pouted. "I trust it must have been something dreadfully important."

"It could not be avoided, Mrs Bennet, but I am gratified by your welcome." These were my words. My thoughts, however, ran to Elizabeth's depiction of the neighbourhood's sympathies after my shameful acquittal at the Netherfield Ball. Would Mrs Bennet have been so eager to receive me if Wickham had just graced her drawing room with his sorrowful face? But, there, had I not fairly purchased such disdain? Perhaps I ought to be grateful that the woman received me at all rather than nervous of her intentions.

As if she had read my mind, Mrs Bennet turned to admire her eldest daughter, standing beside Bingley at the hearth. "Is not my Jane the picture of radiance? The most beautiful bride in Hertfordshire she is sure to be, I am absolutely certain. Do you..." Here, she tilted her head and seemed to lean towards me intently. "Do you not think she is looking well?"

"Indeed, she is. Mr Bingley is a fortunate man," I answered, with not a trace of rancour. Even the most suspicious of listeners could have found no fault in my speech.

"Yes, quite fortunate, although I did think that honour would go to another." More lashes fluttered.

"Miss Bennet chose the most deserving man alive," I replied diplomatically.

"Ah, yes, and that is true. My Jane is very happy, and that is every mother's wish, of course. You truly think she is fortunate?"

"Certainly. Miss Bennet could not have found a more amiable man than my friend." Mrs Bennet was standing still for a moment, and I managed to set my eyes beyond her, on Elizabeth. She was looking away, her hands laced over her skirt as she stood near the tea cart.

"Oh, we all agree that Mr Bingley is amiable, of course!" Mrs Bennet continued. "But that is but one matter. My Jane deserves the finest, everything the finest. I certainly hope she does not find later that there might have been another who could have suited her better. You must think me a flighty matron, Mr Darcy, but it is only my hope that my dearest girl should be happy."

I stopped trying to look past Mrs Bennet and studied her for a moment. "I believe everyone who has ever been guardian of a young lady would share that wish, madam. If it is assurance you seek, there is no finer man in all the world than my friend."

"Oh, Mr Darcy, you are too charming!" she giggled, flipping her hand like a girl. "But what of Miss Darcy? She is not unwell? I hope not, for my Lizzy was terribly fond of her."

"She is quite well, and is eagerly awaiting my return to London."

"Oh," she protested, "You are not going away soon, I hope?"

"Just after the wedding, madam. I would not impose longer."

"Oh." Her voice dropped and her brow wrinkled in disappoint-ment. "Well, I suppose we shall just have to host you for a dinner here before the wedding. It is so dull now that the regiment have gone away. We are all quite despondent! My girls did fancy the red coats, and I thought that if any of them had a few thousand pounds of his own, at least one of my girls would have been quite well suited. It is such a pity about poor Mr Wickham's misfortunes."

My forehead wrinkled, and I thinned my lips.

"Oh, you must not know of it, Mr Darcy! Why, he had some great disappointment. Lydia knows more, I am sure, but it was something quite recent, for he had been expecting any day to have his hopes answered in some respect, but no such thing came to be. That, coupled with his great trial of… well, perhaps I shall not describe all to *you*, but do you know, this second let down absolutely broke the poor man's heart. I suppose you have heard that he found another to take his place and has gone back to London?"

I narrowed my eyes. "I had not heard."

"Oh, but let us not speak of him any longer. I say, Mr Darcy, is not my Lydia looking so well-grown since you went away?"

I turned politely to regard the girl. She was presently leaning over a table her sister Catherine was trying to paint, her bosom spilling from the top of her gown as she laughed in that donkeyish sort of way she had. "Lydia," her elder sister reprimanded her, "do sit back, you are smearing my paints!"

Indeed, it was so, for when the girl sat up, there was a great purple streak crossing her left breast. She looked down in a moment of dismay, then her mouth tugged into a leering smile. She pulled back her shoulders, dipped her chin, and boldly winked at me.

"Indeed," I coughed. "Quite well-grown."

"Ah…" Mrs Bennet was biting her lip. "My Catherine is truly lovely as well, do you not agree, Mr Darcy? And, of course, there is Mary. You know, there is no finer musician in all of Hertfordshire. But I am afraid my poor Lizzy is not quite in looks these days."

I lifted a single brow and wondered where the woman's eyes were. Elizabeth was more ravishing than ever, even hiding her face in rosy shame as she was. Each step was fox-like in its grace, each word as the sweet violin in my ears. "Miss Elizabeth is looking exceptionally well," I replied as evenly as I could, trying to keep the husky undertones from my voice.

"Oh, but she was so greatly diminished when she came away from London. It was the news of poor Mr Wickham going that did it, I am sure. Else she is overcome with concern for my brother, Mr Gardiner. Do you know, it is likely that he will lose his warehouse!"

"Lose his warehouse?" I asked swiftly, but Mrs Bennet was already shaking her head.

"Oh, but you mustn't be interested in that. Surely, you need more tea. Lizzy, dear, look sharp! Mr Darcy's cup is cold." Elizabeth's head came up, and she looked directly at me, then quickly away again as she obeyed her mother.

Mrs Bennet was leaning confidentially towards me. "It is a pity, but it is best that Lizzy serves the guests. Poor Lydia has not the patience for it, you know, but I am sure she never meant to ruin Mrs Long's gown. My dear Lydia has other qualities, as I am certain you must have noticed. She is far more entertaining to talk to than to have pour your drink, if you take my meaning, sir, but Lizzy should be quite steady with the tea pot."

"I thank you, madam." In gasping relief, I leapt at her permission to step away and approach Elizabeth at last. She was pouring studiously, those long lashes grazing her cheeks as if she were afraid to raise her eyes to me. She swirled the pot, coaxing the deep gold to rise from the depths to pour my drink, then proceeded to draw out a sugar lump and to break it.

I surprised her by staying her hand and taking the whole lump from her to drop it into my cup. Her lips curved, but still she did not look up.

"Would it be gluttonous of me to ask for a second lump?" I asked.

Her mouth stretched, and I could see she was biting back an earnest smile as she drew out more sugar. Green-flecked eyes flashed to me for an instant, then dropped again.

"Am I unwelcome, Miss Elizabeth? I had dearly hoped that would not be so."

She looked back up, as if startled. "Unwelcome, sir?"

"Yes, I have been here half an hour, and you have spoken to me only once, when I first arrived. I hope my presence does not distress you."

"Not at all, Mr Darcy."

"You *did* encourage me to write to Mr Bingley."

"I did, and I am glad you have done so. It has made him very happy." She was preparing a second cup now, and I hoped it was to be for herself, so that we could stand aside and drink together.

"Dare I hope he is not the only one to be made happy?" I asked boldly.

She stopped and seemed to catch her breath in the midst of pouring. "We ought always to rejoice when a friendship has been restored," she answered carefully. "Is your tea strong enough, Mr Darcy, or would you like a different cup?"

She looked up to me again, and I could not quite read what was in her eyes. I thought I had known them so well—each changeful shade, each eloquent subtlety, but this was a new light. I could not quite be easy in looking upon it.

"Thank you, Miss Elizabeth, it is perfectly satisfactory," I replied, slowly backing away.

She dipped her head. "You are welcome, Mr Darcy. Quite welcome."

I paused. Complicated Elizabeth. *Love, what did you mean by that?* I yearned to ask her, but she was already turning her attention to her younger sister Mary, who was looking up at me as if I would eat her alive. "Thank you again, Miss Elizabeth," I excused myself.

The only person in the room who was not engaged in some ridiculousness seemed to be Mr Bennet. Again, I noticed that he had been watching my entire exchange with his daughter, and I decided to approach, to try to discover precisely what he intended by that droll look in his eye each time he regarded me.

"Mr Darcy," he nodded as I came near.

I inclined my head. "Mr Bennet. I thank you for hosting us this afternoon."

"Oh, do not thank me, that was all Mrs Bennet. She has been going out into the streets as it were, pressing friend and stranger alike to come in and drink to the couple's happiness. Had I my way, this wedding nonsense would have been over and done with a month ago, and I left in peace in my library."

"I believe the purpose of such gatherings must be to bring pleasure to the engaged couple. Do you not agree?"

He chortled. "I presume they must, although I have tried to block out the memory of my own betrothal. You have more recent experience than I, so perhaps you can inform me."

I looked back at the man. Blue eyes twinkled with disturbing insight, but he simply raised his brows and waited for me to answer.

"I am afraid I cannot satisfy you, for upon the occasion of my first marriage, there were no such celebrations."

"No? My, my, Mr Darcy, however did you do without daily revelry of this sort?" Mr Bennet sipped from his cup with a smug look on his face and appeared to be watching someone across the room. "How very fascinating."

"Mr Bennet," I addressed him directly, "it has been brought to my attention that I was less than amiable when last we met. I would seek to make amends for any offence I may have caused you or your family."

"Would you!" Another sip from his cup. "I should have thought that book of poetry would have been quite enough evidence of good-will on my part. Or, perhaps you have read it by now, and you have come to believe the opposite. Such a dreary thing, that Hope poem. I much prefer Byron's cynicism to the romantic swooning of some milk sop. What do you think Mr Darcy?—for you have read both now. Which viewpoint is the more valid, the cynic or the optimist?"

I sipped from my own cup and considered. "If it is a question of validity, I should say both. But from the standpoint of edification, and the pleasure of soaking my spirits in one or the other, I should choose the latter."

"Indeed?" he chuckled. "Most curious."

He spoke no more, merely continuing to smirk to himself and gaze across the room as we stood beside one another.

"Mr Bennet," I said at length, "if I may, I should like to ask you a question."

"Pray do, Mr Darcy."

I turned to him, and then I fell mute. What I wanted to ask—what I died every minute to know—I had no right to speak of. I hesitated, then fumbled for some harmless question I might ask.

"Are... Mr and Mrs Gardiner planning to come celebrate Miss Bennet's nuptials?"

The man's nostrils flared with an indrawn breath as he regarded me speculatively. "We are hoping so. I understand you met them in Town."

"With much pleasure," I agreed.

Bennet narrowed his eyes again and his expression became even more enigmatic. "I hear you have a fondness for ice-skating on the Serpentine, Mr Darcy. Most amusing." He chortled again to himself as he drew another sip—exactly how large was his cup? I began to wonder if it was just as much of a prop as Lady Matlock's cane.

"Well, well," he decided after a moment, "no harm done. I look forward to speaking with you again during your stay, Mr Darcy."

He wandered away then, walking towards Elizabeth and dismissing me entirely. I watched after him, but he never looked back as he spoke to his daughter. I caught only occasional glances from her —veiled curiosity, open scepticism. I would have given a genuine fortune to know precisely what he was saying to her.

CHAPTER 22

I rode out the following dawn, borrowing one of Bingley's horses, as I had not brought my own. He did not accompany me, for he wished to call on Miss Bennet during the course of the morning. After my reception on the previous afternoon, I was less desirous of calling at Longbourn. What I really thirsted for was a chance to speak with Elizabeth. Without others present to humiliate either of us.

I trotted in the direction of Longbourn, for the weather had not yet turned for ill and I hoped—perhaps in vain—that she might be out that morning as well. It was her way, after all. If she had been a student of my habits when we both stayed at Netherfield, I had been doubly so of hers. She always walked out when it was not raining, and sometimes even when it did, but either her habits had changed, or I had missed her somehow.

Well… There had been little hope of success anyway. Disappointed, I turned my mount and started back over the fields by another way.

The paths were all familiar, for these were the ways we had taken on that dreadful ride. There was the tree I had tried to stare at, instead of her terror-stricken countenance. There was that slight hollow in the ground, where she had clutched at the reins when her horse took a larger step across a small creek. And there was that stile, where I had held her waist, lifted her in my arms…

This was madness. If I did not cease, I would be fit for nothing but Bedlam! I touched the horse with my heel and cantered easily over the low stone fence. Each landmark, each tuft of grass seemed to recall her… And then, there she was.

She was just ahead of me, walking on as if she had not a care in the world; her hand on her bonnet, her face turned up to the overcast sun. Her back was to me, but I knew that gait and I knew that manner. No one else could be so easily energetic, so graceful and so strong all at once but my own raven vixen.

She stopped and turned at the sound of my horse's hoofbeats. I could not tell with what emotion she received me until I drew near, but then I could see the minute smile, and that inscrutable sparkle in her eye.

I halted my mount, and we merely exchanged silent looks for a moment. I lowered the rein, resting my hand on the pommel and allowed the horse to be at ease. She tipped her face back, her skin radiant as the loveliest light I had ever seen broke forth over her features.

I could not help it. She was so pert, so captivating, standing there in the fresh dawn and smiling up at me like that. "Minx," I greeted her with a low chuckle.

She laughed and curtsied. "Swine."

I swung to the ground and waited, my hand resting on the horse's wither. If she gave me the slightest bit of warmth, any indication that my presence was welcome, I would hook the rein in that old oak tree there and walk with her. But if not…

She tilted her bonnet to survey me from under it. "I was sorry to learn that Miss Darcy did not come with you."

I slipped the rein from over the horse's head and secured it, my soul leaping in triumph. When I turned back to her, I had schooled my expression, but my voice hardly sounded like my own. "It was her own resolve. She did wish to see you, but found that another duty was more pressing."

Her answering smile was one I had not seen before—her lips scarcely moved, but her cheeks and eyes reflected her approval. "It is a sad reality, I am afraid. We must all, at one time or another, give way to duty when our desire is for the opposite."

"But if the carrying out of such duty is designed to bring greater pleasure, then there is some consolation."

She dipped her head. "Quite."

She turned, and I feared at first that she meant to walk away from me, but instead she waited for me to come beside her. We ambled slowly over the remaining rise together, then merely stopped and stood, not two feet apart, gazing out over the mist rising from the valley below.

I stole frequent glances at her, and I caught her doing the same, but neither of us seemed to know what to say. I cleared my throat at least twice, thinking I had come upon some notion that might allow me to express myself, but my tongue was a tangle.

"Mr Darcy," she ventured after some time of exquisite discomfort, "there is something I have wished to ask you." Her voice was soft, hesitant, and she did not turn to me as she spoke.

"You may ask me anything, Miss Elizabeth. I will answer as earnestly as I am able."

I heard her catch her breath, and release it in a long, trembling exhale. "Will you tell me a little about your wife?"

I glanced over to her. "Why would you ask that?"

"You puzzle me so greatly; I cannot understand much of what I first knew of you in light of what I know now. I was hoping to make sense of the contradictions. If the topic is distressing to you, then you may defer."

I was a moment in answering. The prospect seemed to have lost nearly all of its horror. In fact, I believed I would have one day begged to tell her the whole truth, so greatly did I yearn for her to understand. "It is distressing, but I am willing to lay the facts before you. Where shall I begin?"

"Oh, always at the beginning, for if you jump into the middle, we shall be obliged to retrace our steps until I am quite caught up."

"I hope you are not cold, for it may be a long tale."

She shrugged her mantle a little higher up on her shoulders and smiled.

"Very well." I frowned and tried to decide precisely where the beginning was. "It was May of the Year 'Ten, just after I had returned from a brief tour of Northumberland. A gentleman—Sir Edmund Benedict—had invited me, as well as a few others I knew, for a month-long house party at his estate in Bedfordshire.

"Ordinarily, I would have gone to spend some weeks that spring with Lady Catherine and my cousin Anne, but my aunt's demands for a marriage had become more and more insistent, and I was only too glad of an excuse. Sir Edmund had been a friend of my father's, and I felt myself justified in accepting his invitation when he pressed me so. I wish to heaven I had simply gone to Kent!"

"Is this a commentary on the palatability of duty again?" she asked, a bit of levity in her voice.

I laughed, but it was a forced, unnatural sound. My hands were already beginning to shake as I relived that spring two years earlier.

"Perhaps. I had two rather close friends I had known since Eton, named Ramsey and Carlisle. They were among the other guests, so their presence was some inducement. Bingley was invited, but it was too soon after the death of his father for him to consider it. The rest of us saw it as a perfect opportunity for some amusement. Sir Edmund was a spectacular falconer, and thought to be an agreeable fellow in general, so we expected to be well entertained.

"We all knew the real reason for the invitation was that his daughter had not made a match that season—her third— and he was becoming anxious to capture a husband for her before we all retired to the country for the summer. Nevertheless, we accepted, or many of us did. Two of our companions were married men who brought their wives, and I think they were only invited to make Sir Edmund's intentions a little less obvious. The remaining five of us were bachelors.

"I was delayed over a week in arriving by some business in

London, as I had been travelling previously and many matters demanded my attention. Within a few days of my arrival, I began to suspect that Sir Edmund was not the gentleman I had always presumed him to be. For one thing, he drank heavily, and played excessively at cards. That alone would not have troubled me, but there were other signs in his personal habits that gave me pause."

"Such as?" she asked.

"He kept unpredictable hours, and the servants all seemed terrified in his presence. That is as good an indicator as any you will ever find about a man's true nature. Even the dogs would not enter a room where he was the only occupant."

She turned her head slightly—not enough to meet my eyes, but enough for me to read the hint of encouragement there. "I recall when I made the acquaintance of your Mrs Elliott, how she could not cease praising her employer. Did you pay her to make such remarks, Mr Darcy?"

"I was rather embarrassed, to be quite truthful." I waited for her to look at me fully and dip her head in amusement.

"Pray, go on, sir."

I looked back over the fields. "Where was I? Sir Edmund—his manner seemed more curious by the day. Forgive me for the comparison, but his wife and daughter would have made your own mother and younger sisters seem quiet and retiring—" here, she stifled a short laugh, but did not interrupt me—"but when Sir Edmund was about, they spoke hardly a word. Or, so I thought, until one day I happened to be walking in the orchard where I overheard Lady Benedict and her husband in the midst of some violent disagreement. I left the area as quickly as I could, but I could not help learning from that encounter that the family were quite different when they thought they were alone. And that Sir Edmund kept a mistress in a cottage nearby.

"I dared not speak of my misapprehensions, but it was three days before Lady Benedict came down from her rooms. I saw no outward signs of any mishandling, but her entire demeanour seemed surly and discontented, where before she had at least made an effort at being a proper hostess.

"We all noticed it, and the situation became so uncomfortable that a few of us had begun to speak of going away. I only delayed because Georgiana was due to travel back to Cambridge at the end of the month with some friends, and I intended to meet her there before going on to Pemberley for the remainder of the summer.

"All this while, I had scarcely spoken with Elizabeth Benedict. She was crass, vulgar, and loud; moreover, she thought herself quite the wit when, in truth, my horse's hind end was better informed. She was the sort of creature who delighted in setting others at odds. She would issue peculiar orders to one maid, then demand of the housekeeper that the unfortunate maid be punished for doing precisely what she had asked.

"Her behaviour among guests was little better, and she provoked many a ridiculous argument between my companions without them ever recognising how it had all begun. There were two or three domestic rows along the married couples due to her multitude of improprieties towards the men, occasionally before the eyes of their wives.

"I believe she fancied herself the object of everyone's desire, and in truth, she was not unattractive at first glance. She looked rather like you—thick dark hair, light figure—but her eyes were... I cannot describe them. Have you ever peered into the eyes of someone and thought their soul appeared dead within? That was how hers were, and it chilled me to the bone when I was required to speak to her."

Elizabeth shivered; her arms crossed within her mantle. It had fallen low at one place, and I boldly reached to draw it closer to her ears. "Are you certain you are warm enough?"

She stared up at me as I withdrew my hand, her expression a mixture of astonishment and gratitude. "I—I am well," she stammered. "Please, continue."

I was a moment in speaking again. How much more would I have preferred to simply take her in my arms! Her eyes were dilated as she looked up at me, her lips full and softly parted. I knew—*I knew*—for the first time, that she would not refuse me if I removed my gloves and brushed her cheek with my bare fingers. She might just lean into my hand and permit me to stroke that lush lower lip with my thumb. Even now, she was leaning forward, her balance still not recovered after I had touched her shoulder.

But it was not yet time. One last duty to perform... and then she would decide my fate, if she could withstand the truth of everything I would ask her to bear. I drew a ragged breath and plunged ahead with my tale.

"Well, as matters with the family seemed to be rather tense, some of the guests began to take their leave. The men who had brought their wives both made hints that their ladies had developed 'interesting' conditions during their stay and wished to return home while travelling remained easy. Huxley and Sanders also departed on some weak excuse. There were only Ramsey and Carlisle and me remaining, and Sir Edmund started to display more and more of his temper as the eligible gentlemen slipped from his grasp. I think there was not enough gold under the sun to persuade any of us to wed his daughter at that point, though both of my companions had shown some degree of interest before.

"You discovered that I have long been in the habit of riding each morning. I was going out exceedingly early those days, in hopes of avoiding any of the family. I would even dress myself, because I did not wish to disturb my valet. One morning, only two days before I was set to depart to meet Georgiana, I had just come from my room dressed for my ride. It was barely after four in the morning. I had my greatcoat over one arm and my riding crop in my hand, so there could be no doubts about my intentions.

"The house had a balcony off the main hall where my room was located. A series of stone steps led down one side of it, and on the other was a low railing with a bench where one could look out over the gardens. On this day, I chose to leave the house via the balcony rather than through the central stairwell. Once out the door, the balcony had several overgrown shrubs and ornamental trees in pots and brick planters, and behind one of these I could plainly hear Sir Edmund and his daughter in the midst of a heated exchange.

"I gathered that he had been returning from his mistress in the wee hours, and had caught her also out of the house, doing heaven-knows-what. He drew his own conclusions, which I learned later were all too accurate, and he was infuriated beyond sense or recall. He was using all manner of epithets, all of which were well applied to her actions, and none of which I care to repeat. Her tones were filled with just as much vitriol, and I felt it wiser to leave them to one another. I stepped back towards the door, but then I heard him slapping her—at least twice; I do not even know how many strikes I heard."

Elizabeth gasped. "He did not misuse his daughter!"

I thinned my lips and looked down at her. When had she come to stand so close to my side? Or was it I who had moved, instinctively seeking her shelter as I opened the door to my demons? She saw me glancing at the remaining distance between us, and something in my manner must have convinced her that I was also cold, or desiring comfort. She hooked her arm through mine and looked up.

My heart almost stopped. As it was, I felt a great seizure in my chest, and my mouth was like cotton. What I would have given to end my story and wrap my other arm about her, and simply hold her close in that grey dawn! Why walk into the darkness again?

"Mr Darcy?" she asked softly. "Did you wish to stop there?"

I blinked and tried to swallow. I owed her the whole truth. Either I would finally gain her trust... or lose her forever. I forced myself to answer. "No. But, if you will be so kind, I quite forgot where I was."

She tightened her arm through mine until I could feel her body pressed against my elbow. "You heard the father abusing..." her lips trembled, and she broke off, her brow furrowed in anguish.

"Yes," I sighed. "Perhaps you do not know, but there is some primal call, some profound understanding that shatters a man's core when a woman is in distress. It is something deep within a man's being, if he be any sort of a man at all. Turning away then would be to imperil my immortal soul... and so I rushed around a potted bush.

"It was too obvious what was taking place. She was holding her hand to her cheek, raising the other to ward off his next blow. I pitied her—truly pitied her. Who was there to defend her from her father? She was shouting her profanity back at him, for I suppose cursing him was the only defence remaining to her. I came towards them, demanding to know the meaning of all this, and that was when Sir Edmund struck her in earnest. She fell to the ground and covered her head.

"I cried, 'Sir Edmund desist at once!' and cast my coat aside. I was preparing to drag the brute away by main force, if needed. I still held my crop, and I remember pointing it at him like a sword—instinct, I suppose. 'Stand aside, sir!' I ordered.

"'Darcy!' he spat at me, '*you* were her liaison? I shall see you at the altar within a fortnight or meet you on the field of honour in an hour!'

"'I would have nothing to do with that baggage,' I snarled back, 'but I cannot allow you to beat your own daughter.'

"Miss Benedict was weeping by then, and she collected my coat as if she could hide herself in it. She scrambled to her feet and hastened to stand behind me, which enraged Sir Edmund even further.

"'Beat her! She deserves worse than that,' was his answer. 'Where were you, you little whore? With him?—' he pointed to me—'or did you have an assortment of lovers tonight?'

"'And where have you been, Papa?' she retorted from behind me.

"I tried to hush her, to send her away, but she had seen her chance to return abuse for abuse. Some of the pavers in the balcony had worked loose—in fact, many small things about the estate were in disrepair. She took up one of the ill-fitting stones nearby and threw it at him, and I suppose I could hardly blame her, if that was the treatment she had known. But the little fool was too twisted, too vicious to take the wiser course and leave when she could.

"'Where were you?' she kept demanding of her father. 'With that woman again? You have no right to scold me!'

"He reached beyond my shoulder and grabbed her by the hair, then dragged her to himself and shook her. 'You little slut! You are a whore, and that is all you will ever be. Just like your mother!' He got his hand round her throat then, and I do believe he meant to choke her until she was unconscious or worse.

326

"I managed to pull her away from him, and she crumpled to the pavers, gasping and spitting in his direction. 'Go!' I ordered her, but she would not. She recovered enough to sit up and jeer at her father, though I repeatedly called for her to leave.

"'You think to make the fool of me, Darcy?' he demanded. 'You can have her, for a price.'

"'Never,' I said. 'That wench is your problem, and no man in his senses would have her now for less than a hundred thousand. Find her lover, if you can. Better to wed her to whatever farmer she was rolling with than to bankrupt yourself paying someone else to take her.'

"He lost his head at this. He had been drinking, that much was clear, and he had decided in his fury that I was the one who must make reparations for his ruined little hussy. He charged at me and got his hands around my throat. I remember slashing at him with my crop, but soon I was forced to drop it to defend myself.

"I am more than a fair boxer, and few men can best me at the pugilist arts, but Sir Edmund had no intention of fighting by any rules. He was nearly as tall as I, and carried a solid thirty pounds more about his middle, which he employed to great advantage. Nevertheless, I was returning blow for blow; not only that, I was forcing him back towards the stone railing, away from the wench so she would be able to flee down the steps. I heard Lady Benedict coming down, and I assumed she would take her daughter to safety. I could not leave off the fight, for Sir Edmund had me by the clothing, and by that time, my ire was up. In my own vanity, I wished to punish his vile behaviour. Would that I had wrested from his grip and fled!"

Elizabeth was trembling, her cheeks wet with tears. "It is in every way horrible!"

I gave in to my earlier desire and tugged my glove from my hand to soothe her tears away. "Do you wish me to stop?" I asked gently.

She shook her head, gazing up at me with those chocolate eyes. "Were you much hurt?"

"Some. My forehead and my nose were both bleeding from cuts by his signet ring, and I did not see when his knee came up to strike me…" I cleared my throat, and Elizabeth narrowed her eyes. "Well, er, when a man sustains a blow to his…" I gestured feebly, and her cheeks reddened, but she nodded in understanding.

"I dropped to my knees, and then I recall him falling upon me, striking about my head with something heavy—one of the loose pavers, I think. I remember rolling back, grabbing at his body to flip him off me like a barnyard cat. And then, something hit my head again, and that was the last thing I recall."

"You were unconscious?" she cried. "How long?"

"I do not know. It must have been some minutes, but it could not have been longer than a quarter of an hour. Had I been dressed by my valet, he could have confirmed the time I left my room, but I was not. Nor had I looked closely at the clock.

"What I do know is that I awoke some feet from where I last remembered being. I was rolled over on my stomach, near the railing of the balcony. I remember opening my eyes and just gazing stupidly at my riding crop, lying nearby. I was so numb, so dazed that I only stared at it for a moment, trying to recall what had happened. My face and chest were bloody, more blood was pouring from a great knot on my crown, my knuckles were scraped, and there were tufts of hair clenched in my fists. And then, I heard the sounds of weeping.

"Lady Benedict was sobbing, wailing like a banshee that I had killed her husband. When I sat up, she beat me over the head, and I was obliged to put up my arm to shield my face. 'He is dead, you have ruined us!' she kept repeating."

"Dead!" Elizabeth lamented. "Surely not! Oh, pray tell me it was not true!"

I pulled my arm closer, my teeth set grimly. "I could not understand, for my last memory was of Sir Edmund perfectly alive and well. I fancied he must have had a heart seizure, but when I struggled to my feet, I discovered the horrible truth. There he lay, two stories below the balcony, and quite still. He had fallen on his back, so I could see his slack visage and the blood spilling out over the paving stones."

"Dead!" she cried again. Her tears were cascading in earnest now, and she held a hand to her mouth.

"Elizabeth?" I closed my eyes, prepared for the end of all my hopes. "If you wish to turn back to Longbourn now, and never see me again, I shall accept your wishes."

She shook her head vehemently, a choking noise rising in her throat. "No," she whispered. "What happened? You did not truly…"

"I had no way of knowing. A terror gripped me, the sort of horror and fear that a man never thinks to experience in the whole of his life. A murderer! It could only be true—it *must* have been true—but I had no memory of throwing him, no recollection of his fall. I would have thought a man's death scream would be something I should never be able to forget, but I do not even know if he cried out as he fell.

"Well, I expect you know the rest. I could only think of my family —of the disgrace and the mortal sin I must have committed. I feared for Georgiana, if I were hanged or transported. My estate and all my holdings would be forfeit, so she would not even have a home to return to! This naturally set my mind to work for all those under my care, and I believe right then I would have sold my soul to the highest bidder, if it would have turned back the clock only a few minutes. So frantic and disoriented was I that by the time the magistrate arrived to investigate the death, I had witlessly agreed to Lady Benedict's demands."

"And those were?" Elizabeth asked softly, her voice strangely nasal, as if she were choking back sobs.

"What do you think? That I would marry that filth of a daughter of hers and she would swear that Sir Edmund had fallen after too much drink. That I would cover all Sir Edmund's debts, which I discovered later were considerable, and provide for his widow. And what she demanded! She is better funded now than she ever was during her husband's lifetime.

"I was sick, furious, and thoroughly bewildered. How had I, Fitzwilliam Darcy, fallen to murder? And what of this creature I was now shackled to? That I should have to give her my name and live the rest of my days bound to such a base, contemptible wench was bad enough, but that was not the worst of it."

Her brows raised. "There was more?"

I gave a bitter snort. "Oh, indeed there was. I sent an express to meet Georgiana's carriage, and an urgent message to Colonel Fitzwilliam, asking for Georgiana to be taken to London. I would not have her there, exposed to... that.

"The wedding was got up in three days' time, so I would have no opportunity to change my mind. And then, the day before the proceedings, my valet learned from one of the maids that my soon-to-be bride was already increasing. There had been accusations, of course—there always are when such a quick ceremony is in the works. How I bore the shame of that, I shudder to recall, but then to learn that the rumours were true, and that I would be claiming as my own some other man's bastard—that was not to be borne.

"I took it up with both women, and I assure you that if you had ever thought me hateful before, you could not fathom my behaviour that day. Yet, I was helpless to protest, for my choice was between a hangman's noose and a pair of witches. God help me, I chose the occult over my just penance."

"But you had only been trying to help!" Elizabeth protested. "Any man who would declare himself a gentleman could not have failed to do the same. Surely, you could not be held at fault."

I gazed affectionately down at her. "Noble Elizabeth! If only the world were as you wish it could be. I would gladly accept even your wrath over what others call mercy."

She sniffed back another sob; her eyes glassy with unshed tears as she gazed up at me. "What did you do?"

I traced my thumb over her chin, then dropped my hand. "What could I do? I pledged myself to one I despised, to a woman I could not even look at without feeling the bile rise in my gorge. I took her as far from London and everyone I ever knew as possible, because I could not bear to see the looks on their faces when the tramp opened her mouth. I could not stomach their laughter when they looked upon her fetid, swollen belly and knew it was no seed of mine, and I could not tolerate the disgrace of everyone knowing that I, who had been so outspoken about the sham marriages all around me, had been ensnared by a woman who could only be described as villainous.

"My family all counted me a rascal and a liar. My uncle was more enraged than I have ever seen, claiming I had purposely ruined his alliances and intentionally betrayed old family loyalties.

"Fitzwilliam dragged me into a dark room and pried the whole story out of me, with the aid of a great quantity of spirits. He was livid, threatened to call for an investigation against all the Benedicts, for as I had discovered by then, Lady Benedict and her daughter were at least a match for Sir Edmund. The heir, Robert, was out of the country at the time, but when I met him later, I discovered him to be his father's son in every respect. Unpredictable, self-serving, and corrupt.

"Of course, it was too late by then for Richard to help. At least he would still write to me, but I did not see him for the better part of a year. I lost all my friends, save Bingley—even him, really. And I lost Georgie... you know her, what life in such a house would have done to her! I could not allow her life to be ruined as mine had been, so I kept her away. It was well that I did, for Pemberley became a living hell."

"You... you even lost the joy of your home," she whispered in sympathy.

"Worse—I abhorred every wall and every rock of the place because there was not a prospect from which I had not seethed and gnashed my teeth in impotence over my fate. We fought every single day. How we battled and raged! My home that had once been a sanctuary, and the fount of my parents' deep affection for one another, became a battlefield.

"Once, not long after the wedding, she tried to make it appear as if I had been to her bed. She had got some blood from somewhere and splashed it on her sheets. When that failed to convince anyone, she stole the key to my room and defiled my own bed. Fortunately, everyone at Pemberley is loyal, and that never happened a second time.

"You never..." she gasped and bit her lip.

"Good heavens, no! I am sorry to be so crude in your hearing, Elizabeth, but it would not have even been possible for me to… no. A thousand times, no."

Her gaze fell, and she shuddered in what appeared to be relief. "Go on," she whispered.

"By the time her condition became obvious, she gave up on trying to make it look as though the child was mine. She resorted to far crueller acts—kicking my pointer until she miscarried her pups, slashing up a painting that Georgiana had done, and smashing a priceless vase that my father had bought for my mother.

"Her imagination was limited only by her growing belly and my vigilant servants. When they thwarted her efforts, she tried to get them dismissed—loyal servants whose families had been at Pemberley for generations. Mrs Reynolds, the housekeeper, has perhaps more salt than is good for her, and defended them ably. You can imagine how well this reversal pleased the Jezebel.

"One day, after a particularly nasty fight, she broke into my study and burned most of my father's journals. A lifetime of experience and love and wisdom, gone in a moment! I found myself overcome with the desire to choke her until she could never speak another vile word… and so I left. I was afraid of myself, what I would do if I had to look at her again, and so I left Pemberley to her mercy, and I disappeared for two months.

"I went nowhere in particular. I just travelled, passing myself off as a common businessman, sleeping in one shabby post inn after another. I could not return to London, for everyone would know the truth, and I should never escape hearing of my own downfall. I toured Scotland, and when I tired of that, I crossed over to Dublin for a fortnight.

"Nothing absolved me of the guilt of abandoning everything as I had done. My only consolation was the knowledge that if I were not there for her to insult and abuse, everyone else at Pemberley would have an easier time of it. But I knew I could not stay away, so I came back, loathing every mile of my journey… and within hours of my arrival, her travails had come upon her. Less than a day after that… she was dead."

My breath misted in the cool morning air and rose away, carrying with it the leaden weight of secrecy that had stained my conscience all these months. I closed my eyes and savoured that lightness, that freedom for a moment, then I turned to Elizabeth.

Even her lips were grey. Her eyes were round and black with horror and pity. "All this," she choked, "you have borne all this?"

I looked down at her hand, felt her grip on my arm slipping away. Her features were wooden, her expression desolate. "You are disgusted," I sighed. "You should be—with all of it, and not least my selfishness in imposing this upon you."

She nodded; her brow creased. "I am. But not by your account, Mr Darcy. By the actions of those who claimed the honour of their position, despite their immoral conduct. Your only shame was in not leaving the house party when your mind told you that you should. This alone should be the burden to your conscience."

"Do not presume I am an innocent, Elizabeth. Heaven only knows what portion of the guilt is mine, but I assure you, my hands are not clean."

She drank in a steadying breath, then hesitantly reached for my gloveless hand. I gave it, and watched in fascination as she spread my fingers, palm up, and traced the lines she found therein. "Hands can be washed," she mused at last.

"But can a soul? For, if you did not doubt me before, you surely will when I confess the worst. How wicked does a man have to be to feel relief when a woman agonises and dies the most miserable of deaths? But I did. I would not say I rejoiced, but I certainly did not grieve. I am truly a wretch, Elizabeth, and until I told you these things, my eyes were never even opened to it."

"Mr Darcy, after what you have told me, I would question your sanity if you did not feel relief. It is not as though you caused her death."

I gazed down at her—so confident, so willing to absolve me—and my heart quailed within me. "You would be wrong to suggest that I did not bear some blame," I replied huskily. "Elizabeth, I want nothing more in this world than your trust, but you would be unwise to give it."

"Unwise to trust one who confesses something so painful that he is trembling as he speaks?" She pressed my hand one last time and returned it. "I do not doubt the truth of what you say."

"It is more than that. You are too intelligent to think otherwise. Elizabeth—Elizabeth—my life, all my hope belongs to you, but I may have just robbed you of yours. I am freer now than I have ever been, but at the expense of your innocence. I shall never forgive myself for that."

She lifted her chin faintly, and her eyes seemed to consider. "You believe that sorrow must be borne by one person or another? That it is a physical thing that can never disappear, but can only be divided and shared?"

I shook my head, touched her cheek. "Something this ugly never just disappears. It only spreads, multiplies, and poisons everything around it. I cannot think why you would..." I hung my head and looked away. "You... you must be wanted at home by now."

She shifted to look into my eyes, then held my gaze as she seemed to search the depths of my soul. My breath died in my throat as I waited... waited for her grace, her sweet ways to touch and heal and make me new, if she would.

"I... I should go, Mr Darcy."

My spirits sank. "Of course."

She lowered her head and moved away but turned abruptly back. "This is a favourite walking path of mine."

I blinked in mild surprise. "I know it is."

She tucked a wisp of hair back into her bonnet and smiled one last time at me—a half-smile, one of uncertainty and pain, and then it faded. But her eyes—I was watching those speaking eyes, and they held compassion. "Good day, Mr Darcy."

I mounted the horse again and stood on that rise, watching her as she wandered slowly away. Gone was the spring in her stride, the proud brow no longer set against the heavens. Her face was turned down, her steps heavily burdened by the weight I had set on her shoulders, and once, I even saw her stumble faintly, as if she were not heeding her path.

A quarter mile or more I could see from that knoll, and I watched until she vanished from sight. I could not bear to turn away until I knew whether she would look back at me before she dropped down into the valley below.

She did.

CHAPTER 23

$\mathcal{T}$he early spring rains began that afternoon and promised to deluge the whole of the valley for days to come. I lingered at the eastern window, my hand at the drape as I gazed forlornly through the rivulets running down the glass. There would be no more secret encounters with Elizabeth for the foreseeable future, and I mourned the impossibility of discovering the leanings of her heart.

"Oh, Mr Darcy, do come and join us," implored Miss Bingley from the card table. "Mr Hurst carries all before him, and I am quite over-wrought."

"There, there, Caroline," soothed her sister, "Mr Hurst is sure to have a bad hand this round. It is only the rule of chance, to be certain."

"What on earth are you going on about, Louisa?" was the queru-lous retort.

"Why, it stands to reason that when he has had so much of good luck, it is bound to turn sooner or later. And for you, the same—your chances for a favourable hand must naturally improve after each time you have a poor one."

"I cannot see how that makes any sense," Miss Bingley sniffed. "Bad luck does not create good luck."

"But that is not what I said at all," protested Mrs Hurst. "I only meant to say that you have equal chances of winning cards or losing ones each round. You keep drawing that queen of spades, but are you not just as likely to find the queen of hearts in your hand this time?"

"How terribly silly you are! And no, my dear Louisa, I believe that contemptible card must have my name on it, else I am fated for disappointment, for it seems to plague me."

Mrs Hurst sighed loudly. "Oh, Caroline, must you be so tiresome? Mr Darcy, do come and educate my dear sister on matters of chance, for I have not your vast experience in the matter."

I half-turned. "I am afraid you are applying to the wrong person if you wish for me to lend you some hope regarding a card game."

"Indeed," Miss Bingley seconded with energy. "Mr Darcy does not approve of games of chance. He makes his own fortune, to be sure."

"I said no such thing. There is nothing in it I disapprove of, so long as one does not stake moneys beyond their means. I simply do not appreciate the thrill of chance as others do. I prefer to have some measure of confidence in my own abilities to direct the game as I please."

Hurst grunted and spoke for the first time. "How very singular. Even at a game of skill, you must be dealt a workable hand. And what if the fellow across the table from you possesses equal skill and better luck?"

"Then I would do best to keep my eyes open for opportunities or mistakes."

"How droll you are, Mr Darcy!" Miss Bingley tittered. "Oh, but do come advise me, for I must make some choice as to which card to play."

I demurred, tried to produce some plausible excuse, and was serendipitously spared by Bingley's return from Longbourn. He had shed his wet hat and greatcoat, but even so, he possessed a damp, windblown appearance from his short carriage ride and walk into the house. He entered the room with long strides and his face all aglow.

"Good heavens," he huffed as he turned about, in an apparent desire to alight somewhere, "I ought to have left at least an hour earlier! Mrs Bennet insisted that I stay for luncheon, and before I knew anything, three o'clock had come and gone. Such a downpour! —it looks as though we are in for the rest of the day. How have you all been keeping here?"

"Ghastly," lamented Miss Bingley. "Whatever could have been so amusing about the Bennet family that you would remain the whole of the afternoon?"

Bingley shot me a jocular grin—the look of a man who had found a more pleasurable activity than I had. "You might be surprised, Caroline. Mary Bennet has been studying a new composition, and she kept us well entertained for the better part of an hour."

Mrs Hurst choked, and Miss Bingley rolled her eyes with a groan she did not even bother to conceal.

"—And Miss Kitty and Miss Lydia were diverting, as always," he continued.

"Did Miss Lydia manage to string three words together for a change?" Miss Bingley sneered.

"A good many more than that, as it happens. And Mr Bennet was even quite amiable. Why, I believe we spent half an hour over drinks in his library."

This time, I did not notice the derisive remarks of Bingley's sisters. I was watching him; the faint shadow that had crossed his brow, despite the smile he always wore. "Bingley—" I turned away from the window at last—"as you mentioned it, a quiet drink sounds just the thing. Do you mind?"

He tilted his head and looked carefully at me before he answered. "Why... indeed, it does. Er, Hurst, Louisa, Caroline, I expect you all mean to continue your game? Yes, capital notion, Darcy. The library, perhaps? I trust you were there earlier and there is still a good blaze. I am chilled to the bone."

We adjourned and settled ourselves accordingly, and this time, I poured the brandy. Bingley sighed in gratitude as he stretched in his chair, and we both drank.

"Well, Darcy." He leaned his head back and savoured his brandy. "What was it you wanted to ask me?"

"What makes you believe I wished to ask you anything?"

"Ah-hah. I know that brooding look in your eye. You were bored as a corpse until I said Mr Bennet's name, and then you got that—that look. Yes, that one there, where you believe you are so sly."

"Exactly how much did you drink already today?"

He laughed. "You forget how long I have known you. What was it that crossed your mind so suddenly?"

I savoured another swallow of my drink before I answered. "Did Mr Bennet have something to discuss with you? You see, I have known you just as long as you have known me, and there was something in your look when you mentioned him."

He smiled faintly and brushed his lip. "Do you know, I never thought Mr Bennet capable of a serious conversation before. He always seemed to me as if he were playing a never-ending round of chess, but his opponents were not aware that there was a game afoot."

"An apt description. I find the man most vexatious."

"But he was not as he usually is today. I suppose it goes to show you that even a fellow like he has his cares. Did you know that his brother-in-law, Mr Gardiner is in the business of importing goods?"

"Yes, I have spoken with him at length about it."

"Did he happen to mention any unlicensed—I should say 'smuggled' cargo?"

I lowered my glass. "Mrs Bennet said something yesterday about some trouble, but if you must know, I brushed aside her comments."

"As I usually do as well, and indeed, as of yesterday it was all simply rumour—not even worth repeating. The news came today, however, that there is some truth to it. It seems that when one of his ships was unloaded in port three days ago, there were five unmarked barrels found aboard by import authorities. When they were opened, they were found to be tea—tea that he had not purchased the tax stamp for."

I squinted down into my glass. "Well, what merchant has not brought in a contraband barrel or two? But to be honest, I had not expected it of Mr Gardiner."

"It turns out that it was far more than that. A subsequent inspection of his warehouse yielded more smuggled tea and a substantial quantity of opium."

I sat upright. "What?"

"Gardiner maintains his innocence, of course, but he has the Company officials now demanding to see documentation on every crate he has ever imported. They are threatening legal repercussions if he cannot produce proof that every barrel in his ships was not from one of their factors in India or the Orient. They take their trade monopoly seriously. It adds up rather quickly—enough to ruin him, Darcy."

"Does Bennet believe Gardiner to be guilty?"

"No, that is just the thing. I have never seen him so troubled as he is now. He insists there must be some mistake. In fact, that was the reason he asked me into his study, because he wanted to find out if I might know any contacts in town—friends who know people, that sort of thing. I was sorry to disappoint him."

"But what good can come of that? Either Gardiner can produce the evidence, or he cannot."

"This is the interesting bit. Gardiner claims he had nothing to do with that cargo, and that someone had been glimpsed sneaking aboard as other barrels were being unloaded, but was not caught."

I made a face. "Do you mean to say he believes someone implicated him falsely? Preposterous. How does one bring five barrels aboard when all the other dock hands are removing cargo? And then do so without being noticed until the deed is done?"

"Oh, perhaps it is not so complicated. Ships restock almost at the very moment they are unloaded, but I agree, it sounds a bit incredible."

"However—" I finished my glass—"I find it equally incredible that Gardiner could be guilty. To be sure, I have spent only a couple of hours in the man's company, but you know how the character of the master of the house influences all who live there. What is more, Miss Elizabeth holds her uncle in the highest esteem, and she is not easily fooled."

Bingley pursed his lips and looked directly at me. "She was not below stairs for much of the afternoon to lend her opinion on the matter."

I glanced down, tried to appear nonchalant. "Oh?"

"Yes, something about a long walk this morning, and feeling indisposed after. However, when she did come down, I thought she looked as hale as usual, save for some sadness about her eyes. I assumed at first she was merely distressed over her uncle, but after her father drew her aside, she appeared even more shaken."

I was silent a moment. My poor Elizabeth! Any disgrace or trial endured by those she loved, she would take as her own. "She is very fond of both aunt and uncle," I answered shortly.

"Such sympathy is warranted, but the danger to the family demands more material resolution. Bennet expects that if things go badly, the Gardiners will lose all. They will have to come somewhere, and the only place for them to come is Longbourn. No one would turn them away, but think what that does to the Bennet family?"

"The financial distress of their support would only be the beginning. Bennet has little enough in reserve, from what I understand."

"Almost none whatever, by what Jane tells me," he agreed. "But neither is he in debt at present. That will change, as will the neighbourhood's treatment of the family. At a time when the elder girls will most need to marry and leave the house, they will find no one to take them."

"Indeed," I mused in almost a whisper.

"Of course, the elder sisters could come here, once Jane and I are wed. Perhaps the younger two as well, but that is all the aid I would be capable of giving. Darcy, do you know anyone in a position to look into matters and see if something of Gardiner's assertions are true?"

I drew a slow breath. "Perhaps."

"Then I wish you would write to him. It may be that nothing is to be done, but I should like to do what we can. Poor Mrs Bennet was in a dreadful state when I left, and I was terribly sorry for it."

I thinned my lips and raised a brow at him.

"Oh, yes," he sighed, "I well know that she is often 'in a state,' but this was something worse. Another disappointment on top of the previous. You know she had her hopes set on finding a husband or two for her girls among the militia, but they have gone to Brighton. I had not the heart to tell her it was just as well, for none of them can afford a wife anyway."

I uncrossed my legs and leaned forward. "Bingley, forgive me for changing the subject, but what happened with George Wickham after I left? I heard he managed to get out of the militia."

"That is what I heard as well. He must have paid someone to take his place, but how he afforded it, or how Forster was persuaded to it, I cannot answer. I know very little—you know, he was no intimate of mine, but he was a frequent guest at Longbourn when I would call. Everyone was quite fond of him, but I did hear after he left that he had accumulated substantial debts in town, and even more among his peers. Perhaps he found better paying work to settle those and start over?"

"More likely, he has merely found someone else to extort."

Bingley shook his head. "He does have a knack for seeking... opportunity. One wonders what genius he possesses, and what might come if he would apply half his efforts to honest living."

"Honest living does not pay quite so well. No, I imagine he has once again attached himself to some woman with low standards and high expectations." I peered down into my glass for another moment, and then a physical shock seemed to torch through my body. I leapt to my feet and stared at the opposite wall as my mind grappled with this new idea.

"Darcy?" Bingley rose, more hesitantly.

"I may know the person to speak to about Mr Gardiner's troubles," I breathed. "But a letter will not be sufficient. I must leave at dawn tomorrow."

OVER MISS BINGLEY'S protests and against my personal inclinations, the early morning light saw my carriage well on the road to London. The coachman had been instructed to spare the horses where he might, but to stop as little as possible and to keep up a steady pace where the roads were good.

The one exception I permitted was to attend some business in Meryton. The innkeeper there affirmed my suspicions, that Wickham owed money to nearly everyone in town. I pledged myself to the debts, provided he would act as my agent in the matter of collecting all the receipts. I then gave him a crown for his trouble and made for London with all speed.

All the while, I could only think of Elizabeth. The thought that she might believe I had gone away, intending to leave her, had been too sickening to bear, so my final words to Bingley had been meant for her. "If you would," I had exhorted him, "please give my regrets to your neighbours, and tell them… I should like to accept Mrs Bennet's invitation to dinner when I return."

He had adopted a knowing look as he nodded. "And perhaps an outing, once the weather turns again. A walk in the meadow might be just the thing."

I checked myself in the midst of turning away to study him. He merely smiled and extended his hand. "Godspeed, Darcy."

I never even stopped at my own house once I arrived in London. Instead, I directed the coachman to B— Street, to a threshold I had sworn never to darken again. The maid answering the door fell back, apparently too astonished by my arrival to think quickly enough to report that her mistress was not at home. She merely looked at her toes as voices from the next room verified all I needed to know.

I found Lady Benedict reclining on a sort of divan. I could see most of her profile, and her features were suffused with that same languor as on the occasion of my last encounter with her. Resting in her arms, his cravat loose and hair slightly mussed, was George Wickham. She was caressing his brow, petting him like a lapdog, while he leaned his head against her satin-clad bosom with closed eyes. The entire scene made me want to vomit.

"I trust I am not interrupting anything?" I spoke from the doorway.

Had I poured cold water over both of them, I doubt I could have startled them more. Wickham jolted and slid from the divan, tumbling gracelessly on the floor before he scrambled to his feet. Lady Benedict snatched her hand away in guilty astonishment, and likewise tried to lurch upright, but Wickham was falling all over her skirts. She sought to straighten her gown and smooth back her hair, but her paramour gave her two or three unintentional bumps as he recovered his own balance. Consequently, it was he who composed himself first.

"Darcy!" he cried. "What a pleasure to see you again. Come to revisit old acquaintances?"

My lip curled faintly, but otherwise I did not answer as I strode into the room.

"How dare!" accused Lady Benedict, as she stood off to one side like a martyred saint. She brushed her hair once more and then raised her palm, as if shunning me. "I thought you passed yourself off as a gentleman, Darcy, but what gentleman invades a lady's parlour uninvited and unannounced?"

"The sort who has paid for it," I returned in a surly tone.

Wickham snickered, put up a hand, and then laughed in earnest, nearly doubling over. "So, you *have* kept a woman, Darcy! Oh, then pray forgive me, I did not know I had infringed upon your private nest. I should have never expected—"

He cut off the filth pouring from his mouth when I shot him a glare that would have frozen Hades. One more half-chuckle of disbelief, a quick darting of his eyes, then he fell silent.

"Well, Darcy," Lady Benedict inquired, somewhat more smoothly than Wickham, "what do you have to say for yourself? Surely, this is no social call. Have you come to make amends for your reprehensible conduct when last we met? Do you mean to return what is mine?"

"I have come to ask for the truth," I retorted, "and to demand that you learn to keep out of my affairs."

She looked wounded. "Your affairs? Why, how should you think that I, a widow of modest means, could possibly trouble you?"

"I shall put it more simply. Where is Daniels, and how much did you pay him to hire dock hands to misdirect cargo?"

Her eyes hardened to black coals. "I haven't the least idea what you are accusing me of, Darcy. I have had no contact with Daniels in two months, and I certainly would never think of cargo from the docks. Filthy place. The very idea!"

"She speaks the truth, Darcy," Wickham interjected. "At the least, it was not Lady Benedict, though I have a fair notion of what may have transpired. I am certain we might be of help," he grinned.

"How is that?"

"Oh—" he examined his fingernails—"I hear things."

"And report things too, no doubt," I snapped. "Whom did you tell about Edward Gardiner?"

"Gardiner?" His eyebrows lifted, and he scanned the ceiling. "Gardiner... I have never met such a person."

"Then you are of no help to me," I announced, and turned as if I meant to go.

"Wait! Gardiner—yes, I recall now. Miss Bennet's uncle, the one Miss Elizabeth stayed with in Town. Indeed, I heard all about him. A shame, what they say about his ship, a dreadful shame. Ah, well, it does not pay to be dishonest, then, does it?"

"I would not know," I said in a low voice, then turned to face him. "But perhaps you could tell me." I drew out a signed statement from my breast pocket and displayed it. "I estimate your debts in Meryton to be at least five hundred pounds, and I dispatched a letter last night to Colonel Forster in Brighton to learn if there be more. I presume you do not have the means to cover all these obligations?"

He paled slightly, then darted a hasty look to Lady Benedict.

"Oh, she will not help you," I informed him. "But she will help me, if she wishes to see another farthing. As for you, I shall purchase your cooperation when I hold all your debts, or at least a sufficient quantity of them. The outstanding credit from Meryton alone would be enough to send you to the Marshalsea for the rest of your years."

"It was Robert Benedict!" he cried. "Was it not, my love?"

She withdrew, distancing herself from Wickham. "I knew nothing of this! And who are you, to accuse my own son?"

"Who am I?" he rounded on her, his face awash with innocent dismay. "Have I not been your defender, madam? The one man upon whom you could rely for a kind word, when not even your own son or son-in-law could be bothered? Was I not there to comfort you at your husband's death, and have I not sought to serve your interests all that while?"

She dismissed him airily. "A plaything, that is what you are—an amusing one, to be sure, but you are far too young, Mr Wickham. I think I should fancy a man whose head is not turned by the buxom tramps at the coaching inns."

"And this is how you would treat me after all my loyalty!" he cried.

"What of how you have treated me? You would hand over my son to save your own wretched neck?"

"Be seated, both of you!" I roared at last. They fell mute and reluctantly chose seats on opposite sides of the room, still glaring at one another.

"Now," I directed, glancing back and forth between the pair of reprobates, "I will have the truth. All of it."

TRUTH WAS AN UGLY THING.

By the time I left Lady Benedict's flat, my stomach was roiling with the infamy of it all. A mother and son—what ought to be one of the closest human bonds—feuding over money. Pathetic.

That same mother taking one of her son's companions as a lover and employing him to inform on both her own child and me. Revolting.

And Wickham! The lecherous filth! Attaching himself to a widow twice his age as a means of skimming whatever he could from me was vile, contemptible... but it was nothing compared to the rest of the story.

I needed to find Robert Benedict. I needed to pin his loathsome flesh to a wall and exact my revenge upon him for what he sought to do to me... to my exquisite Elizabeth and her family.

Lady Benedict had known—indeed, had been the very puppet master behind the screen, playing her lover and her own son as pawns in her brutal chess match against me. *She desired more?* I set my jaw and clenched my fists. She deserved abject penury, but the trouble was, she would likely have everything she sought and then some. Still, I would do it all and more, if it meant protecting the one who held my heart.

I ordered the carriage to drive to my own house and fumed every minute of the journey. The despicable harridan! To attempt to harm Elizabeth, whose only wrong was to thoroughly bewitch me! And to use Mr Gardiner as their means, a family man who had probably never shorted his taxes so much as a penny! Why him, and why—

I suddenly felt as if I were reeling. Dizzy, almost, and short of breath, I clutched the side of the carriage as another notion began to tickle my brain. Robert Benedict ought to have had a fortune tucked away somewhere. The fact that he did not—and everyone could testify to that—meant that he was either a much poorer gamester than even Wickham had ever been, or he had brought back his wealth in another form. Perhaps it was no accident that smuggled East India goods had appeared on Gardiner's ship, for he must have needed some means to get it into the country. This lot was merely sacrificial bait.

I fumbled around in my pocket until I found that satin ribbon and clasped it like a talisman. Ridiculous, really, but that little memento of Elizabeth always helped me to be still, to collect my thoughts. And just then, the predominant thought in my mind was to discover exactly what it would take to rid my life of Benedict and his turpitude forever —and to start again. *Fresh.*

That last notion—for I was so perplexed and agitated that I could not think on only one object—called to mind how very far from fresh I felt. The affair with Wickham and Lady Benedict—the lecher and the termagant—had left me in great need of cleansing both my flesh and my mind. A hot bath would be just the thing, and a rational companion would be welcome as well.

I tried to cheer myself by thinking what a pleasure it would be to see Georgiana again. Though only a few days had passed, I had thought so often of her, and of how she would have liked to be among her friends, that I determined before I even entered the house to prevail upon her to come back to Hertfordshire for the wedding. It would please Elizabeth, and that would please me.

The footman seemed surprised by my arrival, and well he ought to be, for I had sent no word. He bowed quickly and took my coat, then informed me in a low voice that my sister and Mrs Younge were in the drawing room with a caller.

"Indeed?" I replied. "I shall look in and greet them myself. Is it Lady Matlock?"

A peculiar expression passed over the footman's face. "No, sir..." He hesitated. "It is a Mr Benedict."

I turned back. "What? Did I just hear you say..."

"Yes, sir," the footman answered miserably. "The ladies have received him each afternoon since you have been away."

"Benedict?" I repeated. "Robert Benedict? Are you quite sure, James? Miss Darcy would not even know the man. How could it be he?"

"It was Mrs Younge who knew him, sir. Miss Darcy declared her wish that Mrs Younge might have the privilege of receiving her own guests—it is her right as a lady, Miss Darcy said, and she told Mrs Elliott that it was not necessary to ask for instructions from you. She assured us that all would be well."

"All is most certainly not well," I growled, already casting my gaze down the hall and feeling my spine tingle. "Do not announce me, James, I will greet them myself."

He nodded. "As you wish, Mr Darcy."

I found the slithering eel comfortably ensconced in the centre of my drawing room. His back was to me, but Georgiana's face altered so remarkably upon my entry that he twisted round at once.

"Brother!" Georgiana rose and hurried to take my hand. "I had not expected to see you again so soon."

"I see that," I answered, more coldly, I think, than I had ever spoken to her. She shrank, and I turned from her. "Benedict? I am surprised to see you here."

He bowed slightly. "I assure you, Darcy, I mean no harm in calling at your home."

"Do you not?"

"Indeed, no. You see, Mrs Younge is my cousin. Or rather, her husband was—a second cousin—and we have kept up the acquaintance, have we not, my dear?"

Mrs Younge had risen to her feet and bore a look of profound astonishment. She lowered herself in a curtsey when I regarded her, and then drew away, apparently too taken aback to speak.

"If she is your cousin, why not receive her at your own home, and why call here every day? You know very well you are not welcome here."

"Why, that is most unneighbourly, Darcy! Do not friends receive one another mutually, rather than one always playing the host? Besides, we met quite accidentally at the park a couple of weeks back —the very day Miss Darcy received her new chaise, if I am not mistaken. Miss Darcy is an enchanting young lady, and I wished to know her better. Can I help it if you were not in town?"

"Georgiana—" I called my sister to my side without looking at her. "I will speak with you alone later."

"Yes, Fitzwilliam." I glanced down at the quavering flatness in her voice. She was pale to the lips, but she turned and obediently fled the room without another word.

"Mrs Younge—" I gestured for her to come near. "What have you to say for yourself?

She lifted her chin and looked me in the eye, brazen and unashamed. "It was by Miss Darcy's pleasure that we received Mr Benedict, sir."

"And were you or were you not employed as her adviser?"

"I was, sir. You did say that she might receive any of her relations as guests, as she chose, and you gave no explicit instructions against receiving Mr Benedict."

"If you can excuse your actions," I snapped, "you are not fit to remain in service as my sister's companion, nor a companion of any young lady! You may pack your things at once, and Mrs Elliott will have your final pay."

She caught one last defiant breath as if she would protest, then meekly curtsied. "Yes, sir."

"One more moment. If you would like to be paid in full rather than having your rather substantial modiste's bills withheld from your salary, I would know the truth of one question."

Her eyes shifted to Benedict, but she merely nodded her head. "Yes, sir?"

"How many times did you and my sister 'encounter' Mr Benedict in town?"

"Three or four, sir. I was pleased to introduce Miss Darcy to a relation who had been previously unknown to her. As Miss Darcy was charmed by his company, and as Mr Benedict has ever been kind to me, I did not expect there should be any objection."

"By 'kind' to you, do you mean he paid you to bring Miss Darcy under his influence?"

Her mouth opened to protest, but then she closed it.

"Mrs Younge," I stared at her for a moment until she swallowed and some of the insubordination left her eyes. "You are not fit to impose your dubious counsel on any impressionable young lady. You may be assured that I will share my opinion with Lady Matlock, and she will see to it that you never work for another respectable family."

Her voice was barely a whisper when she replied, "I understand, sir." She began to walk away, with her cohort following her, but I stopped him.

"Benedict, I wish you to remain."

"What is this, Darcy? You think you can order me around like one of your servants?"

I whirled on him. "When I return to my own home expecting to find only my sister and my own servants, then yes, I shall treat you as I see fit! You ought to be relieved that I do not call you up for trespassing."

"Trespassing! I was invited!"

"By whom? A traitorous employee and a girl who is not yet out! And what can you mean by imposing yourself upon my sister?"

He laughed and jerked back his shoulders. "What does a man usually mean by showing interest in a female? Charming girl, Darcy. Absolutely charming. A trifle naïve, though."

A murderous rage overtook me, and in a trice, I had his cravat between my fists and his shoulders back against the door. "What have you done?" I snarled.

"Perhaps you should ask Miss Darcy that!" he retorted, and jerked away from me. "Unless you think she would deceive you, as you have her."

"Do you expect to force my hand through her? What do you want?"

"Ah, so now we are come to it. I want what I have always wanted, Darcy. I want what my father left, I want my estate restored, and I want my name back. And to have it, I must have justice from you."

"I have done nothing against you," I spat.

"Still you persist! You have slandered my father and—"

"Your father used to beat his wife and daughter! There, what do you have to say to that?"

He took a step back. "You lie."

"Do I? Ask your mother."

His eyes hardened. "Is that why you killed him, Darcy? You pushed him from the balcony to exact vengeance?"

"I did nothing to the man. As far as I know, his fall was divine judgment for his sins."

"My mother saw! She saw you attacking him—a man twice your age, and on the balcony of his own home!"

"Attacking him!" I barked derisively. "I was defending myself, and faring poorly, if you must know. How can a man murder another when he has been clubbed in the head and lies senseless on the pavers?"

"Are you implying my mother first beat him then pushed him over the railing—a man of nineteen stone? Or my sister, who by your account was already battered and bruised? Are you saying that the two women who were most dependent upon him conspired to have him killed?"

"I made no such accusation; the conclusion was all your own."

"You are wrong, Darcy! I am not afraid to declare you what you are —a murderer and a liar, and my mother was a fool to enter a bargain with you. Had I been there—"

"No!" I interrupted. "I was the fool. I ought to have chosen the noose right then!"

"Then, why did you not?"

"Why do you think? We all have our reasons."

"Ah," he nodded knowingly. "We come back to the matter at hand. Very well, I shall do as my mother did, and make a pact with the devil. Give Miss Darcy to me in marriage, she and her thirty thousand, and I will forget everything I know about my father's death."

I stepped close, my bared teeth near his ear. "Go to hell."

"After you, Darcy. No one was ever tried for my father's murder. I can still make accusations. Your name will be disgraced forever, your property forfeit, your miserable corpse sold to be dismembered by the barber surgeons, and Miss Darcy will be mine anyway."

I had turned away in disgust, but I stalked back towards him. "Do you truly want to test me, Benedict? I warn you now, you will regret it."

"I think not. You truly are so prosaic, Darcy! I can even predict what you shall say next. For example, I knew you would have said nothing of me to Miss Darcy. Any other man would have forbidden his sister ever to have contact with his foe, would have told her all manner of goblin tales to set her off of me, but the sweet and fair Miss Georgiana Darcy received me like family. You never told her a word, did you?"

I narrowed my eyes. "Some things are too hideous to tell anyone."

His features hardened. "Do you mean the part where you allowed *my* sister to die? What did you do to her, Darcy? Everyone says you used to fight. Did you strike her? Throw her over the balcony as well?"

"I told you what happened to her!" I exploded.

"And I should believe you—" he shot back—"a man who already killed once in a fit of passion?"

I shook my head and looked on him in contempt. "There can be no reasoning with such a cloven-hoofed cretin. What do you really want, Benedict? For I shall disclose something you do not know—I have just come from your mother and George Wickham. Yes, I found them together. Did you not believe me before?"

He blinked and shifted his feet, but I did not permit him time to collect himself adequately to make some glib response.

"Amazing is it not?" I goaded him. "How fast even cherished blood and old friends will sell your dearest secrets for a few hundred pounds?"

He straightened his shoulders again. "And what do you fancy you have learned? I thought you would know better than to trust Wickham."

"Enough," I answered simply, my sense of calm and control beginning to return.

His eyes widened faintly—the flare of his nostrils and the hammering pulse at his throat told of his unease, but he drew a short breath and laughed it off. "I suppose Wickham mentioned that little task he performed for me. Ah, well, I meant for you to find out sooner or later. No point in going to all that trouble if it never provoked you to negotiate. Good show, Darcy, coming round at the first breath of trouble. One might almost think you cared about the welfare of that tradesman more than a man of your own class!"

"What do you hope to gain, Benedict?" I hissed.

"I will give it to you straight, Darcy. Twenty thousand pounds, and I shall forget I ever knew you."

I paced round him, glaring intently as a lion stalking his prey. "Twenty? Why not fifty? Why not a hundred?"

"The only reason is because I wish to leave the country in a hurry. I ask for what I think I can get, and I happen to know from your former banker—yes, I have my connections—how quickly you can access that amount."

I walked away from him, not responding for a moment. "How

much unmarked tea and opium do you have stashed away, ready to be sold on the black market?"

The lightness and oily sneer returned to the vermin's tones. "What makes you think I still have it?"

"If you did, you would not be presently in need of money."

He shrugged. "Here in London, I had only ten barrels of tea and four small chests of opium remaining. All those are now the property of your friend Mr Gardiner—or, rather, they were for a few hours."

"So, either you spent the rest of your ill-gotten earnings at the card tables, or someone else found them first, before you could sell them quickly enough. And now, you expect me to fund your licentious existence."

"You know, Darcy," he sighed with an irksome roll of his eyes, "you really are tedious. No man is as sanctimonious as you pretend to be. Come now, do we have a bargain or not?"

"Not."

"Very well, then I shall call Miss Darcy down and ask this very moment if she would like to elope with me to Scotland. She likes me very much, you know, and will not fail to consider the spot on her reputation if Mrs Younge spreads rumours of a liaison. Her thirty thousand pounds ought to see me in good stead, though I imagine you will drag your feet some in releasing it."

"If you ever speak to her again," I threatened, "you will not leave this house alive!"

"I do not need to speak to her. Perhaps I shall report at the club what a fine, sweet morsel Miss Georgiana Darcy was? No, no, no, her reputation is worth more to you than that. And what of this Mr Gardiner? Your haste in returning to London, and your very presence here tells me how keenly interested you are in his affairs—or, rather, in his *niece*. Perhaps I must make her acquaintance? Wickham told me where I might find her. What shall it be, Darcy?"

I stood back, unflinching at his threats, though they made the blood rage in my veins and my head pound with fury. Casually, I half-tucked my thumbs into the pockets of my waistcoat. "Ten thousand."

"Ten!" he protested. "Not half enough for my needs."

"It is the best offer you will receive. What, did you expect your friends to finance you? Your mother? I have tightened my watch on her. She cannot even have a fit of the vapours that I shall not know of it, and she will not dare lift a finger to help you, or she will find herself inhabiting the hedgerows."

He rocked back on his heels, glaring unblinkingly, as if he expected me to flinch. "Do you know the secret of negotiations, Darcy?" he asked after a moment.

I merely raised an eyebrow.

A rakish sort of triumph appeared on his face. "Ask for twice what you truly want. Very well, you blackguard. I accept."

"Done," I agreed. "Whatever contact you have at the East India Company, I do not wish to know. But you are to call them off Mr Gardiner and his business. The investigation on him and the persecution of his family will cease instantly, and you must be out of the country by the end of the week."

"Out of the country?" he protested. "How am I to collect payment?"

"I have an agent in Amsterdam. Once you arrive there, he will dispense your funds. Two months I will give you, which is more than enough time for your travels. If anything goes amiss before then, you shall not see a penny. All this with the agreement that we never set eyes on one another again, in this lifetime or the next."

He snorted. "It must be convenient to be so wealthy, able to pay for whatever whims and pleasures you wish."

I turned away. "Not convenient. A responsibility. I expect to have word from you by this time tomorrow of Gardiner. That is all."

CHAPTER 24

Georgiana had been weeping for at least two hours by the time I went up to her. This was the report of the maid who had been standing just outside her room. I could hear her even now, sobbing as if her heart would break, and I groaned in pity as I stared at the door.

"She carries on like that, sir," the maid whispered. "For long spells, then she's gone still like she went to sleep. I just start to think I might go in and fluff her pillow or put on the coverlet, but then she sets off again. Shall I fetch her some tea, sir?"

"Not just yet. I will call if tea is wanted." I dismissed the maid, then stood uselessly on the wrong side of the door—my arms hanging at my sides and my head reeling as if I had been struck by a boxer.

The damnable thing was that it was all my fault. To acknowledge that much cost me dearly enough, but that the recognition came at the hands of a man I detested made my skin crawl and my conscience squirm. What an arrogant ass I had been! Not to tell her, to equip her to be on guard for herself, was as grave a wrong as I had ever done her.

Another truth afflicted me even more than this, for I could not decide what to do with it. Any well-brought up young lady would have known better than to receive a gentleman without her guardian's permission. Whatever I had, or had not, told her about Benedict, Georgiana should never have considered carrying on with him! She ought to have understood it was wrong, dangerous, and rebellious to have a man in the house without my knowledge.

But who would have taught her such a standard? Mrs Younge, presumably. I had assumed no one would have to state the matter so explicitly, that she would understand what was expected of her. Again, I was forced to acknowledge that Lady Matlock had been right— Georgiana was tender and sensitive to a fault, but she suffered from a deplorable lack of maturity and social prudence. And it was I who ought to have known better.

Had I only warned her... any halfway informed female would know not to trust a man who waited to make his move until her guardian had left town! And any Darcy, as I expected her to be, should have the temerity to set down her paid companion when that woman recommended an unwise course! Or... had Georgiana herself designed it? A chance to defy me and exert her own will? I began to seethe in rage all over again when I recalled Georgiana's words to me, her excuse for sending me off to Hertfordshire alone while she carried on her dalliance behind my back.

Even now, listening to her tears, my spine stiffened—unmoved by the great laments pouring forth from her door. Did she mean to manipulate me still? My determination was swift and indignant. I would chastise her like the child she was, send her back to Pemberley with Richard as a guardian, if I could find no one else to trust. It would be worth finding someone to buy his commission and funding his retirement from the army—even giving him a small estate of his own, if need be! That would be a pittance compared to the irreparable damage Georgiana could do to herself and to everyone else around her.

So resolved, I raised my knuckles and rapped hard on her door. The dry, gasping moans ceased for a moment, and there was a short hesitation. I heard her tumbling from her bed, then dragging herself to the door to open it. The face that greeted me was downcast and puffy with tears. She said nothing; only stood back and stared at the floor.

As the door slowly closed, I glared at her—my own sweet sister, who had never given me a moment's grief in her sixteen years. Georgiana, namesake of both the wisest man I had ever known and my graceful mother, a woman of impeccable manners and discernment! I held her in a cold gaze as her posture slumped, and then when the latch finally clicked, I spoke.

"What explanation have you?"

She sniffed and lifted her shoulders, but did not speak.

"What? No excuses? No casting your blame on Mrs Younge, decrying her as a poor influence? No mournful pleas begging me to have mercy on your lover?"

She looked up at this, her eyes wide. "He is not my lover!"

"If you believe that, you are even more naïve than I thought. How badly did he compromise you?"

She shrugged again and sucked on a swollen lip. "Not at all."

"Do not dare!" I held up a finger just short of her face. "Do not dare to mock me! Do you intend to protest your own innocence? Do you claim ignorance of how a young lady receiving clandestine visits from a man would be damaged forever in the view of society?"

Her eyes filled with tears and her voice quavered when she answered. "I have... I did worry about that. A little."

"But your passions overcame you?"

"Passions!" she protested weakly. "Why, no—"

"Then what was it?" I demanded. "Imagine my dismay when I returned to my own house and found my sister entertaining a man—I assure you, you cannot! But to discover that you were entertaining a man who is not welcome in my house, to whom I would never have permitted you to be introduced!"

"I—I know you despise him," she mumbled.

"Despise! That is not even the right word. He is sheer malevolence, a repugnance in my sight, but there are many such men, and they are all suffered to continue breathing and walking among us. Were it only myself, I would behave the gentleman. I would find some way to ignore him and forever distance myself from him, or even display indifference if we were in company. But it is not just about me! Do you not know the danger you have placed yourself in? Do you not understand the sort of man you had befriended?"

She sniffed and daringly raised her eyes. "How should I? You never told me of him."

"I am telling you now!"

She dropped her gaze again, and a remnant of her sobs shook her. "Oh... I understand."

"Do you! Do you truly?"

"I..." she hesitated, her brow pinched. "I suppose not."

"No." I answered flatly. "How could you? You presume to act as a woman, a being of wisdom and maturity, and yet you yield to childish inclinations that can only be destructive. Good lord, Georgiana, what were you thinking, having him here at the house?"

"I th-thought he w-was f-family!" she wept. She gasped and wiped her eyes hastily on her sleeve. "H-he told me h-he w-was. That his b-be-beloved s-sister w-was your—"

"Beloved! He cursed his own sister's grave! You have fallen for a lie—worse, you have deceived me! What were you thinking, remaining in London just so you could consort with this viper?"

"That is not how it happened!" she protested, visibly offended. "I told you the truth! I only wanted you and Elizabeth to—"

"Do not attempt to mollify me right now, Georgiana. I have not the temper for it. Pray, tell me how he ingratiated himself to you, if it was not by your design."

"Well—" she clamped her teeth into her lower lip in thought. "Mrs Younge said that he was a very agreeable young man who had met with terrible misfortune, and she felt sorry for him."

"Pity! Yes, of course. Always the most reliable means of securing a young woman's sympathies."

"But it was more than that," she added.

I sighed, and a tremendous ache seemed to open up in my chest. "Curiosity? You hoped he would tell you what I would not?"

She was blinking madly, still unwilling to meet my eyes, but looking at my shoulder now, rather than my feet. "Yes," she whispered.

I pressed two fingers to my forehead, trying to collect my thoughts, to make my voice calmer. "Do you suppose there might have been a reason I did not tell you these things, Georgie?"

Her lips parted, and she finally looked me in the face. She nodded.

I glanced about and chose a seat beside her hearth, inviting her to take the opposite chair. "What did he tell you?"

She drew a long, trembling breath, and stared at the hands folded in her lap. "That... that his father's death was no accident, and neither was your wife's."

"And you believe these things?"

She raised her eyes hesitantly and shook her head.

I leaned my forehead on my fist as I watched her. "Do you say that only because I am sitting here and presently put out with you? You tell me what you think will appease me?"

"No," she responded quickly. "Because I know you."

"Do you? What about the year and a half I kept you away from me? Are you so convinced that I could have done no wrong in all that time?"

"I know," she answered more boldly, "because you always seek to do right, to do your duty. You are incapable of deceit or wickedness."

"No one is incapable, Georgiana. Least of all one who had just cause for his wrath."

"But not you," she insisted, "for you are a man who defends even dumb animals. I have seen you angry, it is true, but you could never truly harm another person. You always check yourself and do the right thing."

"Then why—" I leaned forward, my elbows on my knees—"Why would you entertain Benedict in this house? What could you hope to gain by it?"

She shrugged. "Information."

I raised an eyebrow. "Information."

"Well, yes. Naturally, I was curious about his family and everything that happened, but I learned quickly that he thought me ignorant. I—I mean not merely uninformed, but I believe he guessed I was incapable of logical reflection. He must have thought that, I suppose, for as you say, I... I acted the fool. But it was enough to persuade him that he needn't be on his guard against me, and he said a number of things I do not think he would otherwise have done."

"Such as?"

"He spoke of India, of his time there. I was fascinated by the tales of the people, so he told me much of that. One day, he talked of his father. How well did you know him?"

"Sir Edmund? Not as well as I should have, and better than I would have liked."

She nodded eagerly, as if that were a material point of information. "I believe he felt the same way."

"About his own father? I am hardly surprised, but it would be the first I have heard of any discord between father and son."

She shook her head. "I had the impression that he distrusted his father. In fact, one day he mentioned something that was almost disastrous, that could have ruined... something." She squinted, gazing off into the distance. "He stopped himself there, but I remembered that. He laughed it off, saying it was a good job he had gone to India when he did, and that all had turned out right. I thought that was strange."

I bit down on my tongue to keep from blurting the obvious—why had she continued to permit him to call, if she found his words inconsistent? But such a question would avail me nothing at the moment, so I merely nodded and said, "Go on."

"He... he spoke of his mother some, and—oh, he did not mention you specifically, but he said she was left quite helpless after his father's death, but I knew that... that must not have been true."

"How did you come to that conclusion?"

"Because I knew you would not leave her so, no matter what her offences against you had been. If... if she had any claim upon you at all, you would have looked after her. Would you not?"

"I would, and I did."

She seemed pleased and smiled faintly before nervously sobering again. "I thought you would have. And then he said how beautiful his sister was, how when you first met her you were overcome with desire for her, but I knew that was a lie, as well."

"How so?"

"The way you talked about her," she answered, with growing energy. "I believe he meant for me to think you had compromised her, but you had already assured me that you had not. He was not there to see it, by his own admission, so he must have made it up. And I have seen you when you talk about Elizabeth Bennet. You are not the same, you are... it is like you are finally happy when you speak of her. So...." She released a trembling breath and looked down at her hands again. "I am the stupidest girl alive."

I regarded her a moment, trying to decide if this rapid shift was some emotive display, meant to engage my sympathies, or if she had suddenly happened upon this conclusion based on the events as she related them. Her head bowed, and she began to weep again; racking gasps soon cutting off any hope of rational speech.

"Georgiana," I spoke gently, but to no avail. She continued to sob, and it was rapidly apparent that this was no ploy on her part. Her face contorted, she attempted a word or two, but her cries were all inarticulate, and soon, she had lost any prospect of composure.

There was nothing for it but to comfort her until she had done, and so I did. I moved from my chair to her slightly longer seat, wedging my frame into the furniture somehow, so I could put my arms around her as she wept. For a while, I was glancing at odd intervals at the mantel clock. My instinct was, and always had been, to rise her up and set about the business of repairing the damage done, trying to mend affairs between ourselves, and reclaiming order. My very body quivered with the need to do just that, for I could see, if Georgiana could not yet, how delicate and urgent a task lay before me.

Yet, a more imperative cause bound me to my place. Before I could carry out another duty, peace must be restored, and it could only begin in this way. I cradled my sister close and tried to imagine what

Elizabeth would have done. Yes, Elizabeth would know just what to do. How I longed for her in that moment!

I felt overwhelmingly unqualified, and yet, convicted by the knowledge that it *must* be me, *could only* be me. I had tried to enlist others to do what was mine, but though Georgiana had ached for a dear friend, though she craved the counsel of wiser women, what she had needed more than anything was myself. It was I who had pushed her away when she had most needed a stable voice in her life. It was I who had laid expectations upon her she had no hope of understanding. And it was I who had withheld the full truth, treating her as a child even while I expected her to behave as an adult.

I stroked back her hair and felt the worst of her cries abating. Perhaps it was exhaustion more than anything else, but as I continued to brush the curls from her temple with my fingers, her sobs diminished to sniffles and her great quaking stilled to minute trembles. At long last, she drew a shuddering sigh and wrapped her arms around my neck to bury her head in my chest.

I patted her back—somewhat uncomfortably, for I had never held her in such a way, even in her tender days of childhood. And, perhaps, that was where I had first erred. What girl of eleven should not have felt frequent, affectionate embraces such as this while she mourned the death of her father? What a pompous, stiff-necked oaf of a brother I had been these five years! Too rigid, too fixed in my own cares to truly see her, to comfort and nurture her as she deserved. I tightened my arms around her and wept bitter tears of my own for all my mistakes, the time I had lost, and what I had almost destroyed.

We passed some while in this way, simply clasping one another until her breathing had quieted. At length, she made a feeble effort to straighten, and I permitted her to pull away, to investigate my face.

"Georgiana," I said, my voice low and earnest, "I am sorry."

She dashed the back of her hand over her cheek and blinked. "I thought I was supposed to say that."

"I believe the one who has committed the graver wrong, and who fancies himself the more mature of the two, ought to take his part." I drew out my handkerchief and raised it, silently asking permission to wipe away her tears. Her face softened, and I gently dried her cheeks.

"I was stupid," she mumbled.

"Yes," I agreed, but my tones held no recrimination. "Are not we all, from time to time? But yours was a mistake spanning a mere few days, an error in judgment that stemmed from my own tremendous oversights. Or, rather, my arrogance, which I am assured, is a marvel to behold."

She sniffed again, but her throat seized, and a small chuckle bubbled forth. "That sounds like something Elizabeth would say."

"Where do you think I learned of it?"

She giggled softly, looking down. "I am sorry too, Fitzwilliam."

I raised her chin with my fingertips. "Then let this be the end of it. I shall never speak of it again, unless you wish to."

She shook her head, gesturing helplessly. "How can you not? You said it before, I have damaged my reputation already! What shall become of me?"

"You were misled. You allowed it to happen, that is true, but had I bestowed on you the care you deserved, you would never have done so. I do not view this as your fault, Georgiana. Rather, it is a failing on the part of those who ought to have borne their share." I brushed a fresh tear from her lashes, and added, "Let us speak with Lady Matlock. Where matters of a young lady's reputation are concerned, there is none better."

Her eyes flew wide. "Oh, no, Fitzwilliam, not Lady Matlock!"

"No fear, Georgiana. We cannot pretend nothing happened, but we can find out how to proceed."

She shivered. "Oh, how I wish I had never listened to Mrs Younge! I knew, Fitzwilliam. Truly, I did, but I suppose it was too thrilling… what will my aunt think of me?"

"I am more curious how Lady Matlock was also deceived in Mrs Younge's qualifications," I answered. "She came with the highest of recommendations."

Georgiana tilted her head. "She did? But she told me she had never served in such a capacity before. I am quite sure of it, for she said she had been abroad until six months ago."

I stared, puzzled. "With her husband? Did she come back at his death?"

She made a helpless face. "I am not sure she was married. I thought the title was an honorific, like Mrs Jenkinson."

"Georgiana—" I reached to take her hand in mine and squeezed it tightly—"I do not know what any of this means, but I intend to find out."

MY FIRST ACT was to send for Richard, for I had wished to apprise him of the events concerning our ward before others became involved. I thought he would charge out of the door and murder Benedict in his bed, so enraged was he when I reported all that had transpired. After a moment, his fury had redirected itself to me, for permitting Georgiana to remain in London alone.

"Did you not recommend she have her own establishment?" I argued. "Your notion was even more dangerous, for you suggested a seaside town, away from her family. At least this way, no real harm was done, and my own servants were in the room to see that propriety was observed."

"But she is far less prepared than she ought to have been!" Richard pointed out, his ears still red with anger. "I did not realise until she came to London how very immature she was. You ought to have taken her with you."

"And never give her a chance to flourish, to spread her own wings?"

"Georgiana is not a young colt to be improved through exercise and exposure! Think, Darcy, what one mistake could cost. If she is ill-equipped, then we would do better to keep her on a short lead, protect her like chinaware until you find her a husband!"

"No," I sighed. "I would do better to acknowledge my own part in this. She is not a hopeless case, Richard. In fact, she might be made all the stronger for this, but only if I do not break her in the process."

He narrowed his eyes and sat back, scrutinising me, then tilted his head to tap his ear. "Excuse me a moment, I believe my hearing is playing tricks on me. You did not just admit to some fault, did you? I must have been mistaken."

"I have my share of faults, as you well know."

He snorted. "You have a colossal array of them. I have composed an alphabetical list, if you care to survey it one day, but I shall have to tell my batman to summon the carriage to bring it all to you."

"That will not be necessary, for all my faults share the same fatal sins at their root. I am too prideful and too obstinate by half. It is a bitter acknowledgment, I assure you, but I can no longer afford to turn a blind eye to my own flaws."

"Humph. I know where this is coming from. That impertinent minx from Hertfordshire, she enumerated for you the litany of your failings, did she not?"

"With great frequency and vehemence," I confirmed.

"Well, then, God bless every female ever born under the name Elizabeth. When shall I wish you joy?"

I felt my expression darken once more. "My present concern is Georgiana. I would control or redirect whatever gossip might come out of this. Moreover, Mrs Younge was not what she represented herself to be, and though I wish for her perfidy to be exposed, I am concerned for what further harm that may do to Georgiana. I desire for you to attend us when we bring it before the countess."

"She will not refrain from exenterating you on my account, but very well. Father wished to speak with you anyway, for he had learned a bit more about… something to do with your former bank?"

"Ah…" I repressed a groan. It seemed more and more London entanglements conspired to restrain me, when I wanted nothing more than to return to Hertfordshire.

Lord and Lady Matlock received us together, which was a first in my experience, and did little to alleviate Georgiana's obvious apprehension. She entered the drawing room with her head hanging and her toes scuffing reluctantly on the carpet. Richard gave her a sympathetic look as he chose a seat for himself, and I remained by her side on the sofa while we related the pertinent facts.

Lord Matlock's deeply furrowed countenance resembled a cigar-puffing bulldog by the time I had done. His eyes glittered to small, black points and his complexion had assumed a purplish hue. Lady Matlock's face was even more terrifying, with her offended chin set high and her generous bosom rising indignantly with each breath, as if at any moment she meant to unleash such a diatribe as might blister flesh from the bone. She kept still, however—unnervingly silent until I was quite finished with my tale.

Both my aunt and uncle had been casting frequent glances at Georgiana's morose countenance, but I diverted their attention to myself. "I have naturally dismissed Mrs Younge," I informed them, "but I am curious who recommended her to you, Lady Matlock."

"Lady Templeton, and Lady Margaret Downey," she answered at once.

"And do you know how she came to their notice?"

"She presented her character—a letter, as is the usual. She had not been seeking a place overlong, which is always pleasing, if you ask me. One does not wish to be in the position of giving consequence to ladies' companions who have been overlooked by other families. One wonders what can be the matter with them."

"Of course. Her letter, was it from a source known to you?"

"Well! Fitzwilliam Darcy, if you mean to insinuate that I would not verify her claims, I must inform you that I spoke to four different ladies on her account. All praised Mrs Younge's experience in the most glowing of terms. They had all met with her personally, for naturally, all wish to have the distinction of being able to recommend some useful person to a family of consequence, should the opportunity arise. Why, I myself was able to find a place for a Mrs Leighton, and who do you think is most grateful to me for bringing her to their notice? The duchess of Monmouth herself! I assure you; no one would intentionally put forward a fraud." She sniffed. "The damage to my own reputation is not to be thought of!"

"Someone did," the earl groused, speaking for the first time. "Come now, my dear, who first brought out her name?"

"You can be sure, it was no one of *my* acquaintance. Surely, if she *is* a fraud, she is quite a well-connected one. I mean to investigate, of that you may be absolutely certain," Lady Matlock intoned with a heavy scowl. She shifted her gaze to Georgiana, and I felt my sister shrink beside me.

"Mother—" Richard cleared his throat—"while you are looking into the matter, have you any other prospective companions to recommend? I think we must seek a replacement for Mrs Younge at once."

She frowned at her son and shook her silver head. "Richard Fitzwilliam, do not try to distract me from my purpose. Georgiana Darcy…" she sighed, flicked a guarded glance towards her husband, and thinned her lips. "I presume Darcy has already discussed the matter at length? Then I shall forbear for now, save to admonish you to keep up your looks. If the world should work to cast reproach upon you for your actions, then look them in the eye and dare them to speak it to your face. If you do not cower when they expect you to, they will have nothing more to say. Who knows but that you may put them to shame next?"

Georgiana blinked and sucked in a shaken breath, darting her eyes to me. "Yes, your ladyship," she gulped.

"Very well. Come and let us speak privately." Lady Matlock rose grandly, casting a withering gaze over me. Georgiana followed in meek obedience, but, I noted with some degree of hope, her chin was no longer ducked low.

"Well—" Richard craned his neck, watching the countess and Georgiana out of the room—"Mother took that better than I expected."

The earl narrowed his eyes. "That was only the opening skirmish. I pity Georgiana in the weeks to come, and Darcy—" he grunted wryly —"I shall see to it that you have a fine tombstone when she has done with you."

"If you seek to heap burning coals on my head, I assure you, it will be unnecessary."

"Better for you both if you married at once," he declared. "That would quiet any other gossip for a time, and provide Georgiana with some..." he cleared his throat... "proper guidance. Now, let us have no more of delays and indecision. Shall I write to Lady Catherine to expect you?"

"No."

The earl seemed to have anticipated such an answer but was unprepared for the shortness of it. He tipped forward, still fixing me in a dictatorial stare. "Then, shall it be Lady Sarah? I rather fancy the notion of an alliance with Dewhurst."

"No, your lordship. I will not be making an offer to Lady Sarah, nor to any of the others."

Lord Matlock slammed his fist on the table beside him and commenced uttering a string of colourful expletives. I sensed Richard's apprehension, as he drew back and shifted his attention between his father and myself, but I was nonplussed by the performance. The earl thundered about my unfitness as a guardian and the dubious allocation of intelligence granted at my birth. He abused my character with an inventive selection of obscenities and railed eloquently about what misfortunes I deserved to my account until the veins stood out on his forehead.

After three full minutes, he was not yet done—his ingenuity at framing insults limited only by his extensive vocabulary and the expanse of his considerable vexation. He went on to express most ardently his opinions of my parentage and my likelihood of being cast forever out of all 'good' society—of which he considered himself a member, while I could only doubt the desirability of such a distinction. I waited, biding my time until he had jerked to his feet to pour himself some soothing libations. As he drank—an act which required him to cease his obloquy for half a moment—I made a steady answer.

"I regret your lordship's displeasure over the matter, but my resolve is fixed. If I do marry another woman, she shall be of my own choosing. Perhaps one day I may be fortunate enough to present you with the happy news that a woman of noble character and distinguished mind has accepted my troth, but it will not be this day."

The earl gaped in perfect abhorrence, his chest heaving, and his fist still clenched around his empty glass. His head shook, and he instinctively sought his son for some sympathy in his outrage. "Do you hear this bacon-brained half-wit?"

Richard was disguising whatever expression his mouth might have betrayed behind his hand, but he composed himself to answer tolerably well. "Indeed, Father, he spoke quite clearly."

"Bloody fool," the earl growled at his son in contempt, then he turned his attention back to me. "Darcy, do you still fail to appreciate your place? A man of sense—or so I thought—and what I once took for reason, could do much as an MP. A Derbyshire seat is all but assured; all you need do is speak for it! But it will avail you nothing if you are intent upon slighting every ally you might gain."

"Take heart, Uncle," I answered with a fair degree of cheer, "for after this incident with Georgiana, I may not even be able to be elected. Perhaps it is just as well."

Another volley of calumny and vituperation accompanied my statement, but this time, my uncle calmed himself more quickly, and without the aid of his spirits. He was pacing, and at once he ceased and scrutinised me. "Of all the... you set me off intentionally," he realised, squinting one eye and twisting his face into an incredulous grimace.

"I confess, I did."

"Why? Have you some more disastrous news to report, that you thought to exhaust me on another point first?"

I glanced at Richard. "Perhaps. It is not unlikely that my erstwhile brother-in-law might re-think our most recent arrangement and feel himself dissatisfied enough to wish to do me greater harm. I fear that it is time I enlightened you about my previous marriage. Matters were not as you presumed."

His lordship frowned, then returned to the decanter to pour, and then dispense, three glasses. He resumed his seat but set his glass aside without touching it as he said, "I am all attention."

CHAPTER 25

$\mathcal{I}$ remained in London four more days, each hour weighing like an anvil upon my shoulders. My fortitude and endurance were severely tested—most particularly when I found it necessary to confirm and transact matters pertaining to the Benedicts, whether mother or son.

By late afternoon of the second day, Benedict had sent a letter by courier, confirming that his contact—whoever it was—had managed to hush up and cry off the Company's outrage against Edward Gardiner. Paperwork had been magically procured to verify the goods were shipped by a factor-contracted importer, and then "restored to the rightful owner," for, as the documentation alleged, there had been some frightful mix-up at the dockyards.

I could not help but read it all with a sick sense of repugnance. What underhanded dealings and corrupt persons must have been at work to make Benedict's ploy possible in the first place, and then so quickly resolved, I could but guess. The only thing that mattered, that I could have any influence over, was that Edward Gardiner was cleared of any suspicion.

Wickham had disappeared, which surprised me not at all. No doubt, he had decided to make himself scarce, knowing that I already

371

held the power to lock him away for good. At the latest figure, his obligations totalled nearly a thousand pounds in both London and Meryton, and I had yet to hear from Colonel Forster whether he had debts of honour—or, rather, how high such debts were. Lady Benedict grudgingly supplied me with enough information to track him, if I desired, but I did not.

On the third day, I decided to confirm for myself that Gardiner was, indeed, relieved of his trials. I took the liberty of calling on him at his home, in the manner of a casual acquaintance. He had been in his study, but came eagerly to greet me when his butler announced my arrival.

"Mr Darcy! How very good of you to call. I had not expected the pleasure."

"The pleasure is entirely mine, sir," I bowed.

Gardiner offered me a seat, then asked if I would like something. I accepted, and we drank one another's health.

"I heard you had gone to Hertfordshire to celebrate your friend's wedding," he said. "I should not have thought to see you again in London before the ceremony."

"It was a matter that could not be helped. I intend to return to Netherfield soon, and Miss Darcy shall accompany me this time. She will be pleased to see her friends again."

"Very good, very good. I am happy to say that Mrs Gardiner and I will be going to Longbourn day after tomorrow. I had not thought it would be in our power to do so—indeed, I feared much worse, but... well, we will be delighted to pay our respects to our dear Jane."

"Certainly, Miss Bennet will be gratified by your presence," I replied.

"Yes, I believe so. The dear girl! Poor Mrs Gardiner was heart-broken to have to tell her niece we might not be able to attend, but matters seem to have resolved for the better. I tell you, Mr Darcy, it was the most peculiar thing, and I thought I should never see my way clear of it, but I count myself a fortunate man this day—at least, I must have some friend, I am sure of it. At any rate, I was able to write only this morning that all is well, and we are very much looking forward to wishing Jane joy on her wedding day."

"I am glad to hear it. Though it is but a short journey to Hertfordshire, Georgiana and I would be pleased if you rode with us."

"Oh!" His modest pleasure shone forth, and he stammered a polite rejection. "I would very much have liked to accept your offer, Mr Darcy, but Mrs Gardiner wishes to bring the children. They are so fond of the country, and you know, the fresh air is immeasurably healthful. They would be disappointed to miss seeing Jane and Lizzy, I know."

I smiled. "I quite understand. Then I shall look forward to speaking with you again in a few days."

"As shall I, Mr Darcy."

We rose, and he walked with me into the hall. Just as I gave him my hand in parting, a peculiar expression passed over his face. "Do you know, it was the oddest thing, that—a business concern, Mr Darcy. Nothing to trouble yourself over, naturally, and so I shall not describe it for you, save to say that it was a precarious situation, indeed. But have you ever thought to yourself that you must have a guardian angel?"

I returned his firm grip and nodded. "Frequently. Good day, sir."

THE FINAL DAY before our return to Netherfield was spent ensuring that all was arranged with my solicitor. Upon certainty of that, and after my most gratifying visit with Mr Gardiner, I dispatched an express to my agent in Amsterdam to release the funds specified. Afterwards, I washed my hands of it, and expected never to see Robert Benedict again so long as he lived.

The matter of Georgiana was more perplexing. I had not yet settled it with myself what I was to do with her, save that she was not to be out of my sight. She seemed repentant, and indeed, I believed her to be in earnest, but I felt she little knew how greatly vexed I truly was. It was not merely for the sake of her perceived "value" as a bridal prospect for some wealthy man, nor did I suffer chiefly for my own public dignity. It was my personal shortcomings connected to the event, and how I had failed at my first duty to her. How was I to see that she got on better in the future, without casting such a pall over her current existence that she might never recover?

Richard withstood it all far better than I did. He took it upon himself to cheer her, escorting her out for a drive while I was occupied with other matters. When they returned, she appeared as if she had even smiled once or twice before vanishing into her room. We watched her up the stairs, then looked back at one another with deadpan, yet expressive countenances.

"Father sent this for you," he said, by way of changing the topic from Georgiana. He extended a note. "I shall tell you what it says without the trouble of reading it. He is more determined now than ever to prove Wallingford—that is, Percival Ramsey—culpable in some scheme to defraud bank investors. It is all political, of course, but after hearing your story about one mysterious cover-up, he is perfectly convinced there must be more. I am afraid that rather than appeasing his offended sense of family honour, you have only enraged the titan."

I took the earl's note and read it before Richard, scanning quickly over the generalities he had already related and seeking the details. "He has proof now," I murmured as I read. "A secretary working for the bank verified that I was not the only customer to question certain sums. So far, though, it appears I was the only one the bank declined to do business with any longer."

I turned the page, for the note was close-written both front and back, and continued. "Now, this is odd. It seems that in each case, mine included, the customers were perplexed by their accounts showing *more* than they ought to have."

"What?" Richard pulled the note, and my entire hand, close for his own scrutiny. "That makes no sense. If someone were skimming pence here and there to line his own pockets, should not the accounts reflect a lower total?"

I studied the words again, my brow furrowed thoughtfully. "Perhaps he was not skimming. Think how many measures are in place to prevent that exact thing. But if someone were flush with ill-gotten gains and needed a place to dispose of them until their source could not be traced, a simple 'accounting error' might suffice."

"Do you know," Richard breathed, "you might be on to something. I shall mention it to Father."

I narrowed my eyes as I read the earl's final lines, then shook my head. "No need, for he has thought of it as well. I trust you will write to me at once if anything more is heard?"

He stepped back with a lopsided grin. "I will do better than that. I will gallop all the way to Hertfordshire and drag you out of bed in the dead of night."

"I trust that will not be necessary!"

He was still smiling, but his look turned from the jocular to the confidential. "Give Miss Elizabeth my regards, will you?"

I stilled, then nodded solemnly. "I hope I shall have the opportunity."

"Oh," he laughed, "I have no doubt of it. I think I shall like coming to know her better. Do not take too long in going about courting her, though. She might decide you are not worth the effort."

"Your confidence is inspiring," I retorted.

He clapped me on the shoulder. "Best get to it, man."

AFTER RICHARD LEFT, I ought to have been cool-headed, contented, and steady to my purpose. Instead, I was an anxious knot of worry and nerves. I fancied that my organs must have been overworked and my limbs ready to quake from my frame.

A book of poetry would not answer for such distress, so with a quick word to my butler, I sent for my horse. Here in London, I could not gallop the open fields to soothe my nerves, but a long, brisk trot through the park settled me somewhat. When I finally returned to my house, I could breathe, and think on the following morning with some equanimity.

Georgiana and I were both eager to set out at dawn, and as is so rare when one is impatient, our carriage seemed to have wings as it swept along the way. We had left so early and had such good roads that we arrived at Netherfield just before eleven. I had been peering steadily out the window, my nerves very nearly aflame as we approached the place where I had discovered the difference between intention and desire.

As we rounded the final bend, I started and pressed against the glass pane with a fresh burst of urgency and apprehension. There was a carriage in the drive... and I laughed, low in my throat. It was as much a product of uneasiness as it was joy, for I did not know what it portended, but that was the Bennet carriage. Elizabeth was at Netherfield... waiting for me.

Georgiana appeared to be similarly afflicted by uncertain hope, and she offered a nervous smile when she also saw the vehicle. White teeth tore at her upper lip, and she nodded in response to my unspoken question. "I am well, Fitzwilliam," she managed brokenly.

I reached to clasp her hand, and then our carriage was rolling up beside the other, and the door was opening. Bingley had not come to meet us this time, but a footman escorted us into the house. Piteous and frenzied fool that I was, I caught myself counting the steps until I would set my gaze upon her, composing my features so I would not look like an impetuous and ungainly pup when I came into the room.

"Good day, Miss Elizabeth..." No, too stiff, and not half what I wanted to express. I closed my eyes briefly and thought again.

"A pleasure to see you again, Miss Elizabeth." Dull, stupid... Time was drawing close, and I clenched my fist as the footman reached to open the door to the drawing room.

"Thank you for still speaking to me, after all I have done..."

"You smell as fresh as the spring rain over the mountains..."

I looked down at my boots at the last second, chiding myself for a mooncalf and imploring, beseeching my own brain to cooperate, to form a coherent sentence when I finally beheld her. The door was open now... Georgiana was passing through before me, and I watched her to learn in what part of the room my attention should land first.

"Darcy!" Bingley cried, rising to greet us. "And Miss Darcy, delighted you came back to us." He took Georgiana's hand to kiss it and then made me some salutation, but I scarcely heard him. I was already looking beyond him, to the dusky-hued Venus sitting demurely beside Miss Bennet. Her eyes fixed on me—so clear and alive, snapping with that peculiar kind of brilliance that was all her own. She rose, catching her sister's hand as an afterthought, and they came forward together.

"... And my dear Mr Darcy, how dismayed we all were when my brother told us you had gone off to London again so soon! You are full of surprises, sir, bringing back Miss Darcy to bless our happy company at the very last hour."

I blinked, startled from my reverie as Miss Bingley deposited her tall, angular form directly in my path. I fumbled for some polite response—I believe I expressed my gratitude that she approved, or some such nonsense—and was forced to retract my hand behind my back, lest she lay claim to it.

"I thank you most kindly for your warm reception, Miss Bingley," Georgiana answered for me. "I did so long to see you and Mrs Hurst again. Is that a new fashion for your hair? It is terribly fetching!"

"Oh! This?" Miss Bingley touched her coiffure and arched her neck until it met her shoulder in a manner she must have thought seductive. "Why, it is the simplest thing; I only asked my abigail to try something modest and understated. I am sure she can show your girl how it is done."

"I would be most obliged, Miss Bingley." Georgiana slipped an elbow cosily through Miss Bingley's and urged her towards a seat, but as she went, she cast me one brief, almost giddy look of triumph. I watched her go in astonishment. One day, perhaps, I would learn who it was with whom I had to deal—the insecure and heedless girl who too easily yielded to impulse and melancholy, or the calculating and observant mademoiselle who might someday eclipse even Lady Matlock's dominion.

I turned back and almost flinched when my gaze touched on Miss Bennet. I bowed at once, clasping my hands behind my back, and waited for her to speak. Her milky brow seemed troubled, and she was a moment in meeting my eyes, but when she did, she spoke more clearly to me than she had ever done.

"Mr Darcy, I am pleased by your return. It was good of you... very good of you to... to bring Miss Darcy from London, and then to come back in time to wish us joy." She tilted her head, her lips twitching as if she wished to think of something else to say, but she fell silent.

"The honour is mine, Miss Bennet," I answered. She seemed satisfied by this, and with a glance to her sister, pardoned herself to go take the arm of her betrothed.

Elizabeth had been watching me with a steady, earnest gaze—lips parted softly, with just the hint of a turn at each corner where their rosy fullness blended to creamy dimples. Her eyes had darkened again, but rather than glinting with the flaming passion of former days, her lashes fell gently low as she looked up to me.

All the words I had meant for her abandoned me. I could utter nothing—mute as a newborn, I merely returned her long look with all the ardent yearning I could express. My breathing quickened—I only recognised so much when my lungs failed to keep pace with my body's craving, and I was forced to draw a ragged breath as I admired her.

She blushed, looked down for a moment, and was smiling in truth when she raised her eyes again. "You have come very early from London, Mr Darcy."

"Yes," I agreed readily, grateful for something to say. "We were fortunate in our travels."

She nodded and brushed absently at a troublesome spiral of satin hair falling over her brow. "Your timing is most fortuitous, for we should not have seen you, had you been five minutes later."

"Oh?"

"Yes." She cleared her throat softly and caught her lip between her teeth—a nervous gesture I had only seldom witnessed from her. "Jane and I only came this morning so she might have an opportunity to tour her future chambers... ah, without our younger sisters present.

We were just bidding our adieux, since my aunt and uncle are due to arrive today, and we wished to be at home to greet them."

"Of course." My spirits sank, for I would have much preferred to lure her to a chair, ask if she knew how to play chess or whist, and while away a protracted visit with her while Miss Bennet lingered with Bingley. "Do give your uncle my regards, will you?"

She leaned slightly forward, and a quick shifting of her eyes seemed to indicate that she did not wish her voice to be overheard. "I will, sir. We are grateful—*most grateful*—that he could come at all."

"It was thoughtful of him to arrange his affairs so he might attend the wedding," I answered neutrally.

"It was, but the task was more than he could bear himself. I believe he has a friend… a very faithful and generous friend… who was of material assistance in the matter." She looked up to me then with startling intensity, her shoulders rising irregularly with each breath.

I drew back, a dread falling within my very centre. *She knew.* Damn Bingley and his great, flapping gums! She knew, and her tender, eager reception of me was only a product of misplaced gratitude and obligation! I wanted to weep, to retreat in a black cloud of self-pity, for this was not how I had hoped to win her approval at last.

"A—a friend?" I gulped, the stain of guilt tainting even the shades of my voice. "To assume such would be to discredit Mr Gardiner, would it not?" I attempted weakly.

One of her eyes twitched and her lips tightened. "On the contrary, if he does have such an ally in his troubles, I would count it a credit to both. I only wish I knew whom I could thank, on behalf of my family. They do not even know they are indebted to anyone, but I cannot think they could not be."

"If it is so," I answered with energy, "I am sure the party in question would desire no recognition whatsoever. Certainly, if it were true —and it is improbable—it was done for the interests of *one* person alone, and no credit or debt would ever be presumed. Truly, any expressions of the kind would render the gesture both inconsequential and supercilious."

"But to fail to recognise the magnanimity and humility that

inspired such an act of friendship would be a dishonour to myself, and, indeed, to this true and noble friend—if he does exist."

I swallowed, discovered myself to be trembling, and drew a steadying draught of fresh air. She was standing close—so very close. I could see the fluttering pulse just at the groove of her throat, the delicate curve of her nostrils as she, too, apparently struggled for composure. Some phrase from the other occupants of the room caught her notice for the barest second, then her gaze returned—easier now, with a touch of sweetness she had so rarely bestowed on me.

"I suppose it is fruitless to argue the existence of a person whose very being is debatable, unlikely, and secretive," she said. "But if I could ever speak with him, I would tell him..." Her brows drew together, and she tilted her head as her eyes scanned my face.

"Tell him what?" I asked, with more eagerness than I had intended to betray.

"I would tell him that no one could ever doubt his goodness. No proof was necessary to demonstrate his upright character or benevolent ways, but that does not erase my own gratitude that he might find my family worthy of his notice and care." She blinked, smiled thoughtfully, and continued. "That is what I would tell him, but as you say, it is unlikely that there is such a person."

"If there were," I added huskily, "I am certain he would be sufficiently honoured by your words that he would move heaven and earth to please you, if ever granted the opportunity."

She repressed a chuckle, and her eyes darted to her sister and Bingley at the periphery of my vision. They were withdrawing, and that meant Elizabeth must go, too. "Do you not know, Mr Darcy? No lady desires for heaven and earth to be broken loose from their foundations in her honour. She only wishes for one who would walk by her side in the rain."

"With or without an umbrella?" I asked.

She laughed. "Without. Decidedly, without."

I walked her down to the carriage, glorying in the way her light hand rested almost possessively on top of my arm. Bingley handed Miss Bennet into the box, and then it was for me to let Elizabeth go.

She turned back just before the door closed, and the look in her eyes answered every question I might still have.

Warmth flooded my senses, tingling through each sinew and muscle until I felt the only relief would be to leap for joy. But I did not wish to be relieved from the sensation. I savoured the burning of my thirst, clung fast to the sting of my own impatience. If desiring was the first pleasure before having, I would anticipate the fulfilment of the promise I found in her eyes with a fervent hunger, learning to cherish each excruciating moment, each exhilarating glance, for their purpose now was to lead her into my arms.

Some blessed day, some day not far distant, I would call her my own dearest, loveliest Elizabeth.

CHAPTER 26

The final week before Bingley's wedding flew by in a delirious haze for me. The first day after our arrival, we remained in for a quiet dinner and lazy evening in the drawing room. Cards were set out, and Georgiana made a fourth for Miss Bingley and the Hursts while Bingley and I stood by the mantel.

"I say," he mused with a significant cant to his head, "that was a marvellous relief about Mr Gardiner. I suppose Miss Elizabeth told you all about it."

"She did."

"The family are all most pleased, and not least myself, for I shall not now be housing all the younger sisters, should the worst have happened."

I nodded quietly, refusing to look at him. I knew well what he wanted, but this was no longer a matter between ourselves. My deepest cares, my most intimate thoughts, I felt I should preserve for Elizabeth, that she might be the first to hear them.

"Although," Bingley continued, "now that I consider it, I wonder if Jane would prefer for one of her sisters to come and stay. What do you think, Darcy? We had spoken of the possibility of *all* of them coming, out of necessity, but never the prospect of just one coming for companionship. Until she is married, of course, for I expect Miss Elizabeth will leave us one day, but ought I to bring the matter up with Jane?"

"Your house is your affair," I answered. "I should have thought Netherfield quite full enough for the tastes of a newly married couple."

"Oh, as to that, Caroline wishes to remove to London. She will live with Hurst and Louisa, and I have agreed to do something for her that would permit them all to move to a larger flat. It may be a permanent situation, for Caroline has been out for four seasons already." He shrugged, and said, "Ah, well. Are you certain her twenty thousand are not appealing enough to you? And she is still quite a handsome woman, is she not?"

I turned a caustic gaze upon him.

"Never hurts to ask," he sighed. "But what of Miss Elizabeth?"

I felt my own pupils dilate and my pulse skip. "What about her?"

"Why, what I was speaking of! Do you not think she and Jane would both be pleased if she came to Netherfield? They are so fond of each other, and I do not like to be the cause of their separation."

"It is only three miles," I scoffed, looking down into the fire so its glare might conceal the redness of my complexion. "Miss Elizabeth has already proved that she can manage the distance."

"I suppose that is true, but I thought to delay their parting as much as I could. I was assuming they will sustain a greater separation one day—you know, when Miss Elizabeth marries. It does not seem likely that she will choose any of the local men. She may, in fact, go some distance from here when the time comes."

I met his eyes, studied the way they danced in amusement while the rest of his face remained serious. "I hope she does."

I rode out the next morning, in hopes that Miss Elizabeth would be walking in the fields, despite the light showers and heavy morning mists. It was no surprise that she was not there, for even if the weather had not kept her indoors—and I was not certain that it was the weather—surely, the demands of preparing for the wedding had required much of her time. We were not to see the Bennets that day, for Mrs Bennet had sequestered all her girls—even the rowdy, quarrelsome ones—along with Mrs Gardiner for a final fitting of the bride's wedding clothes. This much, Georgiana had gleaned from her conversations with Miss Bingley and Jane Bennet herself, the day before.

I sat my horse on the rise, overlooking the narrow valley in which lay Longbourn house. Contrary to my whimsical fancies, no raven-haired goddess slammed the door and ran for the mountains with her skirts streaming behind her in the wet grass. I wondered, however, if she was at that very moment wishing she could do precisely that. I tipped my hat to the house, turned my mount, and cantered back to Netherfield.

The following evening, we were all invited to Longbourn for a formal dinner. Georgiana did not attend, but she had commissioned me before I set out to employ my time with Elizabeth well. We arrived just on the heels of the Philipses, and the modest house was nearly stretched to its seams with company when we entered.

Bingley's sisters immediately surrounded the bride and made much of her, though a careful inspection of Jane Bennet's countenance revealed a coolness that had not been there at our arrival. I reflected on that with satisfaction, for the soon-to-be Mrs Bingley would not easily be taken in by her future sisters' false affections.

Elizabeth had been occupied with Mrs Gardiner upon my first entry, but a sudden warmth, almost a golden presence seemed to hum at my side, and I turned to find her standing at my elbow. Her countenance I could not attempt to describe, save to say that the welcome reflected there served as honeyed confirmation of all my delirious hopes.

"Miss Bennet is looking well this evening," I said, by way of greeting.

She flicked her eyes over her sister, then back to me. "I recall a time when I might have been tempted to slap you for such a speech."

"Why? You are not jealous, Miss Elizabeth?"

An arch brow lifted, and her chin tilted. "And just what do I have to be jealous of?"

I grinned openly. "Nothing whatsoever, but I am vain enough to wish that I were capable of inspiring such a feeling in you."

"Impossible," she declared, "for to experience jealousy, one must also know uncertainty. I believe you have left me no room for that sentiment."

I laughed and offered her my elbow. "I am pleased to hear it. Dare I hope that you would consider being my dinner companion this evening?"

She accepted it easily, even draping a second hand over the first as she drew close. "I was hoping you would ask, sir."

I could not recall a more sumptuously contented hour in my entire life than the one I spent seated beside her at dinner. Good fortune—or Elizabeth's own manipulations—had placed Mrs Gardiner on my left, and I believe I had never had such agreeable, merry conversation with two females as on that occasion. Most of the company's attention was quite naturally fixed on the bride and groom, leaving us to our own pleasures. Mrs Gardiner was a charming and easy companion, and Mr Gardiner occasionally leaned forward to engage us as well, but for the greater part of the meal, I spoke exclusively with Elizabeth.

That freedom could not go unobserved for long, and I had expected my attentions to be noted by the ever-vigilant Caroline Bingley, at least. What I had not foreseen was for her to publicly snipe at Elizabeth after dinner. I had been standing close to Elizabeth and her sister Catherine—I could not quite bring myself to address her as 'Kitty'—when Miss Bingley drew near.

"My dear Eliza," she purred, "I am so pleased to see you and Mr Darcy getting on better. Why, I recall when we were all together last fall, you found him most intolerable."

Elizabeth blinked innocently. "I do not recall that. Was there some particular incident that stands out in your memory?"

Miss Bingley forced an incredulous laugh. "Why, nearly each time you were in the same room! I thought you and our most excellent Mr

Darcy here were fit to draw swords at each encounter. You did have such a way of provoking him!"

"I believe you are mistaken, Miss Bingley," I put in. "Miss Elizabeth and I have perhaps had a peculiar acquaintance, but I was by no means provoked. I have always taken great pleasure in her conversation."

Elizabeth had been attending my words, but now she looked back to Miss Bingley with serene agreement writ over her features. Caroline Bingley's face changed hues, and her mouth opened in helpless protest. "But what of how you spoke of her in private? And the ball!" She shook her head with a bewildered snort. "I thought we should have to engage our friends from the militia to keep the peace!"

"It's true, Lizzy," the younger sister, Catherine, added. "Why, I remember how you used to abuse him day and night last year. You even ran out of dirty names to describe him, and I have never seen *you* at a loss for words!"

"Indeed!" cried Miss Bingley. "We all thought it was that charming Mr Wickham that you favoured, Eliza."

Elizabeth's face sobered, and she regarded the other seriously. "Allow me to advise you, as a friend, Miss Bingley, not to trust Mr Wickham's assertions. I am not privy to the details, but he has treated friends of mine in an infamous manner. I would not see you suffer disappointment."

Miss Bingley's eyes widened in shock and outrage. "*I* suffer... Eliza Bennet, I believe you forget yourself!"

"Quite the contrary, Miss Bingley. I recall perfectly each of my interactions with both Mr Wickham and Mr Darcy. While one has the *appearance* of goodness, the other possesses it in earnest. Were it not so, we could not have sported so contentiously and yet remained friends. Is that not true, Mr Darcy?"

"True, indeed, Miss Elizabeth," I agreed.

"Why, I..." Miss Bingley gaped, her mouth opening and closing. She blinked, looked about for some distraction, but I was happy to provide it myself.

"Miss Elizabeth," I said, tilting my head faintly, "I had hoped to speak more with your father about Thomas Campbell. Would you care to join me?"

"Delighted, Mr Darcy."

~

THE REMAINING days until Bingley's wedding were some of the most glorious I had ever known. Each morning I would rise, pleasantly drunk on rapturous dreams from the night before and dizzy with anticipation of what the day might bring. A full understanding? The promise that would ransom the rest of my life?

The reality was always more prosaic, for I would not permit myself to interfere with all the pleasures of others. I need not be the centre of everyone's focus; I could be patient. The waiting was at once excruciating and precious, for I now felt some assurance that when the time was at hand, I might truly gain the treasure I sought.

Meanwhile, preparations for the wedding kept us all occupied, for Mrs Bennet would tolerate nothing less than an opulent occasion. Bingley bore it all with good philosophy, and even I found my sources of pleasure. Though Elizabeth could rarely spare a private moment for me, the whole party from Netherfield were frequently in company with the Bennets. I saw Elizabeth every day, and it seemed the astonished whispers of her other sisters and the neighbours diminished each time we were together.

On the afternoon of the twenty-third, we were all settled comfortably in Longbourn's drawing room, engaged in various pursuits of leisure, when Mr Bennet rose from his seat with sudden decision. Every eye went to him, but he only looked about as if he had misplaced something, turning round and absently patting his waistcoat. Then, he squinted thoughtfully and said, "Mr Darcy, would you join me for a drink?"

I glanced at Elizabeth, who had been decorating a bonnet with Georgiana. Her hand froze in mid-air, and she gaped blankly back at me, then her eyes shifted mutely to her father. I felt the silent stares of the whole room—most particularly Bingley's and Mrs Bennet's—as I accepted with as much grace as I could summon.

Mr Bennet closed the library door behind us and, with a gesture, offered me a bit of whatever was in his decanter. I thanked him and took the seat he indicated as he settled himself. "I understand—" he tipped back in his chair and sipped his drink—"that you are a fine judge of horseflesh, Mr Darcy."

"I... I like to think so," I stammered uncertainly.

"You have some foundation for this belief, have you not?"

"Sir, I should think that no man wishes to be a poor judge of himself, and so yes, I believe I speak truthfully when I say I know what I am about. Is there some matter in which I may be of assistance?"

"Oh, to be sure, to be sure," he mused, rubbing his chin. "It is said that you have some magnificent broodmares and young prospects at... I beg your pardon, what was the name of your estate, sir?"

"Pemberley."

"Yes, yes, that was it. Good stock—the very finest, according to Mr Bingley."

"They ought to be," I acknowledged. "Their breeding has been the work of many generations."

"Just so! And I suppose the same could be said of your hunting dogs?"

My brow pinched in bewilderment. "Naturally. All the Darcys have been sportsmen."

"As well as readers, from what I hear. I am told that my library would fit at least four times inside yours, with room above my head to spare. I take it this, too, has been the product of your fathers and grandfathers all the way back to Cromwell?"

I shifted uncomfortably in my chair. "Farther than that, if you would know the truth."

"Indeed! I should very much like to see it one day. And the grounds are quite extensive, are they not?"

"Yes," I confessed, trying to keep the equal notes of pride and confusion from my voice. "We have many summer travellers who take their pleasure by walking round the lake."

"Ah, yes, the famous lake! Stocked with pike and trout, no doubt, since—as you say—all the Darcys have been sportsmen. Such men must have had fine taste. All counts and marquesses, I should think?"

"No," I replied, now truly baffled. "The males of my house have never held a title, but many are the daughters of earls in my family line. Forgive me, Mr Bennet, but may I ask to what these questions tend?"

He barked a short laugh. "You endured my interrogation with more patience than I had expected. I ask, sir, because I wonder if the halls of your fathers would collapse in upon themselves if you were to bring to them anything not possessed of at least ten generations of blue blood."

My face flushed, even the tips of my ears heating like a humiliated school lad. I had not anticipated that rapid shift in topic, and I was entirely flat-footed. "You are speaking of Miss Elizabeth, sir?" I asked cautiously.

"How could I be speaking of anything else? Do not persuade yourself that you are too sly for anyone to notice your interest in my daughter. Indeed, Mr Darcy, I believe the apocalypse itself could descend upon us, fire and brimstone and all, but you would have eyes for none but my Lizzy."

"I fear you have judged the matter rightly. To answer your question, I believe Miss Elizabeth could be nothing but a source of pride to any man, simply in herself. I would gladly defend and keep her over any other honour ever bestowed upon me. What are a bit of soil and a library of musty shelves when compared to such a woman?"

He snorted. "What are they, indeed? You are a stubborn man, sir, and I see that you are set and determined to do as you please."

"Do you object?"

"Object? Now, I shall ask you, Mr Darcy, would you protest the seduction of your daughter by a man who is generally known in the neighbourhood as the most disagreeable fellow ever to set foot in Hertfordshire?"

I shot to my feet. "Seduction! Sir, that is a vile bit of slander! I would never dream of disgracing Miss Elizabeth!"

He made a sour face of perfect ennui and motioned for me to be seated again. "Come, come, Mr Darcy, let us not raise our blood. And do not protest so ardently, for either a man seduces a lady *before* marriage, or he seduces her *into* it. One way or another, he hopes to pull the blinders over her for the crucial moment of decision."

I was slow and resentful in the manner that I seated myself again, never taking my eyes off my inquisitor. "I must dispute this point also. A man who desires a partner and a companion, as well as a lover, would wish for her to see clearly the decision before her, so that she might determine for herself what she can bear and what she desires for her future life."

"And do you? A man who believes this so vehemently must have shown it in his manner, whenever his lady was about. Let me recall— there was the occasion you refused to stand up with my Lizzy, the one in which you declared her to be—er, I beg your pardon—'the last woman in the world' with whom you could be prevailed upon to dance. And there was that memorable encounter at Lucas Lodge, where you were persuaded by guilt, or so it would seem, to make an agreeable answer to Sir William's request to pass the half-hour with her—do you recall what came of that? Oh, yes! I believe my Lizzy forced you to dance with Miss Bingley instead." He broke off there to chortle in great satisfaction. "That was marvellous, if I do say so."

"It is true," I admitted in profound humiliation. "I was a blockhead and a churl. I have not the words to express my own disgust with my behaviour—"

"Hold there, Mr Darcy, for I am only warming to my subject. I would be dreadfully remiss if I did not recount your lustful manner whenever you beheld my Jane. Truly, that is the way of a faithful and devoted lover," he snorted sarcastically.

"Mr Bennet," I interjected, "I have no excuse for my actions. They were the deeds of a man without sense, a raving fool who still bitterly cursed what he perceived as the world's offences against him. Since that time, I have had a mirror held to my face, and what I saw there outraged and nauseated me to my very core."

Mr Bennet propped his elbows forward on his desk, his hands folded together, and index fingers pointed in interest. "Do go on, Mr Darcy. What heinous circumstances would conspire to make a grown man of—I beg your pardon, how old are you?"

"I shall be eight and twenty in July."

"Yes, very well. What could cause a man who is hardly still in the schoolroom, and certainly well-endowed with material blessings, to lash out at the world and grasp at whatever pleasures he felt himself deserving of?"

"If you would know, it was that I felt myself unjustly robbed of the very thing I just declared Miss Elizabeth deserves—the chance to choose my fate for myself, and with it, the person beside whom I will live out my days."

"Ah, yes, the former Mrs Darcy. Mr Wickham enlightened us about the lady. I understand she bore a strong resemblance to another young lady of my acquaintance."

"Only if one is blind and ignorant," I quipped.

"But to a self-proclaimed 'raving fool,' it must have been something of a shock at first, yes?" There was a twist to his mouth as he spoke, a twinkle in his blue eyes that so clearly evoked his daughter, that I could not help the suspicion that came over me.

"May I ask you a question, Mr Bennet?"

He sat back and crossed his arms, a hint of a smile playing about his lips. "Please do."

"I knew myself to be deluded and mad long ago—I would say 'tortured,' if you can bear such a mawkish word, for I had fixed on precisely the opposite of what I most desired, and my sanity suffered for it. However, I would ask when my interest in Miss Elizabeth became apparent to you."

His lips pursed, and he bent forward to arrange a few items on his desk. "Tut, tut. Would you know the truth, or something more comfortable?"

"The truth, sir."

"The second evening I ever set eyes on you, at Lucas Lodge. I had never seen a man sweating blood as you did, simply to avoid a woman's path. You provided me with a vast deal of amusement over the next two months, always acting as if you held aloft a cross to ward off the very devil, while at the same time practically salivating whenever the temptation neared you. I thought I should go distracted when you had to help her mount a horse!"

"If that is so," I answered in some annoyance, "you were a quicker study of my own sentiments than I was."

"Mr Darcy," he chuckled, "do you not know that love and loathing are almost invariably the same passion, and not always expressed towards different objects? If you would know, Lizzy was peculiarly vexed by you—so much so that I believed there must be something more to it than natural grievances over your atrocious manner. A woman is not so irrational as a man; she cares little enough when her dignity is offended by a stranger, one in whom she takes no interest. But let her pride be wounded by one for whom she nurses some fascination, then she will worry it like a dog with a bone."

I straightened, intrigued. "Are you claiming Miss Elizabeth—"

"I claim nothing," he interrupted. "If you would have the answer to that, you must ask her yourself. But before you embark on such a quest, I will be satisfied in one regard."

"You are wondering if my sentiments regarding your daughter are likely to change again? As well you should, for it is a fair question."

"Not precisely, but a respectable guess, sir. I do not think I can doubt you—and anyway, it is out of my hands, for if Lizzy sets her mind on an object, I shall not be able to deter her. No, what I wonder is how quickly you mean to take her away from me."

I hesitated before answering. "If she agreed to have me, I would marry her this very afternoon, if I could."

Mr Bennet sighed, looking suddenly old and weary. "I feared as much. With both Jane and Lizzy gone, I shall not hear two words of sense strung together."

"Have I mentioned, sir, that Pemberley has an excellent library?"

His grey brows pushed sharply over the rim of his spectacles. "Ten minutes, Mr Darcy. I will send her in for an interview."

"I may have some difficulty in persuading her," I reasoned with a smile. "May I beg leave for twenty?"

He rose from his chair and leaned over his desk. "You have spirit, lad. Good, for you shall have need of it. Fifteen, and not a second longer."

I watched him go in little short of complete astonishment. The sardonic, quirky gentleman who did nothing but chuckle over his tea at social gatherings was more—far more—than I had accounted. What further surprises did he conceal?

This thought troubled me for only an instant. Close upon it came the understanding of what was to come, and I began to sweat.

I PACED Mr Bennet's study, my shoulders bunched, palms itching, and my knees unwilling to support my weight. Sweet glory, the moment was upon me! I tugged at my cravat, wishing for a gulp of something besides Mr Bennet's tasteless sherry to wet my throat and refresh my tongue. By heaven, I was addled as a schoolboy, and overcome with a powerful urge to beat my breast so my heart might resume a steady cadence.

I had been angry the last time I had nerved myself to speak—furious, jealous for my own dignity and sure of my right to insist on her adjudication. Blind, I had been—blind to aught but myself, and the shining vision that had been my notion of restitution, as if she were to be my reward for all the past. This time, my only hope was that I might lavish the remainder of my years on her, seeking each day some new means of giving her comfort or joy. Yes, that would be the noblest pursuit to which I could devote my life!

The bookshelves, the furnishings, even the window all disappeared as I strove for words, trying to piece together something more comprehensible, more suitable than the garbled string of syllables presently clogging my throat. I wandered aimlessly about the room and could not say whether it was only seconds or long minutes before the door opened again, and she slipped inside.

I paused, and simply adored her from afar—her scent already washing over me, her irresistible hold already taking me until the whole of my body warmed in eager longing. Her hands were still behind her back, against the latch, and her eyes lit with mischief. "Having trouble locating a book, Mr Darcy?"

I crossed the room and stopped, just short of touching her. "I *was* seeking something, but it was not a book. I wonder if you can help me find it."

Her chin lifted—not in defiance, but in concession, so her eyes met mine directly. Soft flesh furrowed at their corners, and her voice was light, gentle when she spoke. "Perhaps first, you might tell me what it is."

Slowly, I reached behind her back and found her hands—my inner arms grazing her hips—then brought her fingers up and twined mine through them. I looked down, caressing each slender digit with reverent care, and then turned her palms over to expose her ivory wrists. I brushed my thumbs over those delicate planes, seeking the fine ridges and dips, and following down to circle the sensitive hollow at the centres.

"Mr Darcy," she murmured, her voice tight and uneven, "if you wish for me to help you look for something, I will require the use of my hands."

"In fact, it is I who need them to find what I seek."

She swallowed. Her irises, which a moment ago had been golden pools of light, darkened in an instant. I heard and thrilled to the trembling of her breath as she gazed expectantly up to me. "And what is that?"

"Life," I whispered. "The sort of life I had lost hope of ever living. Elizabeth?"

She hesitated, then nodded shakily. "Yes?"

"I would cling to you, hold fast to none other through the rest of my days. I will fall—I am certain to stumble along the way, but will you catch me? For I promise, I shall ever be waiting for you."

A silver bead had started down her lashes, hovering and sparkling in the light from the window as it threatened to tumble down her satin cheek. Her breathing stopped; her lips parted, and her brow drew into tender awe as she beheld me.

"Elizabeth?"

My hands slackened. Shaken and fearful, I tried to force myself to release her, to permit her to draw back, but she tightened her grip with a startling ferocity. She pulled, insisting and urgent, and then her arm was round my neck, her fingers threading through my hair, and she raised up on her toes to meet me.

"Eliza—"

She cut off my hoarse protest when she tugged my face lower, captured me, and stole my breath. While one hand cradled my head, the other slid over my chest, and she possessed me utterly. I was frozen for but an instant; then I snaked my arms round her waist, my hands cupping the sweep of her back, and my only verbalisation was a heady groan as I savoured the sweet spice of her lips.

Again and again, she overpowered me. I think I had never been so helpless, nor so whole—desperately famished and wondrously sated all at once. I was too dizzy to count, too intoxicated to number her caresses, but they were plentiful... and lingering. At length, she quavered, gasped, and reluctantly lowered herself. I followed, stealing one last taste of her lush lower lip before she spoke.

"I... did not mean to do that," she panted, her breath warm against my jaw. "I meant... I think I meant to say something terribly clever."

I caught the hand resting on my chest and held it there. "I hope you meant it to sound like an acceptance?"

She choked, a sobbing sort of laugh. "Heaven only knows! You do have such a dreadful way of setting me off my balance. I only knew... I could think of nothing but that I... I want you."

I was as a man struck dead—I truly believe that my heart did rupture, and my mortal frame ceased to be for an instant. I had dreamt only of a modest acceptance—at best, a promise to bear with me in good cheer for the next thirty years, or whatever was to be our allotted time on this earth. Was that not all a woman ever really surrendered? But even in this, I had been ignorant, underestimating the magnificence of shared passion.

"You want *me*?" I repeated stupidly; my head still muddied with the wonder of it all. "Truly *want* me?"

She nodded, gazing intently into my eyes, and I became aware of her light fingers, yet stirring in the hair at the base of my neck. Goose flesh broke out all over my body, and the hand I had arrested over my heart was as a flame to my chest—bold and intimate, laying claim to me in a way none had ever dared.

"Foolish of me, is it not?" she whispered, lifting her mouth near my chin so that her breath sent a fresh wave of shivers through me. "But I am fearfully obstinate, Fitzwilliam Darcy, and I am afraid I am quite determined to have you."

"You had me ages ago, Elizabeth. God help you."

Her laughter was all that is beautiful and fine and magical in this world—even more so, because for the first time since I was a boy, I truly laughed with her. I could scarcely draw breath for the great bubbling well of elation that twirled me in its thrall, as I kissed her and wept for joy by turns.

Elizabeth did not give her affections by halves, and by the time Mr Bennet knocked on the door, after our appointed quarter hour was long up, there could never again be any distinction between us. My life was irrevocably hers.

CHAPTER 27

Two days later, I stood before a creaking row of pews in a modest, draughty church and permitted my gaze to wander to the woman standing on the left side of the sanctuary. Her ebony hair was encrusted with tiny white flowers, and the light filtering through the stained windows cast a rosy hue over her skin. I saw her eyes slide in my direction, then she lifted her chin and directed her attention forward again in a teasing effort at ignoring me.

I felt, as surely as if they were physical things, the gazes of the nuptial audience on my back. Georgiana, who had not ceased grinning since two days earlier; Miss Bingley, who had taken up the habit of shaking her head and clicking her tongue whenever she met my eye; Mrs Bennet, who was in such a persistent state of raptures that her middle daughter, Mary, was constantly obliged to remain at her side with salts, lavender water, and fresh linens for her eyes; and Mr Bennet, who seemed to spend a good deal more time staring at me than at the bride and groom.

I sighed and raised myself slightly to look over the heads of Bingley and Miss Bennet—soon to be Mrs Bingley—to admire my own future bride. This time, I caught her. The sly curve of her mouth as she looked guiltily to the parson again inspired a pleased smirk of my own. A pity that two days had been too little notice for us to meet at the altar as bride and groom in a double ceremony, rather than merely the other couple's attendants.

The parson droned on until his task was complete, Bingley placed a ring on his bride's hand, and then, at long last, we walked together into the vestry to enter the lines in the registry book. I stood beside Elizabeth as we awaited our turns with the pen, my shoulder brushing hers in the tight space. I had every intention of sober regard for the proceedings, but just before the new Mrs Bingley turned to give the pen to Elizabeth, I felt the barest tickle of her fingertips grazing the inner curve of my palm. It was like lightning coursing through the very vessels of my arm and straight to my heart. She stepped forward then to perform her duty, appearing to take no further notice of me, but when she turned back around, it was with a decided quirk to her lips.

She was driving me mad, and she knew it.

How I was to endure three more weeks of such torment, I could not begin to guess. I only knew that I never wished for the torture to end.

Mrs Bennet had outdone herself for the wedding breakfast. I believe it was her private hope—or, rather, it was her plainly expressed desire—that the lavish outlay would attract a number of single gentlemen from among their neighbours to look over the generosity of the bride's family; not to mention the quantity of unattached sisters remaining. Consequently, there were a veritable plethora of well-wishers with whom I had not been acquainted, and I was constantly being introduced to a Mr or Mrs so-and-so.

The monotony and fatigue of so many new faces were greatly compensated, however, by the fact that they came to know me as Elizabeth's betrothed. Mrs Bennet even insisted upon Elizabeth staying constantly by my side, so we might be lauded as the next happy couple. Sweet and frequent were the moments when I was able to mollify my sense of tedium and social reluctance by surreptitiously catching and toying with her fingers.

So steady had been the flow of congratulations to both Bingley and myself that we had hardly spoken since leaving Netherfield that morning. I looked over at him, openly clasping the hand of his wife and laughing at some jest by a neighbour. It was no stretch to claim that Bingley had always been the happiest man I had ever known, but the look he bore this day was a delight more profound, more assured, than all my previous experience.

I discovered Elizabeth watching her sister with the same sort of pride and satisfaction I felt. She caught my eye, then her arm slid through mine and she briefly leaned her cheek against my shoulder. I did not even care if we had onlookers—for certainly, we must have. I bent down to whisper in her ear.

"I think you should return to London with your aunt and uncle tomorrow."

"And why should I?" she asked.

"Because if you do not come willingly, I shall be forced to extreme measures."

"Indeed? Are you considering kidnapping, Mr Darcy? Bribery?"

"Kidnapping?" I pretended to give the idea consideration. "No. It would be folly, for the captive would soon overcome the captor, and then we would have a fearful mutiny. I should quickly find myself bound, with your sword pointed at my heart! As for bribery, the notion has merit. I expect I could find some way of persuading you."

"Ah! Your library, of course. But what if I tire of reading, or we squabble over the same book?"

"Then I shall find other activities to hold your interest. Reading is not the only enjoyable pursuit one can indulge in a library."

She turned to survey me with that sultry, provoking look she had already perfected, and employed to great effect whenever she pleased. "Mr Darcy, if you think I can be swayed by the prospect of sitting by the half-hour, looking out the window with a pair of field glasses to observe the nesting habits of swallows or pigeons, I fear you will be disappointed."

"Then all hope is lost," I sighed. "For I am quite assured that I hold no other means of incentive."

"There might just be one thing," she mused lightly as she inclined her head to someone who was passing by.

"Might there? Pray, tell me at once, before I succumb to despair."

"Oh, I cannot do that. Certainly not. Why, perfectly shocking, to be sure!"

I frowned in exaggerated displeasure. "How am I ever to lure you to London if you will not reveal to me the proper bait?"

"Come, now, Mr Darcy, surely that is not very sportsmanlike. But I shall try to provide a hint and see if you can discover it."

I waited, my mouth threatening at any moment to betray me and break forth into laughter as she pretended to deliberate.

"No, I am afraid it is impossible," she decided. "I could not say such a scandalous thing in public, and I most certainly cannot meet with you entirely alone, for my father has taken to insisting that even my morning walks be chaperoned—in case any strange ruffians should be about."

"Then perhaps you might drop one or two veiled suggestions?" I pleaded.

She blinked slowly, her lips curved and her eyes sparkling with mirth. "Mr Darcy... that *was* the hint."

"Ah! I shall ponder the matter and see what I can deduce. If I am greatly fortunate, perhaps I can procure what is needed to entice you to London for at least a fortnight."

"You do realise, of course, that if I were to come, my mother would not tolerate being left behind. All my time would then be spent perusing warehouses for wedding clothes, and not a single moment could I spare for your enlightenment."

"Then I shall have to whisk you away to Pemberley when she is not looking," I declared. "A small diversion should suffice—a single gentleman, I should think. Perhaps Colonel Fitzwilliam will not object to being used as the sacrificial lamb."

Her laughter rippled through the room, causing heads to turn our way with indulgent smiles... But then they were all staring back to the door, for a stranger had presented himself and was looking importantly about. He was not attired in clothing suitable to the occasion, nor even as a gentleman, and no one seemed to look on him with recognition. He put up his hand and hailed Mr Bennet.

"Who is that?" Elizabeth asked as the man pressed his way towards her father.

"You have never seen him before?"

She shook her head. I thinned my lips and released her arm. "Wait here."

Bingley and I reached Mr Bennet at the same moment as the stranger, and we instinctively took up our stations at either side of him. Bennet glanced to each of us with a subtle hint of amusement at our protective gesture, then addressed the newcomer.

"Have you come to drink the health of the bride, sir?"

"'Fraid not, Mr Bennet. You are the nearest magistrate, I take it?" The fellow spoke with the rough brogue common to London's slums, and he cast a disdainful eye about the house. *A thief-taker, by heaven!* What the devil made him so bold to interrupt a wedding breakfast?

"I suppose I cannot deny it," Mr Bennet confessed. "But come back in two hours. Today is my daughter's wedding-day, and unless you come bearing a gift for the proud couple, I shall have to ask you to wait until my guests have departed."

"'Tis one of your guests I've come for, Mr Bennet. Is there a Mr Darcy 'ere?"

All eyes turned to me. I scowled, drew a step closer, and said, "I am he. What is this all about?"

The thief-taker worked his mouth in the way of one who is much in the habit of chewing tobacco, and, finding none of his reserve there, smacked his lips with a self-satisfied grunt. "I'm to bring you up to Old Bailey, on charge of murdering a Mr Robert Benedict."

ALL THE GUESTS had been hurried from the house, the doors bolted, and drapes drawn. Mrs Bennet had been carried bodily to her room, but even below stairs, all could still hear her wails of lament for her poor daughter's lost reputation and ruined prospects.

Bingley had asked Hurst to take the ladies back to Netherfield, but Mrs Bingley exerted a rare display of willpower, and adamantly refused to leave her sister's side. Georgiana's angst and terror were so overpowering that she collapsed in my arms, clinging to me with such fierce cries of defiance and horror-stricken denial that only Elizabeth was able to draw her away.

Elizabeth. How grey and anxious she looked! But she was cool, deliberate in word and deed. She recalled to mind the fighting men I had known, whose training compelled and enabled them to think and strategise at points of crisis, though their very soul might quake in mortal dread. She deployed her younger sisters with a strict urgency in her voice I had never heard from her, exhorting them to comfort Georgiana in her distress while she herself stood by my side to hear the full weight of the monstrous accusation.

Mr Bennet proved to be his daughter's father in every respect. Grave and clearly shaken, he nonetheless commanded us all—Bingley, Mr Gardiner, Elizabeth, me, and the thief-taker—into his study. "Now, then," he charged in a thin voice as he sought his spectacles, "let us have the matter out."

"I should like to ask for the facts," I interjected before the thief-taker could speak. "You say Benedict is dead? How?"

"Well, I'd s'pect you know that, sir," he grinned, then shrugged. "But so's everyone knows, 'e was found dead of a fall. Down two flights of stairs 'e was fallen, and I know nough' but 'e died all t'once."

"And you believe *I* could have been his murderer? Not only is there no foundation for such a belief, but I have been here in Hertfordshire for a se'nnight, and a hundred witnesses could testify to that."

"T'were a week ago this morning 'e was found, dead several hours before anyone cared to notice. I 'ave it on good authority that you left London in 'aste that very morning, ne'er restin' the horses."

A wave of murmurs and gasps rose from our small assembly. Elizabeth slipped her hand into my own and gripped it feverishly, but it was Bingley who cried his outrage.

"How dare you presume Darcy capable of such a heinous crime?

Why, you might just as well declare the Lord Chancellor himself guilty of high treason!"

"My son-in-law is correct," Mr Bennet intoned heavily. "As the magistrate involved, I must request some proof of your claim."

"Indeed," Gardiner seconded eagerly, leaning his rather imposing frame far over the desk and almost baring his teeth at the thief-taker.

The rascal gave a nonchalant toss of his hand and drew a rumpled document from his coat. "I 'ave witnesses who will attest to Mr Darcy and Mr Benedict coming to some argument in the few days prior to the victim's death. One of those witnesses—a lady, sir—avows that Mr Darcy swore oaths at Mr Benedict, stating his wish never to see the man alive again. Another witness attests to a large sum of money offered for the latter to undertake certain duties, and then to leave the country, with the monies collectible in Amsterdam. And both a friend and the mother of the victim corroborate the 'istory of bad blood between Mr Darcy and Mr Benedict."

The eyes of the room turned to me, and I felt Elizabeth's fingers tighten even more. "This is all true," I admitted.

"Yet, even so, this is hardly proof of murder," Mr Bennet surmised. "I cannot place Mr Darcy in custody or permit him to be transported to gaol over no more than 'bad blood'."

"And what if the victim was killed in precisely the same manner as 'is father—an event in which Mr Darcy was also a person of interest? Mrs Benedict—that's the dead man's mother—'as given testimony that it was truly Mr Darcy who pushed the senior Mr Benedict to 'is death. Moreover, she accuses that Mr Darcy contributed to the death of his previous wife, the dead man's sister, and 'e 'as placed a watch on 'erself, robbing 'er of 'er peace of mind."

The room fell silent. At length, Mr Bennet pulled his spectacles from his face to knead his eyes. "Mr er... I beg your pardon, sir, what was your name?"

"Jacobs. John Jerome Jacobs, sir."

Mr Bennet made a wry face. "Very well, Mr Jacobs. I would speak with the accused in private."

Elizabeth made a hasty move, stepping even closer to me and

squaring her chin before her father, but he shook his head. "Not this time, Lizzy. You must leave as well."

Jacobs began to protest the irregularity of it all, but not very forcefully. The sad truth was that if I had been almost any other man, I would have been dragged to his cart against my will and unhappily installed at Newgate by evening. But a man of my position could command certain concessions—a fair hearing by the magistrate, for a start.

I drew Elizabeth's hand to my mouth and kissed it. "Go with your uncle and Charles," I murmured lowly to her. "Go to your sister and see to Georgiana for me. It will be well; have no fear."

She looked dubious but permitted Mr Gardiner to draw her away. Even as the door closed, she was still watching over her shoulder, those dark eyes luminous with unease.

"Sit down, Mr Darcy," Mr Bennet sighed, tossing his spectacles on the desk. "Perhaps you will be good enough to explain what there is of truth to these accusations."

I sat and stared at the floor. "Every word he spoke was the truth."

Mr Bennet raised a brow and crossed his arms. "Rather damning, is it not?"

"Mr Bennet, do you know what happens to a man when he is forced to wrestle with the pigs?"

"He becomes covered with filth. Yes, yes, but let me know more of how it came about. I am neither judge nor jury in a case such as this, so if the evidence against you is compelling enough, I shall have no choice but to surrender you to the proper authorities. However, I remain sceptical."

"To tell all would take some while, sir. If you have the patience, I shall detail my entire history with the Benedict family."

"I have no qualms against asking a thief-taker to wait, although I do not relish the fact that he may well eat all my remaining feast. I had my heart set on a bit more of that ham."

Despite the dire situation, I almost smiled. Instead, I began as I had with Elizabeth, and with the earl, and laid before Mr Bennet the whole of the shameful truth. He listened intently, making neither sound nor expression that might yield his thoughts, until I had concluded with the moment of finding Benedict in my own drawing room, calling on my sister.

"And is this the point when you allegedly threatened to kill the man?" he asked.

"I never threatened to kill him. I was angry enough to, and I certainly swore at him and expressed in the most vehement terms my desire never to see him again. I have no doubt that Mrs Younge managed to eavesdrop on our conversation before she was discovered and escorted from the house, so there is no telling what a dismissed servant might report."

"And what of this widow, the mother? She sounds a ghastly sort of woman."

"But she is not a fool. I expect her to put on a convincing act, playing the wronged woman to great effect. She will attempt to gain sympathy, and I have no doubt but that it was she who hired the thief-taker in the first place. With my money!"

"You claimed Mr Wickham was her lover? Has he any grievance against you, apart from his claim of a denied living?"

"Indeed. I bought a significant portion of his debts, and I hold them against any future displays of poor conduct on his part."

Mr Bennet released a weary sigh. "Oh, dear. Odd, is it not, how such antagonists have a disturbing capacity to form confederacies of sorts? Now, I must ask the question which you probably think has been canvassed already, but I assure you, it is not yet to my satisfaction. Did you have any connection to the son's murder?"

"None. So far as I knew, he was on his way to Amsterdam and living off his new revenues."

"Mmm. Interesting, I should say, that son and father were both killed in the same way. Though, you claim the father's death was an accident?"

"I believed it to be. There were only myself and two women present, and I was unconscious. I still do not know how his fall occurred, unless he lost his balance at our last blows."

"And what of your wife, sir?"

"Dead in childbirth," I answered shortly. "Not *my* child."

He replaced his spectacles and narrowed his eyes. "Indeed. And you have no idea who the father could have been?"

"A simple examination of the calendar suggests that she must have conceived during that same month. It could have been any of the other guests—and I do not claim she had but one lover. She may have spared the married men her attentions, but any others would have been prospects. Her wish was to secure a husband by any means possible and to escape her father. I doubt she was discriminating in her tastes, nor do I suspect many men would reject out of hand what might have been freely offered."

Mr Bennet stuck his tongue into his cheek and looked up at the ceiling. "I still say there is no proof. It looks bad, certainly enough to colour all the gossip for years to come, but I cannot in good conscience permit an arrest. Even were you not my future son-in-law, I would send this worm packing without his prisoner or his fee."

"One thing I do wonder," I said. "If Benedict has been deceased for a week, why are we only hearing of it now?"

"Oh, who knows. I have not even examined the paper all week, but I should not be surprised if there was no mention made of it. It sounds as if there was some to-do with securing witnesses and the paying of the thief-taker. He said nothing of other suspects, did he?"

"Nothing."

"Well, let us speak with the man again, shall we? Like as not, it was merely a matter of seeking the first name that came to hand, and he must simply find another."

The thief-taker had gone outside to wait at his cart, but everyone else remained in the drawing room when we emerged. Elizabeth and Georgiana both rushed to me, each taking one of my hands, while Gardiner stood by with a broken, solemn expression.

"Sir," he addressed me with a quaver in his voice, "I have just been made aware by Elizabeth and Mr Bingley that you acted a valiant part in my own delivery from certain ruin. Be assured, sir, that if ever I can be of assistance, I shall do all within my power."

I turned to Elizabeth with a look of betrayal, and she shook her head in apology. "He deserved to know. I cannot see you face these charges without knowing who your friends are."

"There will be no charges," Mr Bennet announced. "Jacobs lacks sufficient evidence to convince me of anything but that Mr Darcy may have had motive and opportunity. From what I have heard of the dead man, I expect a dozen others may have had the same. I will go and say as much."

But Mr Bennet had hardly reached the drawing room door when there was another loud knock from outside. Jacobs was shown in again, but this time he was not alone. One of his peers was at his side, this one possessed of more age and dignity. He bowed formally and introduced himself. "Walters, of the Bow Street Runners at your service, Mr Bennet. I've two constables waiting outside."

Bennet returned his salutation with cheerless disregard. "Am I never to regain the sanctity of my home this afternoon?" he lamented under his breath. "Well, what is it, Walters? If you have come on the same errand as Jacobs, I am afraid you lack the evidence to imprison this man."

"I beg to differ, sir." Walters produced an order, signed by a Bow Street magistrate, for Mr Bennet's inspection. I was not near enough to read what it said, but Bennet's face seemed to have aged in an instant. He put a weak hand to his chest, then looked mournfully at his daughter. My heart turned to ice.

"I can do nothing else," Bennet rasped, swaying a little where he stood. "Darcy... my Lizzy... I am sorry."

I FELL HEAVILY INTO A CHAIR, staring blindly at the walls before me. *Murder. Collusion. Embezzling. Fraud.*

And unlike Jacobs, Walters had presented verifiable documentation. He could prove my involvement in the Benedicts' financial affairs, most notably those which involved decisions made to retrench and sell off what could be parted with. The receipts were all for low amounts, because I had sold items off at almost wholesale simply to be done with the affair. I had no way of proving that I had not pocketed double what I reported.

Walters recorded statements from Robert Benedict's friends and servants that I had exerted considerable pressure on him the week prior to his death, and had been sent into a murderous rage when he had 'innocently' attempted to court my sister. Apparently, he had even written a farewell letter to his mother, in which he declared me responsible if he should vanish and never be seen again. "Numerous witnesses" reported Benedict as saying he expected me to be the end of him, one way or another—I suspected these were all drunken ramblings at the club, but that mattered little.

One could not fail to account for Lady Benedict's testimony, nor was I surprised to learn that she claimed the cover-up of Sir Edmund's death was imposed upon her, and that I had made threats against her own life if she should breathe a word. This piece of slander fit so neatly within the rest of the narrative contrived against me that only the stoutest sort of friend could disbelieve it—friends I was not likely to have.

Then, there was that cursed trail of money. Ten thousand pounds sent abroad for a secret reason to be collected by a man who would never live to touch a penny of it. And I, arrogant fool that I was, had imposed a reversal stipulation on the release of the monies, in case Benedict should fail to meet the requirements of the pay-out! Men had been hanged for less concrete evidence.

But the most wretched of all, the part that caused my heart to fail and my eyes to darken, was the last. A midwife, interviewed at some point by Lady Benedict and then sent for again by the magistrates, who could verify that the former Mrs Darcy's birth pangs had been incited by a violent argument. Too early... too brutal... and she and the child had paid for my fury with their lives.

I propped my elbow on my knee, my head bowed into the crook of my arm, and gave way to great, thunderous gasps of panic. I was alone in a guest bedroom, as Bennet had no choice but to "secure" me until the conclusion of his discussion with Jacobs and Walters and the constables. I believed he still sought to purchase time or comforts for me during my trials, but everyone had seen the defeat in his bearing. I had even feared for some minutes that he would suffer a heart failure, for he kept clutching at his chest, but he had remained manfully on his feet.

To think that my best hope rested with a man I had once counted as careless and too contrary to be of use to anyone! But even were Mr Bennet the top legal defender in the kingdom, I doubted he could have helped. My hands were too stained now to determine what was mere filth, and what was blood.

Tears shrouded my eyes, and I buried my face in my palms to weep. So close! I had almost touched happiness, had been nearly able to taste it, hold it in my hands! Undeserving, I must be—a fool who dreams of fortune when in truth, he can claim no more than a few shillings. And now, the fall! I wanted to seethe, to mourn, to rail against the iniquity of it all, but despair had already settled over me.

There came a short knock at the door, and I dashed my grief away and stood. "Come in," I summoned.

Bennet cracked the door, but he did not enter. He could not meet my eyes, and that alone told me all the rest. "It is growing late enough that I have managed to stay your departure until the morrow, but you must remain here," he reported wearily.

"It is a kind effort, but I am afraid it will avail nothing."

"It does grant time for a message to reach your family in London," he suggested. "Mr Bingley has already sent an express to your cousin, a Colonel Fitzwilliam."

I experienced a brief wave of relief, followed swiftly by sinking nausea. "Perhaps he can bribe someone to procure me a private cell in Newgate."

"Have you no other alibi, sir? No friends who can testify to your innocence?"

"Indeed," I answered, "I have some... not half so many as I ought. Now that I think of it, I hardly have any at all. Ramsey, perhaps. Carlisle. Both were present at many of my encounters with Benedict, but I do not count them among those who would exert themselves on my behalf. They would be just as likely to turn the other way."

He sighed, then nodded. "I understand." He finally met my gaze for a second, then shook his head in grief. I saw him extend his hand to someone out of sight, then he withdrew, shuffling down the hall outside.

Elizabeth rushed in, and I scarcely caught a breath before her arms were around me, her muffled tears hot against my neck. She spoke not a word—too overcome for speech—and I was equally afflicted. I clung to her, all coherent thought lost, and sobbed in earnest. I do not know which of us cried out more, for it seemed our sorrow was a unified beast, crouching and waiting to devour us both.

"Oh, love," she choked, "I cannot let you go! They cannot take you from me!"

I stroked down her back, cradling her to my chest in a way I had only dreamed of doing before. I sought words to reassure her, but each died in my throat as I knew them for a lie. Instead, I merely croaked, "Georgiana?"

"With Jane and my aunt. They had to give her a draught of something; she was so overwrought she could not even breathe. She is sleeping now."

I quaked in some measure of relief. "Thank you."

She pulled back, her icy fingers framing my jaw. Her lips were quivering, gasps still shook her, but she struggled to speak. "How can they accuse you of these awful things? How can they not see? You are an innocent man!"

"Elizabeth..." I gently tugged her arms down and rested my hands at her waist. "Come and sit."

She followed, her steps dragging with trepidation, and eased herself onto the mattress beside me. "What are you about to tell me?"

I closed my eyes with a moan. "The rest—the whole of it."

"There is more? More than the horrible things you have already told me?"

"I never finished—never told you what happened when I came back to Pemberley, before my wife died."

"But..." she shook her head. "What can there be to say? I do not imagine she met your arrival with open arms. Even if there was some dispute, as they claim, what is that? A woman does not—"

I shushed her, placing a gentle finger on her lips. "I am guilty—if nothing else, then of this, at least."

She said nothing, only blinked quickly and swept a tear from her cheek as she waited for more.

"I came back after two months, just as I told you. She was expected to deliver some weeks after that date, but she was already heavy and in some distress. That day saw our most explosive fight ever.

"I meant to avoid her. I thought to merely inhabit the lower rooms of the house, as she had been confined above stairs by her condition, but when I came back, I found a good many of my servants dismissed. Mrs Reynolds was near hysterics—a woman I had never seen bat an eyelash even at my own mother's death.

"Two of the footmen had been accused of assaulting my former wife's person, and so they were brought up on charges. Released, thank heaven, but only after much exertion on the part of my butler and steward. At least three of the maids had been subjected to such abuse as I shudder even to repeat. They bore bruises all over their bodies, I was told—beaten by their own mistress! One was even struck repeatedly by a hot fire poker. I thank God it did not injure her face, but I was given to understand that she shall bear the scars forever.

"I charged up the stairs after hearing all these things, ready to do unto her as she had done to mine. I assure you, Elizabeth, I had murder in my heart that day! When I saw my own quarters smashed, some of my prize mementos shattered or charred, I was even more enraged. This was but an insult, a slash at my pride—the real offence was what she had done to those who had always trusted in me. And I was such a selfish blackguard that I left them to her!

"She was waiting for me, smug in her bower with her own deceitful attendant in retainer. Oh, she knew precisely where to strike her blows! And I danced like a marionette on her string, snarling and raging my impotent fury until I wrung with sweat. Our argument was not limited merely to recent events, but spanned the whole of our acquaintance, from the first offence to the most recent outrage.

"All this time, she had refused to tell me who the father of the child was. I thought I did not care, for what would a name avail me, supposing she even knew? But this time, I put down my foot and made my demands, insisting to know whose bastard she meant to present me.

"She only taunted and screamed the louder, so that all in the house might hear, how I had raped her in her maidenly bed, then tried to deny it all. I threatened to make her be silent—I knew not how, but I threatened, nonetheless—but she only cried out with all her strength that I had been caught by her father, and when called to account for the matter, murdered him before her very eyes. No one could have failed to hear every word of it."

Elizabeth's complexion was a sickly green, her mouth rounded in horror. "How could anyone be so wicked?" she breathed.

"It matters not. I... I lost my temper. After so many months of walking the razor's edge of madness and vile hatred, I denounced her at the top of my lungs. Called her any number of black names. I ordered her maid to gather what she could in ten seconds' time, because they were both leaving the house at once.

"I never touched her, even to take her by the hand, for I knew well enough by then that I could never dare! But I was not above intimidating her, throwing her clothing out the window onto the lawn, and creating such a wrathful presence that even she, brazen witch that she was, cowered in my path. I used my size to my advantage, herding her like a sheepdog until she was in the hall, then at the top of the stair.

"It was then that she at last believed me to be serious, and I was. I meant to send her off to the dower house to let her live out her days in disgrace, and if that failed, I would consign her to Scotland or somewhere farther away, and I told her as much.

"She began to plead with me then, but I would hear nothing of it. She saw it, and her manner changed back to violence. She struck me, spit in my face, and then turned to flee from me, because I certainly felt—and probably looked—as though I might trade blow for blow.

That was when she fell. Her foot caught in that confinement gown she wore, and she fell down the top flight of stairs to the landing."

Elizabeth—*my* Elizabeth, was perfectly ashen, her tears grown cold. I stood and walked away from my love, no longer feeling worthy of allowing her to hold my hand and offer comfort. "If I am responsible for a death," I went on, "it was hers. I would have struck her, Elizabeth. I have no doubt of that. Even though I did not, I was the cause of her fall."

The whites of her eyes were startling, and her hand hovered over her mouth. How I wished to spare her this knowledge! But I could conceal it no longer. My infamy, my sins, had all caught me at last.

"She..." Elizabeth drew a shaken sob, her voice hoarse and fractured. "I thought she died in childbirth. That was what you told me."

"The fall did not kill her, not by half. She was still abusing me when we carried her back to her room, but within a few hours, the labour pains took her. The birthing woman said the child was not ready, that he was breeched. A male child, too! He was dead at birth; else I would have counted him my heir. The delivery did nothing to relieve the mother, though. The midwife did what she could, but I doubt even a skilled surgeon could have saved her, the wretched soul. She bled for hours and died cursing my name.

"I am a murderer, Elizabeth. Even if I did not kill father or son, the daughter's blood stands to convict me. I deserve whatever my punishment may be."

She shot to her feet. "But you do not! Whatever happened was her own fault!"

"Do you not see?" I protested, withholding my hands from her. "I am guilty in my heart, as truly as if I had pushed her. No one could hold me blameless!"

"Stop it, William!" she cried, arresting my hand at last and gripping it with the strength of two men.

I froze. Never had she—had anyone—called me that. So simple, so personal; so very much her own! I could only gape in wonder, and the sense of all I was losing broke upon me. I crumbled; my head bowed as my shoulders heaved. I crushed her to me, weeping savagely at the injustice of it all. To lose such a woman, to lose a life, over what had seemed to be beyond my control!

"I will come with you," she promised, her face buried in my hair as she clasped the back of my head in trembling hands. "To prison, to anywhere!"

"Elizabeth, my darling Lizzy." I drew back, fervently kissing her brow and cheeks as if I could capture her sweet tears, her daring, her confidence. "You know you cannot. There is no help for it."

"Then I will seek the truth! I will find out who—" her words strangled there, and she caved into me with helpless grief. "Oh, my William!"

I soothed her as best I could, my fingers tangling irreverently in her hair and careless of any impropriety. "Fear not, love. Richard and the earl will set their wits to the case. I shall be well defended in court."

She pressed her head into my neck as another tremor racked her body. "Will it be enough? It *must* be! Oh, it cannot be otherwise! My father will help, and my uncle and Mr Bingley!"

"Elizabeth," I murmured into her hair, "just now, all I want is you."

She tipped her face up, and her eyes took on that black sheen that always told of some deep feeling. "Now? I would…"

"Would what? I asked for nothing but to hold you."

She swallowed and trembled, nodding jerkily. "I promised to take you as my husband, William. I vowed that in my heart, and it can never be undone. I count myself as yours even now—"

"Elizabeth, do not even think it!" I protested.

"I see it in your eyes, William. You have no hope of a reprieve! I cannot let you go without—" she broke, her beloved features buckling, and she pressed her hand to my cheek as her eyes pooled, and rivulets of sorrow streamed down to her chin.

"Think you that I could dishonour you? Indeed, not if I faced the gallows this very night! And what would become of you, if—"

"I am ruined either way!"

"Then let it be an honest ruin," I pleaded. "Just as mine. Even if I am hanged, my soul would never find rest if I did you this wrong.

Either some miracle will restore me to you, and we may look forward to a life of peace and honour, or I will be taken, and you must seek a new life without the burden of guilt. The less of me to haunt you, the better."

"I cannot!" she sniffed miserably. "It is too unfair, so... so wrong!"

"It is," I agreed in a whisper, twining my fingers through the unruly curls at her temples. "Just hold me now, my Lizzy. Let us not lose a moment—let me keep this much, at least."

Dark had fallen long before, and the groanings of the old house told of the cooling night when Mrs Gardiner finally appeared at the open door of my prison. I roused Elizabeth, who had pitched into a tearful sleep against my chest. At first, she refused to leave me, but her aunt and better sense prevailed.

I kissed her once more—perhaps it was to be the bittersweet adieu to all that could have been—and watched as she trudged heavily away in the night. Then, wrung and exhausted in every way a man can possibly be, I collapsed on the old mattress, and prayed for both our lives.

CHAPTER 28

The dawn was grey and overcast, carrying the last bite of winter frost. I was thankful of my heavy greatcoat and the comfort of my warmest breeches sent over by my valet. Jacobs had apparently left the previous evening, as he had lost his fee to the Bow Street Runner, but Walters and his two constables stood ready in the drive to escort me to London.

Once, I would have been furious at such ignominy. To be forcibly taken from a house where I had been in company, shamefully detained and then marched to such a conveyance with disgrace on my head—I would have bellowed my arrogant complaints, and they would have had more to do with my shattered pride than any fear of what was to follow. Oh! Yes, I would have been perfectly assured of my deliverance, for how dare any lay a hand on me! I would have threatened reprisals, demanded the names of each man's superior, and made a general ass of myself.

Now... Now, everything was reversed. I stood in the cold drive, my eyes lifted to the window above my head where Elizabeth and Georgiana pressed against the glass. I had been permitted a scant few moments with each of them, and for that I supposed I had to thank

Mr Bennet's influence in the affair. Additionally, I was not to ride with my hands bound. How grateful I was for such small mercies!

One of the constables beckoned me to mount the coach, and I turned round for one last look at the men who stood behind me. Bingley, the new bridegroom, had ridden over an hour before and now looked forlorn and hopeless as I was to be carried away. Gardiner and Bennet flanked him, each man looking haggard and grey. I nodded to them and stepped into the coach.

Several hours later, I faced what was to be my reality. The coach pulled up outside Newgate prison, and as the constables urged me down to the cold earth, I could only look up. There, jutting out from the debtor's gate, was the gallows.

"Had fifteen hangings last week," one of the constables noted with a grin. He waited until I had turned to him in disgust, then—"Three of them dumb fellows stole a heifer. Worth thirty pounds it was!"

I set my teeth and looked away.

Within a few moments, I had the dubious pleasure of meeting the Ordinary at the prison Lodge, the man whose task it was to record my arrival, age, physical characteristics, and the charge against me. I told him as little as I possibly could, for the Ordinaries were known for their publication of criminal accounts for profit. Yet one further disgrace from which I could not spare myself.

The Ordinary looked me up and down, commanded my hat and greatcoat removed, and then asked, "How do you plead?"

"Innocent."

He shrugged, for surely everyone gave that answer, and recorded it.

"Drink to your health, sir?" He glanced up expectantly, licking his lips.

I had come prepared for this. "My coin purse is in the pocket of my coat."

"Ah!" he exclaimed in pleasure as I received the purse and counted a few coins out. "Drinks for everyone!" he proclaimed.

My health was toasted roundly, and I was given leave to keep my clothes and proceed into the prison relatively unmolested. "May I ask when the next Sessions are scheduled?" I inquired.

"Oh, you've got bad timin' sir," the Ordinary tsked, shaking his head in mock commiseration. "We've just had 'em. Next starts in five weeks. Won't be no Grand Jury for a murder trial, so you'll wait till first bit of April."

I drew a long breath. Five weeks to rot before I was sentenced. I could not decide if that were a reprieve of sorts or further punishment. "Very well."

They shackled leg irons to my ankles, and I was escorted into the belly of the hulking prison. My senses were offended at every moment by the fetid air, the dank surroundings, the echoes of a hundred coarse voices, and the absolute baseness of my circumstances. The men's quadrangle lay directly behind the keeper's house, so I had not far to walk before all of it crashed upon me—the hopelessness, the filth, the lack of control over any part of the proceedings.

In the centre of the hall was a tight promenade of sorts, and at that moment, about fifteen men were circling the small room for their daily exercise. I was allowed—or, rather, compelled—to join them for the next ten minutes. The odours of their bodies, the unkempt appearance of their persons, I could not possibly describe. With a sinking feeling, I realised I would soon be indistinguishable from any of the others. I marched numbly among them, speaking to no one and being acknowledged by no one. I only watched the floor, and how my boots—I had been permitted to keep my boots, thank God—minced along in the irons between a pair of bare feet before me and the toes of ragged shoes behind.

After the mandatory exercises were complete, a guard took me to a long corridor. Down one length of it, he told me, was the entrance to the courthouse. Down the other, and through a kitchen, was the exit to the gallows. Then, with a gleeful shove and a satisfied cackle, the guard propelled me into a chamber full of half-naked convicts. I stopped just inside the door, staring at the other occupants of the cell, and in that moment all my pride, my self-respect, and my confidence took their leave of me.

The men all stared at me—me, in my silk shirt and fine waistcoat, my buckskin breeches and boots that had been polished only that morning. I was beginning to panic, with black spots dancing in my vision and sweat beading my brow in the cold cell. Beside my feet, through the centre of the floor, ran an open sewer, and the smell was churning my stomach, causing it to roil and storm painfully. I clenched my eyes for an instant, then forced them to the window, high above the other prisoners' heads. A weak shaft of light broke through there, and I tried to force myself to breathe the foul air.

Without warning, some tide broke. Bodies swarmed me, hands pulled at my clothing, but the cries of the mob were all indistinct, raving, and maniacal. One man was tearing at the buttons of my waistcoat, trying to strip it off me, while several hands yanked at my cravat and others plunged into my pockets. I tried to fight them off, but from somewhere in the back of the crush, a wiry, faeces-covered woman vaulted over the backs of her male comrades. She ripped at my side whiskers, clawing at my face and trying to pull me to her as if she meant to kiss me, but her mouth was foaming and she was screaming about how I had abandoned her, turned her in as a whore, and now she would hang for it.

I managed to push her back, but only after the madwoman slashed my cheek with her filthy nails and ripped out a patch of my hair. After she tumbled away, I searched more carefully. The room I had first taken to be occupied solely by males in fact hosted four women— three of whom appeared to have been badly used already, while the fourth looked riddled with disease.

It was then that my knees quaked in terror. This was no ordinary holding cell. It was the cell of those condemned to die.

THERE WAS no fire to warm us. No candle offered when the dusk fell in late afternoon. The window above our heads let in the rain at night, but that much was a mercy when one counted the sewage that was eased away by the small trickle of water.

I was only one man among a dozen crazed, half-animal brutes abandoned to rot in that cell, but I had the advantage of being fit and strong. They deprived me of my waistcoat and cravat, and I only kept my boots because they were shackled to my feet. However, they left me alone after that, and I was able to secure a seat on one of the damp wooden benches lining the wall, rather than the mouldy stone floor.

We were offered no food. I discovered the reason only later, for the condemned received only bread and water, and only once a day. I was not to be permitted even that much, for I had been marked at my entry to the prison as a man of means, and this was my initiation into the brutal ways of the gaol. A terrified, starved, desperate man was more willing to part with his coin.

I put my head back against the wall and struggled to rest, though sleep would be an impossibility. At least with my eyes closed, I could see what I wished...

Elizabeth, that morning as I was torn from her—the beautiful way she cried out for me, wrested from her father's staying arms, and ran back to me. I had kissed her cheek one last time, then tried to let her go, but she held fast to my neck. "What can we do?" she had pleaded, her tones strained, barely above a whisper. "Tell me where to start, whom to call to your defence!"

"Richard," I told her, but how she understood my gravelled and broken voice, I cannot know. "And the earl. Get them, and Lady Matlock. And get Mrs Reynolds from Pemberley."

She had cupped my face then and pressed her sweet lips to mine— not even caring that her family looked on in pity and dismay. "I love you, William, my William, and I always will."

Those were her last words to me... perhaps forever. If I were very fortunate, I might glimpse her beautiful face at my trial, but... tears leaked from my clenched eyes as I considered what would follow. *Please... please God, let her not see me hanged!*

I never slept that night, nor was I ever in danger of it. Even had I not been in agony over losing those I loved, all my hopes scattered to the four winds, the deplorable conditions of the cell made it inconceivable. By morning, the cut on my cheek was already festering and my tongue was thick for lack of water. I was dull, sick, and cared little when the gaolers came for me.

"Dreadful mistake, that," they laughed. "Sorry, sir, we'll get you right up to the Lodge to see what's to be done."

What was to be done, of course, was that I was to pay. Twenty guineas, to be exact, to secure better quarters, with more expected as the weeks passed to retain the privilege. I would pay for food, pay for drink—not merely my own—pay for damp, mouldy bedding, and the comforts of a fire or candle. I had almost... almost... determined to be obstinate and deny my coins to the keeper of the prison, but when I walked into the Lodge and smelled food more powerfully than the aroma of refuse, I changed my mind.

The denizens of the Lodge were fellow inmates, mostly condemned to severe sentences for their crimes, who volunteered to serve as keepers of their fellows to put off their own executions. They knew their business and anticipated what answer I would give when presented the chance to pay for "easement." They held out their mugs, waiting to drink my health once more, and a tin plate stood ready to satisfy my hunger.

"All a misunderstanding," the gaoler assured me as my leg irons were unlocked, just before he offered to sell me a bit of rotten straw to sleep on.

"Oh, sir," he added as an afterthought, "there's a constable to see you."

"A constable? Whatever for?" I asked.

The gaoler produced a greasy, stained grin. "'E wants to know if you can give a statement, so's 'e can find your accomplices."

"Accomplices! How can I have accomplices if I am innocent of the crime?"

He shrugged carelessly. "Might go easier for you, sir, bein' cooperative and all. Not like you 'ave a choice. 'E says 'e's to see you alone, bein' 'ow you 'aven't been to trial yet. Might be a Militia officer involved, 'e says, so 'tis above my 'ead, sir."

He summoned a turnkey who bade me to follow him to a side room. The door opened, and I beheld a short man in a drab suit, but as I entered the chamber more fully, a red uniform leapt out to me. *Richard... good heavens, Richard!*

I nearly cried out in relief, but a stern look in his eye interrupted me. "Is this the correct prisoner, constable Jones?"

The constable nodded. "Yes, Colonel, that's him. I saw him when they brought him in."

"And has his behaviour been agreeable and repentant?" he demanded of the turnkey.

The turnkey lifted his shoulders and looked indifferent.

"Very well," Richard answered, looking satisfied. "You may leave us. I shall send for you when we are finished interrogating the prisoner."

The door closed, and then—only then—did Richard rush forward and brace his hands on my shoulders. "Good God, Darcy, what happened?" he cried. "I received Bingley's express night before last and spent all day yesterday trying to learn what had become of you. By heaven!" He drew back suddenly, holding his nose. "You smell vile."

"Thank God you came," I gasped, eagerly taking the clean handkerchief he proffered to refresh my face... and then I stopped cold when I recognised it. "Where... where did you get this?"

Richard shook his head. "Your fair lady gave me that last night, begging me to give it to you, if I could see you."

I fingered the little white knot at the corner, and the edge of the lace I had accidentally burned. "You have spoken with her?"

"Yes, she came to London yesterday with her father and uncle. I understand she would not be left behind, but there is precious little she can do from a drawing room in Cheapside."

"She has already done more than she can know," I murmured, and tucked the newly scented handkerchief into the corner of my sleeve where I could keep it near. "Will you please tell her?"

"I will. Well, now, no time for sentiment." Richard cleared his throat and gestured to the constable. "Jones here has been investigating some matters, and I have hired three of my own Runners to gather intelligence. Did you know that Benedict had purchased passage to Amsterdam just before his death?"

"I assumed he had. That was where he was to collect his money."

"Yes, but he bought two tickets. One of them has been used."

I narrowed my eyes. "Mrs Younge."

"No, in fact. I paid her a visit this morning before coming here. She took some money Benedict gave her and rented a deplorable address on H— Street. She has tenants in each of the rooms, and I think she means to make a go of it. No, I believe that second ticket must have been for Lady Benedict, but were they on speaking terms when last you saw either of them?"

"I doubt whatever I knew was the truth. The son was a fool, but the mother is hardly so. Do you know where she is?"

"Indeed, I do. Those men you had put to watch her started reporting to me, and they say she had been packing up her belongings as if she meant to remove, but then ceased abruptly at the news of Benedict's death. Jones here thinks she intended to go to Amsterdam with him, but she remains at her flat as we speak. This, naturally, leads me to wonder who left on that other ticket."

"Wickham would be my guess," I answered.

"Mine as well, but curiously, when I called on Carlisle yesterday afternoon to ask what he knew about Benedict's death, I was told he was out of the country. I found out later that Ramsey is gone, too."

"Indeed! By thunder…" I breathed, then it was as if something struck me. "They are after his smuggled goods! I would lay my life on it."

"I hope it shall not come to that," Richard retorted drily. "I assumed, if anything, someone meant to collect the ten thousand pounds in Benedict's place."

"They probably want both. It will cost a deal of money to get that contraband all scattered and sold, if I properly understood how much there is of it."

Richard nodded grimly. "I have not yet told you what Father has found. You speak of black market tea and opium—well, what does one do with all that money to hide it for a while?"

I would have laughed at how obvious it was, but it came out as a sob instead. "Small deposits here and there in other peoples' accounts, to be corrected over time, and in such a way that no one notices."

"Except you did notice—you, and a few others, but your letter was the only one to draw attention. I suppose your history and disposition is such that no one wanted to take any chances of you learning more, so they severed ties with you—made it look like it was connected to personal scandal. It was all very tidy."

"Richard, who do you think actually killed Benedict?"

He thinned his lips and glanced to Jones.

"We have a witness, sir," Jones answered at the prompting. "We thought there were none, as the crime was not discovered until morning, but a manservant in the employ of Mr Benedict's neighbour saw a man going into the flat at approximately seven the previous evening. The manservant reported hearing an argument through the walls, but that the stranger went away after ten minutes or so. It was three the next morning when a char woman found Mr Benedict's body in the courtyard."

"And he was dead out there for eight hours?" I scoffed. "How could anyone have missed him?"

"Most of the residents in that building are widowed gentlewomen and pensioners, sir, so there is little enough that happens. The dead man fell in a dark part of the yard, behind a short wall, and so he was easy to overlook."

"Odd, but go on. What else did the witness see?" I asked.

"He described the stranger as a man in his late twenties, with dark hair and a strong build. The man was tall, he said, and attired in gentleman's clothing."

"Why... that description suits me perfectly," I confessed, my whole body flooding with terror.

"It suits a dozen men perfectly," Richard replied. "Tell him the rest, Jones."

"The, eh, the blow to Mr Benedict appears to have been done with the hilt of an old sword that hung on the wall. Quite a blow, sir. It is likely he was unconscious before he fell."

"A sword... heavens above, they will think it was me."

Richard lifted his brows. "Why do you say that?"

"Because I was the fencing champion at Cambridge! Some scoundrel will see that as evidence that a sword was my weapon of choice, and I reached naturally for it!"

"I think we are looking at this the wrong way, Darcy. Consider: you left for Hertfordshire that very next morning. You would have been home the night before, and your own servants can testify to this. Hell, I was even there! I know you were at home."

"Except I was not," I groaned. "I never told you, but late that afternoon, after you called, and we spoke of what I meant to do—to make another offer to Elizabeth—I... I went for a ride."

He stared. "Alone?"

"Yes. I was much in need of fresh air, and restless, thinking on the following day, and I could not remain in the house. After you left, I was so anxious and desirous of something to settle my nerves that I did what I always do. I ordered a horse to be saddled and set off for the bridle paths. I was gone well over three hours."

"And what time was this?"

"I missed Georgiana at dinner. I suppose it was... just after seven when I returned home."

"Dear God," Richard hissed. "It would have been bloody helpful to know this before!"

"How was I to know I would be implicated in a murder?" I cried.

He looked as though he would punch a hole through the brick but drew his hand back and flexed his fingers at the last moment. "Well," he growled tightly, "we still have a witness. His description may sound like you, but he claims to have seen the man's face. Perhaps he will see and declare that it was not you when he testifies in court."

"After over a month? I do not like depending on his memory after a half-second encounter."

"I mean to keep looking," Richard groused defensively. "If I can get someone to describe Wickham, for instance—"

"No need for that. There is still a miniature of him at Pemberley. Mrs Reynolds knows where to find it."

"Magnificent! I shall write to her as soon as I leave. I intend to have her brought to London anyway. You could use a character witness or two. And a lawyer. Father will see that you have the best in the country. Darcy, they will send me away in another moment, but is there anything else you can think of that may help your case? Or... anything that may harm it?"

I sighed. "Lady Benedict. Find out what happened to those shares she keeps going on about. Where they came from, why she thinks I had them, or if it was all a sham intended merely to incite confusion and hostility. If she gives a statement, she will accuse me of murdering Sir Edmund as well. You know the details, what happened. I..." I gritted my teeth in thought. "Richard, I never knew whether it was he or someone else who struck me with the paving stone that knocked me senseless."

He nodded. "Understood. Ramsey and Carlisle were there at the time, were they not?"

"Both of them, but they were asleep when it took place."

"You know this?"

"I do not *know* anything!" I thundered. I snagged my hands in my hair, then bowed my face in an attempt to master myself. "Forgive me, Richard," I muttered.

He drew near and clasped my shoulder. "Easy, Darcy. We will find a way out of this."

The door creaked open, and Richard snapped back to attention as the turnkey poked in his head. "Time's up, sir."

Jones held up a hand. "Two minutes more, sir. The prisoner has just revealed something of import, and I must have the whole of it to apprehend his accomplices."

The turnkey grumbled, and Jones drew out a silver coin to toss to him.

"Two minutes," the turnkey agreed sullenly, and closed the door.

"Oh," Richard started, as if just remembering something. "I brought you a bit to replenish your purse. I expect you have already been bled dry in this hell-hole." He drew out his own coin purse and emptied it into mine. "And do not bother with buying a candle," he advised. "I am told the rats eat them before you can light them."

"Bloody hell," I spat, and then sneered in disgust at myself. "Listen to me! I am already swearing every other phrase."

"You have a perfect right to. I'd no idea this place was such a purgatory. You will have your own cell from now on, though?"

"I certainly paid enough for one. Or five."

"Probably more than I pay for my flat," he grimaced. "Better do something about that cut on your cheek, or you may not live to see your trial date. Here, I've just a bit of gunpowder. If you will wet that handkerchief of yours—"

"I will rip my shirt tail first. The handkerchief is far too precious to me, burned though it is."

"Burned! I should have thought that would make it even dearer to you."

I looked at him quizzically. "Why should it?"

"Darcy! Are you really so ignorant about the language of courtship? Egad, man, no wonder you have taken so long to find a woman. Do you not know what it means when a woman gives a man a handkerchief with a burned corner?"

"It means something? What?" I asked, almost desperate to hear.

Richard glanced uncomfortably at Jones, then rolled his eyes and tried to make some descriptive gesture with his hands. "Er… It means, 'I cannot live without you.'"

CHAPTER 29

*R*ichard's visit was to be the only such comfort I would have in that dungeon of affliction. For thirty-six days, my life assumed a repulsive pattern. I slept on rot, lived in decay, and shared my putrid abode with vermin. Each day, my own filth worsened my surroundings, yet each day, I noticed it less. Perhaps it was a sort of delusion, one contrived by whatever mercies are allotted to incarcerated men, that kept me from descending into an even more torturous kind of madness.

The only bit of life I could cling to was Elizabeth's handkerchief. I would sleep with it over my face, long after the lavender scent faded, simply so I might feel something of hers close. When my days stumbled into the last week of March, a despair came over me that I could scarcely describe. All my thoughts and energies had turned to spring—taking Georgiana to Rosings, fulfilling my duties once more.

Worse: If I had remained at liberty, the banns would all have been read by then. Our nuptials would have been arranged the Tuesday or Wednesday following, and Elizabeth would have been mine.

Thus, on what should have been our wedding day, I lay prostrate on the slimy stone floor, my face pressed mercilessly into the dank, and wept aloud. I should have been consigning myself to her, standing beside her, calling to her... holding her. *Heaven, how I wanted her!*

But it was not to be... not now, and probably not ever. I was no fool—I knew the odds against me and what would happen after... The bloody code of law would not be satisfied in merely taking my life. No! I would be denied a respectable burial, sold to the surgeons for their unspeakable butchery, and everything I had ever called mine would be forfeit to the crown. Georgiana would be alone and destitute, the impoverished and orphaned daughter of a disgraced house, but at least she would have Richard. Elizabeth would... dear God, someday she would belong to another man... if she was fortunate.

That simple acknowledgement sent me into a fresh transport of demented misery. The longing, the aching, the bone-numbing wretchedness of reaching and not touching... I was fit to run mad. One moment, I could nearly taste her, feel her, smell her, claim her warmth for my own cold body! The next moment, she was so far away, such a vague memory that I could scarcely recall she had almost been mine. I curled up in my rotting straw and wished some prison disease might claim me that very night.

The Ordinary was called to look in on me when I failed to eat and refused to take my exercise with the other prisoners. He sat on the wooden plank in my cell with his pen poised, ready to put down what he must have supposed to be a ruinous and heartbroken revelation— the Confessions of Fitzwilliam Darcy; Murderer. I could almost see the man's eyes glinting with the profits he expected to glean from me, but I had nothing to confess. Nothing, that is, but the mournful ruminations of a derelict man, deprived of his love and entirely without hope.

I did rouse somewhat the following week, wavering between baseless expectation and exhausted melancholy. Dull and listless would have been appropriate descriptions of my attitude, and only an improvement over the prior week because now, I no longer wished for death. I simply did not care. One thing I did know: my despondency and anguish were almost at their ends. A few days more, and I would be set at liberty... through one door, or the other.

APRIL THE FIFTH was to be the day—a Monday, the first day of the Sessions. I paid, and paid well, for the concession of a bucket of water and a rag to clean myself somewhat the night before my trial. I even wrung out my shirt and tried to brush some of the stains from my breeches, but the gaolers did not provide me with a razor for my face. It was just as well, I supposed—I had never been required to shave myself, and most likely would have cut my own throat.

I shuffled in a long line of other prisoners down the corridor to the infamous and oft-cursed Old Bailey. The smell of the room was almost overpowering. It was sweat, and fear, and over all that, an oppressive and sickeningly sweet floral essence. Anxious to ameliorate the odour of unwashed prisoners and reduce the spread of disease, the court officials had decked the room in whatever fragrant herbs and dried flowers came readily to hand. My head had already pained me before that heavy cloak fell over me and I nearly gagged... and then I caught the earthy delicacy of lavender among the bouquet. I forced myself to close my eyes and draw a breath, and slowly, my head cleared.

We were all made to sit in the back of the room. Many of the prisoners were looking up at the balcony, hopeful that some friend had come to see them or speak in their defence. Others merely stared at the floor.

I had no need to look around, for even as I entered the chamber, I could sense her. If I had ever felt her before—had ever known how the hair on my neck could spring afire, or how my very core could billow and foam like a storm-swept sea, when I had sought so fearfully to avoid her—now her very presence in the room was a soothing balm. She was the one place in that whole melee that made sense and felt familiar.

I looked up and found her, crushed between her father and... and Lady Matlock? I squinted and nearly rubbed my eyes to be certain of what I saw. *What the devil...?* It would be odd enough for a lady of Elizabeth's station to attend a trial, but the countess?

But it was true, for there she was, patting Elizabeth's hand and generally looking as though the proceedings were all taking place under her direction. Richard and Lord Matlock sat behind them, and with them I just caught a glimpse of Mrs Reynolds. I gave them each a small nod, then my eyes fixed on my Elizabeth until I was pushed towards a bench.

I had no way of knowing when my case would be called. The judge, the honourable Mr Adolphus, merely sorted a stack of papers, lifting each one by turn and calling out the name thereon. Unless the prosecuting party had secured the services of a lawyer, which was not common, the judge stated the case and questioned the witnesses himself.

By the time half an hour had gone by, twenty cases had been heard and sentenced. Eighteen were for some sort of theft. Two were for keeping a house of ill repute. Only five souls had walked away free.

Another hour and a half dragged by, though the tempo of the courtroom seemed to be nearly frantic. The longest cases were heard for fifteen minutes at most, while some were settled in less than five. After several cases were read in such quick succession, the jury would huddle together to issue their verdict on each, in order. More often than not, the accused stood condemned. I could feel Elizabeth's gaze on my back and almost hear her whispered prayers.

At long last, the judge read from his papers, "Fitzwilliam Darcy, indicted in the first for wilful murder of Robert Benedict; also charged in the second with assaulting by means of a sword with intent, in so doing, to cause grievous bodily harm; and in the third, for inciting Mr Benedict to extreme measures by means of financial duress and, in so doing, becoming responsible for the wrongful death of said person."

I stood and was shown to the rail where I was to stand. The jury all eyed me with interest. No doubt, my name had been in the papers. I wondered for half an instant if Lady Matlock had been waging her own war of public opinion in my defence. I found the courage to glance just once over my shoulder to my family... and to *her*... but then I could not bring myself to look on my Elizabeth again.

"I beg your pardon, your honour," I heard Richard call out. Mr Adolphus paused and looked up. "We have engaged a lawyer, Mr Pence, for the defence of Mr Darcy."

The judge frowned and waited for said lawyer to make his way forward. The crowd rustled—a defence lawyer was an oddity, though the prosecution occasionally employed the services of one. Such novelties always protracted the trial, and the judge seemed little pleased by that. I calculated that I had, perhaps, twelve minutes before my fate was decided.

"Now, then," the judge cleared his throat and cast a suspicious eye at my lawyer. "We shall begin. Let us have the first witness, please."

A court officer stepped forward and called—to my utter lack of surprise—Lady Benedict to the stand. She looked directly at me, a satisfied hauteur blackening her hated features, then affected a mournful face for the jury.

"Who are you, Madam?" Adolphus asked her.

"I am Lady Benedict, widow of Sir Edmund Benedict, and I live alone at my flat in London. The deceased was my only son."

"You have no other children, Lady Benedict?"

She lifted her chin and glared at me. "I had a daughter who was wed to Mr Darcy. She died an unnatural death."

"And was their union a happy one before your daughter's death?"

"No. Mr Darcy treated her very ill, and his discourtesy extended to me, as a dependent widow, and to my son, who was grieving his father."

"Indeed. And your husband, how long has he been deceased?"

"Two years. Mr Darcy was present at his death."

"He died of natural causes?"

"No." She blinked at me. "Of a fall."

There was a rustling among the jury, and one or two exchanged whispers and shook their heads. Mr Adolphus silenced them with a look, but my spirits were already beginning to sink.

"Thank you, Lady Benedict," he resumed. "Were you aware of any animosity between the deceased and Mr Darcy?"

"Yes. Mr Darcy stole my late husband's property and refused to relinquish it to his heir."

"And what sort of property was this?"

"Shares in East India Company stock, worth over eight thousand pounds at present value."

"And was there a record of any transfer?"

"No, but Mr Darcy did sell a quantity of his own shares about the same time. I have seen none of the profits I ought to have, had there been no transfer, so they have been misdirected somehow."

"And your son desired to restore the property to your family?"

"Yes, but Mr Darcy refused to deal with us, and threatened consequences."

"Thank you, Lady Benedict." Adolphus waved a hand and permitted Mr Pence to approach. I gripped the rail at which I stood with no small degree of angst. Surely, the earl would have found someone competent... surely...

"Lady Benedict," said Mr Pence, "You spoke of these shares. I took the liberty of inquiring at the Company Court of Directors, and could find no proof that your late husband, Sir Edmund, had ever owned them. Can you verify that he had them?"

"I certainly can. They were in his strongbox, which disappeared just after his death."

"And do you know where and when he obtained them?"

"From his friend Archibald Doyle."

"And can this Mr Doyle verify the sale?"

Lady Benedict sighed and once again employed her mournful expression. "Sadly, Mr Doyle is also deceased."

"When and how did Mr Doyle die?"

"He was killed in a hunting accident two-and-a-half years ago. Sir Edmund was the one to bring him in from the field—they were intimate friends."

"Can Mr Doyle's heir testify to this?"

Lady Benedict sighed and shook her head piteously. "He had no heir."

"Do you know who the beneficiary of his estate was?"

"He held no ancestral land. He bequeathed his personal property and assets to three of his closest friends, Sir Edmund among them. The shares I spoke of, which were taken by Mr Darcy, were a part of that bequest."

"Thank you, Lady Benedict. And one more question; would you describe your late husband as a violent man?"

Lady Benedict's face reddened, and she looked at the judge. "I do not see what all this has to do with anything."

"Indeed," seconded the judge. "Sir Edmund is deceased, and not on trial."

"My apologies," Mr Pence bowed. "Thank you, Lady Benedict."

I was groaning by this time. The lawyer had only succeeded in making me look more dastardly, while doing nothing to demonstrate that I could not have perpetrated the crime.

She turned to go, and Mr Adolphus looked up from his papers. "Daniel Perkins, please."

A nondescript young man stepped forth, and Adolphus spoke to him. "What are you?"

"I am a manservant, employed by Mr Samuel Bridgeforth. Mr Bridgeforth resides next door to the flat where the deceased lived."

"Did you note anything on the night of the deceased's death?"

"Yes, sir. I saw a tall gentleman of robust build enter the deceased's flat at approximately seven o'clock."

"Was this man familiar to you?"

"No, I had never seen him before."

"And did you see his face?"

"For a second. Mostly, I saw his back."

"Does the defendant, Mr Darcy, resemble the man you saw?"

The manservant turned to study me. His forehead wrinkled and his head tilted. "Yes. At least, he was like him, but he wore a hat, and did not have a beard."

"And did you overhear anything when this man went into the deceased's residence?"

"Yes, sir, I heard loud arguing that started some fifteen minutes after the gentleman arrived. There was a crash, like furniture being broken, and then more arguing, and a few more crashing noises. After that, it went quiet, and a few minutes later, the gentleman left."

"Did you not think to investigate?"

"No, sir," the manservant answered frankly. "Mr Benedict often had visitors. They would play at dice or cards, and occasionally we would hear similar disputes among them."

"And you did not hear the deceased cry out as he fell?"

"No. The argument ended, and the gentleman left a few moments later."

"Thank you," Adolphus said. "Did you wish to question the witness, Mr Pence?"

"Yes, your honour. Mr Perkins—" Pence came forward again, carrying a small tray. "I have here four portrait miniatures. One of them is Mr Darcy without a beard. Do any of these men resemble the gentleman you saw entering Mr Benedict's flat?"

The young man took his time examining each of the miniatures, picking up first one and then another. At length, he appeared to have settled on one, but then shook his head and picked up a different one with an air of certainty. "This looks like the man I saw."

"You are sure?"

"Yes. The man was tall and well-built, but his face was lean like this."

"This is a portrait of a man who is not on trial today. The miniature of Mr Darcy is this one here," the counsellor said, pointing to the one on the extreme right—one Mr Perkins had hardly looked at.

The manservant looked up to me in surprise, then studied the portraits again. "I... am fairly certain," he repeated at length. "I still think the other is the man I saw."

"Thank you, Mr Perkins."

The judge was beginning to look somewhat impatient, and he consulted his paper with a frown. "James Wilcox."

I closed my eyes and tried not to look as if I were despairing. James, one of my newest footmen, and a man whose loyalty had not been entirely tested... I braced myself for the worst.

"What are you?" Adolphus asked.

"I am a footman, and I have been in Mr Darcy's employ for five months."

"What are your duties?"

"I am usually at the front door, and it is my duty to accept calling cards and to assist the master or mistress to the carriage."

"Had you ever seen the deceased calling at Mr Darcy's residence?"

James seemed to grit his teeth, and he nodded briskly. "Yes, your honour."

"Was Mr Darcy at home to him?"

"Mr Darcy was in Hertfordshire."

"Was Mr Darcy in London on the evening of February the seventeenth?"

James blinked. "Yes."

"And was he at home all evening?"

A hesitation—"No."

"And when was Mr Darcy away?"

"He went out on horseback at approximately half past four in the afternoon and returned at approximately half past seven."

"Thank you, Mr Wilcox, that will be all. Mr Pence?"

"Mr Wilcox," Mr Pence addressed him, "please describe your master for the jury, so his character might be understood."

"Well, sir," he stammered, his cheeks flushed and his words tumbling over one another as if he were in a great rush for them all to be heard, "Mr Darcy is considered exceeding fair and honest. Everyone at the house respects him and is proud to be in his employ. He is generous to his servants and to the poor, and I have never heard anyone speak ill of him."

"What more can you tell me of him?"

"He is very protective of Miss Darcy, sir."

"Protective? How do you mean?"

"Only, sir, that he takes great interest in seeing her well cared for."

"Have you ever heard of Mr Darcy losing his temper?"

James appeared to wilt. "Once, sir."

"And what was this occasion?"

"The day he returned from Hertfordshire, and Mr Benedict was calling on Miss Darcy without his knowledge."

"You were at the door on this day?"

"Yes, sir."

"Did you overhear anything?"

"No, sir. I remained at my post, but perhaps a quarter of an hour after Mr Darcy's return, Mrs Younge—she was Miss Darcy's companion—was escorted from the house. A few minutes after that, Mr Benedict left."

"Can you describe for me the manner of these persons as they departed?"

"Mrs Younge was angry and using language unbecoming to a lady. Mr Benedict appeared calm."

"Thank you, Mr Wilcox," Pence said. James looked once more at me, his face red with discomfiture, and left the box. I shook my head in absolution. James had done nothing but to tell the truth. I simply could not discern why Pence had asked certain questions in the way that he had.

Adolphus looked at his paper once more. "Mrs Younge, please."

I groaned. Not a surprise, but an unwelcome face as she came forward and curled her lip at me across the room. I tried to force my hands not to clench, but it needed all my self-control. No matter what came of myself, Georgiana would now be compromised, for certainly, she meant to harm as much as she could.

"What are you?" Adolphus asked her.

"I am a widow, and I presently operate a rooming house to support myself. I was formerly employed by Mr Darcy as a companion to his younger sister."

"What was the duration of your employment there?"

"I began on December the twenty-sixth of last year, and Mr Darcy terminated my employment without warning on February the fifteenth of this year."

"Did he give any reason for such?"

"He was enraged that Miss Darcy would choose to favour the

deceased with her attentions. He held me accountable, and dismissed me at once, with no notice or character given."

"Were you acquainted with the deceased?"

"Yes, he was a relation of my former husband's. A very agreeable young man, and earnest in his suit of Miss Darcy."

"And were you present for any of the discussion between Mr Darcy and the deceased?"

"I heard almost all of it. I heard the deceased address Mr Darcy honourably to petition for Miss Darcy's hand, and Mr Darcy swore at him. The deceased also requested information pertaining to the deaths of his father and sister, but Mr Darcy refused to satisfy him, and abused him further. At one point, Mr Darcy declared his wish never to see the deceased alive again."

"Did you hear anything else?"

"No, but I spoke with the deceased again the following day, and he told me that Mr Darcy had extorted information from him about his private affairs. Mr Darcy then offered to return some of what was owed the deceased's family, but he would be required to go to Amsterdam to claim it. If he did not claim the money within two months, it would remain Mr Darcy's property."

"And while you were in Mr Darcy's employ, did you notice anything in Mr Darcy's manner or habits to indicate a tendency towards violence?"

"It did not occur during my employment, but the deceased told me that a close friend of his, a Mr Wickham, had sustained a bloody lip inflicted by Mr Darcy during a dispute."

"Thank you, Mrs Younge."

Mr Pence came to her then, and I hoped—despairingly—that the fellow would not botch this particular interview.

"Mrs Younge," he asked, "when did the deceased begin his courtship of Mr Darcy's younger sister?"

"Two weeks prior to the altercation in which Mr Darcy confronted the deceased."

"And did Mr Darcy at first approve of the courtship?"

Mrs Younge visibly held her breath, looked down, then confessed, "He was not aware of it."

"Indeed? How was the acquaintance carried forth?"

"The deceased met Miss Darcy in town, when she was out in her chaise. After a few accidental encounters, he was invited to call."

"And was this when Mr Darcy became aware of the relationship?" She paused.

"Pray, Mrs Younge, answer the question."

"No. Mr Darcy had gone to Hertfordshire."

"Just as Mr Wilcox stated. Thank you. So, Mr Benedict presumed to call without asking the young lady's guardian?"

She narrowed her eyes and I could see swallowing. "Yes."

"How many times did he do so?"

"Four, sir."

"And was Mr Darcy's return to London unexpected?"

She scowled sullenly and set her teeth.

"Attend to me, Mrs Younge."

"Yes."

"Did he find Mr Benedict in his house at his arrival, and was this how he learned of the relationship?"

She drew an unhappy sigh and glared again at me. "Yes."

I leaned forward on the railing and tried not to fume. Was Pence *trying* to make it look as if I had just cause to lose my temper?

"And the altercation you spoke of occurred immediately after this?"

"Yes."

"You said previously that Mr Darcy questioned the deceased about another affair, not connected to his attentions to Miss Darcy. Describe that, please."

She blinked and looked around. "I do not recall much of that."

"Describe what you do recall, please."

Her lips puckered, and she stared at the floor. "There was a tradesman, in whose warehouse was found smuggled tea and opium, and he was being investigated. Mr Darcy seemed to think the deceased knew something of the affair."

"And did he?"

She crossed her arms and looked to the side.

"Mrs Younge, you must answer the question," Adolphus reminded her.

"He did," she muttered unhappily. "But I do not know the particulars. I was escorted from the house at that point."

"Thank you, Mrs Younge," Pence said at last, dismissing her.

Mr Adolphus called for his next witness, a Dr Howard Brown. The doctor came, and Adolphus asked him the usual questions to establish his credentials and verify that he had examined the body of Robert Benedict, then asked for the doctor's findings.

"The deceased died of a blunt trauma below the ear, behind the jaw. There was also a quantity of blood in his abdomen and several broken ribs."

"Do you find these sorts of injuries consistent with the report of Robert Benedict falling from a great height to his death?"

"Yes, except for the head injury. He was dead or unconscious before he fell."

"And how do you know this?"

"Because he fell without attempting to catch himself. Also, he landed on his back, and there was a matching contusion on the posterior of his skull, but the mortal wound was on the left side of his head, consistent with a lethal strike by hand or weapon."

"And was anything of interest found on the deceased's person?"

"He had four dice in his pocket, and a card on which had been scribbled bets for what appeared to be a game of Hazard. The beadle who delivered the body informed me he did not have a weapon when he was found, nor did I find that he bore many bruises on his hands, which would have indicated a long fight."

"Was a weapon found anywhere else?"

"A decorative sword was found by the balcony window in Mr Benedict's flat, with blood on the finger-guard."

"And what sort of force would be required if one were to deliver a blow with such an object, with intent to kill?"

"Force would be less important than skill. The head is susceptible to a blow in that place, but to strike from the side, if a man is defending himself, requires some degree of prowess. It was most likely a deliberate killing blow."

"Thank you, Dr Brown." Mr Adolphus then asked if Mr Pence wished to question the doctor, but my own counsellor declined, and the doctor was dismissed.

I stared at Pence, hoping he would notice my growing annoyance without giving the jury cause to think me a temperamental beast. Why would Pence not ask more? What sort of incompetent buffoon was he?

"Mr Pence," the judge asked, "This concludes the court's witnesses. Do you have any others to call?"

"Yes, your honour. I have called two more witnesses," said Mr Pence. "Mr Angelo, please?"

I turned about in surprise. Angelo, my old fencing master? It was indeed he, making his careful way down to the floor. He spared me a minuscule nod as he passed and then faced the front of the room.

"Who are you?" Mr Pence asked.

"I am Henry Angelo, the elder. I own the finest school in London for gentlemen's fencing."

"Were you acquainted with the deceased?"

"No, he was no student of mine." Angelo pronounced this with a decided sniff, as though any gentleman who was not his student was no gentleman at all.

"And what of the accused?"

"Indeed, Mr Darcy has long been a pupil."

"How well do you know Mr Darcy?"

"My acquaintance with him is merely professional, but I have known him since he was a youth, and I knew his father."

"I shall ask more about Mr Darcy's swordsmanship in a moment, but what can you tell me of the man and his character?"

"He has always been a noble gentleman. He is well-spoken of among my other pupils and is not given to much personal vice."

"By which, you mean what?"

"Certainly, sir, you must know that fencing is not all the gentlemen do at my parlour. We have retiring rooms, where the gentlemen may indulge in cards or refreshments. Knowing, as I do, most of the finer gentlemen in society, I am familiar with the man's reputation. Mr Darcy declines to drink to excess or to bet on games of chance."

"So, you are saying that Mr Darcy is not known to play at dice, as Mr Benedict appeared to have been doing on the night of his death?"

Angelo laughed in slight condescension. "That is what I am saying."

"And can you attest to Mr Darcy's skills with the sword?"

"He is a marvellous swordsman for a gentleman, and it is an honour to call him my pupil."

"And what of his personal strength? Has he the ability to inflict grievous harm if he choses?"

"Certainly, Mr Darcy has the height and strength to be a formidable opponent, and he has great speed as well."

"Is it possible that he could have struck Mr Benedict as the doctor described?"

"No," Angelo stated unequivocally.

"No? Why not?"

"I have said Mr Darcy has great skill for a gentleman, but he is no master. He could not have done this thing."

"Why do you say that? Does it require tremendous fencing skills to strike an unarmed man?"

"No," Angelo shook his head and almost chuckled. "But it requires skill beyond what Mr Darcy possesses to do so with his right hand. Mr Darcy is a left-handed swordsman."

There was a stirring among the jury, a rustling of seats that swelled to a great tide of whispers and expressions of awe. For the first time during the trial, I felt the smallest trickle of hope. Richard's lawyer had done his task, and done it well—above and beyond all my fears. I only prayed it was well enough.

"Thank you, Mr Angelo," Mr Pence said, dismissing the fencing master. "Your honour, the defence would call a character witness, if it pleases the court. A Mrs Reynolds, who has been in the employ of the defendant for twenty-four years."

"This case has heard quite enough witnesses," Mr Adolphus decided. "Let Mr Darcy provide his own statement."

Mr Pence turned to me with an apologetic bow, which I acknowledged with a nod of gratitude. I knew not where the earl and Richard had found him, but he had brought more truth to the proceedings than I had dared hope. However, my case alone had dragged out well over twenty minutes, and my clemency was at an end.

I braced my feet apart and raised my voice, and along with it a silent prayer for some grace among the jury. "I am innocent of this crime. I freely acknowledge that my relations with the deceased were antagonistic, and that I was obliged against my will to call him a relative by law. He frequently accused me of theft and dishonour, which were baseless accusations, in hopes of gaining financially from me.

"When that failed, I discovered that he intended to harm an innocent businessman and exert influence over my sister to achieve his ends. It is true that I was angered over his mendacity. However, I made an agreement with him in good faith, one which he upheld by giving relief to the guiltless parties. I am prepared to transfer the proceeds which ought to have been his to Lady Benedict, in lieu of Mr Benedict's decease.

"I regret his death, but I could not have committed this heinous act, for my thoughts on the night of the crime were not engaged in bitterness or resentment. In fact, I was intending to make an offer of marriage to a woman who would secure all my happiness. I had the honour of being accepted, just before being accused of this crime. The true injustice, if I should be found guilty, is not the loss of my own life or dignity, but the loss of the life I could have lived, and all I wished to do for my intended bride, and for my young sister. I implore the court to have mercy on them, if not myself."

The judge raised his eyebrows and made a strange expression with his mouth. "That will be all, Mr Darcy. Will the jury please confer?"

It was over. No more testimony was to be heard, no more evidence brought forward to either condemn or exonerate me, and the jury turned to one another to deliberate. I raised my eyes to where my family sat, clustered together and anxious.

Elizabeth... She was clutching her father's hand and leaning up intently, her colour gone. I could see by the pallor of her cheeks and the blackness of her eyes that she had slept ill, and I ached to comfort her in some way. I tried to offer her a smile, but I feared it was little more than a grimace. She smiled back, and then she did something rather curious. She turned to Lady Matlock with an urgent whisper.

Lady Matlock tilted her head to speak something comforting, and then even applied to Lord Matlock, who leaned forward, and whispered to them both. Richard caught me looking and gave a confident wink that seemed wholly incongruous to the present affair. How assured the Fitzwilliams all appeared, not uneasy at all! They would be the only ones! I waited for Elizabeth to look at me again and took courage from the faltering smile she fought so valiantly to give me.

The jury conferred for only a moment, a blink of time that was to decide the rest of my fate. Then, the chief among them stood to pronounce their decision.

"We find the defendant, Fitzwilliam Darcy, not guilty of the first count of murder. Not guilty of the second count, intent to commit grievous harm. And guilty of the third, responsibility for a wrongful death by means of financial duress, with a fine recommended."

"So be it," concluded Mr Adolphus. "Fine to be set at twenty sovereigns, accused to remain in custody until it should be paid. Next: Bernard Jones, charged with..."

I stood mute, staring, and aghast. Had he really said... was it true? I stumbled forward, scarcely able to believe what I had just heard. But it must be true! A court officer was leading another man to the stand, gesturing for me to move from the place. Another asked—I heard him only vaguely—whether I was prepared to pay the fine immediately. I think I nodded, but I was too dizzy, too breathless to make a full reply.

Free! There was Richard, his fist raised in triumph as he stood to help Mrs Reynolds to her feet... and before him my Lizzy, my beautiful Elizabeth, weeping and laughing all at once. She was struggling to stand, unwittingly pushing back against her father's assistance and waving from her path those who would tell her to wait, to be still. But then I saw Richard take her by the hand and push others out of her way, leading her to the door. I stumbled from the dock, scarcely able to see or to put one quaking limb before the other.

I was taken to a desk where I was to make arrangements for the payment, and that done, I was simply ignored. I was almost fearful to stir my foot to the right or to the left, but the open door to the street beckoned. The sunshine and fresh air, and then the small crowd gathering outside the gate drew me away, and I left Old Bailey behind.

Just outside, Elizabeth rushed into my arms, caring nothing for my bedraggled and foul state. I gathered her to me, sobbing inarticulately as I touched her hair, her cheeks, and tried to drink her in. I held her so tightly, so scandalously, that I later wondered why Mr Bennet did not think to object.

But holding her was not enough. I wanted to see her face, hear her voice, take courage again in her eyes. I wanted to express to her all that was on my tongue and stirring my heart, all that I had longed for, my joy, my hope, my sorrows… but all I managed was one strangled word.

"Minx."

She laughed, tears streaming down her cheeks as she pressed a hand to my face. "Swine."

"Swine indeed," Richard interrupted. "Darcy, you smell positively ghastly. Come away from this godforsaken place and let us get you home to a bath and a shave."

I nodded but refused to turn loose of Elizabeth so I could walk. The earl and the countess were already halfway to their carriage, turning occasionally with incredulous stares at the way I lingered. Mr Bennet was looking purposely away, pretending fascination with the architecture of the structure as if he had not a care in the world. Mrs Reynolds stood by, weeping into a handkerchief and beaming as if I had just returned from the dead, but Richard was drawing out his pocket watch and fidgeting.

I looked back to Elizabeth, and I am certain that never did I look such a preposterous fool as I must have in that moment—unshaven, filthy, and grinning like an oaf. "Elizabeth, is it true? I am free… free?"

She nodded, captured my hand and kissed it. "We are both free."

CHAPTER 30

That evening, I was back in my own house, just as if I had never left. Georgiana had rushed to me, bouncing and sobbing by turns, and bewailing her youth, that she had not been permitted to attend the trial. But Bingley, he had been there to steady and succour her during that awful day—he and Mrs Bingley, who looked more beautiful to me than she ever had as I watched her comforting both my sister and my own love. My friend was a lucky man... but I was even more so, and I shamelessly clung to Elizabeth's hand whenever I could be pried away from someone else.

Mrs Elliott had prepared a feast in honour of my liberty: honeyed ham, head cheese, two different ragouts, white soup, and such an assortment of pastries and delicacies that my stomach ached merely looking at them. I did briefly wonder what she would have done with all that food if circumstances had been the reverse, but I scarcely dared to let my mind linger there. It was all too fresh, too raw, and I preferred instead to think only on what brought me pleasure.

At the moment, what brought pleasure was Mr Gardiner, lifting his drink in a toast; the Earl of Matlock, busily engaged with Bingley on a matter of investment principle; Lady Matlock and Mrs Bingley both laughing with Georgiana over some recent encounter with Lady

Catherine and Mr Collins; and Mrs Reynolds and Mrs Elliott both petting and making as much of Elizabeth as they ever had done for my mother.

There was one moment in the midst of that afternoon when I simply sat back from everyone—detached, and taking satisfaction in the simple things... in people, in fond old memories, in dear hopes for the future, and I counted myself the most blessed man in England.

Later, much later that evening, all the guests had gone away—the earl and countess to Matlock House, Bingley and his wife to Gardiner's house in Cheapside, but Elizabeth and her father had remained. Richard stayed as well, agreeing to act as chaperon while Mr Bennet amused himself in the library, and I retired that evening to the comforts of my drawing room with my own all about me—well-fed, clean, and once again the master of myself. Georgiana and Elizabeth both remained persistently at my side, and every few moments, my sister would burst into tears all over again.

"There, there, Georgie, you must not carry on so," soothed Richard. "There was never any real danger."

"Real danger!" she cried. "He could have been sentenced to be hanged!"

"Not at all. There was far too much doubt in the case. Each of his accusers meant to cast him in a poor light, but they only ended up looking suspect themselves. No jury in the world could find against him."

"You may have been confident," I replied, "but to my thinking, it was a very near thing."

"Near thing! Do you not know what Mother has been up to? Tell him, Miss Bennet. Why, it is almost enough to make me think a woman could serve in Parliament."

Elizabeth shook her head, smiling, and raised her hand in denial. "I do not feel properly qualified. My spirits are far too rumpled now to present it all in an orderly fashion."

"Well then, I shall do it. Do you know those miniatures that your counsellor showed the witness?"

"Yes, I was curious about those. Who are they?"

"One of them was Wickham, as you suggested. Mrs Reynolds brought that from Pemberley, but I thought how clever would it be if I also had miniatures of Ramsey and Carlisle? Of course, such were not to be gotten from their own houses, but I contracted an artist to have them done up."

"From which likeness? I cannot believe you could simply march into their portrait galleries and copy them."

"That was where my mother was useful. You know how crafty she is. She knows everyone and is so careful about maintaining her circle of influence that no one thought a thing about it when she asked certain high-ranking ladies who had done the portraits for their sons or husbands and so forth. Naturally, certain artists are always fashionable, and so it was my good fortune that both Ramsey and Carlisle had had their portraits done in the last year by the same gentleman. He recalled them well enough to work up passable likenesses—indeed, I could have sworn they had sat in his studio for him. He did charge me a rather immodest fee, but I felt sure you would not mind reimbursing me for my trouble."

"You can have my whole blasted vault for all I care. But now, I am dreadfully curious: whose likeness did the manservant identify?"

"It was Ramsey."

"Ramsey! I should have thought it would be Wickham."

"I did as well, but it does not surprise me overmuch. Wickham is too much the coward."

I snorted. "That is an understatement."

"Hah! I shall let Miss Bennet tell you more of him in a moment. Let me finish first. I am quite certain that it was Ramsey, and I suppose we will discover the whole truth when Lady Benedict is called to testify in her own defence."

"What do you mean?"

"Well, naturally I have already shared the manservant's identification of Ramsey's portrait with the constable, who conveyed it to the magistrate at Bow Street. When Ramsey returns to the country, as no doubt he will at some point, he shall be arrested and charged with murder. Naturally, we cannot let that bit of knowledge become public, or he may remain at large forever. A pity we have no evidence that Carlisle did anything truly illegal, but I expect that is only because we have not looked long enough."

"And what of Lady Benedict?" I asked.

"She will be called to testify at Ramsey's trial, and I do not imagine her remaining at liberty after she is compelled to tell all the events regarding Sir Edmund's death. Do you recall that bequest she talked of?"

"Yes, and I thought your lawyer was a fool for dwelling on it."

"Not at all! She was forced to confess under oath certain facts of import. For instance, were you not curious who were the other two beneficiaries of Doyle's wealth at his death?"

I narrowed my eyes. "I was, but I see you have the advantage of me."

"You have already guessed it. Viscount Wallingford, who is Ramsey's father, and was on the board at your bank; and Rufus Carlisle, father of your other good friend and a member of the East India Company's Court of Directors. So, indeed, they formed an unholy trinity of ne'er-do-wells, and their sons were meant to follow in their footsteps. Unfortunately, Sir Edmund did something to cause him to fall out of favour with his partners."

I scoffed. "I think you presume too much. Are you suggesting that Sir Edmund's death was no accident, that he was truly murdered?"

"I am not suggesting it. Father practically has it in testimony from Wallingford himself. The wretched bastard was called up on charges for fraud at the bank—good heavens, Darcy, you have missed all the news this month. Father and his friend Hayworth finally got their way, and Wallingford is ruined—both politically and financially—but he was apparently determined not to go alone. Just last week, he gave a statement incriminating Rufus Carlisle for underhanded dealings. The elder Carlisle is under investigation by the East India Company as we speak, by the way.

"In Wallingford's statement, he blasted Sir Edmund for murdering Doyle on that hunting expedition, and said that it was all done without his knowledge. Some servant had leaked the truth, and

Wallingford was trying to keep clear of the blame. Unfortunately, he only managed to direct more questions to himself. One naturally wonders about Sir Edmund, so father sent a Runner to Bedfordshire, to see if he could scare up a witness."

"And?"

Richard grinned, traded glances with Elizabeth, and seemed to relish the suspense. "Well, the Benedicts are no longer there to terrorise their servants. The Runner found one who was finally willing to speak, and it opened the floodgates of Heaven, as it were. Soon, he had statements from at least twenty servants. Perhaps, Miss Bennet, you might not wish to hear…"

"I would know the whole of it," Elizabeth declared.

Georgiana looked guiltily back and forth between Richard and me, then cleared her throat. "I cannot imagine how there could be anything worse than what I have already heard, but I think I will retire to dress for bed."

Elizabeth caught her hand as she rose. "I will be up in a few moments, if you wish to talk."

Georgiana nodded, then fell into Elizabeth's arms for an impetuous embrace. She came to me next, her tears wet and her kiss sweet on my cheek. She drew back, blinking and hesitant and seeming to search for words, but neither of us had any. I touched her chin, kissed her hand, and said, "Good night, dear Georgie."

After she had gone, Richard leaned forward, his hands clasped on his knees. "It has been hard for her this month, Darcy. The poor child has scarcely eaten or slept."

"I can see that. She is thinner and her colour is fearful. She blames herself, does she not?"

"Of course she does. Mother has done all she could, and Miss Bennet here has been her saving grace. But do you know, I think it was my father who eased her the most."

"The earl! How so?" I asked.

"He got this capital idea of taking her driving in Hyde Park last week. What with everything, she refused to go at first, but Mother fairly dragged her to the coach—after setting at least two maids after her hair and attire."

"An open carriage, no doubt," I chuckled.

"But of course! This was just after Wallingford's disgrace, so Father deliberately sought out his fellows and talked over the matter, then openly praised Miss Darcy's intelligence and virtue, and said how she had been so vital in discovering the final clues to the puzzle."

I narrowed my eyes. "But she was not."

"From a certain point of view, she was. And anyway, the facts matter less than peoples' opinions of them. Mother told me just this evening that now that you have been exonerated, she had three cards waiting for her when she returned home, and that each of the callers had asked after Miss Darcy. It seems that any reserve or doubts about Georgiana are as quickly forgotten as yesterday's newspaper."

I turned to Elizabeth and lifted her hand to kiss it. "I fear, Elizabeth, that in marrying me, you take on the monumental task of guiding Georgiana. Are you up to it?"

"No more than you are!" she laughed. "But Lady Matlock has proved to be a friend whose counsel I shall regularly seek."

"Enough of that," Richard protested, squirming in his seat and looking away as I continued to caress Elizabeth's hand. "I think I shall tell you something less cheerful to turn your minds."

"Ah, yes," I sighed, and tucked Elizabeth's fingers into mine as they fell. "Let me hear the rest. What of Benedict's estate?"

"What of it, indeed. Several of the upstairs maids shared the same testimony, and two or three footmen's statements concurred with them. The, er... the daughter of the house, if one may speak so delicately of the creature, was known to entertain midnight callers to her room. Both your unmarried friends, as it happens, and once even at the same time."

I recoiled in disgust, and I could feel Elizabeth beside me doing the same. "Abominable!" she cried. I looked to her in sympathy and silently put my arm around her shoulders.

"Of course," Richard continued, "neither had any intention of marrying the whore. It seems their true purpose in going to Bedford-shire was not to seek their leisure, but to do something about Sir Edmund at the behest of their fathers. A footman was outside the door when they confronted Sir Edmund—this was before your arrival, since the others were there a week before you. The footman says he heard the word 'murder,' and that the younger gentlemen were furious that if Sir Edmund should be brought to trial for Doyle's death, all might be lost."

"All of what would be lost?" Elizabeth asked.

"Hold there, I am just coming to it. The footman claims…" here, Richard cleared his throat delicately and winced in sympathy for Elizabeth, but he forged on. "Ah, the elder gentleman tried to persuade the younger two to consort with his daughter, even offering to turn a blind eye, in hopes that one of them would be obliged to marry her, thus ensuring their continued allegiance to him."

"Oh, my…" Elizabeth gasped, and clutched my hand in abhorrence.

"Do not feel too much compassion, Miss Bennet, because Sir Edmund only offered what the lady was already providing. But matters took a turn one day, and here I am not certain of what occurred, but I suspect both Ramsey and Carlisle declined to marry the daughter, and that incited both Sir Edmund and Lady Benedict to fits of rage."

"I expect I overheard that particular incident out in the orchard."

"You may have. One maid claimed that after that, Lady Benedict kept to her rooms and Sir Edmund to his mistress, and neither parent took notice when their daughter began to go off by herself to the vacant gamekeeper's lodge to carry on… well, that is sufficient to the imagination, I expect."

"More than sufficient," I pleaded, with a decided twist to my stomach. "Elizabeth, I am sorry you heard—"

"But I have not done! She must hear this part," Richard insisted. "This is where it clears you entirely of any blame, for a footman was awakened during that skirmish you had with Sir Edmund—hardly a surprise, for I know how fearfully loud you are. A jolly good thing you do not have to fight for your livelihood, I say. The enemy would hear you coming for a mile."

"Thank you," I retorted sourly.

"Listen here—you said when it all happened, you awoke several feet from where you had last been, and I do not think either Lady Benedict or... ahem, well, any lady could have carried you thus. Do you?"

I shook my head.

"Of course they could not! There was a gentleman nearby, just out of sight. The footman claimed to have been upstairs at a window, and saw the whole thing from above, so he was able to witness what you never could. You do not imagine that... er..."

"You may say her name, Richard," I told him. "I have long recovered from the horror."

"Very well," he sighed. "I shall call her Miss Benedict, for she never deserved the title of Mrs Darcy." This, he said with a respectful nod to Elizabeth.

"Anyway," he went on, "Miss Benedict had not been out amusing herself alone. She was with Ramsey, and the footman claims he saw Ramsey down below the steps the whole while. No doubt, he heard you struggling with Sir Edmund, and saw his chance to end the affair and neatly shuffle the blame to another."

"I do not understand," Elizabeth mused carefully. "Why would they cast the blame to you? Were you not friends?"

"So we were," I acknowledged. "But where there is money to gain and influence to purchase, old friendships are sold cheaply."

"Indeed," Richard agreed. "The whole thing is more disgusting than vengeance. At least Benedict fancied himself to have a grievance. Ramsey and Carlisle were purely mercenary."

"But why would they want Sir Edmund dead?" Elizabeth wondered. "If they truly wanted him gone, they could simply have borne witness against him for Mr Doyle's murder. It sounds cold, but at least it would be within the bounds of the law."

"Well, a man who has been killed is simply dead," Richard explains, "but a man who is tried and hanged for murder..."

"Loses everything," I finished. "Ramsey and Carlisle could not afford for that to happen, because they still needed Benedict, either son or father. That black market stock—they could not get to it without Robert, and Robert needed some forged paper trail from his father's possessions. But shares are merely that—a right to a portion of the company's profits. They are not import documents."

"No, but if they could forge or steal one and make it appear legitimate, they could bloody well do the same with the other. And that is why someone knocked you senseless from behind, just long enough for everything to come out to their satisfaction. Lady Benedict covered for Ramsey because she still wanted her money, Miss Benedict covered for her lovers, and you bore the disgrace of it all."

"Good lord," I breathed. Elizabeth leaned closer into me, and I turned my face to hide my feelings in her hair while I composed myself.

"Indeed," Richard agreed. "I know it rattled your wits surely enough, but it was rather convenient having Lady Benedict testify against you in court today. She came off looking less than innocent, and Mother has ensured that everyone heard all about it already—everything from the trial, and everything I have just told you. Everyone loves an unsung hero, and you are the toast of the *ton* tonight, Darcy. I imagine you never thought to take pride in that distinction!"

"I do not now, but perhaps I should feel relieved. What of Wickham? What was his part in all this?"

"Ah, well, he was merely an unemployed thug to the others—someone who could easily move from the society of the gentry to the seedier parts of Town. I expect he was to get close enough to you to keep an eye on you, and also to maintain watch on Lady Benedict. It is likely that neither Ramsey nor Carlisle wished for Benedict and his mother to patch things up, and everyone thought they were playing everyone else. Wickham left the country on Ramsey's passage… but here, Miss Bennet ought to resume that tale."

"It was my father and my uncle, truly," she confessed. "I had little to do with it. Mr Wickham returned from the Continent, having failed to collect on Mr Benedict's money in Amsterdam. He was in search of funds, so he came to my uncle with an offer. He said he would give my uncle a generous portion in what he had obtained from Mr Benedict—which, as we found later, was truly nothing—if my uncle would set him up as a partner and help him establish himself as a merchant. His intent, naturally, was to find some means of reclaiming what Mr Benedict had left behind at his death, but of course he did not say this.

"My uncle pretended to consider his offer and asked Mr Wickham to return the next day. My father and I were in London, so they conferred over it. It was decided... oh, dear William, I pray you forgive us!"

"Forgive you for what?" I asked.

"I... that is, my father attended the next meeting my uncle had with Mr Wickham, and they were very amiable with him. Mr Wickham claimed that he held the promised funds—ten thousand pounds—in an overseas account and could not access them at the moment, but he would obtain them soon and my uncle would be compensated. My uncle knew this for a falsehood, but he pretended to hear Mr Wickham out and agree. Then, both my father and uncle suggested that if Mr Wickham were in earnest and quite ready to enter such an arrangement, there might someday be the possibility to cement the alliance by marriage."

I stared, and I felt my eyelid beginning to twitch. "Marriage... to... one of your sisters?"

She cleared her throat. "Ah... not precisely. They told me of it beforehand and asked my blessing on the scheme, but... it was me they suggested, on the reasoning that if my present betrothed were..."

"What!" I leapt from my seat. "You agreed to this?"

"Keep quiet, Darcy, and let her speak," Richard snapped. "You do jump to conclusions too easily. I think the notion was rather ingenious, myself."

I sat, unsteadily, and leaned close to see if I could discern more than her words had conveyed. "What possible reason could you have for considering this thing?"

"It was setting the trap, that was all," she protested. "Naturally, nothing could come of it, for my father had accepted settlement papers from you. You know perfectly well that if Mr Wickham had addressed me with his suit, I would have refused him in the most uncivil way you can imagine—and you have certainly seen that I can be uncivil. But it was enough to stroke Mr Wickham's vanity and to coax him into overplaying his hand, which was their intent. After they had fully gained his confidence, my uncle played the trump card."

"And this was?"

"He asked whether Mr Wickham had other debts that must be settled—any that you had not previously taken over. He reasoned that if they were to be in business and relationship together, old debts were not to be borne. Naturally, Mr Wickham did have such, and a substantial sum of them. My uncle asked Mr Wickham if he could satisfy them, and of course, he could not, and so my uncle and my father did."

"Brilliant, was it not, Darcy?" Richard chuckled.

"I..." I swallowed and looked back and forth between them. "I presume you will tell me next that Wickham is presently lodged in a debtor's prison?"

"The most charming resident of the Marshalsea," Richard affirmed. "And do not think of thanking either Bennet or Gardiner, for they would not hear of it. I believe Mr Bennet is merely content to have the man locked away from Miss Lydia—"

"Pray, Colonel," Elizabeth interrupted, her cheeks red, "I do wish you would not mention my sister's foolish letters to anyone."

I raised an eyebrow. "Is there more scandal I have not yet heard?"

Elizabeth tipped her chin up to me and brushed my lips. "Five weeks' worth, but I will tell you the rest tomorrow, my dearest William."

"Alone?" I asked suggestively, and softly kissed her back.

"I am still here," Richard coughed. "And I have no qualms about sending for Mr Bennet this very moment to tell him he must insist on an immediate ceremony because his daughter is actively being compromised."

I did not take my eyes off Elizabeth's when I answered, "A capital notion, Richard. Be quick about it, will you?"

I heard next—and carried with me all the rest of that wondrous first night of freedom—the most glorious sound in all the world. Elizabeth laughed.

And then, she cupped my face in her hands and kept kissing me.

ONLY A FEW SHORT DAYS LATER, I met Elizabeth at the altar, and she surrendered to me more than I could possibly have ever gifted her. I believe the last broken bit of my soul clicked back into its place in that moment. I took her hand and vowed to belong to her—wholly and irrevocably—before God and our families and in the sight of the law, and then, no one could stop me from embracing her like a besotted fool before the whole congregation.

Lady Catherine was most seriously displeased. Caroline Bingley was in mourning—it was the first time I had ever seen her in black, and the shade did not suit her. Mrs Bennet made me cringe more than once, but I had the grace to smile and nod when, after the wedding breakfast, my new mother-in-law patted me on the cheek and promised that her daughter would give me many sons. Mr Bennet merely stood back in that sardonic way of his and laughed over the matter.

It was a distinction for the entire assembly that the Earl and Lady Matlock chose to attend the ceremony. Richard claimed that his lordship viewed it as a political move—publicly displaying his support of me despite my socially disastrous marriage, in hopes that one day I might be prevailed upon to run for a Derbyshire seat in Parliament. I quipped that if I ever did so, the earl would not appreciate my politics, for I would take up prison reform as one of my first objectives. The truth, however, was far simpler than all that; for the truth was that Lady Matlock desired to come. To his wife's demands, his lordship had never been able to object, and I expected that my life in thirty years would be much the same.

After all the flurry and excitement had passed, the farewells had been given and received, and the last bridal trunk secured to the last coach, I had all the pleasure of giving Elizabeth Darcy my hand into the carriage. We would spend our wedding night in a coaching inn on a north-bound road, which was not as I had dreamt or hoped, but we had both had enough of London.

I longed with every part of my being to show my wife her new home in Derbyshire. For the first time in over two years, my heart swelled at the thought of Pemberley's rolling hills, the jutting blue mountain peaks, the quiet paths, the fondly remembered rooms. Everything, all of it, and my eyes grew moist as I imagined standing beside her, overlooking my home, and giving it to her.

"William," Elizabeth called softly, turning my chin with her tempting fingers, "there is something I have been meaning to ask you."

"Is there? I find I am quite at my leisure now."

"I know that you previously suffered some... unpleasant associations with a name such as the one I now bear."

"Elizabeth Darcy?"

"The very one. I had wondered if you would prefer some other appellation, something that did not call to mind disagreeable memories."

"Do you mean that I might call you my vixen, or my Calypso, or perhaps Queen Bess? Or nymph, or ruffian, or enchantress, or saucy tart—"

"Good heavens, William!" she cried in laughter. "Have you called me all these?"

"That was only the beginning. Shall I continue?"

"I think it better if you do not! But I would not object to something more... respectable. Beth, perhaps, or even Eliza, if you fancy the name."

"I do not dare call you Eliza, for you might presume it is Miss Bingley speaking and draw your sword."

"Then what of Lizzy? My family all call me by that name, and so have you from time to time. It would not do for the sake of introductions, of course, but—"

"No." I stopped her by touching my fingers to her lips. "Elizabeth you are, and Elizabeth you shall always remain. You wear the name as a crown, my love, and no other so perfectly suits both that queenly way of yours and your shocking capacity for provoking me."

"You are quite certain?"

I wrapped my arm around her, traced her cheek in the fading light of the carriage, and rather than to assure her of my resolve in words, I proceeded to show her.

❧

I DEVELOPED a new appreciation for the smallness of coaching inn beds over the next few nights. What I did not appreciate, however, was the dimness of the rooms. What good was it to take a goddess to bed when a man could not see her?

But what I could not see, I could feel, and each velvet inch of skin, every shattered breath against my cheek, and every panting shiver of her lithesome body was glorious. And, perhaps, the darkness lent her just enough boldness during those first few nights that she permitted me more freedoms than she might otherwise have done.

I shall never forget—for the sound shall remain with me until the day my eternal soul is called from this mortal frame—I can never forget Elizabeth's first cry of ecstasy, the first time I was able to give her some small measure of what she had already given me. And I remember the first time we found our rapture in the same moment, for that was also the first time I called out her name in my sudden weakness. *Elizabeth Darcy...* the name I would forever hold as the most perfect string of syllables in the world.

I was still floating on the bliss of the previous night when our carriage crested the rise overlooking Pemberley. I called for it to stop and roused Elizabeth to show her the first prospect of the house. She was drowsy, for we had accomplished most of our slumber these last days in the carriage. The bedchamber had recently become home to far better activities than sleep, but this was a view I knew she would want to partake of.

A light spring rain dusted the fields, so I intended to only look out the window. Elizabeth, however, lifted the latch herself and shot me a mischievous glance as she caught my hand.

Already the obedient husband, I yielded to my wife's wishes and helped her to the ground. "Shall I have the umbrella brought down from the box?" I asked.

"William," she chided, "what woman needs to take refuge under a silken frame when she has a rock for her protection? Tie my bonnet for me and put your arms around me, and I will have all the shelter I require."

I laughed and fumbled with the bonnet I had rumpled some while earlier. Then, she wrapped my arm around her hips—and I knew now precisely how well-formed those hips were—and leaned into my shoulder. I heard only soft hums of appreciation as she breathed deeply and occasionally touched her fingers to her eyes.

"Do you approve of it?" I asked into her ear.

"I think there are few who could not approve."

"But it is your opinion that I find worth the earning. My grandmother desired for the formal gardens to be taken out, as was the fashion then, and these more natural scapes were introduced. I thought you might appreciate those."

She nodded. "I do."

"And the western wing, do you see there, was rebuilt after a fire in '86. Most of the ground floors were not affected, but the upper rooms have been entirely remodelled. Among them are the master's and mistress' chambers, so your room has been completely done over—and was made over again this spring, of course."

"I am certain it is lovely, William."

"And the stables—I know how you fear riding, but I have bought you a very gentle pony and a phaeton. If you should ever feel bold enough to venture back into a side-saddle, I have purchased Nightingale again from Bingley, and she will arrive next week."

"That is very thoughtful of you, William."

"But I believe your favourite part will be the library, where you can—"

"William," she interrupted, turning to me with those amber eyes dancing in a blur of sentiments, "you could describe the majesties of Pemberley for hours, but I should still come to the same conclusion."

"And what is that, my Elizabeth?"

"I love it—every knot-hole, every gilt banister, every dusty book and every uncultured flower in the meadows. I could never have imagined any place more to my tastes. But my favourite part, the part that will keep me here and make me call it my home, is and shall always be you."

I was the one with tears in my eyes when she finished, but I drew out my handkerchief—that burned one that I now carried every day—and touched it to her cheek. "Welcome home, Mrs Darcy."

She smiled, sniffed gently, and took the handkerchief from me. She was looking down and stroking it, and it seemed that her thoughts had suddenly wandered far from me, far from where we stood on that rise, and back to a frosty winter night in Hertfordshire.

"Do you know—" I turned her palm over, then twisted the hand-kerchief until that curious little memory knot was compressed between each of our index fingers. "I have always wondered about this. What were you trying to remind yourself of?"

She chuckled. "You might wish I had not told you."

"Indeed! Now I insist that you tell me."

"Well," she playfully lifted her shoulders—"it was merely that I used to find one particular individual most vexing. I suppose we all encounter such people. They are the ones who try us at every turn, because we wish so desperately that we could have been friendly with that person, but every encounter is maddeningly the opposite. Perhaps they possess a well-informed mind, or admirable tastes, or are simply…" she lowered her lashes and gave a coquettish toss of her head—"the most beautiful man ever seen."

"I had no idea you felt so strongly for Mr Wickham."

"Shameless tease!" she accused. "Indeed, I spoke of you, and you would be appalled to know how many times I wished I could first scandalously kiss you, then strangle you for your odious ways."

"Appalled? I doubt it, but what of the knot?"

"I stitched that the evening after the party at my aunt and uncle

Philips's house, when I learned that you had endured more than I had ever understood. It was my memento to myself that not all things are as they appear at first, and that I should be less hasty to pass judgment."

"And what have you decided since forming that resolve, after coming to know everything?"

She gazed up at me for a moment, golden flecks sparkling in those remarkable eyes, then carefully tucked the handkerchief back into my breast pocket. "I believe I will save that for tonight, after I have seen the rest of my new home, met everyone there, and sampled the comforts of my new bedroom. I fancy the lighting and the bed there will be a vast improvement over my previous experience."

I set my hands on her hips and pulled her to me. "I have always loved the way you think."

She slid her arms about my neck and kissed me, then rested her head on my chest. "Then take me home, my William."

EPILOGUE

I clutched my head in my hands and doubled over in my chair in sympathetic agony for the sufferings from the next room. It was all my doing—the pain, the danger, the humility of it all. It seemed to have been going on for hours, and with each new wave of affliction, it was my name she cried out to come to her, to ease her.

How I ached to answer her call! But every time I tried to spring from my seat to rush to her side, Richard cuffed me about the arm and pinned me back again. "Good lord, man, have a bit of composure," he grumbled. "You act like she is the first woman ever to endure this."

"Would that she were!" I shot back. "I would not then know all the worst."

"Come, Darcy, you mustn't look so green," Bingley soothed. "Everything will be perfectly well."

"How can you say that?" I nearly barked at him. "You have not endured all this."

"I will soon," he gloated. "Do you know, I still cannot believe you bested me in this regard, Darcy. By four whole months! I ought to have known you—" He broke off at a warning glare from me, and from the corner of my eye, I thought I caught Richard frantically shaking his head, urging him to cry off.

"It is not your wife suffering just now," I snapped. "Trust that I know of what I speak, when I say you will be in a deplorable state when it is your turn."

"I will not," he answered tartly, "and neither will you, in a few moments."

"Bingley is right, Darcy," Richard said. "No man likes to hear his wife in distress, but it shall be short-lived, and the reward well worth the trouble."

"It is not always so," I retorted, then I clenched a fist over my mouth and fell to muttering my fretful curses at the floor.

"That was the past, Darcy. This is nothing like that. Everything will come out right, you will see."

Another deep, quaking moan sounded from Elizabeth's room, and once more, Richard was obliged to reach out and push me back against the seat.

"We should not be here," Bingley protested in discomfort. "Can we not go downstairs? Or even to your own sitting room, Darcy? Decency aside, I would not have you in the next room if it were my own wife. Let her have a bit of privacy, man!"

"He did not invite us here," Richard reminded him. "The surgeon asked us to restrain him, and this was as far away as we could drag him. Why the devil did you need to send for a London surgeon, Darcy? I have never heard of such a—"

"Wait!" I cried.

The laments and travails from the next room had all gone eerily still. I froze, my heart pounding as I strained to hear. A moment later, there was a gasp—not from Elizabeth, for I would have known the sound of her breath from the grave. Then, we all heard the shuffle of rustling feet, the creaking of the floor as her attendants flew into some frenzy.

"*No*," I heaved. "No! She cannot be—"

But just then, there was a new sound. We all listened, scarcely daring to breathe, but I was the last to understand. It was a warbling, gravelly sort of noise... weak, at first; no louder than the soft mewing of a kitten. Then, it grew into an insistent peal, and was joined by a chorus of female voices.

I could bear it no longer. Richard was not fast enough this time, and I sprang to the door, but it burst open before I touched it. It was Mrs Reynolds who appeared, her dear old face shining and jubilant.

"All is well, master! You have a healthy son!"

The room tilted, and I put out a hand to steady myself against the door. "A son," I breathed. "And Mrs Darcy—Elizabeth, is she well?"

"Perfectly, sir. Both the surgeon and the midwife declare she is the strongest lass they have ever seen. Oh! There she is laughing. Fancy that, laughing so soon after everything! Pardon me, sir, I must go look in on the mistress again, but I knew you would wish to hear just as soon as ever anything was known."

"Yes," I murmured as she left. "Yes, very well… very well, indeed!" I merely stood in a daze, my body listing first one way and then another, and I was only vaguely aware of Richard bracing against my shoulder to keep me upright.

"Let me be the first to congratulate you, Darcy!" Bingley grasped my hand and began to pump it. "A son, and the very first born of perhaps a dozen to follow. Well done, Darcy!"

Spots were still dancing before my eyes, and my head felt light. "I had nothing to do with it," I managed. "It was all Elizabeth—she deserves all the honour."

"She certainly does," Richard retorted. "Any woman who can abide you—"

He went on, no doubt abusing my character to Bingley, but I was too delirious to attend him. A son… *a son!* My own child; not a fraud, not a lie, but mine in truth. My own Elizabeth's blood in his veins, her light in his spirit—and if I should be so blessed, perhaps I would mark some bit of myself made new again in him.

"Sit down, Darcy, or you will give yourself an apoplexy. Here, take a drink," Richard suggested sensibly.

"Let us have a toast, shall we?" Bingley declared. "To the future master of Pemberley! May he grow in likeness to his father, the finest man I have ever known."

"Hear, hear," Richard agreed.

I merely stared at the drink they had thrust into my hand and listened in awe as the two men I admired most in the world spoke their blessings over me, and over my household. My eyes stung, and I could scarcely believe what I was hearing. Trials, I had some, but I would never again be without friends to help lift my burden.

AN HOUR LATER, they had gone below. The next room had just fallen quiet, and Mrs Reynolds told me I might venture in. I silently pushed the door aside and crept on quaking knees near to the bed.

Her eyes were closed, those thick lashes that had first sent me into tremors of denial brushing her rosy cheeks, her head with its nest of chocolate curls reclining gently on the linens. On her breast lay a swaddled babe, only a flash of pink visible where his face crushed into her.

I drew near, longing to speak, but the peace of the moment was too precious to shatter. Instead, I merely gazed raptly on the woman I adored. What had been my feelings, this year and a half since she had come into my life? I could hardly account for the sweeping course of my sentiments, the cursed absurdity that had almost embittered her against me forever—and justly so!

Since the day she truly became my own, I had tried to form the words, to tell her all I felt. No matter how many attempts I made, how many trite phrases I rejected, I never felt able to do justice to the inspiration that set my spirit aflame whenever she looked at me just so. But now, my body seemed to be overflowing with the outpouring of love from a heart once blackened and charred, and I could no longer keep silent. I bowed my head, more tears starting in my eyes, and spoke in a voice so soft, it was barely a whisper.

"They say it is a feeling common to man, in such cases as these— that he must naturally feel obligation, his instincts press him to cherish that which is his own. But that is insufficient. Since the day I first beheld you, you began a work in me. How I feared you! But you saw what I could not bear to lay before another soul, and in your goodness, you did not crush me, as you might have.

"I was a wretched man once. I was selfish, prejudiced—a bane to my family and too arrogant to conceive of any improvement wanted. I shall never be so deceived again, and I give you the credit for that. I bless the day you first walked away from me, laughed at my folly, and showed me how little I understood of pleasing a woman worthy of being pleased! You, with your wit and good humour and the beautiful way you teased me—even before I knew your character or had seen any of your strength, you discovered precisely how to bend my knee and make me your slave.

"Oh, how I fought you! I still cannot conceive why you were ever willing to listen to me a second time... or a third... but I will tell you the truth. I only fought so hard because I feared losing all, but instead, I have gained more than I could have dreamed. A lover, a friend of my heart, a family—do you know, your family delights me. Your father with his lackadaisical intellect, your gentle and wise uncle and aunt, and yes, even your younger sisters have become dear to me. I love each folly, each aggravation, because you love them, and I cannot bear for my heart not to align with yours.

"And now, you crown all this with the final blessing—how can I be worthy? I scarcely found the courage to even claim you as my own, and yet you give more than I could have asked. My dearest, loveliest Elizabeth!"

"If I had any notion you could speak so well," murmured a drowsy voice, "I should have asked you to write me some poetry long ago."

I raised my head and found my wife smiling at me, her countenance flushed with weary contentment. "You once told me that a poor sonnet would kill love stone dead. I dared not risk it."

"Only if it is but a vague inclination. I fear my sentiments for you are quite too stubborn to be tempered by a bit of mediocre poetry. Besides, I doubt anything you composed could ever be 'poor.'"

"Then I shall put pen to paper this very afternoon." I smiled down into her laughing eyes and traced her cheek with my finger. "I did not mean to wake you."

"I was not fully asleep. I knew you would come. Look, William, you must see him!" She shifted, and I helped her to raise up on the pillow so she could lift our child to me.

I tugged away the blanket and discovered a thick shock of dark, wavy hair. His face was red, and his round cheeks half covered bleary eyes, but then she held him back, lifted him so he could look up, and he blinked at me… and that was when I saw my Elizabeth's changeful and brilliant eyes shining from his face. I began to tremble, my hands to shake, and something dashed against the inside of my ribs as I looked on the face of my son for the first time. "He looks like his mother," I breathed.

"I was about to say he looks like his father. Look at that nose, those fingers! Is he not beautiful?"

"Beauty! I have none of that. It is all from you, my Venus."

"Do you not know? Beauty is said to be in the eye of the beholder, so if I possess it, it was yours first."

I laughed. "I disagree, but I dare not match you in wits. Particularly not now, when you have too much the advantage of me."

"That is wise, William," she intoned gravely. Then, her face brightened as she shifted the babe from her shoulder. "Here—he is yours."

I received him in terror, certain that his head would break off or I would drop him, but Elizabeth settled him securely in my arms and pulled back the blankets so I could see him better. Fascinated, I brushed his tiny hand with my finger and was astonished at the immediacy and force of his grip.

"No," I decided. "He is ours—your flesh and mine. With you, my life is complete, Elizabeth Darcy."

~

Fine

~

ACKNOWLEDGMENTS

From J.W. Garrett

The written word is a powerful tool. If handled correctly, it makes us laugh, cry, shocks us, informs and entertains. JAFF [Jane Austen Fan Fiction], as a sub-genre of Regency Romance, features variations on Austen's wonderful classics, letters, shorts, and unfinished works. She left us way too soon; however, during her lifetime she began a work that is still very much alive today. For many authors, writing is as essential as breathing and to not write is unthinkable. Austen knew this and even as her health was failing, she continued to put words on paper. We will always appreciate her hard work and her dedication to the written word. To the many authors who continue Austen's legacy, we thank you.

This is dedicated to her memory. May she rest in peace. And to Nicole Clarkston for taking a simple idea and creating magic. Bless you, my dear.

J.W. Garrett

ACKNOWLEDGMENTS

From the Author

This book has been a labour of love and laughter. About a year ago, my dear friend **J.W. Garrett** told me about this idea she had for a story. She had written up some initial paragraphs, most of which are still present in the first chapter of the book, as Darcy is venting his frustrations out on the grave of his first wife (Jeanne called her Evil Elizabeth, or EE for short). With that, Jeanne had some ideas of how Darcy had gotten into that predicament, and she very generously offered me her baby.

The story idea blew my socks off, and I told her she should write it herself, but she laughed and graciously declined. I was just finishing *London Holiday* and trying to get back to *Nowhere but North*, so the idea went on the shelf until January of 2019. We launched it as a serial on the **Austen Variations** blog, and the rest is history. Jeanne and I had an absolute hoot talking over chapters, chatting with readers, and giggling wickedly about all the mayhem we were about to inflict in the next instalment. I am sorry now to see the project come to an end, but I am proud of what we have wrought.

I am exceedingly grateful to the veritable army of support I have had. Apart from Jeanne, **Janet Taylor** (who is also responsible for most of the cover art and is a gorgeous woman in every way), **Joy Dawn King** (a top-notch author who regularly needles me, then dries my tears), and **Debbie Fortin** (a sharp cookie who lectures me about those weird sentences I like) practically held my hand as I wrote every scene. Their advice and feedback have been invaluable.

The fun did not stop there! **Don Jacobson**, author of the *Bennet Wardrobe* series, and **Jennifer Altman**, author of *To Conquer Pride*, graciously offered to read through the final draft. As did **Deborah Brown**, the Queen of Commas (and if she is the queen, I'm the kitchen wench); **Carole Steinhart**, whom I affectionately call "Aramis"; and **Betty Campbell Madden**, a whiz of the written word who has forgotten more about language structure than I ever learned. If any errors or deviances have managed to slip through a firing squad like that, then they were "nefarious" rascals, indeed! I am so humbly grateful for each one, and their sweet friendship has made writing its own reward.

Lastly, I must thank the readers at **Austen Variations**. This book is for you, and you cannot know how much delight you gave me each week when the first chapters ventured forth. Thank you!

Nicole Clarkston

BONUS STORIES

If you enjoyed *Nefarious*, I would love to hear from you! Please let me know your thoughts by leaving a review or recommending the book to your friends.

As my personal thank you to readers, I am offering a free eBook of shorts for signing up for my newsletter. To learn about new releases, or just connect over a good book, check out the links below.

- Newsletter: https://mailchi.mp/e2e9ebe98571/nicoleclarkston/
- Blog and newsletter: https://nicoleclarkston.com/
- Facebook: https://www.facebook.com/NicoleClarkstonAuthor
- Twitter: https://twitter.com/N_Clarkston
- Amazon: https://www.amazon.com/Nicole-Clarkston
- Austen Variations: http://austenvariations.com/

ABOUT THE AUTHOR

Nicole Clarkston is a book lover and a happily married mom of three. Originally from Idaho, she now lives in Oregon with her own romantic hero, several horses, and one very fat dog. She has loved crafting alternate stories and sequels since she was a child, and she is never found sitting quietly without a book or a writing project.

ALSO BY NICOLE CLARKSTON

PRIDE AND PREJUDICE VARIATIONS

London Holiday

These Dreams

The Courtship of Edward Gardiner

Rumours & Recklessness

Rational Creatures (Multi-author Anthology)

NORTH AND SOUTH VARIATIONS

Nowhere but North

Northern Rain

No Such Thing as Luck

SPANISH TRANSLATIONS

Rumores e Imprudencias

ITALIAN TRANSLATIONS

Una Vacanza a Londra

Made in the USA
Middletown, DE
13 June 2019